THICKER THAN WATER

Adrian O'Donnell

For my wife Jo, and also for all my friends and family who have supported my writing....you know who you are!

THICKER THAN WATER

PROLOGUE

Luke Woods stood with his back to the mould-spotted shower wall. Three racist thugs had just walked in fully dressed and ready for trouble, one holding a broken metal bed leg in his right hand, once hidden inside a rolled up white towel but now fully exposed and exuding menace.

"We told you to get yourself moved from the wing, what's wrong with you? This wing is run by white people for white people," one of them said, his voice booming around the room unafraid of who might hear. Luke moved forwards and hurriedly made a grab for his own towel to cover himself up, but it was too late. A thick set skinhead with ugly tattoos covering every inch of his muscular arms grabbed it, along with his tracksuit which was sitting on an old, soap-stained, wooden slatted bench.

Standing naked and vulnerable, Luke cursed to himself about how life had got to this stage, his mind buzzing as to how he could call for help. The only route out was blocked and this whole area had become a no go zone for staff to patrol. It was futile to try and cry out for the officers, as from the safety of their own wing office he knew they wouldn't hear a thing. The warm water continued rolling from his shoulders unnoticed as it managed its own escape down a filthy drain hole. The other two prisoners who were just frightened onlookers in the shower area got dressed hurriedly, racing back onto the prison landing before trouble struck. Only one person stayed, a much shorter Nigerian boy named Chris. At five foot five, he was short in stature for an eighteen-year-old, but his solid muscle mass made up for his lack of height. He stood, dressed only in blue prison shorts, and stepped in between Luke and the thugs.

"You fuck with my friend, you need to take care of me too."

The three boys looked at each other. "Ok, if you want to be a hero, you can die like a fucking hero." The leader, a young thug named Shamus McCann jumped forwards, the bar smashing into Chris's forehead. He dropped instantly onto the wet tiled floor, unmoving. Luke stared down in disbelief, blood seeping out from a long deep split in Chris's scalp, the white fragments of skull washed clean by the hot water forming a grotesque scene. A thick red river merged into the soapy suds creating a delicate pattern seen all too frequently in the steamy shower room of this stinking shit hole of a prison.

Luke bent down, feeling for a pulse. "He's dead, you've fucking killed him."

He looked accusingly at the three thugs, expecting to see some kind of reaction or guilt.

They didn't care; instead McCann came forwards again, smashing the bar into Luke's leg, the bone shattering with a sickening crack as he fell in a heap, screaming in agony. He could hear a distant alarm bell sound as the thugs casually walked out, dropping the bed leg and disappearing back onto the landing. The last one to leave turned around and mockingly said, "Try kicking a ball now when they put that leg back together, you mug. Tell them you need to move wings." The door swung shut seconds before health care staff raced in with their emergency bags.

CHAPTER ONE

Six Months Earlier

Jake and Luke Woods, seventeen-year-old identical twins stood in the December freezing rain as it came sheeting over the Reading FC training ground in the small village of Sonning, Berkshire. They didn't care about the cold, or the fact that it was New Year's Eve. It had taken them five years since moving over from Jamaica to be able to train with the first team and this was their chance to shine.

Jake's hundreds of goals scored for the youth teams, and Luke's ability to defend at the other end of the pitch had quickly brought them to the attention of the coaching staff. This could be the year they finally got to run out onto the pristine pitch in front of twenty-four thousand supporters. At least that was the plan. Another more pressing plan was also on their minds, what to do for New Year's eve. An invitation to the pub in town, or welcoming in 1997 at a friend's house party? Which one would it be? Luke tossed a coin as they dried themselves in the changing room. "Heads the pub, or tails the party," he said as the coin spun in the air.

The Snooty Fox pub in Newbury's main street was jumping, the long narrow bar having the reputation of a place that never seemed to close. Music bellowed out through the door as the twins entered, spotted straight away by a group of friends congregating at the far end by the pool table.

Dave Shipton, a stocky little boxer stood and met them with an enormous smile. He had become friends with them both at school. People who knew things thought that he was going to be a boxing star and the signs were looking good with an impressive amateur record building up behind him. A few promoters were looking to sign him, and one had offered him a debut fight at the MEN Arena on the same bill as Rick Hatton. As always Dave was cool and calculated and he was still undecided as to whether he was ready for the step up in class.

"Are you two drinking tonight?" he asked as he headed towards the bar with them.

"No mate, we have a game tomorrow, but we're here until the end whatever." Luke was the one with the self discipline, Jake was the opposite, and sometimes the devil sat on his shoulder whispering sweet nothings in his ear.

"Anyway, I thought that you were in training for a fight?" Luke added. Dave laughed. "No mate, I haven't decided what to do yet, my old man wants me to wait another year." The DJ seemed to whack up the volume, almost drowning out the conversation and he had to shout to make himself heard. "The promoter phoned and offered me three grand for the fight last night, but I've told him that I want five and it's a deal."

Jake looked around, and shrugged his shoulders. "I'm having one Luke, even if you lot are drinking Coke." At the bar he noticed a girl standing alone; he didn't recognise her but the smile she offered was the only invitation he needed. Standing beside her he gave his bar order before looking her in the eye. "Hi, I'm Jake, are you alone?"

She gave a sigh. "No, afraid not." She pointed over to a group of drunken guys sitting around a table. "My boyfriend and his arsehole mates have been drinking all day. I'm so bored with them," she continued, rolling her eyes as she spoke. One of the drunks looked up and noticing Jake, he stood up unsteadily and pushed his way through the crowd before grabbing the girl in a bear hug. "Oy, piss off and find your own girl," he told Jake before staggering back to his friends and a table full of beer bottles. Brushing him off the girl looked back at Jake.

"Sorry about that, normally he's a nice man, but when he gets with this lot......" Another shout went up from the table and she gave a further look of displeasure.

"I have to go - my name is Chloe by the way, nice to meet you." Jake nodded and gave his biggest come and get me smile.

"Maybe chat later?" She half nodded before turning to leave.

Taking the drinks over to his brother and friends, Luke gave him the eye before whispering into Jake's ear. "Yes I know, I saw her. She's fit, but those guys she's sitting with are cussing you. We better drink up and get gone, I can smell trouble."

Almost before he finished the sentence a fight broke out at the far end of the bar. It was Chloe's table again and bottles crashed onto the floor and chairs were tossed across the bar before security staff came running in and escorted the drunks out. Luke nodded towards them. "See I told you, just trust me brother. Drink that beer, we're going."

Putting their jackets back on, to the disappointment of their friends, they forced their way back out through the dancing crowd and over the broken glass, until the winter air outside persuaded them to find a cab instead of the usual walk home. The large market square was still busy with diners insanely eating outside under heat lamps that would melt an ice cap, the chatter reaching all corners of the square as the smell of seared steaks drifted around on the cold breeze. Luke looked around for a waiting cab but the rank was empty, the exhaust from the last remaining car still hanging around the edge of the car park they frequented.

"Are you hungry Jake? We could have a long wait." He looked around at the options for a takeaway.

A small Kebab shop close by, normally empty at nine thirty was packed and Luke saw why. Chloe was standing outside while the rest of her party were arguing with the shop owner over the price of a bag of chips. She spotted the twins and walked over, pressing her number into Jake's hand. "After tonight I'm done with him. Maybe phone me sometime?"

Just then the shop door burst open, her boyfriend running towards them. "I fucking told you," he yelled, squaring up before throwing a wild punch towards Jake. The pair tussled, Jake trying desperately to avoid a fight but the ferocity of the attack made that option impossible. Grabbing onto his jacket, the drunk bundled Jake over a hastily abandoned dinner table, plates and glasses crashing to the floor as more clients sped away from the fight. An older man possibly in his sixties screamed at Luke to "Fuck Off," as the plates on his table hit the floor spilling the food onto the wet cobbles.

Luke looked up at him, wanting to apologise but the intensity of the violence was growing as once again he tried to separate Jake and the drunk.

"Jake, leave it. Let's go home."

The drunk sneered, "Yeah, both of you fuck off back to where you came from." He punched Jake again, the blow deflecting off his shoulder before Jake responded with a full punch to his face, splitting the man's nose instantly. Bending forwards for a second the man watched the blood drip down onto a pile of food on the ground as Jake stepped back, looking for a way to leave. He had no time to move before the drunk sprang forwards again as a girl's voice from the distance screamed for them to stop.

Another roar went up as the twin's friends appeared, Dave leading the charge, and soon ten men were fighting before the sound of a police van winding its way down the busy high street made the crowd disperse. All except one guy, the drunk boyfriend. He stood looking accusingly at Jake, before putting his hands down to his own stomach where a large serrated steak knife protruded from his blood stained shirt an inch above his belt, a dark red stream flowing over his dirty jeans. Seeing the knife, Luke moved to help him as the man fell to his knees placing his bloody hands on Luke's white jacket, leaving a red smear from chest to waist before falling face down onto the wet cobble stones, dead.

Everything fell silent before havoc erupted.

A shout came from the restaurant where one of the diners who had fled inside pointed out Luke and Jake to the approaching police officers.

"It was them, I saw them stab the lad, the one in the white

jacket started the trouble."

Luke put his hands up. "I haven't done anything, he must have fallen on the knife in the fight."

In a haze of slow motion confusion they were surrounded by police officers, the flashing blue lights from the van casting an eerie glow over the watching, shocked faces. Radios crackled as an ambulance raced to the scene, a police sergeant taking control as friends of the dead man returned to the square, adding their voices to the demands to lock up the killers.

"Get these two searched and into the van before we have another fight developing. Cordon off the area and find out if any of the customers saw the killing," he ordered his men. Jake looked at him in horror before glancing back at the body on the ground.

"No, he can't be dead, no one stabbed him."

The slam of the van door abruptly cutting them off from the chatter of the excited crowds brought them back to reality as faces from the street tried to peer in towards the killers, the outside noise replaced with a constant hum of radio traffic from the unseen police officers in the front.

The boys sat silently in the back of the police van, the handcuffs digging into their wrists before Luke finally broke the silence. "What happened Jake? I saw you fighting and the next thing he is stabbed."

Jake looked up, eyes filled with tears. "I honestly don't know, you had hold of him while he tried to hit me. We all fell on the table and the next thing I saw, he was wiping blood down your jacket."

Luke stammered, trying to hold back the fear that was gripping his stomach. "I know, it was all madness but I didn't see the knife at all. This is fucked up, all I did was try and protect us both from that drunk guy. The CCTV will show that we didn't stab him. That old man shouting that he saw us do it, what the fuck was he going on about?"

The sudden halt of the vehicle stopped the conversation as the van pulled up outside the police station. A team of officers wearing forensic suits waited for the order from the person in charge before opening the doors and leading them into the harsh white lights of Newbury Police Station. A young looking inspector stood by the custody desk waiting for them.

"You're going to be placed in separate cells, but first my staff are going to take your clothing from you for evidence. They will be returned to you once the investigation is complete. Do you understand?"

They both nodded before being led separately to different areas of the building, neither one thinking of looking backwards to see what was happening to the other, both caught up in the magnitude of what was happening. Luke arrived at his cell door, a blue paper suit waiting for him on a hard bed. The young male officer who had accompanied him spoke to him gently.

"We need all of your clothing Luke, then put on the suit. You can have your own clothes to wear when your parents come to see you."

In a daze Luke nodded. "When will that be?" he asked, his voice trembling as he tried to control his terror. The officer put his hand on Luke's shoulder in a gesture of his kind nature.

"If you give us your home number, I will ask them to bring some things down for you. After your court appearance tomorrow you will get a chance to talk to them."

Luke gasped in shock, realising he wasn't going home any time soon. "This is getting out of control, we haven't done anything. The guy has had an accident somehow." He ran his hands through his hair in disbelief. "Shit this is crazy."

The officer didn't change the tone of his voice as he explained the situation to the frightened boy.

"Luke, a man has received fatal injuries in a fight with you and your brother. He was stabbed in the stomach and has died as a result. You need to understand how serious this is."

Luke's knees buckled slightly before he regained some control. "I know how serious it is but we haven't done anything. Why will no one believe us?"

Just then, the door opened and two more officers entered the cell.

"We need your clothes Luke, place them in the bags and we will seal them and then we all sign this label." The officer pointed to a white label, already covered in writing. As though in a daze, Luke dropped all of his clothing into separate paper bags, signing each time it was sealed. Eventually he was just left in the forensic suit given to him on arrival as the two officers left without another word.

"Now what?" Luke asked, more from confusion and shock than anything else.

"Everything will be sent for examination," the officer explained, "and you and your brother will remain for questioning and will appear before the Magistrate tomorrow. It looks like you're going to be charged with murder."

"Fucking murder? No way!" He tried to call out to Jake but there was no reply. A hundred metres away in the same police station Jake was facing the same nightmare.

CHAPTER TWO

Desmond and Kim Woods sat in Reading Magistrate's court awaiting the first hearing. A door opened at the opposite side of the room and their sons, Luke and Jake, were led into the dock, both wearing the black tracksuits Kim had dropped off at the police station earlier. Another door opened behind the judge's bench and two middle aged men and a much younger woman filed out and took their seats, briefly looking at the defendants before hearing the charges against them. The clerk of the court confirmed the boys' identities and addresses before reading out the charge, *that on December 31st 1997 in the town of Newbury Berkshire, between the hours of 21.30 and 21.50 they murdered Mr Robert Bell.*

Kim took a sharp intake of breath as these words were read out. The magistrates listened before the woman spoke. "This case will be heard at Reading Crown Court at a date to be arranged. The defendants will be held in custody."

The boys looked shocked as the words sank in, their solicitor standing quickly to address the court.

"Having spoken to the prosecution team and the police, we feel that there is no reason why the defendants can't be released on bail pending the hearing. They have good character, they live three miles outside the town centre and both have employment as professional footballers. They represent an extremely low risk to the public."

After a brief discussion the lead magistrate spoke. "As you are aware we do not have the authority to bail those charged with murder. This can only be authorised by a Crown Court judge. In this case, I'm content that Jake and Luke Woods will return to the custody of the police until this decision is made. If successful, the defendants can be bailed to their home address; however there will be strict conditions that they must not enter the town, nor leave the approved address between the hours of six in the evening and six in the morning. That is unless they need to for the purpose of work, in which case we will look at those reasons case by case."

"All rise."

The look of anguish on the boys' faces drove Kim to tears as she watched her sons led from her sight again and into the grim darkness of the police cells. She tried to call out but the words stuck in her throat as the solicitor approached, her smile seemingly out of place given the circumstances." It will be fine Mr and Mrs Woods, I'm sure your boys will be granted bail today, I'll make it a priority."

A member of the court staff approached and spoke. "There is no more you can do at the moment, the next case is due to be heard so you have to leave. I'm sure your solicitor will contact you when there is news."

Numbly, they left the building, the bright daylight hurting Kim's red eyes as she stepped out on to the pavement as a white prison van pulled out on to the road at the same time. She knew her babies were behind the black glass but just couldn't bring herself to look. The drive back to Newbury was tortuous but the wait was worse. Every second without news seemed like a day as they sat silently in the kitchen, the clock ticking relentlessly through the afternoon. Eventually her phone rang with an unrecognisable number.

"Hello, Kim Woods speaking."

"Mrs Woods, I have good news, bail has been granted. You'll need to go to Newbury police station and sign the paperwork. I'll meet you there.

Des and Kim rushed to get ready, driving directly to the station where a young woman in a police uniform stood behind the desk.

"Good afternoon, how can I help you?"

"We've come to take our sons, Luke and Jake home on bail. Our solicitor phoned us twenty minutes ago and asked us to come here."

The external door opened behind them and Kim turned to see the solicitor from court earlier.

"Hi Mr and Mrs Woods, I was as quick as I could be," she told them before turning to the desk officer. "Are the bail documents prepared yet?"

The woman left for a few minutes before returning with a police sergeant. He gave them a form to read while he instructed them about the bail conditions.

"Neither of your sons are able to enter the town centre of Newbury, they must reside at your address and not leave that address between the hours of six in the evening and six in the morning. They are not to contact any witnesses to the alleged offence or to use any social media while under these conditions. Do you understand?"

Kim and Des both nodded.

"If the bail conditions are broken, they will be taken into the custody of Reading Prison. Please sign here."

A side door opened and Luke and Jake came out together, the sergeant repeating the instructions to them as they both signed, the solicitor watching as they did so.

"Okay everyone, let's just have two minutes outside before I go," she suggested. They walked out towards the family car where the solicitor stopped and turned towards the boys. "Please stick by these rules, I can't emphasise how lucky you are to be bailed on a murder charge, it's almost unheard of."
Luke thanked her, but something else was pressing on his mind.

"How is this looking for us?"

"It's not looking good, I have to say. You will both be on trial for murder and without some substantial evidence emerging which clears you two boys of any involvement in Mr Bell's death, you stand a very good chance of conviction. That will mean a long period in prison and you need to be aware of that."

Luke listened to what she had to say before speaking again.

"You're talking as if we are guilty - what happened to

innocent until proven guilty? If you don't believe us, what chance do we have with a jury?" She didn't respond directly to Luke's question, instead speaking to them all.

"The evidence as it stands is straight forward. In plain sight of fifty diners, you were both involved in a fight with Mr Bell. Everyone else ran away as the police arrived and one minute later Mr. Bell received a single knife wound to the stomach resulting in his death. You were the only three people present. Of course it's going to be difficult to prove that you were not involved but our team will try persuading the jury to see it from a different angle - maybe a tragic accident or at worst, self defence." She looked back at the boys. "Do you have any more questions?"

Luke spoke again. "But how can we both be found guilty? I don't get that."

"If the jury does believe that Mr Bell was killed unlawfully, they can find you both guilty as you were both heavily involved, or they can find one of you guilty and the other not guilty. It's a bit too early to second guess until we have seen the full case against you. Now please excuse me, I have to be back in court in a few minutes." She left, leaving a scent of despair in the air.

5 Months later

Luke and Jake sat outside court number one at Reading Crown Court. Hearts trembling and struggling to compose themselves, a court usher came out to talk to them.

"The jury are coming back in and they have a verdict." Luke nodded as the man re-entered the court, expecting them to follow.

"Here we go Jake, our fate is in the hands of those twelve people. Are you ready?" His face looked grey from worry as he stared at his brother.

"No, I just need a second," Jake told him just as the usher came back out.

"Please, we need you in here at this moment. Follow me."

Jake leaned over and whispered to Luke. "Sorry mate, I have to tell you now, it's been eating away at me and I haven't slept thinking about this. It was me who stabbed him."

Luke looked at him unable to comprehend what he had just heard. Five months of denial, and here he was confessing to the killing one second before the jury were going to give their verdict.

Without time to reply they were hurried into the dock as the jury sat watching them, Luke seething but unable to talk as the judge came out.

"All rise."

He sat behind the high bench, looking over the courtroom as he spoke.

"Have you, the jury come up with a verdict on the charge of murder against both defendants?"

The foreman of the jury stood. "Yes your honour."

"In the case of Jake Woods, do you find the defendant guilty or not guilty of murder?"

"Not guilty." The sigh from Kim was audible from across the courtroom.

"In the case of Luke Woods. Do you find the defendant guilty or not guilty of murder?"

"Guilty."

Kim let out an anguished cry as Luke's legs almost buckled, hardly able to comprehend what he was hearing.

"Very well, Jake Woods, you may leave the court a free man." The court officer opened the door for him to join his parents. Luke's eyes follow his every step into freedom, watching as the guilty man was hugged by his parents, seething with rage as Jake's last words raged around in his head.

His attention returned to the judge as he spoke in an almost theatrical manner.

"Luke Woods, you have been found guilty for the murder of Robert Bell. The mandatory punishment is life in prison and I will set the tariff which you must serve at tomorrow's hearing.

Take him down."

The judge sat staring at Luke as the staff ushered him towards the stairs heading into custody. The family of Mr Bell cheered as he was taken down towards the prison cells for the first time. Luke looked up and caught Jake's eye, just long enough for him to shake his head before a court officer led him away towards his first experience of incarceration.

A well dressed official from the football club appeared in the public gallery and shook Jake's hand, before consoling his parents. "I'm sorry for what has happened Mr and Mrs Woods," he said before turning back to Jake,

"Take a couple of days at home, then phone me on Thursday and we will talk about training." He looked back at Kim and Des. "If there is anything that we can do, please call me." He handed them his card. "We'll need to make a club statement at some point today as obviously we're going to have to tell the supporters that Luke is no longer part of the football club. I'm truly sorry for what has happened."

Neither Kim nor Des were fully taking the words in and they nodded weakly as Jake continued to talk to the club official.

"I'll be okay, just feeling it for my brother. I need to get back into training so I'll be at the training ground tomorrow." The heat from the June day seeping into the courtroom seemed to make Jake sweat as he spoke and the haunted look permanently etched over his young face since the start of the trial had not vanished, in fact he was looking worse. Des took his arm.

"Come on Jake, there is nothing more you can do, don't blame yourself son."
The words felt very hollow within the oak confines of the courtroom and Jake was blaming himself but also plotting how to keep himself out of prison.

It was a very different feeling twenty feet below where he stood as Luke sat in a small cell underneath the court room by himself, the words from Jake still ringing in his head, hardly allowing him to contemplate the consequences of the moment. The solicitor, Sue Cotton came down to see him and tried to reassure him.

"I'm lodging an appeal straight away Luke. Jake was found not guilty so how the hell can they pin this on you?"

He shook his head. "Thanks Sue," he said, his voice sounding dead. "I guess one of us was going to get convicted - two black guys with a knife in Berkshire. It was never going to end well was it?"

She gave an apologetic smile. "Come on, head up, let me lodge the appeal straight away. Let's try get you back on the pitch."

The door opened and an old, craggy-faced court officer poked his head in. "The van is going in ten minutes, if he misses this one, he will still be here at six this evening." He closed the door, leaving Luke and his solicitor alone again for the last time that day. Luke let out a sigh, the reality of the moment finally resting on his tired shoulders.

"Thanks for all that you have done. Try to get me out of here, I can't cope with spending my life in prison. I'd better get on this van Sue, I need to face up to the fact that I'm not going home for a while." The words drifted into silence as he reached the end of the sentence before breaking down with a sob.

"I'm not sure that I can deal with prison Sue, please get me out, at least on bail until an appeal....please Sue, I'm begging you." The tears were flowing freely down his crumpled cheeks as he spoke and holding his hand, Sue Cotton spoke like a mother to a child.

"I'm going to do my best, but for now you're going to have to go with the van Luke. Just be strong and know that I will be doing all that I can out here."

She stood and picked up her bag, hardly able to look at the top of Luke's head as he rested it on the table, almost hoping that the situation would dissolve if he didn't accept it was happening. Craggy-faced man appeared again.

"Get on the van son, it's in your interest to get your shit sorted out and stop sobbing. The people upstairs have lost their son to your actions and now you need to pay the price for what you did." He didn't hear Luke mumbling as he climbed onto the white van and into the tiny box cell wearing heavy handcuffs.

"I didn't do it."

The mechanical rumble of the heavy sliding brown wooden doors signalled that the van had entered H.M.Y.O.I. Reading. It had seemed strange watching the streets which they used to drive along while heading for training disappearing behind him, but for how long? He would find out in the morning, however the figures that he had heard thrown around by other people were scaring him. Some prisoners from the court cells said twenty years, Sue suggested twelve years, ten if he was lucky. Ten years in prison didn't feel very lucky to him, it seemed a lifetime.

The clang of the metal stairs being unfolded from the van and hitting the tarmac floor was followed by the appearance of a smiling Prison Officer.

"Come on son, let's get you through and onto the induction wing. I've seen you and your brother play for the U23 team, you are both bloody brilliant. Fingers crossed for an appeal, we need you in the team."

Luke didn't respond, other than a forced smile, his mind was elsewhere as the reception process buzzed away around him. He paid little attention to anything that was said until a young prisoner sat down next to him.

"Hi Luke, my name's Stu, I'm a helper down here. I don't think that you've heard a word that was said to you have you?"

Luke looked up at him. "No, not really."

Stu laughed. "I didn't on my first night here either, but it'll be ok. After a few days you'll know everything. Have you ever had any thoughts about hurting yourself?"

The question sounded crazy to Luke, no one had ever asked him this before.

"Course not man, never."

Stu didn't flinch. "Well if you do, at any time, just ask to speak to a listener. They are just prisoners trained in helping out people who are desperate...we all need them at some point."

Luke stayed indignant to the line of questioning, putting a suit of armour up against the world. "Not me mate. When do I get up to my cell?" He was almost snarling his answers back, instantly regretting his tone.

Stu looked at him, knowing what Luke was feeling, but disliking his demeanour. "In a second, one of the officers will take you up to the wing. Just lose a bit of the attitude though, there are a lot of people up there who will test you out so take care."

He stood and left as a young officer came and collected Luke.

"Ok Woods, we're going up to 'A' Wing where you'll be in cell 3.25, sharing with another lad who came in this morning. You'll like him, nice lad." Luke considered the information for a second as it rattled around in the fuzz of his mind. "Why would he like the guy? He didn't know him did he?"

Walking through the endless secure corridors, passing a myriad of locked barred gates, Luke tried to take everything in before finally reaching the large open space of 'A' Wing. His first impression was bad, litter strewed the floor and half eaten food was left in trays on a small dirty table. Music seemed to emit from every one of the hundred or so cells and occasional shouts went up from an unseen window as some other poor boy was bullied, sometimes literally to death. The officer spoke briefly to the wing staff sitting in the office before coming back out and calling Luke to follow him. The metal stairs felt threatening as he ascended to the third landing, the grime of decades embedded into the industrial looking metal, the pack of bedding he carried suddenly feeling heavy.

"Here we are, this is your new home, Woods."

The blue metal cell door opened and Luke looked in. The walls were covered with peeling paint, graffiti and blobs of toothpaste previously used to hold up photographs of family and friends from the last occupant. He took a deep breath as he looked at the state of the Victorian cell which looked as though it hadn't been cleaned since the first occupant a century before.

A dirty, lidless, stainless-steel toilet sat in the corner beside an equally filthy sink, the stainless part of the description failing miserably. His small, gray, metal-framed bed stood on the right hand side next to a wooden locker with a broken door balanced unsteadily at its end, stains and burns covering the top. An old ripped blanket covered the broken cell window, trying valiantly to keep out the dust and heat coming from the concrete exercise yard below them.

Lying on the left hand bed was a large, red headed prisoner who didn't acknowledge Luke's presence, instead reading a newspaper discarded by a member of staff.

"This is your cell, Woods, you're sharing with Mitchell here. He's a regular visitor so can show you the ropes." The guy still didn't acknowledge anyone as Luke turned and pleaded with the officer.

"The place is filthy, have you got a better cell? This one hasn't even got a proper window." The officer's sarcasm cut through any further requests.

"Well maybe you should have thought about that before you stabbed that guy to death. It's a prison, Woods, get used to it. This is where you're going to grow up. Do you realise something? My twelve year old son will be married and with kids by the time you set foot out of prison again. Mad thought isn't it?"

The door was banged shut, Mitchell finally putting down the newspaper and turning to face Luke.

"Don't listen to that little prick, I heard about you on the news. You have just been given life, but that doesn't mean that your life stops, it's just a state of mind." Luke dumped his bedding pack on the broken locker and lay on the uncomfortable bed. "I don't share that view, I'll be a middle aged man when I'm released."

Mitchell sat up. "Bullshit! Okay, the first couple of years are going to be different for you. Yesterday, the boundary of your world was endless but forget that, the boundaries are now within the walls of this prison. They have shrunk, that's all, they haven't disappeared." He lit a thin roll up cigarette before continuing. "You need to treat the next couple of years like a secure university, grab everything that you can for free. Get every exam, degree or qualification they offer you. Let's just say that you get twelve years, the first three are behind a wall, shit-holes like this. The next three will be in an adult jail, Category 'C', still banged up but with a fence around you instead of the wall. Get through that and you're half way through." He took a long pull on the cigarette, watching the smoke hit the stained, flaking ceiling. "Then aim for some work outside the jail, it doesn't matter what you do, just get out and do something. Work on the gardens, anything is better than this." Another smoke ring spiralled its way upwards. "After that you head towards Cat 'D' status which means going to an open jail, the sun on your back all day long, working outside unsupervised for eight or more hours a day. Only sleeping in the prison at night and weekend trips home, everything will be better, then before you know it you're home, sentence done. Use your qualifications to get a job, get on with life and forget this crap."

Luke shrugged disbelievingly. "As easy as that, how do you know this stuff?"

Mitchell finished the cigarette and put the butt in an old jar by his bed.

"My brother did the same thing as you, killed a man in a fight when I was younger and he was given ten years. At the moment he's in an open jail. Just like I said, you need to play the system." He stood and held out a large freckled hand. "My name's Lawrence. Trouble is, I never listen to my own advice - that's why these pricks keep banging me up." He let out a long laugh.

Luke shook his hand and smiled. "What if I told you that I didn't kill anyone?"

Lawrence laughed and lay back down. "That's easy, the longer you deny your part in the crime, the longer you will serve. These fuckers want you begging for release and forgiveness from the off so if you didn't do it you have two choices. Find the person who did do it, or shut up bitching and do the time - simple really."

CHAPTER THREE

Luke stood back in court number one, listening to the judge addressing the people sitting in the courtroom, describing how he had balanced the serious nature of the offence against Mr Woods' previous good behaviour. He finally turned to speak directly to Luke.

"After careful consideration and deliberation, along with the view that knife crime must be tackled seriously for the safety of our community, I have come to a decision in regards to your tariff." He took a moment to observe the public gallery before continuing. "That, in plain terms, means the minimum number of years which you will serve in custody. My deliberations began at twenty years, this would not be disproportionate to the offence that you have been found guilty of. However, after careful thought, and reading the exemplary reports from Reading Football Club, I have decided that a tariff of ten years would be suitable. I trust that you will use this time wisely, and on release, once again become a useful member of our community. Take him down please officer."

A cry of, "Ten years is not enough!" came from within the public seating. A figure was quickly removed from the court, muffled shouts echoing from the corridor outside. The silence which ensued in the courtroom was disturbed only by the shuffle of his feet heading down the wooden stairs and back to confinement for a very long time.

He looked around at the other cells in this dank dungeon of a court building, not wanting to spend another minute there. The officer stopped outside cell number ten, the court staff's last dig at him. The metal cell door opened and the unspeaking court officer ushered him back into the secure setting that was to become his home for the next ten years.

Luke fought back the panic that slowly built inside his mind as he looked around the sterile, white - tiled cell, the back of the door covered with graffiti from long forgotten hands. He mumbled as he paced, "The rest of my life in places like this, I can't do it," before hammering on the back of the door with the palms of his hands. "I can't do this, please let me go home, I didn't do it." He fell to his knees sobbing, "I didn't do it, please believe me."

The door finally opened and the same non-caring officer looked down at his red eyes. "Get a grip of yourself. I have your family here to visit, do you want to see them?"

Luke nodded, and wiping his eyes with the palms of his hands, he slowly stood and followed the officer into a larger room that contained a cheap, wooden table and three chairs. Noticing that his mum and dad had been crying as well, his stomach flipped and his throat tightened as he struggled to hold his own emotions together for the sake of his parents.

"It's ok, everything will be alright Mum. I'll be home before I'm twenty nine years old so I'll still be a young man."

She tried to smile through her tears. "But you're still my baby, only just eighteen years old and thrown in prison, all because of an accident." Luke hugged her and stroked the back of her head as he looked at his father.

"Where's Jake? I thought that he might come to see me off."

Dad wiped his eyes. "He's gone back into training. He said that he needs to sort his head out. Apparently kicking a ball about is more important to him at the moment. I guess he just thinks that he was the lucky one."

Luke nodded, wiping his eyes with a tissue that had been left in a half finished box on the table. "I think he was the lucky one, maybe he thinks that he should have been sitting here instead of me." Dad shook his head.

"Who knows Luke, he said he's coming up by himself on Saturday to see you. We'll come and see you next week sometime, whenever you are allowed to send us a visiting order."

The court officer who stood by the half opened door cleared his throat. "We need to leave now, I'm sorry Mr and Mrs Woods, you have to go."

Standing, they all hugged one more time, Kim feeling strong again. "And we will chase an appeal Luke, we will never let this go." She turned at the door with a smile. "Believe it Luke, we will come back and pick you up one day, just hang on in there."

The familiar feeling of loneliness wrapped itself back around his shoulders as the hollow sound of them walking away sapped the last of Luke's resolve. He placed his forehead on the table as he considered what had just happened to him. Jake had got away with murder, and here he was doing the time for him. The tears were long gone by the time the guard came back for him.

The monotone cold voice, the type that almost sounded automated, droned into the silence of his despair. "Come on Woods, the van's waiting for you."

Luke stood with his hands to the front as the handcuffs were locked shut around his wrists, flinching as the weight rested on his wrist bones again. The clang of the steps being unfolded to allow him to board sent a shiver down his back as he moved forwards towards the darkness. This was his new reality, no longer a potential football star, now just another black prisoner with no future. One of the tens of thousands of bright lights who were extinguished by grief, his thoughts were interrupted as the vehicle engine fired up and the white van slowly made its way from Reading Crown Court and past the waiting media teams hungry for a photograph of a killer, before merging into the daily traffic, people unaware of the heartache contained within that secure van.

Looking through the small, meshed window, he caught sight of a young boy, maybe only five years old and still full of optimism, going into a park with a football. The enormity of the fact that he might never be able to do this with a son swept over him, hitting him like an icy wind. He shuddered and tried not to cry again as he looked down, hoping that the scene would disappear as quickly as it had come.

His attention was drawn to the beeping of a car horn beside the van. A red car had pulled up alongside as the traffic lights turned red and a group of youths jeered towards the windows. Luke recognised them as Robert Bell's friends from court who must have followed the van. Behind them was the familiar car of his parents, oblivious to what was unfolding, and as the lights changed, they drew alongside for a second and Luke banged on the window hoping that they would look up. As if in a dream they drove past, caught up in their own troubles and unaware of his plea for one last glimpse of their faces.

And then, unwelcome but inevitable, the foreboding walls of the prison loomed back into view giving him a few more seconds of freedom and public spaces before the great brown door closed securely again behind them, leaving him in another world - a place that the public would never see, a land of violence and survival of the fittest.

The smells of the reception building flooded back into his senses. He hated it but it gave a little comfort in the face of adversity, some sort of normality to this very unnatural environment for him. He looked through into the holding area and saw a group of new inductions waiting for their first taste of jail. Staring at the faces, nervous and already embracing the grey flesh tinge that all prisoners inherited while banged up, Luke gazed at them all, considering the short sentences that they would have in comparison to him, and he was the only real innocent one there.

A large reception officer stood waiting, grinning. "Ten years son, that was a result, trust me." He scribbled a signature on a document and handed it to the escorting officer.

"Just go in and see the healthcare staff and we will take you back to the wing," he instructed, pointing Luke in the direction of an office with an open door. Knocking, he could see an older male nurse typing on a keyboard before looking up. "Take a seat, name please."

"Luke Woods."

He checked the paperwork in front of him. "Oh yes, life sentence today, recommended ten years. How do you feel? Do you have any thoughts of self harm?"

Luke shook his head, "No, I just want to get back and arrange an appeal. I didn't kill anyone, that's the truth."

The nurse laughed. "It isn't me that you needed to convince, it was the jury and they said that you did do it. Any other issues?"

Luke shook his head again.

"Good, go back to the desk and they'll take you back to the wing." Looking towards the reception officer he shouted out, "Next please," dismissing Luke to his next ten years of misery as though he had just shooed away an unwanted caller. An officer came into reception, looking around before spotting Luke in a holding room. "This way Woods, I'm taking you back to the wing which saves you from sitting here for hours."

Luke followed him, unspeaking while they returned to his cell where he found the other bed empty. "Where has Mitchell gone?" he asked the officer who barely bothered to answer him.

"Bail, went this morning," he muttered before slamming the door shut with excessive force, causing small pieces of plaster to fall onto the already dirty floor. Luke stood, staring around at the confined space before noticing what looked like a hastily scribbled note lying on his pillow. It read:

Keep your head Luke, remember what I said, and watch your back. Some guys on here were asking too many questions about you. Take care. Mitchell.

The door reopened thirty minutes later to reveal a small black guy standing holding a bag of property. He walked straight in and tossed it onto the spare bed. "Fucking place is filthy," he stated before fist bumping Luke. "I'm Chris, from Tottenham, where you from?"

"Newbury, just down the road."

"Never heard of it. Why are you in here?"

"Murder, a guy died in a fight. He got stabbed in the

stomach."

The boy laughed. "You stabbed a man to death, rah. So did I bro, fucker was asking for trouble. Kept running from paying me what he owed. Caught him yesterday in a shit-hole town called Basingstoke....his face when he saw me."

Luke listened in shock at the way a murder was being described so blatantly to him, before adding, "But the difference is that I didn't do it."

Chris laughed, "Course not bro, we are all innocent. Difference is that if you don't accept that you are guilty, the parole guy ain't never letting you out, so even if you didn't do it bro, you might as well just say you did."

Quickly unpacking his bag he looked around again. "This is your first time isn't it? I can tell, the place is filthy. We either clean it up, or we move. I say we move, everything here is shoddy," He rang the cell bell and a short time later a young officer opened the cell flap. Chris stood in the middle of the cell, topless, flexing his huge torso. "We need to move out of this cell. The place is broken, I ain't staying in here."

The officer didn't have time to discuss it with him. "You haven't got a choice, keep off the bell." He slammed the flap shut as he left. Chris laughed to himself.

"Ok, these guys haven't realised that I don't play games. Keep close to me Luke when we are unlocked the next time." Silently Luke shook his head. Confrontation wasn't on his agenda today.

Later on that afternoon, the rattle of a key signalled that the cell door was being opened. "Come get your tea meal. Bring a bowl, you have soup as well."

Chris and Luke walked down the stairs, taking in the activity around them before joining a queue in a long line. Three boys pushed to the front as the staff ignored them. Chris nudged Luke. "See them white boys at the front? They're going to cause us trouble. Look around, nearly every face is white."

They slowly moved forward as people picked up their meals and walked back towards their cells. The three men stopped as they got level with Chris, soup slopping out from their bowls.

"You two can fuck off my wing, we don't have blacks on here, understand bro?" Shamus McCann sneered at them as he spoke. Chris ignored him, but McCann continued. "Don't let me down, by tomorrow you need to be on 'C' Wing. If you don't move we will fuck you up." He tipped his bowl, letting soup fall on Chris's trainers and two officers, noticing the confrontation moved closer.

"Bang up McCann," one told him but he ignored them, continuing to eye ball Chris. Chris threw up one of his massive arms, smacking into the bowl and causing the soup to go all over McCann. Some of the other prisoners laughed.

"You better fuck off and bang up McCann. If you bother me again, I'll knock your ugly arse on the floor." A group of staff now gathered and separated the two men facing up to each other.

Turning to Luke, Chris laughed. "See, I told you that they were trouble. Now, when we get our food, follow me." They took a plate of stew, ignoring the brown liquid the servers called soup. "Come with me, don't worry, just watch," Chris instructed a bemused Luke.

He sat on a pool table eating the food as Luke sat next to him. Two staff tried to move him back to the cell, but he refused.

"I told you earlier, we are not banging back up in that broken cell. Find me another clean cell and I will go, it's simple." The officer attempted to reason with him, but Chris wasn't listening.

"Just go get me the Governor, I'm not moving without seeing him."

Soon all the other prisoners were behind their cell doors, apart from Luke and Chris. Staff were mumbling, it was time for most of them to go home and this could cause them some delay. The wing manager walked over, an overweight man with a strong Welsh accent.

"What's happening here you two? Go back to your cell now."

Chris carried on eating, "No, the cell is a shit hole, we aren't going back in there. If you want us to bang up, either fight us and move us back in there, or find us a clean useable cell with windows. Trust me though, if you try to move us, you're going to need a lot more people than are staring at your flabby arse from the office."

The man looked around, seeing his staff watching him. "Ok, have it your way but one way or another you are going to go back to your cell, it's your choice."

The manager walked back to the office and picking up the phone, he made a short call while Luke sat on the table watching the game play out in front of him. Day two of a life sentence and already he was in trouble.

A man in a suit appeared at the gate. Chris whispered, "That's the duty Governor, let's see what sort of man he is."

He walked down towards them and sat on the table with them both. "Do you want to show me your cell? You said it's broken."

Chris laughed. "Yeah, and when we get there, your boys push us in and shut the door. No, that's not happening."

The Governor shouted down to the office. Mr. Evans, what cell are these two in?"

"3.25 boss." The Governor walked up onto the landing and looked into the cell before leaning over the landing rail and calling down.

"Mr Evans, that cell is a disgrace, put it off line and report it for repair. Where can these two go until it is fixed?"

Evans looked at the board in front of him. "4.15 is free boss, try that one."

Opening the door and inspecting it, the Governor shouted down again. "Yep this one is OK, come up here lads and have a look."

Chris sat his ground. "Go have a look Luke, let me know if it's okay." Standing up, Luke climbed the stairs to where the governor was waiting. He looked in at the spotless cell before shouting down, "all good Chris." Collecting their possessions quickly, they moved into the fresh, clean cell, the door closing

30

behind them. Chris burst into laughter. "See Luke, lesson number one, if you don't stick up for yourself, no one else will." He lay back on the bed still smiling.

"Now we just need to worry about those racist idiots - that might be somewhat harder."

CHAPTER FOUR

Jake strapped on his heart monitor and jogged out onto the pitch. Reading had suffered the heartache of losing a playoff final and the prize of promotion to the Premiership had been cruelly snatched away from them at Wembley Stadium. Ian Woodford, the manager stopping him briefly as the two chatted in the June sun. "How is it going Jake? Is Luke holding up alright?" Jake shrugged; even talking about Luke made him feel hollow,

"Yes boss, I'm going in to see him this weekend. Ten years and he didn't even do anything."

Ian looked at his clip board while still chatting. "Just count yourself lucky that you aren't with him. Get your head straight, I'm taking you on the pre-season tour with the first team where you'll get some match time. My plan for next season is to use you as an impact substitution, give you a few starts from the bench and a couple of cup games. Let's see how they deal with your strength and pace....defenders will bloody hate playing against you."

Jake nodded with a grin. "You better believe it."

The training session had passed by in a blur, but at least Jake had some focus in order to escape the burden of guilt he felt. The rest of the squad had gathered together in the training ground restaurant area, Jake sitting with another two Under 23 squad players who had been invited into the training session to assess their characters. A pair of hands clasped firmly over his shoulders and Jake turned to see that it was the club captain, Steve Evans.

"Jake, a little birdie has just told me that you will be coming to Sweden on the pre-season tour. You know what that means don't you?"

Jake's friends laughed. "Oh my God, man, you have to give them a song."

He smiled, somewhat nervously. "Shit, when do I have to do it?"

Steve pointed at the manager. "Boss, can this be a special one, like last time?"

Ian put down his fork. "It looks like it Steve. I will leave that to you."

Jake had some panic in his voice as he asked, "What's a special one?"

Steve pushed out his chest, showing the club badge off on his training top.

"Ok Jake, you'll like this. Gatwick Airport departure lounge, the entire world will see it on YouTube and Facebook, so it better be good old son." He strutted back to the tables where the first team players were sitting.

"Oh, one more thing Jake, if you're coming on tour, you'd better get your arse over onto these tables. If you want to be in the first team squad you need to eat with us as well."

Jake looked at his Under 23 squad team mates as though for approval. One smiled at him before adding, "You deserve the chance mate, get over there and do well. Good luck buddy."

Jake picked up his plate and walked towards the first team table where a space had been cleared for him to sit down and join them. Steve looked over at Ian and winked; Jake was one of them now.

A few miles away Luke picked up a very different type of meal and walked back to his cell, kicking his metal door shut with a resounding thump as he entered. He had no thoughts of fame and fortune, just on lasting another day without getting hurt in this jungle he now lived in. Only one more day and he would see Jake for the first time since court, and his mind raced to the conversation that they would have. How the hell do you greet someone who has just dumped you in prison for life?

Jake woke with a knot in his stomach on Saturday morning,

he would be visiting Luke for the first time in prison and looking at his new watch he saw that he had only an hour before the visit session would start. Mum and Dad were planning a shopping trip around Reading while Jake had the visit and Kim called up to him from downstairs. "Twenty minutes and we're leaving, have a shower before we go please."

Jake knew what was coming, in his mind Luke was going to ask him to admit the stabbing, face the court and get a lot longer than ten years. He had lied to the judge, told him that he didn't know what had happened and he could expect at least twenty years if he were lucky. In less than two hours his dreams could be dead.

Desmond and Kim noticed how silent he was in the back of the car. "I hope that you're going to be a bit more talkative with Luke, what's wrong with you?" Kim asked. "You haven't stopped chatting about the football tour since you found out that you were going and now we can't get two words out of you."

Jake continued looking out of the window wondering if this would be the last time he saw the countryside.

"It's just different Mum, I don't like the thought of him in there, I feel bad for him."

Kim turned in her seat to half face him as she spoke. "It's the same for us, but if you're not going to enjoy the visit, me and dad will take your place."

Shaking his head he half smiled. "No, I need to get this done. It'll be fine, honestly."

The tall, brick walls of the prison soon loomed over him and the greasy smell from the McDonalds burger bar drifting across the main road from the car park opposite suddenly seemed a more attractive proposition. He looked around, unsure about where to go or what to do before seeing another family of visitors entering a doorway by the large main vehicle gate. Following them in, he copied what everyone else seemed to be doing and noticing an overweight white lady push her visiting order through the hatch in the sealed gate area, Jake pulled his from his own pocket. He listened as instructions were given to her. "Do you have a mobile phone in your possession? Please place all bags in the secure lockers on your left."

Mentally he checked through his pockets, thankful that he hadn't brought anything with him, while an array of signs on the walls signalled the secure environment that he was entering. He felt a knot of apprehension in his stomach as suddenly it was his turn at the window.

A tired looking man wearing an ill fitting uniform of white shirt and black trousers stood behind a thick glass counter and took the Visiting Order from him. "Do you have any of these items on you?" he pointed to a long list on the wall.

"No, I haven't got anything," he answered.

Scanning the visiting order and identification, the officer pushed the papers back towards him without looking back up. "Ok, go through the door behind you and wait," he told Jake.

The buzz of a sliding door opening showed him the way into a waiting area. Jake entered and sat with another twenty or so families, keeping his eyes on the floor, not wishing to make conversation with anyone. He didn't feel as though he belonged in this environment, it should just be for other people, not for him and his brother.

With a click, a door at the far end of the room opened as visitors were called forwards and again Jake showed his visiting order. This time the staff searched him and he hated the process instantly; strangers rubbing their hands over his body seemed both intrusive and embarrassing. A disinterested voice gave a command. "Step onto number one please."

Looking at the numbers written on the tiled floor, he stood feet astride the number one as again the monotone voice instructed him what to do next.

"Do not move, and do not touch the dog please."

A Springer spaniel worked his way around the five visitors standing in line.

"Ok thank you, move through to the visits room please, next

five people please."

An officer stood by a blue wooden door, watching as the visitors came towards him. They congregated for a moment before the dog handler gave him the thumbs up. The door swung open and Jake found himself in a large visits room where each table had a prisoner sitting at the far side, all wearing orange bibs. He quickly spotted Luke sitting near the desk where the staff were congregating. A cheap grey track suit seemed to hang off him and an orange bib, similar to the one he had last worn for football training, shone brightly, but an expression of desperation was etched deeply across his unsmiling face.

Pulling out a chair and sitting down, they bumped fists.

"Fuck Luke, this is difficult. I don't know what to say man." He looked his brother in the eye, hoping for any sign of forgiveness.

Luke just shrugged. "How about starting with sorry? I'm sitting here for ten years for something that you did. Do you know what it is like in here? This place is dangerous, it's not a joke Jake."

Jake's eyes clouded for a second before he composed himself. "I'm sorry, I didn't mean to end our last conversation like I did, it wasn't how it sounded."

Luke gave a look of mock surprise. "It sounded to me like you admitted stabbing the guy to death, you know, ten minutes before you walked free and I was banged up."

Whispering quietly, Jake responded. "No, it wasn't like that. The guy was trying to choke me on the table and you were pulling him off. I didn't know that I had picked the knife up and when he struggled free from you and fell on me, that's when it happened. What do you want me to do?"
They stared at each other for a second before Luke replied.

"You could have told the truth, but there's nothing we can do now. I'm not going to let you go to the police, you'll get twice as long as me for lying so let it go. I'll just do the time, I won't give you up. You're my brother, my best friend."

He stood and they hugged, both crying. An officer separated them, as he spoke to Jake.

"Sit down please, otherwise I will have to ask you to leave."

As Luke sat back down he noticed that McCann was having a visit three tables along. Two skinhead thugs and a heavily tattooed woman with a baby were talking loudly, McCann pointing towards Luke and the entire table turned before laughing. Jake looked at them, confused.

"What's that all about Luke?"

Luke kept his head lowered, trying not to look over at the other table.

"That prick is a racist, my cell mate had a row with him during the week. He's bad news and I'm trying to stay clear of him until I get a move to my next prison." Taking a sip from a plastic cup of water he changed the subject. "How's the football going? Any news on starting a game yet?"

A beam appeared across Jake's face. "I'm going on the pre-season tour. Ian Woodford told me that I'll play in Sweden and if it goes well, I'll get some game time in the season. Worse thing is, I have to do the initiation song for the first team squad."

Luke managed a smile. "Oh my God, that could have been me as well bro, at least there are some good things happening."

Jake nodded. "If I score this season, I'll do a secret celebration for you. Watch the TV when I score."

Luke smiled, but cringed inside, listening as Jake detached himself from what he had done. "Just don't forget me in here when you become famous and remember to send me a little bit of your million pound pay cheque."

A voice sounded out of nowhere. "Time please, everyone finish off your visits."

The call from the staff made everyone hurry their conversations. Luke fist bumped Jake before glancing over at McCann just as the woman visiting him passed something under the table. He took it and pushed his hand into his tracksuit bottoms. It all took just a second and as he sat back up, he noticed that Luke had spotted him and gave him a look of hatred. Luke looked away hurriedly, wishing that he hadn't seen anything.

Jake stood as the remainder of the visitors began to leave the room. "Ok brother, are we good?"

"Yes Jake, it's all good. Listen, be brilliant in Sweden, I'll keep in touch through Mum while you're out there."

They hugged again before Jake turned and left. Looking back as the visits door closed, he saw Luke's smile disappear from his face as the two worlds separated once more but there was nothing else he could do to help, not unless he wanted twenty years.

The rumble of traffic outside the prison gate seemed a welcome distraction as he mingled with the other visitors leaving. The three visitors who had just seen McCann barged into Jake in the car park area, one of them laughing at him as he spoke.

"Careful boy! Oh and by the way, we know who you are, football star. Your brother is going to get fucked up in there soon. Next time you come to see him, you will bring a little package in with you. If you don't, things will be really tough for him, do you understand me?" He pushed a phone number into Jake's hand.

"Two weeks time, phone me and I'll meet up with you and give you the stuff. Your brother can pass it onto my friend. I'm sure a clever superstar like you can work out the rest." He didn't wait for an answer, running over the road to join his friends before heading into McDonalds. Jake looked at the number before throwing it into the bin. "No thanks," he muttered.

Luke stood in line, waiting for his turn to be searched by the officers before he was allowed back to his wing. McCann stood beside him.

"Next time your brother comes to visit you, he'll have a package for me. You saw what I did with mine, you do the same."

Luke stared back at McCann. "I will never allow him to bring anything in here for you, I would rather go without visits."

McCann laughed. "Of course you would, but if you and your brother value your health, you will do as you're told. My boys outside can hurt your family, I can hurt you. And if you want to test me, I can have someone knock on your mum's door tonight, 66 Southdown Street. Does that sound familiar? Right next door to an old bird who does the gardening in her bra - one of my boys saw her yesterday."

Inside, Luke deflated like an old birthday balloon, the address was correct and the description of his nosy old neighbour was spot on. McCann must be having the family watched.

McCann laughed again. "Don't play poker Woods, I can read you like a Sunday paper. My people live in your town, we are everywhere. Phone your mum, tell her to expect a visitor tonight."

Luke stuttered, "No need, we will do it just this once, understood?"

McCann grabbed him by the throat, his powerful fingers biting into Luke's neck. "No you will not black man," he spat the last two words out. "You will do it when I say," he said, pausing for a second before letting Luke go. "Understand?"

Luke didn't respond, angry for not standing up for himself. An older male officer searched him as he passed out of the visits area, looking at his neck as he checked through his pockets.

"Why have you got all of those scratches on your throat? They weren't there when you came in."

Luke shrugged his shoulders, "Just had an itch while I was waiting, no big deal sir."

The officer looked at him suspiciously. "Bullshit son, something has happened, I'll come and see you later," before waving him through and back onto 'A' Wing.

Chris stood by the busy pool table, jeans hanging round his backside, looking every inch a London gangster. Two big white lads played another game as a group of smaller boys waited. This had been their third game and Chris didn't even want to play, but enough was enough and a point needed to be made. He walked over and took the cue from the biggest guy, a six foot twenty-year-old man with a full beard who looked down on him as Chris took it off him, and then glanced around at the people watching. He felt silly and it was obvious to everyone what was in the process of happening as half heartedly he complained.

"Give me the cue back, you can play next, we're doing the best of three." His friend walked round the table and stood by him, also staring down at Chris.

Unmoved, he stood his ground. "I couldn't give a fuck what you think you are playing, what I'm telling you is that I'm playing now, and so is my friend Luke over there." Luke heard his name and walked over, unaware of the situation.

The big lad tried to grab the cue back from Chris before a heavy punch to the jaw sent him crashing over the green cloth. He looked up at Chris dazed, not wanting to feel anymore of his power and blood trickled from his nose as he shook his head in submission. Chris had smashed one part of the racist thug's gang.

"Like I just said, me and Luke are playing." He stared at the other white lad.

"Give Luke your stick, you have just finished," he ordered him.

Ten seconds later Luke was setting the balls up for his break and two new enemies were slinking back to their cell to lick their wounds. The crowd around the table dispersed allowing them to play as many games as they liked as McCann walked past, noticing that his friends were not controlling the table anymore. He headed directly to their cell before walking calmly back down the stairs to talk to Chris.

"You may think that you're going to come onto my wing and take over but I will not allow it. If you don't move, I will move you myself." Chris sized McCann up before replying; he was a powerfully built, twenty-year-old man, thrown out of the Parachute regiment after a court martial for the death of a civilian in a bar in Aldershot. These two were destined to fight, just not today.

"Ok McCann, we have a problem, I'm not moving, and I don't think that you or your boys are going to make me change my mind. You've just seen what happens to your boys when they don't listen to me…." They stared each other down before McCann turned and went back to his own cell leaving Luke pale with concern.

"Chris, I've just got ten years, he's threatening my family already and if my brother doesn't bring in a package on his next visit he's going to hurt my mum and dad." Chris played his shot, the red ball missing by a mile before standing up straight and facing Luke.

"I'm not here to fight your battles, Luke, in case you haven't noticed I only fight my own. You have ten years to do so it's time to stand on your own two feet. You need to stand up to McCann yourself – I'll have your back, but I'm not doing your work for you."

An officer walked past, yelling out at the top of his voice - "All away 'A' Wing."

The sound of doors banging echoed around the wing until a voice called out. "Not you Woods."

It was the officer from the visits room and he took Luke into an office, the remainder of the prisoners now safely back in their cells.

"Ok Woods, I'm Mr Davies. I saw what happened back in the visits room, why was McCann threatening you?" Luke remained silent, considering what he should say. Seeing his dilemma, the officer reassured him.

"Look, there's no need to worry, the guy is a bully. If you tell me what's going on, I'll have him and his little gang moved a long way away, but you need to be brave and speak out."

"Does this come back to me? The prison is a small place and if I'm known as a grass I'll be hurt." Luke looked worried as he spoke.

The officer smiled. "It's not grassing Woods, this person needs to be dealt with. Why is he threatening you?"

Luke told his story for the next two minutes as the officer listened.

"Ok Luke, go back to your cell. Tell your cell mate that I was talking to you about your appeal and leave the rest to us. Okay?" Luke nodded and headed back to his cell where the rattle of the food trolleys arriving on the wing told him that it was nearly time for dinner. Chris looked at him as he walked in, but didn't ask him any questions, he didn't need to. The answer was written all over Luke's face - he had grassed up for the first time.

The line for the evening meal was subdued, the news was spreading around the wing that McCann was unhappy with the two new guys. Luke held out his tray for his meat pie. The prisoner serving him leaned forwards and barely audibly whispered, "McCann is planning to fuck you up, he thinks that you've grassed him up to the staff."

A knot tightened in Luke's stomach as he wondered how McCann could know. Did the officer go directly to him to tell McCann what was said? Or was he just guessing, knowing the officer from the visits room had witnessed the incident and later came onto the wing to talk about it. Either way he would need to talk with Chris and took his opportunity as they sat in the cell eating and watching TV.

"Chris, we have a problem." Chris looked up.

"No, you have a problem. I'm not stupid, you grassed that kid up to the screw. I could see it on your face. The whole wing knows what it means when a screw takes you into an office when everyone else is banged up."

Luke put his half eaten meal on his locker top. "I didn't know what to do, he put it on me. I didn't have any choice and anyway, they're going to move him and his gang to another prison."

Chris laughed. "You'll meet up with him again as you're both young offenders serving life. There are only a few prisons that you can go to. Trust me, within the next few years you'll meet up again so just be ready because he's going to have to hurt you badly. Plus every other prisoner will have you marked down as a grass. That makes you a dangerous person to mix with so after today we go our own ways."

Luke looked on in disbelief. "What are you saying?"

"What I'm saying is that I have a long sentence to do as well and I need to do it as easily as I can. If we are banged up together everyone will suspect me of grassing as well and I don't do that stuff. I understand why it happened, but it was a bad mistake."

Luke nodded although this was the last thing he needed to hear. "And what about tonight? I'm having a shower and those bastards will be after me."

Chris sighed and threw his towel on his bed. "Stop worrying, I'll be there. I didn't say that we weren't friends, just that I can't be living in the same cell as you."

Luke lay on his bed reading a book as the cell door unlocked and a young cheerful looking female officer stuck her head into the cell.

"Ok lads, association time. You have two hours out tonight so if I were you I would grab a shower quickly as the whole wing are out."

Chris looked over at him. "You hear that Luke? They have enough screws on duty to get the whole wing out, that means that your friends are going to be out as well."

Luke put the book down on the green sheet on his bed.

"Shit, I need to get in the shower quickly, hopefully before they come out of their cells." He grabbed his towel and shower gel. "I'm getting in there now, are you coming or am I on my own?"

Chris picked up his own towel and threw it over his shoulder. Dressed in just his blue prison shorts and flip flops he looked an imposing sight with his short cropped hair and bulging muscles. "No, you're not alone, but this is the last time Luke.

You're on your own from tomorrow."

They walked down the three flights of metal steps to reach the showers that were on the ground floor level, seeing through the window that two other prisoners were finishing up, just washing the shampoo from their hair before drying themselves.

Chris pushed the blue wooden door open and the smell of stagnant drains hit his nose. The room was around half the size of a badminton court with white tiles covering the walls which were discoloured and in need of cleaning and grouting.

A knee high wooden bench covered three walls while at the far end was an open shower area with eight shower heads and no privacy from a casual gaze. Two smelly mops and a metal bucket were leaning against the wall as a drain filled with empty prison shampoo sachets did its best to collect any water making it that far. Luke stripped off before pushing the steel button to start the shower and a steady stream of warm water poured over him. In another half an hour it would be replaced with cold as the boilers lost the race with the demand, so it paid to be first.

Chris sat on the bench watching through the window over the landing outside while the two other occupants dressed quickly feeling the tension and knowing they would rather be anywhere else.

The shampoo stung Luke's eyes as he heard the shower room door open again. He rinsed his face before looking out, instantly wishing he hadn't. McCann and two of his best men were standing blocking the door and he was armed.

McCann moved forwards before seeing that Chris was sitting behind him. Luke stood in silence as the well orchestrated ballet of violence began to unfold in front of his eyes. Chris had stuck to his word, his courage immeasurable as he placed himself in the way of danger, a miscalculated attempt to make the gang back down and leave.

"I told you and your racist friends to fuck off, I'm not telling you again McCann," Chris said as he stood facing all three of the attackers. "You fuck with my friend, you need to take care of me too."

Not taking his eyes from Chris's face, McCann spoke as he moved forwards.

"Let's do the cunt."

The bar crashed into his head, almost without a sound. Chris partly spun around, Luke seeing that his eyes were shut as he hit the floor. Something about the way he lay crumpled and bleeding told Luke that he was dead, even as he bent to feel for a pulse. The blood lust had not yet been satisfied as McCann and his henchmen moved towards Luke, ignoring the devastation that lay at their feet. The second crash of the iron bar was different, designed to damage and destroy flesh and bone. This was pure vengeance.

The following events passed in a blur as Luke lay crumpled and in agony on the wet shower room floor, Chris's dead body still spilling blood across the filthy tiles, the wail of an alarm bell magnified as the door burst open and staff ran in.

A nurse shouted at Chris, "Can you hear me?" as she tried to find a pulse while the automated voice from a defib machine gave her the commands of what must happen next. The thud of the shock was followed by a panicked voice.

"Nothing."

The machine buzzed into life again as another shock was given.

"Nothing."

A trolley was pushed into the shower and Luke found himself lifted into the air. The pain was intense as a mask was placed over his face, the harsh lights burning his eyes before he drifted into an assisted sleep.

His eyes flickered open again, the pain once more sweeping over his body. He was in a place he didn't recognise and a tugging on his wrist made him look down drowsily. A handcuff was attached to him with a long chain secured to a fat officer, his stomach hanging below his black leather belt and the signs hanging from the ceiling spelt out that he was in the Royal Berkshire Hospital in Reading. He had only been in here three months before for a knee scan.

Wincing as the trolley banged through another set of doors, Luke became aware of the agony from his leg again, the deep pain making him look down towards his shin where a white bone sticking from his naked leg made him feel sick. His entire body began shaking from the inside out and a cold sweat broke out across his forehead. Seeing his agony, a doctor leant over him and slid a needle into his arm and the pain drifted away.

He awoke again and this time things felt different although still confusing as he looked at the face of a nurse talking to him. "Evening Luke, we have just operated on your leg and it's all fixed. You just need to rest now. The surgeon will see you later." The tug on his wrist reminded him that they were not alone.

"You'll be moved to a ward in a bit where the two officers here will be staying with you. Try sleep if you can."

CHAPTER FIVE

Jake sat in the changing room in the Madejski Stadium, Reading FC where the team were about to play a friendly match against Spurs, the last game before the Sweden tour. The manager, Ian Woodford, came in with the team sheet.

"Okay lads, listen in. Everyone is getting a run out tonight, that includes you Jake." His heart thumped - he had thought that he was there just to soak up the first team atmosphere. The manager continued.

"We're putting out a strong starting eleven and I want you to work on the formations and set plays. Be brave and get on the front foot. They are putting out a full strength team tonight which shows the respect that they have for us."

Desperately wanting to phone his parents to tell them he was going to be playing, Jake hunted for his phone as Woodford smiled at him.

"I've already called them, your parents are both here Jake. You will get the last twenty minutes."

The changing room door opened and the kit man came in, hanging up a fresh kit from a spare peg. Jake read the name on the back of the first team shirt, *'Woods'*, as the manager continued.

"Okay lads, let's get out there and warm up as we need to have a good intensity from the start. We'll have around eighteen thousand in the ground tonight so let's show them what we are all about."

The captain, Steve Evans walked over.

"Come on Jake, soak it up. A Wednesday night game under the floodlights - what a way to make your debut."

Jogging out, Jake looked up into the stands where he guessed his parents would be taking advantage of some hospitality before the game. The East Stand stood proudly and directly in front of him, the blue and white seats beginning to fill up. Jogging over the closely cut grass, he took in the buzz from all around him, even looking at the seat in which he used to watch every home match. He heard a young lad ask his dad who the new player was and the answer sent a little shiver down Jake's back.

"He's an academy player, scores lots of goals. Number 36, Jake Woods, he's really fast and can use both feet. Watch what he does, you can try out his tricks on Sunday."

Jake's heart swelled as he looked over at the father and son, the boy holding out the programme with a pen. Jake jogged over and signed for the first time in his life before starting the warm up. The mood changed and became more intense, the crowd noise drifting away as he concentrated on getting the drills right. He didn't want to make himself look silly on his first ever warm up routine. Another couple of shuttle runs and he was back down into the changing rooms with five minutes until kick off. The academy manager walked in and spotted Jake as he sat nervously, waiting for his debut.

"Jake, I have some bad news mate, follow me to the office." Jake's stomach turned cartwheels, trying to figure out what had gone so wrong. The manager closed the door and turned to face Jake.

"Your parents can't come tonight, Luke has been involved in an incident. He has just had an operation on a broken leg so the boss has left it up to you if you play or not, he understands." Jake sat shocked, "Shit, is he okay?"

"I think so, I'll leave you to give your parents a call. Let me know what you decide, I'll need to tell Ian." He left the office, leaving Jake to make his call.

His mother picked up the phone on the first ring.

"Mum, what's happened? If you want me to come I will. The manager says that it's alright if I miss the game tonight." He was speaking in a high pitched stressful tone that Kim recognised all too well and he could tell that she had been crying as he listened to her reply.

"A gang of thugs in the prison have just attacked Luke and his friend. They have broken Luke's leg badly, but his friend is dead. How the hell can that be allowed to happen in a prison?"

Jake looked down at his phone in horror, the shock making him feel cold and shaky. "How is he? Was the operation successful?"

His mother started sobbing again, and unable to make herself understood Jake then heard his dad's voice on the phone.

"Hi Jake, your brother is ok, we're on the way there now to speak to the surgeon. You can't do anything over here anyway and the prison officers are not allowing visitors to see him at all. Play tonight, but promise me that you'll get the official club recording of the game. Luke will want to see your debut as much as we do so don't worry, just be brilliant for us all."

Jake ended the call looking at the blank screen as though all the answers would present themselves to him. There was a knock on the office door and
Ian Woodford came in and put an arm around Jake.

"What do you want to do? I will leave it up to you to decide if you want to play."

Determination and resilience flowed back, showing in Jake's body language as he looked his manager in the eye.

"I want to come on and score the winning goal, boss. There's nothing that I can do at the hospital and I want to show Luke the recording of it after."

Ian smiled. "I knew that you were a winner from day one Luke, get yourself ready, son."

Sitting on the bench was an exciting experience as he listened to both managers barking instructions. The players flashed past him at a speed above anything he had seen before and Spurs were magnificent, scoring two early goals before the Reading captain was fouled on the edge of the penalty area. It was on the stroke of half time, the referee telling him that this would be the last kick of the half. Steve Evans carefully placed the ball down, a five man wall standing in front of him forming a solid white shirted barrier. A shout from the Spurs French goalkeeper bellowed out, trying to position his players to protect the goal. Evans drove the ball over the left hand man and it arrowed into the top corner, evading the keeper's desperate effort to claw it over the bar. Three sides of the ground erupted, Jake's spine tingling at the sight of the crowd celebrating wildly, even though this was only a friendly game. The whistle blew even before the keeper managed to pick the ball out of the net. It was half time and Reading were back in with a chance.

The superstars of Spurs strolled off the pitch while the blue and white hoops of Reading jogged past them, itching to get back onto the field to get the equaliser. Ian Woodford was buoyant back in the changing room.

"Brilliant lads, if we had another five minutes left in that half we would have been level, keep up the pressure."

Jon Cushing, the small striker came walking into the changing area, his boots and socks off. "I've pulled my calf boss, I need to come off." Ian looked at him with disappointment. It wasn't the first time that this had happened in a big game and the papers had questioned his attitude after the Wembley final. Jake saw Ian look in his direction before speaking.

"Jake, I can't bring you on yet. Sam, go warm up, you're coming on for Jon."

Jake's heart sank for a second before Steve sat himself down beside him.

"Head up Jake. I know it's tough but Sam is our second choice striker. Keep positive, you will come on, the boss has told you."

The second half flew by and when Jake looked up at the large scoreboard seventy minutes had passed with twenty to go. The game was finely balanced at 2.1 to Spurs so there could be no way the manager would risk a change. Sam was causing confusion in the Spurs defence and had just hit the post with a diving header. Jake marvelled at his positioning around the area, he seemed to be a league above him in ability.

"Jake!" The word rumbled along the bench and he looked up.

"Warm up, you're coming on son." Jake jogged down the line, supporters shouting his name as he did so. He gave a long look at the Spurs defence before he took his tracksuit top off; three England internationals, each paid in excess of ten thousand pounds a week just to stop him scoring. He would make them earn every penny.

He stood listening to Ian giving him last minute instructions. "I'm leaving Sam up front, I want you to play on the right, but cut in whenever you have the chance. Good luck son, take this chance to show us what you can do."

The pace of the game was so much faster than the Under 23 games and twice he was beaten to the ball before he could run with it. In any other game he had played in the last season he would have made the ball and been in at goal, but these guys were a different sort of animal, their anticipation and reading of the game almost super human.

Steve Evans picked up the ball in the half way circle and spotting Jake in space he sprayed a fifty yard ball out to his feet. Without thinking about it Jake took it down and knocked it past the defender. Sam was busting a gut to get into the penalty box as Jake sailed a beautiful cross over onto his head and a powerful header thumped the crossbar before the Spurs captain hacked the ball out of play. The crowd rose to their feet as the ball came to Jake again and he could feel the excitement from the fans as he controlled the ball and beat the defender again. This time he cut into the box himself, ignoring Sam's calls to pass before thumping an unstoppable shot into the bottom corner. The roof of the stadium almost exploded off as he threw his arms in the air, the team mobbing him in joy as the opposition re-gathered themselves for the restart.

The main screen below the scoreboard showed the goal again as he jogged back and it was only then that he realised he had gone past the Scottish International captain, Don Dooley as though he were standing still.

Spurs kicked off with the scoreboard showing two minutes to go. The Reading goalkeeper, Lenny Fuller, caught a lame effort of a shot and noticed Jake in space. He punted the ball out to him, Jake killing it dead before turning to run at goal. Don Dooley had other ideas and took Jake out with a two footed tackle, the referee showing the red card without hesitation. Dooley turned to Jake before he traipsed off.

"Try to make a mug of me son and I will snap your fucking legs." Steve Evans bundled over and grabbed Dooley by the shirt. "You're past it Dooley, and you tried to break his leg. He's a kid! Fuck off the pitch idiot, it's supposed to be a fucking friendly." Dooley turned and walked, he knew better than to argue with Steve.

Jake lay on the pitch, a crushing pain in his ankle. A couple of team mates wandered over before waving quickly towards the bench for help. The trainer ran on.

"What's up Jake?" The tear down his sock and the blood seeping onto his blue boots told the story as the trainer inspected his leg. "Yep, a few stitches needed and a scan. Let's get you off."

Jake hobbled around the pitch to a standing ovation from the home supporters. He had tasted the highs and lows of professional football all in twenty frantic minutes.

Sitting back in the changing room with the club doctor, he felt as though he was part of the first team at last, the adrenaline masking the pain from the gash and the feeling of his first goal still fresh in his mind. The doctor finished his examination and brought Jake back down to earth with his next words.

"This is a job for the hospital Jake, I'll get transport arranged. The cut is too deep for me to deal with here and I'm afraid the Sweden trip is off for you. We need you fit for the first game of the season in three weeks time and if this is as bad as I think, you're going to be out for a while." He patted Jake on the back as he left.

The car pulled up outside the A&E department and Jake

hobbled through the sliding door on crutches, the team physiotherapist accompanying him. Two corridors away there was a very different story being played out.

The door opened to the family restroom at the end of the ward and a stocky prison officer came in and sat opposite Kim Woods. Although he had the physique of a MMA fighter he had a kind face.

"Mr and Mrs Woods?" he enquired. They both nodded before Kim asked the question. "How is Luke doing? We've been told by the hospital staff that you're not letting us visit him."

He nodded. "It's not that simple, the security department and the Duty Governor have told us that he can't have visitors. They're worried that he was the witness to a crime. If the gang know that he's here, they could come and find him. We just need to cautious." He gave a sigh. "But if you're quick, and promise to not tell anyone, my manager and I will let you have five minutes."

Kim stood and hugged the officer while Desmond held out his hand. "You're a good man, Officer. I promise that we will not say a word."

Following him into a private room they saw Luke asleep on the bed, a heavy chain attached to his wrist. A smaller female officer fastened to the other end of the metal chain with a single handcuff, sat reading a book but looked up and acknowledged them both as they stood by the bed. Luke didn't respond, still firmly asleep. Desmond turned to the male officer.

"Do you know what happened in the prison? Have they caught who did this yet?"

The officer nodded. "This is off the record but a small racist gang targeted Luke and his cell mate. They were due to be moved to another prison tomorrow and they should have been locked up all evening but someone made a massive mistake and unlocked their doors."

Kim gasped. "So someone in your prison knew that Luke and the other boy were in danger and still let it happen?"

The female officer interjected. "We don't know for sure that that's what happened, there will be an investigation." Desmond looked at her shoulder epaulets and saw she had different markings from the first guy. "Are you in charge here tonight?" he asked, his anger rising with what he was hearing.

"Yes, I'm a Senior Officer, and if anyone gets wind that I allowed you in here, I will be a former Senior Officer." She put her book down and looked at them with sympathy in her eyes. "The police are investigating and they will speak to Luke when he's awake. Until then, all we know is that a gang targeted your son and his cell mate. I promise that once the facts are known, you will be informed instantly."

A muffled voice came from the crumpled sheets. "Mum? Dad?"

Kim leaned over the bed as a chair was pulled up for her. She held Luke's hand and stroked his hair. "We were so worried Luke, we spoke with the Duty Governor at the prison earlier when he phoned and told us that you were here. They're going to move you to another prison tomorrow."

Luke shook his head, thinking about what Chris had told him. "No, they'll find me. They are all getting moved as well so we might end up in the same prison again."

Stroking his cheek Kim smiled. "No, he has promised us that the three boys who did this will all go to an adult prison and they've been charged with murder tonight. You're going to a special unit near Henley-on-Thames where they have a small place for boys like you. He told us it's called Patterson Unit in a Young Offenders prison named Huntercombe. Apparently it's great for sport and education." Luke gave a weak smile before closing his eyes again, the painkillers doing their job.

Three hundred yards away Jake sat oblivious to his brother's condition with a doctor looking at the wound to his leg.

"I think that you're a very lucky chap as normally with injuries such as these we have to operate and the recovery time is months rather than weeks. However, with this one and your age and fitness, we'll be able to opt for rehabilitation work at the club. The operation would have been a very different prospect, put it this way, you wouldn't have kicked a ball for months and it would most certainly have put an end to the first half of your football season. It's deep but we can give you normal stitches and you'll be back on your feet playing in a couple of weeks. A young lad like you will retain plenty of fitness." The doctor looked at the physiotherapist. "Get him on the exercise bike in a couple of days and he can do some upper body exercises as well to bulk up slightly."

Opening his wallet he took out a Reading season ticket and waved it proudly.

"We need this lad on the pitch, my son has told me about your goal this evening, very exciting times young man." A nurse appeared pushing a small suture trolley and the doctor spoke again, this time with a wide smile on his face.

"Now do a good job please Zara. That foot could be worth a few million pounds over the next few months." His white coat disappeared back through the curtain as he made his way to the next patient.

CHAPTER SIX

The prison van drove the short drive from Reading along the leafy roads just outside Henley-On-Thames. Luke felt the van slow down as it prepared to take a right hand turn down what appeared to be a single track, private road. Peering through the small window, he saw the green metal fence of the prison loom into view while beautiful gardens adorned either side of the main gate as the van pulled in before stopping by the reception building.

The metal steps clanged down as the van cell door was unlocked and a middle aged man dressed in prison uniform leaned in and grabbed Luke's property which had been hastily packed by a member of the prison staff. It was sealed in a thick plastic bag with a blue plastic tie securing the contents. The officer looked up, his Scottish accent cutting through the hum of the vehicle engine.

"Get your arse down here son, I have a nurse waiting who is going to tell me if we're going to keep you here with that wound on your leg. We don't have a hospital wing here, so if it needs too much treatment, you're heading straight back to Reading."

Luke hobbled down and through the reception entrance where a kind looking woman in her mid forties sat in a side office, her blue uniform giving the clue that she was the person who would be making the next decision.

"Okay love, take a seat, let's see what we have got here." Her cheery Yorkshire accent made Luke feel at ease as she took a large brown A4 size envelope from the officer and carefully opened it. Luke could see the hospital details written on an official letter and held his breath while she read on, hoping that she would give the authority for him to stay. Eventually she looked up over the top of her glasses. "You have been in the wars, chuck. Looking at the hospital discharge letter it seems that we can look after you here but it's important that you come to our clinic every morning so that we can keep an eye on you."

She turned to the officer. "Okay Mr McGrath, we can keep him here." She turned and looked at Luke, giving him a wink.

"You'll be okay here, just relax a bit, this place is nice," before adding, "for a prison."

The sound of the vehicle engine starting up and driving back through the gates without him was possibly the best sound Luke had heard in a long time before Mr McGrath shouted through to the nurse from his desk, his gruff voice making Luke jump. "When you are finished with Woods, send him round to me. I need to process his property before he goes onto Patterson Unit."

She looked at Luke and smiled. "He isn't really as horrid as he sounds," she reassured him while still reading through the remainder of his paperwork. "That has been some break in your leg, they must have hit you with something very heavy. The doctor thinks that it may take a year or more to completely repair so no more football for you Luke."

He had anticipated that the break would have serious consequences, just not for a full year. "I guessed as much. Can I ask you about Patterson Unit? What's it like?"

She took an intake of breath while she considered what to say.

"It's a sixty bed unit and only lads receiving long sentences are allowed to go on there. You'll get a chance to have a good education programme; they have their own gym on the unit and you get a cell to yourself, but it does get a bit hectic on there from time to time. They are mostly London boys caught up in gang stuff so stay away from that if you can." She looked at him before carrying on. "But I don't think that you are a gang member are you Luke?"

Luke sat back in his chair and shook his head, "I've never

joined a gang in my life, apart from the football team. How do I keep out of trouble as whatever I'm doing hasn't worked out so far?"

She smiled again, Luke finding her relaxed attitude comforting. "You'll have to work that one out for yourself, but don't lend anything to anyone and on no account ever, ever, ever borrow anything. It will always cost you double to pay back. Keep yourself to yourself until you find your feet. Oh, and one last thing, stay out of the way of a lad named Bellingham, he's very bad news." She sealed the letter back up and looked back at Luke.

"See you tomorrow chuck. Tell the officers on the wing that I need to see you at nine in the morning." She stood to leave. "Now you have to go and see the officer at the front desk."

Luke made his way slowly towards the gruff talking officer. Mr McGrath had his head down checking documents until he finally looked up. "Come on then Luke, let's get your sorry arse down to the wing."

The metal barred gates at the end of the secure corridor had a sign bolted above them which read, *Patterson Unit*, but there wasn't the hum of noise that Luke expected to come through the double wooden blue doors behind the gate.

Mr McGrath looked at him, seeing the puzzlement on his face. "All the prisoners are locked away at the moment so don't worry yourself, but it gets a lot more rowdy in ten minutes time."

McGrath dramatically pushed the doors open, revealing a small corridor in front of him. Luke tried to take in as much as he could in the first few minutes as if this prison was like Reading he could be locked up for the next twenty-four hours. Immediately to his right was a classroom with desks and a flip chart. It could have been any classroom in any school in the country if the course content displayed on the board hadn't contained advice on how to stop hurting people. It had the look of a group therapy room with areas where small groups had obviously sat to work out a solution to a problem set by the

tutor. The words on the paper showed today's course content -
Anger Management.

The next room on the right made Luke's stomach sink….the
shower area. It looked smaller than the one in Reading Prison
and much cleaner, and it was also only feet away from the staff
office, but it was still a place largely unsupervised.

To his left, three silver phones were attached to the wall,
each with an individual hood for some privacy and a sign
screwed to the wall informing callers about the Samaritans'
phone number. McGrath spoke again, this time not looking at
Luke, just waving a hand to the left hand side, his tough man
persona back on show. "And this is your association and dining
area."

Luke gazed at the room where eight long tables sat in
uniform across the floor, each table taking eight people. At the
far end of the room two pool tables sat empty, balls and cues
kept safely away in another area. It had a sports hall feel to
it, the ceiling thirty plus feet above his head adding to the
basketball court feeling but it was also light and airy, somehow
giving the impression of cleanliness and space to breathe.

Leading Luke through to the office, Mr McGrath instructed
him to wait outside while he went in and closed the door,
speaking to the staff inside. Luke stood, taking it all in and
feeling it was entirely different to Reading. This place felt
controlled, organised and professional. The door opened and a
young female officer came out and smiled at him.

"Hi, my name's Miss Myers, and I'm your personal officer.
Anything that you are unsure about, you can ask me. I'm going
to take you to your cell now, you're on the ground floor, cell
twenty-five so whenever we call for bottom two landing, that
means you." She led him to a cell close to the office.

"We'll be unlocking for dinner in around five minutes.
Follow the others on your landing as you must sit at the
correct table. Once you have taken your meal, remain seated
until we tell you to move. It's very simple, follow the rules and
everything runs well. Your landing will be out on association

this evening, and I will give you a phone call to your parents from the office. After that, all calls must be made on the official card phones. Any questions?" Shaking his head, he couldn't think of anything other than his aching leg.

The door to his cell closed and Luke unpacked his few belongings. The walls were free from graffiti, the windows were not broken and the bed came complete with a duvet. Everything spelt out a well maintained modern wing, a polar opposite to the rundown Victorian buildings of HMP Reading. Kicking off his one training shoe, he laid back on the comfy bed looking at his filthy toes sticking out from the bottom of the white plaster cast. A cell to himself, a TV which seemed to be working and only sixty people to worry about…maybe this wasn't going to be so bad. Soon though, the all too familiar sounds came drifting through his window.

"Oy bottom 25, are you listening?" He lay still while others waiting for his response chattered and laughed. The deep voice bellowed out again. "25, answer me or it's on when we come out." A chorus of encouragement swept up the outside walls of the unit but still Luke ignored the shouting. He knew that to respond would lead to bullying. They would ask him to sing and each request would become more ridiculous until he would in the end refuse, and then they would be at the same impasse as they were at the moment.

The voice sounded out one final time. "Ok, it's on at dinner, and guess what new boy? That's around about now." The sound of the door opening one minute later filled him with anxiety as he sat up and grabbed his crutches. A line of young faces looked in through his door as they passed by, blue plastic plates and white plastic knifes, folks and spoons in hand.

Taking his 'plastics', he followed them around to the food servery area in the association room. His landing was the first to be unlocked so they were the only ones out at that time, and taking the meal given to him, he approached his table where there was only one chair empty. It was between a lad with thick ginger hair and a terrible complexion and a skinny lad with black hair who, when he spoke to Luke, apparently only had two teeth left in his mouth. The smell of stale tobacco breezed over Luke as the boy tried to whisper his message.

"You're going to get fucked up in a minute, that lad who you ignored is called Phillips, we call him Bigger. He runs a gang from Tottenham called *No Remorse* and he's a nightmare."

Bigger was not given his name for nothing, he was an imposing black guy, six foot plus and notorious for running his gang with brutal discipline. That was how he treated his own friends, cross him and he would have you killed. Brought up by his single mum on the Broadwater Farm estate or *'The Farm'* as locals called it, he had served two prison sentences before receiving a life sentence at seventeen for the kidnap and murder of a pizza delivery driver who had refused to hand over the food until he was paid. His mutilated body was found weighted down with bricks in the nearby River Moselle, a narrow stretch of water heading past the estate and through Tottenham cemetery, the pizza box lodged deep in his throat.

The top landings were unlocked and the crowd gathered at the serving area while a huge black lad stood alone, two gold teeth glinting as he scanned the tables for the new face. Seeing Luke, he called over. "New boy. Where have you come from?" This time Luke answered. "Reading, this morning."

"Fuck that place, my friend was killed in there, a white man's prison. Why are you disrespecting me by not talking? You trying to make me look like a little boy?"

It wasn't a question which required an answer, he was stoking himself up for violence, not noticing that Luke had a broken leg, not that it would have made any difference. It was rumoured that Bigger had once pushed a drug user confined to a wheelchair over the top of a balcony fifty feet from the ground. The wall of silence that followed prevented the police from ever prosecuting anyone.

"I was banged up with a guy called Chris, we were friends."

Bigger looked at him suspiciously, not believing the excuse. He checked out the story with a quick fire question. "What was he in there for, new boy?" he spat out the words, ready to pound on this idiot's face. Luke thought for a second. "Stabbed someone who owed him money in Basingstoke. He was doing life."

Bigger took his plate of food while everyone watched, expecting the normal beating to explode from nowhere again.

"Come see me later, I want to know what happened," he ordered Luke as he breezed past, staff and prisoners breathing a sigh of relief. As he reached the skinny lad sitting next to Luke, he leaned over and took his cake. "You come and see me too Bellingham, I have something for you."

Bellingham tried a weak smile, showing his only two teeth. "Okay Bigger, no worries, enjoy the cake," he replied before muttering threats under his breath that no one could hear.

Luke watched as Bigger walked to the end table, sitting with his back to the rest of the room as two of his friends sat beside him, both of equal size.

Bellingham saw Luke watching them and whispered, "His two friends are as bad as he is. The one on his left has a massive scar across his throat but don't mention it, he's called Blue, the other guy is called Spider. I don't even know their first names, only the street names they have." He held out a hand to Luke, "My name's Charlie Bellingham, but the screws call me Rat Boy."

Rat Boy was a skinny nineteen-year-old kid who had obviously had a drug problem. Caught up with a gang who robbed lorries and lorry drivers as they slept on the road side overnight, Rat Boy's calling card was to open the cab and pour petrol over the sleeping driver until he handed over everything he had while the others stole the goods from the back. The plan had come unstuck one late night when he flicked a match at the driver and the fuel ignited. He died a slow death as Rat Boy watched him burn trying to escape. The police first named him Rat Boy due to his looks, but then because he had no family and scurried from place to place at night time trying to find a place to keep warm. Nobody liked him and he would sell you down the river if he thought that it could benefit him.

The rest of the table laughed at the nickname, before Bellingham protested. "It's because I'm small and have bad teeth." A voice from the far end of the table spoke up. "No, it's because you are a fucking rat, Bellingham. Everyone hates you." Again the table laughed as Bellingham focused on his food.

Luke took the moment to make his own introduction. "I'm Luke Woods, good to meet you all. What happens after dinner?"

The ginger haired lad spoke up, his breath taking Luke back a few inches. "We bang up for thirty minutes while the staff have their dinner, then we come out." His thick Welsh accent stood out amongst the southern voices and a bread roll bounced off his head as he finished speaking.

"Shut up you ginger fucking nonce. He's only been here for a week, Luke, came from Cardiff. I think that he's a paedophile, my sister is checking out his name in the papers and I'm talking to her tonight." A thick set, short haired boy named Byles glared down the table, "And I'm telling you something, if you've been touching kids, I'm going to slice your face open."

The wing manager walked over to the table and all chatter stopped. "And if you keep threatening people like that, you will be staying behind your door, understand me Byles?"

Byles sat back down. "Yes Miss Knights." She nodded, looking at the others on the table.

"Now piss off back to your cells, any more nonsense Byles, you and I will be having a chat." The table rose as one and sauntered back to their cells, Byles eyeballing the ginger kid the entire time. Luke was happy to hear his door close behind him and placing the crutches to one side he sat on the bed thinking. Prison was prison, regardless of the environment. A bunch of dysfunctional people who you wouldn't want living next door to you, all in one tiny space..... what on earth could go wrong with a system like that?

Tiredness overcame him due to the pain killers and he

briefly slept before waking and checking the time on the TV. The evening news was starting on the BBC so he judged it would soon be time to unlock for association. Almost as soon as he had the thought, the noise of the doors unlocking made Luke stand to start getting himself ready. His head was still foggy but the overriding thought he had was that Bigger wanted a chat with him this evening. He looked to be the only threat on the wing and if they could get on, perhaps his two friends would tolerate him as well.

A voice boomed down the corridor, it was Byles again.

"I fucking told you all that he was a nonce. Look, his cell is empty. They moved the dirty bastard out because he was about to be found out, crafty bastards. I didn't hear a thing."

The officer smiled as he continued to unlock the doors as Bellingham pushed Luke's door open. "Come on Woods, Bigger wants a word, he's already out and on the pool table and it doesn't pay to keep him waiting."

Luke hobbling out and past the now clean tables, Blue and Spider watching his every move as Bigger took a shot before watching the ball disappear into the pocket. He handed the cue to another lad who was watching him play. "Finish the game for me," he ordered before taking a seat by the far wall and beckoning Luke and Bellingham over. Bigger spoke to Bellingham first.

"You've got a visit this weekend, I need your visitor to bring in a parcel again and then give it to my friend from Howard Unit when you go to the chapel this Sunday. You know the guy, don't fuck up, don't steal from me and I will look after you again. You listening to me Rat Teeth?"

Bellingham didn't argue, he just nodded and headed for the phone to make the arrangements. No one said no when they were asked to do Bigger a favour.

Luke sat still, praying that he wouldn't be asked for the same thing. If he was, he would refuse and the same trouble would start again. Bigger spoke first.

"I can see it in your eyes , you think that I'm going to ask you to do the same. Don't worry, I only pick dispensable idiots to do that type of work. All I want from you is the truth about what happened to my boy Chris. People are going to pay the price, but I don't want it to be the wrong people."

Luke sat and recounted the entire story, just leaving out the informing to staff part. Bigger sat back and looked at his two friends.

"That works out with what I already know, they're all in Woodside prison at the moment in Milton Keynes." He turned back to Luke. "I guess that you're going to give evidence against them in court?"

Luke shrugged his shoulders. "I guess so, I was there when they split his head open."

Bigger shook his head.

"Well make sure that you do your job right. At some point over the next twenty years, me and McCann are going to meet up and then I'll be looking at another life sentence." He passed Luke a sealed envelope. "You'll have another hospital appointment at Reading next week. You might not know about it yet, but I've already been told. Take this note and hide it behind the toilet system next to the doctor's room in the hospital, my boy will take care of the rest."
Luke took it and slid it into his pocket, heart racing. "What if I get caught?"

"It's a note and some cash, nothing else. If anyone looks likely to find it, eat it or burn it before they can take it. Don't let me down, and don't try and read it." He waved Luke away and took the pool cue back from the boy who was playing and continued with his game, business over.

CHAPTER SEVEN

Jake peddled away on the exercise bike at the training ground, his ankle still sore but beginning to heal. He looked up as the door opened and Ian Woodford entered, his Reading tracksuit showing the grass stains from a hard morning's training. At thirty-eight he was one of the youngest managers in the league and still enjoyed taking part in the six aside games.

"Hey Jake, how's the injury feeling?" he called across to his youngest player. After an extensive playing career, the last ten years spent with Liverpool, there wasn't much Ian didn't know about the long and lonely road of recovery.

"It's feeling sore boss, but better than yesterday. I'm struggling to be ready for the Sweden trip though," Jake admitted.

Ian laughed. "Forget that one son. We want you firing on all cylinders for the opening of the season. I'm serious about you this year, this could be big so let's not take any risks. We have a full programme of exercises that you must perform because when we get back, we have only five days until our first game at home to Blackburn. We'll make an assessment on you mid week and if you look ready to go, you'll start on the bench. Okay, keep your head up and I'll see you in ten days or so." His thick cockney accent sounded reassuring to Jake and he knew that regardless of missing the first big opportunity, he was still in the manager's thoughts.

Ian turned just before getting to the door. "And one more thing Jake, we have a new contract waiting for you to sign; the director of football will be in touch with you today. We want to keep you here for the next three years so either get an agent, or bring your dad down to the ground to run an eye over it." The door swung shut as he left whistling some long gone 1980s pop song.

Jake sat in the board room at the Madejski stadium dressed in the only suit he owned. Ironically the last time he wore it, Luke received life in prison and here he was, enjoying life to the full with a promise of at least three more years at the club. His dad sat proudly beside him; he had rushed home from his taxi driving job in the West End and was still dressed casually for work. Sat alone in the room, they spoke in hushed tones, Jake feeling as though he were back outside the headmaster's office at school, waiting for a telling off.

After what seemed an age, David Decker, the Director of Football at the club came in and sat down opposite the pair.

"Hi Jake, Desmond, sorry to keep you. We thought that we should look at a new contract. At the moment you're still on the same deal as every other scholar at the club. We do see a bright future for you Jake, and as a result we would like to offer you a three year deal, with the option of a further two years if things work out as we hope. The bottom line for you will be this." He pushed a piece of paper over the table towards Jake. "Your pay will increase significantly. At present you are on £155 per week and as you can see, this will increase to £500 per week, and if you are involved with the first team it will be £800 per week. After year one it will increase to £1000 per week and £1600 if involved with the first team, and for year three it will be £2000 per week and £3200 with first team appearances. We need to be cautious though, Mr Woods." Here he looked directly at Desmond. "We anticipate that Jake will be hot property after a successful season so we will demand a thirty percent sell on fee from future buyers should he be bought by another club and then resold."

Desmond nodded; the figures suggested in the contract were stunning, but he was not getting ahead of himself. "If we sign, and Jake is sold in two years, what percentage of the fee will he receive?" he asked, sounding as though he knew what he was talking about. One of the other cabbies had a son playing for Millwall and he had tipped Des off about the minefield of contract negotiations.

David looked down the contract. "Jake will receive five percent of any transfer fee. If he turns into the superstar we all hope, that could add up to a substantial amount of cash."

Desmond nodded again. "And will he receive a signing on fee if he signs this contract?"

"I would have preferred an agent to have been here, you're robbing me blind,"

David laughed, before continuing. "No, normally the signing on fee comes when Jake moves to another club." He looked at his laptop.

"I can on this occasion give Jake some back pay? I see that he has had involvement with the first team so how about a £2000 one off payment?"

Jake nodded, feeling uneasy that his dad was pushing too hard and his dream of a professional contract would be pulled away from him at any moment. He sat nervously on his chair watching the two of them spar out the details before feeling unable to keep silent.

"Dad, I'm happy with the deal, this is where I want to play my football. Can I sign please?"

Des looked at him and handed Jake the pen. "Sure Jake, sign. Well done son, I'm very proud of you."

Decker picked up the phone and a photographer from the team entered the room, taking pictures of the done deal as Jake sat with the pen poised over the contract.

"Jake, I work for Reading FC news, can we just have a few words from you before you leave?" Composing himself for a second Jake tried to remember his media training.

"Sure, I'm so happy to be part of the set up and I'm going to show the fans why the manager has put his faith in me. I'm strong, fast and can score goals so hopefully I'll get my chance to shine this season." A second question was fired back, Jake concentrating on the wording,

"And why aren't you involved in the pre-season tour this

year? The fans are interested to know. Someone told me that you have damaged your knee already."

Jake smiled, this was his first introduction to the world of media and distorted truths. "I picked up an injury at the end of the Spurs match. I got caught on the ankle and needed some stitches. I will hopefully be ready for the first game of the season if selected."

The reporter smiled and clicked the camera a few more times before shaking Jake's hand. "Glad to have you stay at the club Jake, you'll be a huge hit with the fans."

Des placed his arm around Jake's shoulder. "Come on son, we have to give Mum the news before it's all over the local papers."

Leaving the confines of the stadium, Jake's mind galloped ahead of itself. He had made it, a three year deal with a massive pay rise. He braced himself for the first real batch of autographs as he left the main entrance where a small gathering of fans stood outside the ticket office, not interested in anything other than organising the season tickets for the forthcoming campaign. No one noticed him and he felt a little foolish as he drifted past preoccupied faces, just as the main door opened again and fan's favourite, Steve Evans walked out in his tracksuit. Immediately engulfed by a bevy of kids within his first ten paces, he looked up as he signed autographs and noticed Jake.

"Jake, come over here mate, the fans need to meet you," he called as he continued signing a few autographs as Jake slowly walked over. Steve pulled him to his side and put an arm across his shoulders.

"Listen everyone, this is Jake Woods. This season he is going to score a bucket load of goals for our team and fire us towards promotion. You should be getting his signature as well, before he gets too famous."

The fans cheered the famous urzzzz chant before congregating around the two players, Desmond watching on in pride. Jake laughed as a pen was thrust into his hand. He looked up as Steve winked at him, whispering into his ear,

"Enjoy every second Jake, it doesn't last forever."

He signed everything, looking at the smiling faces surrounding him, children asking him questions and adults wishing him well, before realising that there was nowhere else that he would rather be. That dreadful night in Newbury town centre with his brother suddenly seemed a long way away, and so was his conscience.

Meanwhile in Huntercombe Prison, the adulation of Jake was a galaxy away from the experience Luke was going through as prison staff escorted him to the medical centre. Luke had been due to go at nine, but a violent disturbance over rival gangs on Mountbatten Unit had ensured that all the medical staff were needed to patch up the wounded, and there had been lots of those. Luke was just happy that it had not been on his unit. Mountbatten was always the place where the violence exploded as so many London gangs on two large connected units was a melting pot for trouble. He heard another shout from a member of staff's radio asking for more assistance as prisoners from other wings shouted encouragement from hidden windows. And then, as quick as it started it was over and Luke was on his way as though nothing had happened.

Spotting the nurse who had been kind to him the day before, Luke waved and smiled as she greeted him in her usual way. "Alright chuck, let's have a quick look at that leg before you go to the hospital clinic."

"Today?" Luke was surprised, suddenly remembering his promise to Bigger, the letter still hidden in his cell.

"Yes chuck, we're booked in for eleven o'clock, the staff will come onto the wing and pick you up in ten minutes, just enough time to go to the loo. See you tomorrow at nine and you can tell me all about it."

He thanked her, but Luke's brain was spinning out of control. He needed the letter or a broken leg would be the least of his worries. Walking back to the wing with an officer, Luke made his move.

"Can I just go and get my book sir? We could be waiting for ages in the hospital."

The officer grunted back a response which Luke took to be, "If you make it quick."

Racing back to his open cell, he hurriedly grabbed the book and stuck the letter down inside his cast where it was just out of sight of the officer. If he bothered to look, he would see the tell tale clues, a thin piece of thread which was stuck onto the envelope tucked just inside the rim of the cast so he could pull it back out in the hospital toilet.

Checking himself over Luke was surprised at his own level of devious thinking; prison was teaching him some valuable lessons but he also realised the risk he was taking. The letter could say anything, and given what Bigger had discussed, Luke thought the worst, that it was a death warrant.

Two staff who Luke didn't recognise were standing behind the reception desk, both young and professional, checking through his paperwork as an older manager lurked behind them. The manager checked through everything again before speaking.

"Name and number?"

Luke answered as though on auto pilot.

"Date of birth?" he continued as checking the photograph, he nodded at the escorting staff waiting to take him. "Take him into the search room please." Even after this time, Luke still hated taking his clothes off in front of staff, no matter how nice they were as they did it.

"Okay Woods, jumper and shirt please." Luke complied as he slowly turned around with his arms in the air as the staff looked at him, tossing the clothing back as he redressed his top half.

"Trainer and sock." Sitting down he slid his trainer and sock off, the staff turning his sock inside out and checking the inside of the shoe.

"Tracky bottoms and boxers." Luke hated this part but

taking them off, he stood again as the staff inspected him.

"Thank you, get dressed." Inside his own thoughts Luke was shaking his head, he was putting up with these liberties just to protect his brother. The officer opened the search room door and guided Luke back to the desk.

"Okay Woods, I need to put handcuffs on you, hands out please."

The heavy metal cuffs were placed on his wrists, the weight of them pressing onto a bone reminding him of the first time it had happened as the older man stepped from behind the counter and checked that they were attached correctly.

"Thank you very much, take care. Any problems phone the prison." The officer in charge of the escort nodded before heading out of the reception building, Luke struggling to use his crutch with the restrictions of the cuffs.

A four-seater taxi sat outside the building, its engine idling as the driver leaned against the bonnet smoking a cigarette. Luke climbed into the back seat, one hand handcuffed to an officer, the other holding his NHS crutch. The other officer sat to the other side of him; three in the back seat was a squeeze when the other two were sixteen stones of non-exercised flab.

The man in charge of the escort spoke with the driver as the car pulled out of the prison driveway, the car travelling another mile before pulling into a layby. Quickly the officer climbed out and got into the front seat, looking around as he fastened his seat belt.

"It's not that I don't want to sit next to you son, just it's a bit of a squeeze with your pot leg. Any trouble and you will have two pot legs, get it?"

Luke smiled and nodded, the man seemed to be a decent guy and made the threats while smiling. Escape was the last thing on his mind, then it came back into his brain….the letter, what the hell was so important that he had to smuggle it out, but on top of that, the fact that someone was willing to drive from London to pick it up worried him. The words from Bigger echoed around in his mind; this really was an order for someone to commit murder and Luke was the person passing sentence. A shiver passed through him as he considered the consequences.

The taxi sped through the countryside, the staff chatting with the driver about a cricket match that was happening outside the prison that weekend. Luke couldn't imagine these two playing any sport other than an eating challenge and he closed his eyes for a second before the car hit another pot hole, jolting them open again. Staring back out of the window as the tree lines began to fade, Luke soon recognised the roads that they were using. The Reading training ground was only a mile away and he felt a rush of nausea as he realised that Jake could be running around a free man only two minutes away. Looking down at the car floor and taking some deep silent breaths, he composed himself. He would have given anything to be able to stand on that pitch waiting to train again as they had both done, just after last Christmas. Closing his eyes once more, he visualised the entire training facility which he would never see it again....he just had to accept it.

The familiar skyline of Reading soon greeted them as they drove across Caversham bridge, the Thames flowing slowly underneath as they peeled into the right hand lane. Only another five minutes with good traffic and they would be there. Luke took in every second, enjoying the familiar sights again and his imagination charging ahead. *Another few years and I will be walking these streets again*, he repeated again and again in his head. *One day I will be back out there.*

The infamous Reading road system, the IDR loomed up ahead, the cab jostling for position until it reached the signs for the Royal Berkshire Hospital. Pulling up outside the entrance to the building, the officer in the front checked his documentation before telling the driver he would call when they were ready to be picked up again. They climbed out in full view of the public and Luke saw a small child banging on his mum's leg while pointing towards him. He wanted to smile at the child and tell him not to worry but it was futile, as scurrying her child to one side, the woman looked back at Luke in disgust.

The cab pulled off as the officer chained to him spotted a free wheelchair sitting just inside the doorway.

"Here we go son, get sat down in there and I'll get you up to the clinic in no time. We have twenty minutes to spare."

Finding himself in the outpatients department, Luke contemplated his next move. If the officer remembered that he had just used the toilet at the prison he might get suspicious so Luke clutched his stomach as if in pain.

"I'm sorry sir, the tablets they gave me have upset my stomach. I need to go to the toilet please." The officer grunted before pushing the chair to the toilet door and getting out a long escort chain from his bag. It rattled as he pulled it out, like something from a scene in A Christmas Carol.

Fastening one end to Luke, he secured himself to the other.

"No funny business lad, I'm waiting just outside of the door. Five minutes, no more."

Luke needed thirty seconds. "No problems sir," he replied and entering the cubicle, he pushed the door closed as far as the chain would allow. Making the noises the staff might expect to hear, he took out the envelope as curiosity got the better of him and he gingerly opened it, looking at the contents. There was only one line written on the piece of paper inside.

Shamus McCann's family. Twenty Three, Lyndhurst Road, Thatcham.

Obviously nothing else was needed and his first thoughts had been correct. It was a death warrant for the family. If he didn't leave it in behind the cistern, someone else would and Luke would be in a world of pain. Resealing it, he pushed it behind the unit before flushing the toilet.

The officer searched him as he left.

"Seen this too many times son, hope that you haven't been stupid." Luke stood with his arms out wide as the officers searched him in the toilet area, the second officer watching the door. "Now drop your bottoms, and I will be checking that cast of yours Woods. If you have anything, hand it over now." Luke shrugged and showed them that he had nothing hidden, breathing a sigh of relief that they hadn't shown this zest for security with his plaster cast before he went in. Satisfied he had nothing on him they moved back into the waiting area.

They took three seats twenty feet down the corridor and after ten minutes a nurse came out of an office and called them all into a small consultation room where Luke was asked to shuffle himself onto a bed. After a few minutes the surgeon entered and Luke recognised him immediately, thanking him for fixing the bone. The surgeon smiled at him.

"Oh, it wasn't hard to repair, the tougher part was keeping it in a good state so that you could play football again. Fingers crossed it looks like a good fix so the prison can take care of you from here. I'll see you again in one month, any questions?" Luke shook his head before the surgeon packed up his notes.

"Take care Luke, and keep out of trouble please, we need the repair to carry on knitting together."

The staff stood and wheeled him out of the room, almost colliding with a large black guy who was walking out of the toilet as they passed the door. He gave Luke a glance, not acknowledging him in any way, but his cruel face, dead eyes and a fuck you expression as he looked at the staff told the story of who he was. Bigger's assassin, a stone cold killer.

Two hours later Luke sat in the association area where Bigger and his band of brothers paid him no attention at all. Obviously knowing that that the job had been done, there was nothing else to add. If for one moment he suspected that Luke had backed out on the deal things would be looking a lot bleaker. Bellingham came and sat next to him.

"I have a package coming in on Saturday, I need you to hold it in your cell until Monday when I can deliver it to Bigger's mate."

Luke didn't hesitate. "No way Rat Boy. If you want to bring stuff into the prison, that's on you but I'm having nothing to do with it." A sharp prick in Luke's side made him look down to where a homemade knife sat just below his third rib. Bellingham's face contorted and Luke could see his real personality - a streetwise, wild kid, someone who would do whatever was needed.

"I'm not asking you Woods, I'm telling you. Saturday tea time before lock up I am giving you a package, you will take it to your cell and stash it until I ask for it on Monday." He pushed the shank back into his pocket before strolling away as though nothing had happened. Luke assessed his options, the drugs were ordered by Bigger and his gang. If they didn't get delivered because of him refusing to play ball he was in trouble. Bellingham, despite weighing nine stone wet through, would put a blade into Luke's stomach if he refused to hide the package. Whichever way he looked at it he would lose. The only other option would be to tell his personal officer but grassing didn't work out too well last time.

Hobbling back to his cell, his head thumped with stress as he tried desperately to find a solution to this shit storm. If Reading prison had seemed bad at the time, this unit was a pure fucking dog fight. Sixty people under the age of twenty one, most serving in excess of fourteen years were rubbing shoulders with each other 24/7, and everyone was holding their breath hoping for the best. Turning the TV on, he watched the normal mind-numbing shows which had taken over evening viewing until he heard Bellingham's voice hiss from his window. Of all the people to live next to, he got Rat Boy.

"Woods, look at the local news on TV." He sounded more excited than normal so Luke turned over to the ITV station, just as a reporter concluded their piece.

"Police still have no clues to the cause of the blaze which took the lives of both parents and two young children. Witnesses report a disturbance in the house earlier before the thick black smoke billowing from a downstairs room alerted them to the fire. Fire fighters are still on scene damping down the flames from what is described as the most ferocious house fire they have faced for a very long time. This is Tony Williams reporting from Thatcham, Berkshire."

Luke sat staring in disbelief as he heard Bellingham laughing from inside his cell.

"I know what you did Woods, do what I tell you or you are never getting out of here." Luke took a deep breath before calling out a reply. "Ok Bellingham, just this once."

CHAPTER EIGHT

Desmond and Kim Woods sat at the pine dining room table, Kim with tears spilling down her cheeks as she repeated the story again.

"The whole school know about Luke. I went into the staff room this morning and no one spoke to me, it was as if I had committed the offence myself. In my classroom, some child had sneaked in earlier and wrote on the board. *Luke Woods - murderer, RIP Robert Bell.* I can't go through with it any longer, one of Bell's family attends the school and I feel as though I'm being blamed for his death."

Des put his arm around her. "Do you want me to come up to the school with you? The Head should be giving you some support." Pulling another tissue from the box she blew her nose.

"No point, he isn't interested. He suggested that I find another school in the county." Des threw up his hands.

"That's not the point, you love teaching in Newbury. They can't force you out."

The sound of a car pulling up outside stopped him talking and he looked through the lounge window overlooking the small driveway.

"It's Jake back from training. We need to be strong for him, let's talk about it later."

The door opened and Jake bounced in. "My ankle is feeling good, Dad, the club doctor thinks that I could start the first game of the season. Any news from Luke?"

He was chattering as though nothing else mattered in the world to him. Kim gave him a smile, she understood his excitement.

"He phoned last night. He's settled in the new unit ok and we can visit him at the weekend. Do you want to come?"

Jake took off his tracksuit top, throwing it over the back of a chair. The season was starting on Saturday and he was expecting to play.

"I can't, there's football this weekend and the boss has promised me that I'm in the squad."

She smiled. "Don't get too ahead of yourself; as my mother used to say....many a slip between cup and lip."

As normal Jake didn't understand the meaning of what she was saying, only adding, "Can we go on Sunday? I'll be free then."

Kim nodded. "We booked Sunday just in case we were watching you play," she said before glancing down at his wrist. "Jake, is that a new watch?" she asked, her playful expression giving way to disapproval.

Looking down at it proudly he nodded and laughed. "A few of the guys wear them. Some of them are worth thirty or forty thousand pounds but this one was only three."

She puffed out her cheeks. "You have enough money to buy a three thousand pound watch? Just you take care what you're spending or it'll all be gone before you know what's happened."

Des took hold of Jake's wrist and looked at the watch and then at him, a flash of annoyance in his brown eyes. "Just keep your feet on the floor, Jake. You've only had the money for a few days and it's gone already."

Jake pulled his hand away sharply. "There's plenty more to come, you saw the figures Dad. I'm earning more than I could have ever dreamt of earning and I make more in a week than what you and Mum do together in a month." The sound of a growing ego was clear for Des to hear and Jake went silent for a second, contemplating how to present the next question.

"One of the guys has an apartment in West London, he asked me if I wanted to move in with him. Would you be annoyed if I moved out Mum?"

She shook her head. "Jake, you've only just signed your first contract. It means nothing and already you want to move out.

You're still only eighteen."

Jake exhaled loudly. "Mum, there are loads of lads living around Chelsea Harbour, it's only in West London, not the other side of the world. They are all my age and I'm the only one still living at home."

She banged her hand on the table. "And maybe they are not from families as caring as ours. In case you have forgotten you could have been in a cell with Luke only a few weeks ago. He has taken all the responsibility for what happened on that night, not once did he mention that you started the trouble in the bar by chatting to another boy's girlfriend. And now you want to skip off and forget about everything, just leaving us to pick up the pieces of our lives while Luke serves ten years in prison." She paused for a breath but the verbal tirade was far from over. Des sat back watching, knowing this thing had been brewing for a while.

"If you want to go traipsing around the West End with your expensive watch dangling from your wrist, carry on. That watch is worth five times what Dad earns in a week. All the miles in the car and hours he spent at training with you two boys, the weekends we spent standing on the side of a football pitch in the freezing cold, and the first thing you do is spend everything on yourself and tell me that you're moving out. We didn't bring you up to have stars in your eyes, some other fool has put them there for you."

Jake felt really small for a minute, every word spilling from his mother's mouth smashing into his conscience. He was lucky, lucky to have great parents, lucky to escape the punishment that should have been his, and very lucky that Luke had kept his mouth closed. Kissing her on her cheek he took her by the shoulders and looking into her tearful eyes, a lump gathering in his throat.

"Sorry Mum, you're right and I'm sorry that I've upset you." He turned and went upstairs to his small bedroom where he took out his new phone, too scared to show his parents that he had spent another thousand on a new model. He dialled a number and left a message on the answer service.

"Hi Micky, I've been thinking about your offer of the room. I need to stay where I am at the moment, my Mum is having a hard time coping with Luke being in prison - sorry buddy."

Saturday came around quickly for some, and for Luke the knot of apprehension in his stomach for what he was about to do for Rat Boy was making him feel sick. Every evening he heard the same whispers coming from the next cell, threats of disclosing the note which he had left behind the cistern and the danger he faced if Bigger was to lose the package.

Losing track of time was a difficult thing to do in prison. Life was regimented, Luke had learned the routine and always knew what was coming next. It was either bang up, food, work or association. He was not enjoying the food, bored with the inane babble of association and the only thing he hadn't experienced yet was work. An interview with the education manager on Monday morning would hopefully resolve that issue.

His door opened and he knew that it was ten o'clock and therefore association time again so, putting on his training shoe, he made his way around the outside of the wing office to the pool tables. The top landings were already out and Bigger was playing table tennis with Blue, the pair of them building up a sweat. Writing his name on the board to take his turn in playing pool, Luke saw there were five names above him, the winner staying on, so while he waited, he sat on a large blue chair reading a chapter from his book. When his attention was distracted by someone sitting next to him he looked up as Spider took the book from him and read the cover. "I've read that one Luke, it's a good book, he's my favourite author."

Unsure as to whether this was a wind up, Luke agreed, asking Spider about other books that he had read. He thought for a minute before looking Luke in the eye, his intelligence shining past the thuggish attitude which normally smothered all other senses.

"The Power of One, it's a great book, about a young boy growing up in South Africa." Luke was shocked, he had misjudged this lad from day one, writing him off as a drug dealing thug with no other ambition. He smiled before replying; this was a nice change from the normal crap spouted from prisoners.

"Yeah, I've read that one too, and the sequel. I didn't have you down as a book person." He shrugged his shoulders hoping that Spider wasn't offended. He wasn't.

"No, it was only when I came into this place two years ago that I started. I couldn't read when I came in but the education woman got me interested, and before I knew it, I had some qualifications and an addiction to books instead of crack." He laughed a deep belly laugh. "Anyway, enough of the nice stuff. I hear that you're going to be holding a package for Bellingham tonight?" Luke shuffled in his seat, the cosy chat about books had quickly ramped up into his own personal nightmare. His smile vanished and a worried frown took its place.

"I didn't have much choice, Rat Boy was threatening to stab me if I didn't, and Bigger would smash me if it got lost." Spider looked around the association area before speaking again.

"It isn't your parcel to keep hold of, it's between Bigger and that piece of shit Bellingham. Stay out of our business unless you want to be involved. And let me give you a little advice.... involvement with us isn't a nice place to be as you will see in a moment."

The frosty atmosphere disappeared as quickly as it came and his book was handed back to him. "I'll read that sequel if I can find it in the library." Spider stood and nodded at Bigger as he walked past the table tennis table, heading towards the shower room where Bellingham had just entered. The sound of the alarm bell coincided with Bellingham falling through the wooden door and onto the floor near the office, his nose bust open and blood flowing over the lino floor. He looked up at the officer walking towards him, his eye already swelling from the beating he had just received.

"Sorry Miss, I just slipped in the shower."

CHAPTER NINE

Ian Woodford had called the players together. It was lunch time before the opening day fixture and Jake sat in the briefing room tingling with anticipation. Today would be his time to shine and a packed stadium would see him tear Blackburn Rovers to pieces. Or that's how he had planned it during a restless night's sleep. With the stitches removed, he had trained with the team for the past two days, stories abounding about the Swedish trip he had missed. The team had recently taken on two decent sides and won both matches so confidence was high ahead of the expected promotion push. Jake had an uneasy feeling that things had changed a bit while his leg was mending - ten days ago he was in no doubt that he was already accepted into the squad, but with their return to Reading, he felt a little distant again. The young Irish academy lad, Lance Fallon, who had taken Jake's place, had played well and scored an important goal in the final game, and the first team seemed more at ease around him. All thoughts of his blossoming career seemed to have taken a step backwards as he fought for some attention again.

Ian stood and spoke to the squad.

"Okay lads, listen up while I tell you the squad for the Blackburn game. It will be the same team who started against Malmo in the last match on tour. Lance, you'll be on the bench again, you did well out there and took your opportunity well." He didn't acknowledge Jake at all.

"Some of you will be disappointed not to be involved but your chance will come, it's a long season. Those selected for the game please stay here, the rest of you can take a well earned weekend off. See you on Monday." A small murmur of discontent came from one of the senior players not selected but Ian ignored it. Jake picked up his bag. The thought of no longer having involvement had hurt him, but seeing this, Ian stopped him before he left the room.

"Jake, you need to get used to this. Lance performed well and I can't overlook him. You'll be playing for the under 23s on Tuesday to keep fit."

Jake couldn't be sure if the disappointment was showing but he nodded and thanked the manager. Instead of running out in front of twenty thousand at the Madejski Stadium, he would play in front of a dozen people at Brighton's training ground. His deflation was immense but worse still, he had to tell his parents that they wouldn't be watching him make his first championship start. After the chat he'd had with his mum earlier in the week, this one would really prick deep into his pride, but the worse thing was that she would be happy that he had been taken down a peg or two.

The hum of the wing in Huntercombe had built all day, weekends were always a tense time with plenty of hours to waste and not a lot to do. The officer looked at the clock in the wing office before shouting out his instructions.

As normal everyone had to sit in their seats before being called up to their landings. Rat Boy slid in beside Luke, his eye a vivid shade of dark blue and purple and almost swollen shut. The small amount of eye ball which could be seen was streaked red with ruptured blood vessels and a strip of tape across his nose held the torn skin together.

"Did you grass me up?" he hissed.

Luke looked up, seeing Spider staring at their table. "No, I didn't grass anyone up, I was just warned not to get involved in their business." He shrugged in a *What do you expect me to do?* gesture.

Rat Boy grunted and felt his eye. "Well, no need to keep that parcel for me, I'm going to look after it myself."

The cry went up. "Bottom two landing," and Luke set off to his cell with half a smile on his face. He had enjoyed seeing Rat

Boy squirm, and doubly happy that the pressure was off him for a while.

The visits room was bustling as Luke entered. He could see the family sitting at the far end, Mum looking as though she had just come from church, Dad and Jake looking far more casual. Kim and Des stood and hugged him. Unlike at Reading, the staff here seemed to be a little more relaxed, plus if it didn't get too busy there was a chance of a full two hours together. Jake fist bumped Luke while Des went to a table selling sweets and drinks, coming back loaded up with snacks.

"How did the game go yesterday, did you get any match time?" Luke asked Jake as he tore open a bag of salt and vinegar crisps.

Jake shook his head. "I didn't even make the squad, Lance Fallon got the call up in my place. We won 1:0 and he didn't get on, the manager just kept it tight at the back. I'm back with the U23 team on Tuesday playing at Brighton.... gutted."

Luke smiled before generously adding, "Your time will come, you're too good to keep out of the team. Anyway, you scored ten more goals than Fallon did last season so it should be an easy decision for them to take." Just then a man wearing a suit approached the table and smiled at Luke's parents.

"Afternoon Mr and Mrs Woods, I'm the Duty Governor. We didn't realise that Luke had a twin brother so could I please ask that you stay on opposite sides of the table at all times, and that only Mum or Dad go to the coffee bar." He then looked at Luke, "please keep your orange bib on at all times."

Luke nodded while the others looked on at this intrusion into their conversation. "Sure sir. Sorry, I didn't know that I had to tell you about Jake."

The Duty Governor nodded before turning back to Luke's parents. "Sorry for butting in, have a nice visit," he told them before speaking to the person in charge of visits and leaving the room. Luke just shrugged his shoulders at his family. "It's just how it is, this is prison life and nothing is private anymore."

The visiting time passed seemingly in a second for Luke as stories about the prison were swapped with training ground incidents. Luke loved hearing about home and for a brief moment they felt like a family again.

"Time please ladies and gentlemen, finish your visits please." Jake looked at his watch, seeing they'd had nearly two hours of chatting. Luke caught sight of it. "Bro, that's a serious watch."

Jake looked a little sheepish. "The club gave me some money when I signed the new contract. I might take it back, I don't like it too much."

Luke laughed. "Don't like it? Are you crazy? You always wanted to buy one of those things, you never stopped talking about it. Keep it, or if you don't want it, give it to me."

Jake took it off and handed it over. "It's yours Luke, take good care of it."

Luke shook his head. "I can't do that Jake, it'll be stolen in a second in here... the place is full of thieves." Kim nodded, not realising that Luke was joking. "Good idea," she said as the boys struggled to keep a straight face.

An officer walked briskly over towards Jake. "Sir, I'm sorry, you can't give your brother your watch." He took it from Luke and handed it back to Jake. "Maybe buy him something slightly less expensive and post it in. I'm afraid the visit session is over so say your goodbyes please."

Everyone stood as the visits room door opened and people filed out, leaving just the prisoners and staff.

Byles came across and spoke to him. "First proper visit is hard Luke, when you see everyone leave it's horrible. I remember my first time and how bad I felt. Your family look nice, I didn't know that you had a twin brother."

Luke rolled his eyes. "Nor did the prison so I expect it's going to cause me another problem."

Escorted by staff back to his cell Luke felt hollow, as though everyone he cared for had been ripped from him again. For two hours things had seemed normal as he lost himself in the conversations families have, but now the reality of what he faced for the next few years kicked back in. He looked despondently at the drab walls of the secure passage way as he walked back in a crowd of prisoners all having similar thoughts.

His self pitying thoughts continued once he was back in his small cell with a locked door. While his brother was wearing watches worth thousands of pounds, with a new contract worth more than most eighteen year olds could dream of and a life without horizons, here he was, banged up for a crime that he didn't commit, looking at the thick end of ten years and with no plan B. Who would want a twenty-eight-year-old man, with a criminal record for murder and no work history other than having kicked a ball around a football field?

Staring around the bleak walls, listening to the senseless crap shouted from the cell windows, the enormity of what was occurring hit him hard for the first time. This was not a brief stay away from home, this would be his entire youth spent behind a metal door, looking forward to a visit every two weeks and living in fear of attack for the rest. He wasn't like the other lads here. He was normal, kind; he was fucking innocent and he didn't belong here.

For the first time since his conviction he cried, tears of frustration, anger and sorrow for what he had lost. He buried his head under the pillow so others didn't hear. If Rat Boy smelled weakness he would attack again. He cried until he felt that his heart would explode with sadness, his sheet becoming wet with tears.

He visualised his family driving home; he could see inside the car, Mum and Dad in the front and Jake looking at every girl who walked past. He could smell the food cooking at home as Mum sang in the kitchen while Dad took a shower after a day's driving.

He could feel the softness of his own bed, and the gentle hum of vehicles as they trundled past on the A4. All these things that he had taken for granted, all snatched away by the toss of a coin in that dressing room in December. Why did he ever agree to take the fall for his brother? Why should he suffer for what Jake had finally confessed to? That gutless admission before the verdict was reached, and he walked out a free man without a backwards glance. For that one split second in that lonely cell he hated Jake, and then the door opened.

"Luke." It was his personal officer standing in the doorway and she stepped in and slid the bolt on the door to stop it from locking her in. She sat on his wooden chair as he emerged from under the pillow.

"Are you ok? I could see that you were upset at the end of visits. Do you want to come into the office for a chat, just you and me?"

He did want to talk, he wanted to tell the whole story and phone his Mum, just for a minute. But instead he told the most common lie ever told in prison. "No, I'm fine." Even in this darkest moment of desperation, the fear of weakness overrode his need for comfort.

"I'm fine Miss, my leg was hurting so I'm just trying to get a bit of rest until the pain has gone." Looking at him in disbelief she nodded, throwing a chocolate bar onto his bed. "Ok, if you change your mind I'm on duty tonight. Otherwise I will see you tomorrow morning with the Education Manager."

He nodded, just hoping she would ask him one more time, knowing he would break. "Thanks Miss, see you in the morning."

The closing of the door crucified him, the help was there and he had turned it away. Now he couldn't ring his cell bell, everyone would hear and know that he was a little boy who couldn't do his time.

The sun dipped below the metal fence surrounding the prison and darkness crept into the cells. He hadn't turned his light on as the gloom engulfed him and lay watching the flickering shadows from the small TV set create patterns on his ceiling. The blackness felt lonely, cold and cruel, and darkness came with a companion, a frequent visitor to a gloomy cell, that of despair.

Rat Boy whispered through his window. "I can hear you crying, you fucking baby, everyone can hear it. Why don't you just kill yourself? Look what I've got for you, look out of your window." He'd swung a line between the two cell windows, an unofficial way of delivering things between cells without the staff seeing. Luke looked out and saw the thin torn sheet swinging in front of his window and grabbing it, he pulled it in.

The whispered voice continued. "What do you think of that Woods? Ten years at least in prison, probably closer to fifteen by the time your parole hearings are held. What's the point? Everyone else in here will be long gone, except you."

Luke looked at the gift, a noose made from a ripped blanket. The evil hiss of Rat Boys whispering continued. "Tie it around the bars, put the noose around your neck and just fall to the floor. Simple as that and it's all over. I have one as well, let's do it together, let's show these bastards."

Twisting it between his hands Luke looked at the green strands of torn material, pondering the meaning of everything. "No, I can't do it. I have too much to live for," he whispered back.

Rat Boy laughed. "Like what? More of the same, another whole lifetime behind bars? Come on, do it with me, I will count us down." Crying once more Luke whispered, "Okay, okay I'll do it," half choking on the realisation of what was happening. A buzz came from some of the other windows and excitement started to crackle from all sides as he slid the noose around his neck, tying the other end to a white painted bar. Sighing, he felt all hope leave his young body.

"I'm ready Rat Boy."

"Let's do it. One, two, three." A thump came from the window of the cell as it took the weight, followed by the hush of anticipation before an unseen voice from a dark cell called out. "Rat Boy, what's happening?" It was met with silence before a lone cell bell sounded.

The door opened. "Miss, I know that I said that I was ok but

I'm not. Can we talk?" As Luke made his way to the office, Rat Boy cursed him through his door.

"Fucking idiot, don't tell me that you're going to do something and then back out." The booming voice of Bigger cut through the night air.

"Rat Boy, you had better get yourself off this wing before morning or you are getting fucked up again at unlock."

A second cell bell sounded and this time it was Rat Boy. "I want to go to the block."

CHAPTER TEN

The soft rain of a summer evening shower dribbled down the window of the team coach as they pulled into the car park of the Brighton training ground, the familiar seagull emblem flying inside the sign for Brighton and Hove Albion.

Jake had received a few jibes as he'd boarded, the last time he had played with the team was when he'd thought that his professional career had kicked in and he'd made sure everyone knew about it. A couple of the lads had not forgotten that and chipped away with the super star chat for the entire journey. Jake was sick of hearing it and put his ear phones in and listened to music, anything to dull out this tedium of a U23 game. He was changing in silence when the manager came up and spoke with him.

"Jake, the boss has asked me to give you the full ninety minutes tonight. He's thinking about you for Saturday's game away at Millwall. I know that you were disappointed not to be playing for the first team, but Lance didn't cover himself with glory after the game. He wasn't happy that he didn't get on and his entire family had flown over from Dublin. He had a go at the boss in front of a few people in the player's lounge so he's now finished, stupid lad." Jake listened, excited that another new door had opened.

He felt a release of nervous energy as he ran out onto the pitch and playing as though he had something extra to prove, and with a fiery determination, he was sensational. He scored two goals and won a penalty for the third in a 3:2 victory for Reading. At the end of the match a small but stocky man with a pronounced limp stopped Jake before he could leave the field. Holding out his hand he introduced himself and once Jake heard his name he recognised him instantly - Jay Thompson,

Liverpool and England winger from the eighties.

"Hi Mr Thompson, how are you doing?" Jake greeted him in surprise and shook his hand vigorously

Thompson clung on to Jake's hand as he spoke. "I was doing okay until ninety minutes ago. I was asked to watch your captain playing in midfield and prepare a report," He let go of Jake's hand. "But the problem I have now is that I haven't made one note about him. Do you know why?"

Jake shrugged. "I don't know, I thought that he had a good game."

Jay nodded, "Yep, he had a good game, but so did the Brighton lad who was up against him. You, on the other hand were unstoppable - fast, strong and you knew where the goal was. One sweet shot with your left and an unstoppable one with your right." He held open a note book, the pages full of written notes. "All this information is about you. I work for Southampton and I'm going to recommend that the club put in an offer for you."

Flattered, Jake didn't know what he should say. "Thanks Jay, that's really kind of you, but I've just signed a new contract with Reading."

Thompson made a *pah* noise with his lips, almost as if the Reading contract meant nothing to him. "We can treble whatever Reading have offered, and I can promise that you will be playing with, and training with international players all of the time, in world class surroundings. Our training ground in Staplewood is one of the best in the country. If you're as good as I think you are, the sky's the limit."

Jake shook his hand again. "As I've said Mr Thompson, I've just signed my contract, but thanks for sparing me your time." His head spinning, he walked back to the changing room and sat on the bench, oblivious to all the chatter around him. Jimmy Dean the interim U23 manager came and sat beside him.

"I saw you chatting to Jay Thompson, he's a scout from Southampton. What did he want?"

Jake kicked his boots off. "He wants me to sign for Southampton, apparently they're going to put in an offer to buy me. Triple my money, all the normal stuff that happens to anyone who has a good game." Jimmy took out his phone. "We will see about that, he shouldn't be tapping you up."

The short coach ride back to Reading was a more humorous affair than the drive there. It seemed that Jake had been forgiven for his temporary first teamer stance although he didn't pay much attention, his head full of the conversation with Thompson. The banter flowed around the bus as the team buzzed with exhilaration; they had just gone toe to toe with a top U23 side and beaten them in their own training ground.

Jake became more subdued as the journey progressed, his head was full of the earlier conversation and he juggled with the pros and cons of the offer. If he stayed where he was, he would be guaranteed a shot at first team football, plus he lived close to the ground and knew everyone. If he took a chance and left, what opportunities would he have to play? As Jay pointed out, the team was filled with internationals and on top of that, there were some brilliant players not even getting into the starting eleven.

The decision was about to be forced upon him as the coach pulled up at the Madejski Stadium player's entrance where Ian Woodford stood by the main doors looking up at the coach windows. Before anyone could get off, Jimmy Dean walked down the aisle to Jake. "I phoned the boss on the way back, he's fuming and wants a chat with you."

Fear shot through his body again, although this time he had done nothing wrong and regretted ever mentioning what was discussed. He got off and grabbed his boot bag from the luggage hold before approaching the manager.

"Hi boss, Jimmy told me that you wanted a chat." Ian nodded. "Come to my office, I have something that I want to show you." On his board was a long list of names which he had obviously written down that evening. Jake recognised five or six of them.

"All of these players, Jake, were taken from us before their Reading career even started. How many of these names do you know?"

He looked down the list wondering where the conversation was going.

"Maybe six or seven at a push," he replied, looking for some kind of response from Ian. He got it. "Exactly! Out of a list of seventy five names, only six of them went on to play any decent level of professional football." What do they all have in common?"

 The penny dropped. "They were all academy players who left before they were first team players."

Ian nodded. "Exactly, teams like Liverpool, Chelsea, Southampton and other supposedly bigger clubs took years of investment from us in one flourish of a cheque book. Plenty of empty promises and a fist full of nothing to spoil the development of young potential stars, people like you Jake."

Jake held up his hands in submission. "I'm not going anywhere Boss. I told him that I had just signed a contract."

Ian flipped a sheet of A4 paper at him. "It's eleven o'clock at night and I should be in bed with my wife. Instead, I have an offer sent to me and the Chairman of Reading from the Chairman of Southampton saying they are willing to pay five hundred thousand pounds for you Jake." Woodford looked him square in the eye. "I want you to stay here and continue developing. When the time is right for you to move on, I will not stand in your way. What do you say?"

Jake took no time to think about the reply. "I'm a Reading player and I want to pull on the Reading shirt and represent my team. I don't want to go anywhere Boss, tear it up. I'm not moving to Southampton or anywhere else."

Ian clasped Jake's shoulder. "And that is the very reason you will be in the squad for the Millwall game."

CHAPTER ELEVEN

Luke sat in a large brightly lit office on the unit, a room the manager normally worked from. His personal officer, Miss Nevis, sat behind the desk, an attractive woman in her twenties with Irish looks, soft dark brown hair and brown eyes. She had a gentle looking face with a faultless complexion which lead to a lot of the lads chatting about her when they were locked behind their doors, everyone dreaming that they would have a chance of hooking up with her if they were outside. The ring on her finger spelt another story, as she picked up the phone and made a brief call.

"Hey Vicky, it's Imelda. I have a lad with me at the moment who is a bit upset. I wondered if you fancied a chat with him?" Putting down the phone she pulled an ice cold can of diet coke from a drawer. "Just taken this out of the fridge but I don't fancy drinking it, do you want it?"

Luke didn't need a second invitation, his throat dry from the crying. "Yes please."

Handing it over, she fixed him with a stare. "What was going on in there Luke?" she asked, her voice a mix between sympathy and disappointment.

He paused for a moment before pulling the noose from his tracksuit pocket. "Rat Boy wanted me to hang myself. He just kept on about how I would never be allowed to go home and how I could be in prison until my mid thirties."

She tossed him over a box of tissues as he continued to talk before finally adding her own comments.

"He knows nothing, in fact he's sitting in the segregation unit as we speak. The other lads were furious with what he tried to do." She smiled showing her perfect teeth, her words helping Luke feel more at ease. "Guys like you, Luke, just need to start finding your feet." A knock at the door stopped her, and slightly older woman came in, her broad northern accent reminding him of the nurse.

"Hey Luke, what have you been up to?" She looked at the noose on the desk. "Bloody hell, that's a bit drastic! What were you planning? Do you really want to die?"

He shook his head, tears bubbling out again before he composed himself. "No, I don't want to die. I was just being an idiot. Someone was trying to get me to do something stupid."

Vicky showed little facial expression as he spoke, she had heard this story one too many times. "Bellingham again! This is the third time he has tried to do the same thing, the little bastard. I warned him last time that I would move him to another prison if he tried again." She made a note on her notepad before looking up at Luke. "We're going to have a chat again tomorrow Luke and I'm going to invite the chaplain and the probation officer to come in as well. Is that okay?"

He nodded. "I'm seeing the education manager in the morning as well."

She smiled. "Good, do you still feel like hurting yourself?"

He shook his head. "No, I'm fine, honestly."

She patted him gently on the hand. "Great news but what I'm going to do tonight is ask staff to keep an eye on you. They will look through your cell flap at least every hour tonight. If you're feeling a bit shaky, tell them, don't do anything daft."

Luke vigorously shook his head. "No way will I try and hurt myself again. How long will staff keep checking on me? The others will notice."

"Just until we have a chat tomorrow, then I'm sure that you'll be fine," she reassured him. "And don't worry about the others, every lad on here has been through the same thing at some point." She pushed an orange folder over the desk at him and he drained the last of the cold drink before opening it.

"This is a form we use when we need to keep an extra eye on you and give you some support," she explained. "The staff will have this tonight and it tells them what they need to do. Read this part here and sign in that box."

Luke read through her neat handwriting. She had identified him as a risk due to his new life sentence and a bullying prisoner making threats. He took the pen and signed.

"And tomorrow, when you have calmed down, I will let you phone your parents. You can do it from my office, okay?"

His spirit and resilience grew as he listened, and no longer feeling alone, he held out his hand to shake hers. She took it and looked at him sternly.

"You seem to be a nice kid Luke, get all you can out of this place, we have a lot to offer you."

The words from his first cell mate at Reading bounced back into his head and made more sense now. "Yes Miss, see you tomorrow."

Miss Nevis his personal officer stood. "Come on then, time to get you back to your room. No one else knows about what we have talked about, if you tell anyone it's up to you." Leading him back on to the wing, she shut his door without a word. Two seconds later a booming voice came from above, it was Bigger.

"Woods, are you listening?" Luke didn't have the strength to ignore him and knew he just had to accept the abuse that was coming his way. He walked over to the window. "Yeah Bigger, I can hear you."

The voice came back. "Don't try that shit again, come speak to me next time." He then raised his voice even further as if that were possible. "And if anyone else tries any shit like that on you again, I will deal with them. Now all of you, go to sleep, I'm tired."

The chatter from the windows stopped straight away and Luke collapsed back onto his bed, the occurrences from the evening running through his head. One thought kept coming back to him.....*The guy who runs just about every illegal act in the entire prison has my back. What the hell does he want with me?*

CHAPTER TWELVE

The floodlights from the New Den, home to Millwall FC, illuminated the area around the ground as the team coach pulled up to the player's entrance. It had always seemed a hostile ground to visit as a fan, but stepping off the coach into the throng of supporters who stood watching as the players came down the steps was nerve tingling. Ian had gone back on his promise to start Jake, but he sucked it up and prepared himself for when he was needed, concentrating on what he was about to face,

He needn't have worried, a few funny comments and an awful lot of happy children collecting autographs was all Jake had to deal with. He took time with every request, posed for every selfie as the other players walked past, headphones on and faces pointing down. He remembered how it felt to be an eight-year-old and meeting players for the first time. He never forgot when David Beckham stopped when he called out his name at the old Leicester City ground, Filbert Street, as he was walking towards the player's entrance before the game. Beckham smiled and rubbed his head before posing for a picture. Moments like that stuck with you forever. He wasn't Beckham at the moment, but perhaps one day.

There was something special in the air as they all sat in the changing room, a silent belief that this would be a good season. The squad had stuck together after the disappointment of the Wembley defeat, and with the addition of a steely defensive midfield player named Lloyd Case from Leeds United, and the attacking right sided midfielder, Craig Russell from Norwich, they had a solid shape with plenty of attacking threat.

Jake jogged out to warm up with the team, the friendly feeling from the young fans now replaced by the famous chants from the home supporters. He had never played against Millwall but it seemed that the fans didn't like him very much, vile abuse spilling over the wall as he went to pick up a stray football. Looking up into the crowd to see where it was directed from, he spotted a young lad who an hour ago had posed happily with Jake. Only now he was giving him the two fingered salute while his dad laughed and patted him on the shoulder.

We are Millwall, no one likes us, rang out around the ground. A few hundred Reading fans who had made the trip tried their best to drown the song out, but they were outnumbered and out-sung.

The whistle blew, and the first forty-five minutes seem to flash past with no damage to either side until the second minute of additional time when a soft free kick led to a curling twenty three yard shot, straight into the top corner of the net. The Millwall fans erupted as though the game was won and before they could restart, the referee blew his whistle.

One nil down at half time and the Reading players sat in disbelief. They had hit the post twice and a certain penalty was not given with two minutes left of the half. Ian walked through the door; he had come from the referee's room where he had obviously been making his feelings known.

"Okay, we need to keep pressing them - we gave away a stupid goal from that free kick. No more fouls in silly positions." He looked around at the player's faces.

"Let's get at them, I'll give it another fifteen minutes and if we haven't got back into the game, we throw the kitchen sink at them. We are not walking away from this ground without three points. Forget the first forty-five minutes, go out and win this half for the fans."

The clatter of studs on the floor added to the war cry from the manager as they ran back out onto the pitch. A chorus of boos was broken only by the cheering as the Millwall players ran on, saluting their fans as they did so. Ian held Jake back for a second. "If we don't score in the first fifteen Jake, you are coming on. I want everything from you son."

Jake nodded. "Boss, I can win this game for you," he promised, his youthful self belief evident in his words.

The New Den exploded as an attacking move was crudely thwarted and the Millwall striker was sent tumbling inside the penalty area. The referee pointed to the penalty spot without hesitation and thirty seconds later the lead was two nil.

"Jake!" He looked around towards the manager. "Get warmed up, you're coming on."

The player's heads were down and the away supporters silent as Jake jogged onto the field, a mountain to climb ahead of him. The big central defender for Millwall made Jake feel welcome by kicking him directly onto his injury the first chance he had. The pain was intense but Jake didn't show it, he didn't need to as the giant Welshman just laughed. "Plenty more where that came from son, you'll be crying for your mum by full time."

The time ticked by and with less than twenty minutes left on the clock, Jake still hadn't touched the ball. Suddenly Millwall broke forwards again, the attacker bearing down on goal only for the goal keeper to dive down bravely and take it off his foot. Looking up, he noticed Jake in the clear, punting the ball down towards him and his new Welsh friend. Killing the ball on his chest, Jake turned and darted towards goal, the defender unable to keep up with his pace. Entering the area and ready to fire the ball into the back of the net, Jake's legs were kicked from under him, leaving his sprawling on the damp turf.

"Penalty!" The referee pointed directly to the spot, flashing the red card at the lumbering defender. Steve Evans picked up the ball and placed it on the spot before calmly stoking it into the top left hand corner.

Two-one and still fifteen minutes to play, Reading had a spring in their step with Millwall down to ten players and still a reasonable amount of time left on the clock. Reading drove forwards again and this time the Reading midfield player,

Billy Sayer, saw Jake making a run into the box. He played a wonderful pass which Jake collected and smashed high into the net. Two-all and the Reading fans were in great voice, willing the team forwards again with only five minutes left to play.

Ian screamed from the touchline. "Get the ball forwards to Jake." High in the stands Desmond and Kim watched on in amazement. This was their boy, taking the game by the scruff of the neck and getting them back level.

Millwall were desperate, punting the ball into the Reading penalty box at every chance, the Reading keeper coming out to collect another hopeful cross. Jake made a run straight towards the Millwall goal, knowing what was coming. Sure enough, the ball flew from the keeper's boot into the night air, Jake watching every spin and sprinting in quickly to beat the defender to it. One beautiful pass and he put Craig Russell through on goal where he rounded the keeper and smashed the ball home. Three-two to Reading as the final whistle blew and the away supporters spilled down towards the celebrating players where they became one frantic scene of excitement.

The atmosphere in the changing room was electric and Jake lost count of the number of people who came in and hugged him. What he did know was that he had made an entrance that evening. Scoring one goal, winning a penalty and setting up Craig for the winner, it would be a brave manager to leave him out of the team for the following game. Ian finally came into the changing room and addressed them all.

"Okay lads, great result, but it's only good if we can follow it up with another win at home against Preston. Stay focused, one game at a time."

Steve Evans came and sat beside him for a moment. "You played well tonight Jake, drove the team forwards. It's all in your hands now; you can get carried away with a good half hour, or you can buckle down and play like that all season. I've seen a lot of promising young lads get stars in their eyes before they have done anything. You could be a different class buddy, just keep your feet on the ground." Steve pulled his towel over his shoulder and headed for the shower, leaving the words to soak into Jake's brain, before Craig came and slapped him on his bare back.

"Me and you buddy, we can take this division to pieces. A couple of the lads are staying over tonight, sleeping over at Billy's place in Chelsea. What do you say? A night out and back for in for training fresh as a daisy?"

Jake didn't need to think twice. "Yeah, let's do it. I just need to see my mum and dad first. They're in the bar waiting for me." He dressed quickly before heading out to find his parents.

Ian stood in the corridor leading to the player's lounge blocking the way in. "I hear that you won't be joining us on the coach back Jake. Bit of a strange decision to make after only thirty minutes of football - do you remember me telling you all to stay focused?" His voice rose a little above what seemed comfortable for Jake. "Makes me wonder what you will be like if I give you the whole game. We are a professional club and I don't expect my players to be out on the town midweek, so what do you think?"

Jake could feel himself blushing as the gravity of the conversation hit home and Ian continued.

"I'll tell you what we'll do Jake, while me and the boys are playing Preston at home on Saturday, how about you take a weekend off to decide if you really want to be a player for my team?"

Jake didn't need time to think, he knew he'd messed up and stammered, "No, I'll come back with the guys. I wasn't thinking."

Ian tapped him on the head. "And that, my son, will get you into a lot of trouble. Now go see your parents, they are waiting in the bar, and then get on the coach with the others." He turned and walked away, leaving Jake to ponder his decision. He needn't have worried, Craig appeared in the corridor, just as red faced and followed him into the bar.

"Jake, I've been having a think about it, perhaps we better

give tonight a miss.

CHAPTER THIRTEEN

Luke slept deeply all night after listening to the commentary of the game on Radio Berkshire, soaking up the excitement that football can bring when your own brother was the hero of the hour. This was followed by a twinge of envy as he listened to a short interview with the manager in which he praised Jake's performance. In truth, he had always realised that Jake's turn would arrive first, but he also knew that in time, fame would distract him from home, and more importantly for Luke, Jake's rising profile would keep him away from prison visits.

He brushed his teeth before breakfast, the rumble of staff and prisoners getting ready for the morning growing around him. Alarm bells were tested before the unlock and the sound of the food trolley entering the server area signalled that breakfast was imminent. His door was unlocked along with the other sixteen cells on the landing and Luke was still washing and shaving as he heard the rest of the prisoners file past his door towards the table. He finished quickly, and pulling his t-shirt on he turned to leave and saw Bigger standing in his doorway.

"Luke, I've got your back while you're on my wing. My contacts in Reading told me that you and Chris were close and he lost his life trying to protect you."

Luke had no idea where this conversation was leading. "Yeah, it's just like I told you a few days ago, Bigger."

He nodded at Luke, "I need you to do some things for me Luke, just so that our relationship keeps sweet. Indirectly you cost me the life of one of my friends so you need to repay some of that goodwill back to me." He stood waiting for an answer from Luke.

"What do you want Bigger? I can't do much to help."

Bigger laughed. "The staff are calling for us both to get to the tables." He threw a heavy package onto Luke's bed.

"Look after this until Sunday when someone will collect it from you. Mess up and you will need to join Rat Boy in the segregation. Understand?"

Luke nodded weakly as Bigger left and took his seat for breakfast. He then hastily lifted his mattress and hid the package underneath. He cursed to himself as he sat down at the table where Bigger eyeballed him intently. A frightened Luke didn't know where to look and the pressure facing him seemed insurmountable with no realistic chance of stopping. He had folded and taken the parcel and knew that this situation would repeat itself until either Bigger left, or Luke was caught. Bigger still had a year until he would be moved to an adult jail so the odds were very much against Luke.

Just then, the main unit gate banged open as three staff came onto the wing, one holding a small, black case. Byles whispered along the table. "It's a search team, anyone got anything hidden?"

Silence followed as the men spoke to the wing manager, prisoners trying to overhear any clues as to the targets. Holding a sheet of paper containing names, the manager looked around the tables before nodding at the staff and carrying on as though nothing special was happening.

The normal routine continued, those lucky enough to be working were escorted to work while the remainder returned to their cells. Bottom two landing were the last to move.

"Byles, Robertson and Woods, stay where you are." The search team came over to the table. "Byles, follow us please."

"I fucking knew it, you won't find anything on me, mugs." Byles was in full voice as two men shoved him ungracefully towards his cell. Luke's stomach dropped, knowing they would find the parcel in no time and that it could contain anything. Its contents could be so serious that all hope of parole or even staying on the unit could end - why did he have to always pick up the blame for others?

Byle's voice was still audible to everyone still on the unit as he was led away while the remaining staff strip searched Luke and Robertson individually in the shower room. Luke hated this process, he felt violated every time he was ordered to remove his clothing in front of grown men.

"You two will wait here until the team are ready for your cell. Woods, you will be next, do you have anything in your cell that you shouldn't have?"

Luke shook his head. "No, of course not."

At that moment the main gate opened and the education manager came in and approached the wing manager.

"I have a meeting with Luke Woods this morning, is he on the wing?" Luke lifted his hand.

"Yes Miss, it's me."

She could see what was happening, but was clearly in a rush. Luke watched her speaking to the wing manager, and seeing that they seemed to be on friendly terms, he prayed with every ounce of faith he had in his body, not believing it when his prayers were answered.

"Look I can see that he's due to be searched, but please, just this once, can I take him for this meeting? I'm really pressed for time today."

The wing manager looked over at the search team and nodded. "Lads, you'll have to pick another cell to search. Woods has an important meeting."

The education manager looked at Luke and smiled. "Come on then Luke, let's get you on some good courses."

Inside, he was still shaking with the fear of the package being discovered, but outside, he tried to remain composed. "Thanks for coming to get me Miss, another five minutes and I would have been in a cell search."

Returning to the wing two hours later, Luke was met by Bigger.

"You are a fucking liability man, but you are also the luckiest man on earth. I thought that you had lost my stuff. They'll be back for you later so go get the package and bring it to Blue, I've got a better place to keep it safe."

Luke returned to his cell, stuffing the package into his boxer shorts before handing it over to Blue in the shower. "Tell Bigger I'm sorry, I wouldn't have grassed on him."

Blue laughed, the prominent scar across his throat hinting at the ferocious nature of his life. "He knows that already, we wouldn't be having this conversation if he didn't trust you."

Luke was walking out of the shower area when an officer took his arm. It was the leader of the search team.

"We missed you from the list this morning Woods," he said and a glint in his eye told Luke that this man didn't like him. "I can just tell from the look on your face that you have got something that you don't want us to find so let's go."

Another officer standing chatting in the office was beckoned to and he stopped his conversation and came over to the shower room door before the pair of them escorted him back to his cell, the stench of expectation and enjoyment dripping from every pore of their bodies. They had their target and knew they would hit gold.

"I have asked you once already, but I will ask you again. "Do you have anything in your cell that you shouldn't have?"

Luke almost laughed inside but kept his face straight. "No, I don't have anything at all."

"Great, well let's see if my friend here can find what you're hiding. And guess what Woods? I have been told that you are hiding something."

A Springer spaniel came to the cell door, tail wagging and almost pulling its handler into the cell. The searcher turned to Luke once again.

"Just wait outside Woods, while the dog does its work. You can watch if you like."

The handler released the harness as the dog sniffed the air around the cell before leaping onto the bed and sitting over the exact point where the parcel had sat ten minutes earlier.

"Good girl," the handler said as the staff pulled the mattress from the bed, examining every lump of foam. The dog still remained interested in the scent and the search leader turned to Luke. "Why would my drug dog become so excited about your mattress Woods? What have you had hidden?"

Luke kept calm while others on the landing listened. "I've only been here a few days, it could have been the last person in here."

"Bullshit, when the dog gets a hit like that it's a fresh scent. You're hiding something Woods so where is it?"

Luke shrugged his shoulders. "I don't know who told you that I had something hidden, but they were wrong."

The officer checked the mattress one last time before throwing it onto the floor, his anger evident.

"Today was your day but I will catch you, and when I do, I will make sure that you have years added onto your sentence." He eyeballed Luke before pushing him firmly back into the cell.

"Stay lucky Woods, you will need it."

Luke sat back in his cell, scared but laughed through the relief of not getting caught. "Oy Woods, are you listening?" The familiar call came down.

"Yes Bigger, I can hear you."

"Are we all good Woods?"

"Yes Bigger, we are all good."

But what he hadn't told anyone yet was that he was better than good. Freshly enrolled in the education programme, Luke was going to sit his A-level English and maths exams over the next two years. He also had an opportunity to start work on a media studies degree if his studying went well.

Luke's door opened again and he looked up to see that it was the woman who had talked to him the night before about self harm, Vicky Anderson. "Luke, we are ready for your meeting, follow me."

They went back to the wing manager's office on the unit where two other people who Luke didn't recognise were already sitting waiting. Vicky introduced the first. "Luke, this is our prison chaplain, Derek Willis."

A scruffy, skinny looking man with black straggly hair sat looking at him. He appeared to be in his forties with a terrible complexion. Luke noticed that other than him wearing a thread bare jacket with elbow pads and strange orange trousers, he actually had odd shoes on, one brown and one black. Derek looked at him and smiled.

"I see from your expression that you have noticed my fashion faux pas this morning Luke. It was very early and I got dressed with the lights off." He stood and shook Luke's hand warmly. "But despite my appearance, I do give a good church service every Sunday. I hope to see you there at some point," he said, his thick Liverpool accent putting Luke at ease. He was amused by the chaplain's approach to life. "I will come and check them out Mr Willis."

The other lady in the room introduced herself, she had a well educated southern accent, from somewhere around the M25 was Luke's initial guess. She was immaculately dressed and seemingly armed with all the information they would need.

"I'm Lynn Trotter, Senior Probation officer at Huntercombe and I'm here really to see that you have all the support that you need. Shall we start?" She opened a file.

They spoke for forty minutes, covering every issue from football, his life sentence through to his feelings of self harm. It wasn't at all what he had expected, no preaching or telling off, just support and a little advice sprinkled into the mix. Luke told them nearly everything, only leaving out the very simple fact that he wasn't a murderer, but his famous football star brother was. He also omitted the fact that he had given the name and address of the prisoner who had killed his cell mate in Reading Prison before stopping to break Luke's leg, to Bigger's on-tap contract killer, who then murdered the entire McCann family in a revenge killing. Oh, and the minor detail that he had hidden a large supply of drugs under his bed that same morning as a favour to someone who would probably kill him if he hadn't. Apart from these small details, everything in his first couple of weeks had been uneventful as he informed those listening.

Lynn and Derek had a brief discussion with Vicky before concluding the meeting, Lynn speaking to him again.

"I think that we can safely take you off the self harm process. We feel that you were a little low in mood yesterday, but that's normal in your situation. Just be cautious about other prisoners on the unit, they can be very persuasive sometimes. We will leave it there if that's okay with everyone. Enjoy the education course, it's a good choice Luke." He stood and shook her hand.

"I'm hoping so Miss, and Derek, I will be coming to your service on Sunday so can you book me in please?"

Desmond and Kim had settled down to watch Thursday evening TV when the phone rang. Des didn't recognise the number calling but sensed that it might be something important.

"Good evening Mr Woods, David Decker speaking. It was good to meet you for the contract talks but I have an issue that I need to discuss with you if possible?"

Des looked at the clock, it was eight thirty in the evening, a strange time to be receiving this kind of call. "Sure, go ahead."

"I know that at present Jake doesn't have an agent and you are helping him deal with his matters. I just need to give you a head's up as they say."

Kim noticed a puzzled look come over Des's face as he spoke.

"A heads up on what exactly Mr Decker? Do we have a problem?"

There were a few seconds silence, as David thought about how to phrase what he wanted to say. "It's from two angles really. After Jake's performance against Millwall on Tuesday, we have received a fair bit of attention from other clubs on the lookout for potential stars for the future. But also the Reading Post is going to run a story about both boys, Jake and Luke. They have spoken to me this evening, and from what I gather, they will be phoning you tonight to arrange a meeting.

111

They are in contact with the prison, but the Home Office have declined them permission to go in and interview Luke. This means he needs to be aware that if anyone, even staff, tries to get his story from him, he must decline."

Desmond shook his head, the pressure of representing Jake and all that involved becoming larger by the day,

"Thank you David, that's good of you to tell us."

Again there was a short silence. "That's not the whole story though Mr Woods. I did say that we have attracted interest from other clubs and I have had an offer from Southampton. They would like to buy Jake and this is the second time that they have tried. His price has gone up though since last time. They are now offering us two million pounds for him, which is a lot of money for an untested player. We have rejected the offer, but it will appear in the papers in the morning. A German football agent has also contacted me, it seems Jake has set off some alarm bells over there and without a doubt they will be over here scouting him over the next few weeks. Again, we have no intention of selling Jake for any price. Can you make that clear to him before he reads these stories elsewhere?"

Des was not shocked, his involvement with the academy for the past few seasons had shown him how competitive it was within other clubs, but it was now blindingly obvious the impact that the Millwall game had made on people.

"Yes, I'll tell him tonight but I think that we probably need to think about getting some professional advice for Jake. The world of football is too ruthless for me and I can see that I'm going to be out of my depth very quickly."

"Good idea Mr Woods, tell him to speak with me on Saturday after the Preston game. We will see what we can sort out."

Des ended the call and was explaining the situation to Kim when the phone rang again. This time Kim answered.

"Good evening Mrs Woods, this is The Reading Post. We would like to run an article about Jake for next week's papers. Is that possible?"

Kim was a smart operator and she had seen too many con

men in her time to get caught out by this approach.

"Of course you can run a story on Jake, do what you always do when you want an interview. Go to the club's media department, I'm sure that they can help you."

There was a slight pause. "Of course Mrs Woods, we would normally do that and we have a great working relationship with the football club. Just this time Jake's story is a little different to most and we wondered if you would give us some information about Luke as well?"

Her heart wanted her to rip out the tongue of this reporter but her common sense held her back and allowed her to reply calmly. "I'm sorry but this is too fresh in everyone's lives. What happened was a tragedy and has ruined the lives of a number of families. We feel incredibly sorry for the family of Robert Bell and have no intention of putting them through any more pain than they have already suffered. Now I have nothing further to add, so good evening sir."

She put the phone down, put her head in her hands and sobbed, just as Jake walked into the lounge. "What's happened Mum, is it Luke?"

Desmond answered for his distraught wife. "No Jake, the press is trying to run a story about you and Luke, trying to make some quick money about misery. We need to have a talk, son, before you see some stories in tomorrow's news."

Jake looked confused, his brain wondering what had been said. Had Luke told the real story about that night in Newbury? Jake could hardly hold his anxiety back as he questioned his father.

"About what Dad?" He almost didn't want to hear the answer to the question. Then, when it came, a relief swept over him.

"A few football clubs are showing an interest in you. Southampton have offered two million pounds to buy you. Some German teams are interested too, Bayern Munich and Borussia Dortmund to name only two. Reading have told them all that you are not for sale. David Decker wants to speak to you after the game on Saturday when he's going to talk about football agents. I think that you might need one soon."

Jake rubbed his hands together. "Two million? That's gone up a bit. Anyway, I have already promised Ian that I'm staying where I am, I have a lot to learn about football. If they still think that I'm good enough in another two years then that will be different."

Desmond looked at him, the words sounded sincere, but the eyes were giving a different story.

Jake pulled into the training ground in his newly purchased second hand Honda Civic. It was his first car and suddenly he felt more like a first team player and less an academy boy. It was only a year old but the showroom dealer was a big Reading fan and gave him a two hundred pound discount and an easy repayable finance package. Jake had bitten his hand off for such a good deal.

A couple of the players pulled up at the same time, laughing at the car. "What colour do you call that Jake?"

He laughed and polished the bonnet with an imaginary cloth. "That my friend is Iced Teal Pearly." He said proudly.

"No mate, that heap of crap is grey. I swear to God, if you leave that unlocked for half a second, I will fill it with rotting fish."

Turning to check the doors, Jake wondered if Billy was being serious, but then turning back and looking him in the eye, he saw it was a real threat.

"Where are you going to find enough rotten fish to fill my baby?" he half heartedly laughed, sharing the joke.

"You leave it open, I'll find the fish, and that sounds like a challenge Jake."

He backed down straight away. "No Billy, no challenge, I bloody know that you will do it."

When Billy had gone out of sight, Jake moved his car to a secluded part of the car park behind a large wire cage containing the rubbish bins, where even Billy wouldn't look to vandalise it. He had the label of team joker but there seemed no limits to what he would do to get a cheap laugh.

The training session was as intense as Jake had ever seen, repeating drills increasing in technique until every player knew where they needed to be. The strange thing for him was that Ian involved him in everything; on Tuesday night he had been told that he was dropped and it looked like it would be a long road to get back in the squad, and now here he was, the one finishing off all the moves.

Sending the players to get a drink of water, Ian collected up the training equipment, speaking intently to the other coaching staff as he did so. Players began to reappear in dribs and drabs, Billy trotting on as the last person again. Ian clapped his hands and gathered everyone round. "Okay, for some of you this is the worst kept secret, for others it will be news. You would all have noticed that Jon Cushing hasn't been around for a couple of days; Birmingham City came in and offered the club five million for him. Strikers with twenty goals a season are hard to find, and well, we have just lost ours. That leaves us with Sam and Jake to lead the attack until we strengthen the squad and Lance Fallon will be called back up for the bench. Any questions?"

Billy put his hand in the air. "Just one boss, where is that smoke coming from?" He pointed to a plume of black smoke appearing from behind the metal cage containing the bins.

Jake looked at the spiral of smoke billowing into the sky, directly where his car was parked, a guttural scream rising from deep inside of his belly. He had only been the owner for one day, and now Billy had torched it for a joke.

"Billy, what have you done? My dad will kill me," he managed to stutter, trying hard not to show that he felt like bursting into tears.

Billy was laughing so much he thought that he would hurt himself. "That Iced Teal Pearl is looking a bit hot under the collar Jake, you want a lift home son?"

Jake raced across the pitch towards his car to see if he could salvage it, almost skidding as his studs hit the concrete car park surface. Tears running from their eyes, the squad members joined him as they pointed to the far side of the car park to where Jake's car had been recently moved by the kit man, a pile of old tyres smouldering away where it had previously been parked. It seemed that Jake was the only one not in on the joke and Ian gasped for breath as he slapped Jake on the back. "You have to admit, that was a good one Jake, your face was a picture." He composed himself before continuing more seriously. "You've trained well the past two days and you'll be starting against Preston. Just keep your feet firmly on the ground. You have a lot to learn, but trust me. If you give me everything for two seasons, I will let you go to a bigger club if you still want to."

CHAPTER FOURTEEN

There had been a strange feeling around the prison for the past two days, the word spreading around all six units was that a police informer was amongst them. This suspicion grew after two of the more prominent gang members from neighbouring unit 'Rich' had been arrested by the murder squad for a high profile killing that had happened in Peckham, London, the year before.

The police had questioned them about conversations they'd had on the unit that could only be known to prisoners who were within ear shot. As both prisoners worked in the gymnasium helping to keep it clean, the only person who could have been privy to this information was a young traveller named Jimmy Flynn who worked with them.

What they, or no one other than the Governor and the Head of Security knew, was that the police had placed listening devices in all areas that these two prisoners used during the day and night, and this even included the table at which all of their family visits were held every other weekend. The police were listening to each and every conversation that the boys were having and they didn't have or need any other prisoners to inform.

Jimmy was a smartly dressed eighteen-year-old traveller from an East London site, recently convicted for the theft of a number of caravans from driveways in and around Kent. He was caught towing one of the stolen caravans on the M25 when the white transit he was driving had a blow out in the middle of a section of road works, causing a seven mile tail back. The police quickly pieced together the evidence before the court sent him down for twelve months.

He brushed off the sentence as 'something that happens to

all travelling lads,' but his heavily pregnant girlfriend didn't share his sense of flippancy. With no money coming into the family, she had to lean heavily on the other travellers on the site. The men didn't give her money for nothing, and although ready to give birth, she still gave sexual favours to put food on the table.

Bigger and the rest of the *No Remorse* gang were handed Jimmy's name one Sunday afternoon during a visit from two of their business associates. Jimmy Flynn's fate was sorted over a can of warm coke and a packet of cheese and onion crisps in a stuffy visits room, and they had just the boy to take care of business.

Rat Boy was now resident on Mountbatten unit, a separate newly built wing which housed a hundred and twenty prisoners. The Governor's hope was to isolate him out of the way of Patterson Unit until a space could be found for him in Portland Young Offenders, a place that had a reputation for dealing with dangerous little thugs such as him. The routine was hard and the staff enthusiastically ensured that the rules in place were vigorously reinforced at every opportunity.

But no matter where anyone was located within the fence of Huntercombe, Bigger could find them and get to them. At eight thirty on the Thursday evening, Rat Boy had his orders given to him, along with a small bag of the heroin he tried so hard to avoid while in prison. He scurried back to his cell and greedily smoked the entire contents of the small roll of cling film. Within the rolled up towel that had been pressed into his hand sat a large folding knife, the blade razor sharp. He had one job to do and the slate with Bigger would be wiped clean. What Rat Boy didn't know was that on that Friday morning, Jimmy Flynn would be staying in his cell, awaiting a doctor's appointment.

The last few stragglers came out of the unit gates and into the secure passage which ran up the spine of the prison. Staff stood at various points to supervise, but in general prisoners were able to move around during these set times in what was described as free flow movement. Once all prisoners had arrived at their work places, all gates would be secured and no more free movement was allowed.

Rat Boy hovered around the bottom of the corridor despite repeated requests by staff to move. Nearly everyone was accounted for in their workplace when the Orderly Officer, Bob Rogers, in charge of movements spotted him acting suspiciously. It wasn't unusual for him to behave like this, normally to try get drugs or to borrow something from somebody,

"Rat Boy, get to where you are supposed to be."

Just then, an officer shouted up towards Bob, "Last one coming up for the gym."

A smartly dressed white lad with his gym kit in his hand jogged along the corridor, not wanting to miss his football session. Rat boy allowed him to get alongside him before producing the knife and slashing the boy's throat wide open, hitting the main artery in one slice.

Micky M'cDonnagh put his hand up instantly to try and stop the flow of blood before falling to his knees, and then on to his back before passing out. It was like a horror show being played out in front of three watching staff and a silent CCTV camera, and the men were momentarily rooted to the spot before hurriedly trying to cover the twenty metres between them and Rat Boy. He hadn't finished, and holding the knife high in the air, he plunged it through the heart of the prostrate lad, totally oblivious to the fact that he had killed the wrong person.

Standing covered with blood and still holding the knife in his right hand, he raced at the staff who backed away from him, one drawing his baton in an attempt to disarm him. It was too late and he sprinted through the open gate which seconds before had seen prisoners leaving to go to the education building which sat in the prison grounds.

A panicked call came over the radios held by every guard.

'Urgent message. One prisoner armed with a knife is running towards the perimeter fence section twelve and one prisoner

stabbed in the secure passage way. Code red, we need medical assistance immediately.'

Rat Boy had no intention of heading for the fence, knowing that the razor wire at the top of the fourteen foot steel barrier would cut him to bits. Instead, he threw himself onto the window bars of the building and hauled himself onto the roof of the secure corridor before running along and ascending the higher roof of the gymnasium. The staff lost sight of him and were scouring the roofs when again a call came over the radio.

'All stations take up fixed posts, we have an armed prisoner on the roof. Unsure about his location; do not approach him under any circumstances.'

Rat Boy huddled behind an air-con unit around twenty feet from the ground, directly above the main sports hall. He was out of sight but could see the staff taking positions around the fence. Anticipating that this would happen he had prepared himself for a long standoff, pockets filled with sweets and enough warm clothing on to withstand the colder night time. He sat back and waited, knowing that his time was coming.

The clatter of a police helicopter overhead was the first real sign that anything of substance was happening. He had sat up on the roof for an hour and twelve minutes according to his watch and as of yet nothing had happened other than the staff standing on alert around the fence. He had counted five in the three hundred metre stretch to his front and it would make sense to him that the other areas would have the same cover. Another half an hour passed before the helicopter hovered directly overhead and any doubt in his mind about getting found was dispelled one minute later.

An officer stood at the bottom of the building and shouted up to him.

"Bellingham, we know that you are up there, the police have seen you. We need you to come down."

Bellingham stood up, no longer seeing the point in hiding.

"Fuck off! If I come down, you lot will just give me a beating again. I'm staying here."

The same voice shouted up. "My name is Miss Nevis, you know me from the wing, Bellingham. No one is going to hurt you, you need to throw the knife down onto the grass and when you have done that, we can talk a little more. I just need to know that we are both safe, okay?"

Rat Boy had been around too long to fall for this line.

"No chance, I know what happens. A team will come up here and try to restrain me. If anyone comes close to this roof I will stab them, then I will kill myself. Do you want to take that risk?"

A few hundred metres away near the Governor's office the command suite had opened up. The senior managers on duty initiated the contingency plans and the rest of the prison was closed down. Any prisoners presently locked in the education block would stay where they were until it was safe to move them. All other prisoners were locked back in their cells and nothing else was allowed to happen within the prison without the permission of the Silver Commander sitting in the room. Today that was the Governor, Miss Sue Bridges, a stern Yorkshire woman who took no nonsense from staff or prisoners. Straight forward and plain speaking, everyone loved her. She checked through the contingency plans carefully before taking off her glasses and asking for silence.

The chatter stopped instantly and she spoke to the staff in the room, briefing them precisely about what had happened. She had seen a lot during her thirty years of service, but this was the first time a prisoner had been murdered in any of her establishments. Looking around at the gathered group, she explained how she wanted to proceed

"Our primary concern is to keep the staff safe so I want a rapid reaction team organised. If this chap comes down off his own steam and starts waving the knife about, I want him dealt with straight away. I also need a plan for if he surrenders, and another one for if he starts to hurt himself. We will need to get up there and restrain him quickly. I want all those plans within the next ten minutes please. We also have national resources on their way. A control and restraint team trained to work at height will be here in an hour or so, and until then, if he stays up there, we just keep talking to him, Any questions?"

Rat Boy chewed on a snickers bar; he knew that the boy he stabbed was dead, there was enough blood on the floor of the corridor to have a bath in but he didn't care. It was his destiny anyway. Fumbling in his pocket he looked for another small ball of cling film, to have one more smoke before the action started.

"Bellingham." A voice echoed up before he had the chance to heat up his silver foil. He folded it up, thinking he would maybe save it for the night time. Leaning over the gutter, he saw Miss Nevis standing around twenty feet away on the grass, the sun now shining down directly on him and warming him up.

"What?" He looked down at her as she continued the conversation.

"Why are you up there? We can sort out any issues you have down here. It will be easier."

He shook his head silently. "Easier for who? I know Flynn is dead, I killed him. I will come down when I'm ready." Taking the drugs back out he prepared them and inhaled deeply, the calmness creeping over his entire body.

The negotiator stuttered briefly, forgetting her brief as she watched the haze of smoke drift from his mouth. "Flynn isn't the boy you killed, you stabbed someone else." She paused for a moment before exclaiming,

"You killed the wrong person Bellingham."

Rat Boy let the words sink in, and as they mixed with the heroin in his brain, the realisation that he had screwed up again pierced his conscience, this time with drastic consequences. Prisoners started to shout from their cell windows as they heard the conversation developing.

"No, I killed Flynn, he was going to the gym. Smartly dressed, it was him,"he insisted as he struggled to recollect the description Bigger had given him.

A prisoner listening from another unit shouted from his window, his voice drifting over the exercise yards. "No, you fucking idiot, Flynn is sitting in the cell next to me. You killed that Irish kid who came in last month."

The helicopter flew over one more time before heading back to its base. Rat Boy looked around; it was almost midday and he had nowhere to go. Scanning the fence one more time, he noticed that something had changed. A large man wearing black overalls stood looking up at him from the path beside the wire fence. The tactical intervention team had arrived. Picking up a stone from the roof he threw it towards him.

"I know who you are man, if you lot come up onto the roof to get me, I will jump. If I see one person coming up here, I will kill myself. I haven't got anything to lose."

He sat back down on the roof as the voice of another negotiator shouted up to him. Looking down, he didn't recognise the face.

"Who the fuck are you? Where is Miss Nevis?" The man took a long drink from a can of Fanta and looked up. Rat boy could see the condensation running down the sides of the cold can; it was hot up there and he was getting thirsty.

"Miss Nevis has been out here for hours, she needed a break. You have got me for a while, my name's Bryan, I'm from another prison."

Rat Boy found a metal bolt in the gutter and tossed it to the ground, contemplating his options. Life in prison with no hope of release, or jump and kill himself? He scanned round his potential drop zone and noticed a few crash mats had been positioned under where he sat, but they were useless as he could jump from anywhere.

A voice shouted out to him from the wing next to the gym where a prisoner on the top landing was watching everything. "Don't jump man, fight them. I can see that they have a team with shields hiding near you. Fucking stab the first one who tries it."

A few more shouts of encouragement made up Rat Boy's

mind. He was going to go out in a blaze of glory. He had messed up the only job Bigger had given him so he might as well go down fighting.

In a blur of speed, he got up and ran out of sight of the negotiator and back to the lower level where he had first climbed up. He could see staff running frantically to catch up with him and a team of five officers, one with a shield, raced across the concrete basketball court between two units in the hope of catching him. He was too fast and leapt down, knife in hand. The prisoners watching erupted into the cheers of a football crowd as they egged him on.

A teacher from the education unit, unaware of what was happening, walked out of her office as he ran towards the fence. Seeing the knife and dropping her books, she screamed as he made a grab for her. The blade rested against her throat as Rat Boy hissed his stale breath in her ear.

"You are going to get me out of this place. Do what I tell you or I'll slice your head off."

Sue Bridges sat with her head in her hands as the news came through on her radio. She lifted her head and glared at those around her. "And how the hell did we have a teacher working in an office who knew nothing about the incident? Now we have a hostage on the move, an education block still full of prisoners waiting for lunch, forensic staff all over the secure passage way taking evidence and a dead prisoner."

She phoned the Gold Command Suite in London and calmly explained the developments before speaking to her team.

"The teacher has keys. I want every gate double locked or chained shut. He must not be allowed to take her anywhere else. Clear all the staff out of the gate except one officer who must hide out of sight. If Bellingham gets to the gate, I don't want him to be able to see or talk to anyone at all." A few members of staff hurried out of the room to carry out the tasks, all feeling the beginnings of controlled panic.

Stella Davies tried to remain as calm as she possibly could, given the fact that she had the sharp point of a knife digging into her throat as she tried to control her breathing. She tried hard to remember the advice that the security manager had given to all education staff should this very thing happen.

Forcing her down onto a curb, Rat Boy looked at the staff standing in the distance. He held all the cards, all the power, as voices kept floating from cell windows telling him where the staff were standing and more importantly where the intervention team was heading.

Taking her metal key chain and looping it around her neck, he sat with his back to a post, twisting the knife slightly to keep her aware of the danger he posed.

"Listen to me, we are both going to walk out of this prison together. When we get outside you will take me to your car and drive me to London. Do you understand?"

Stella nodded, trying to remember to be compliant without making him angry.

"I'll need my car keys, they're in my bag, in the office."

Again twisting the knife, he spat, "Let's go for a walk then, doggy."

She hesitated before he kicked her hard in the ribs. "Get on your hands and knees and walk like a dog to the office."

The knees on her jeans were soon green from the grass stains and she stopped. "I am forty-five years old and my knees won't let me crawl anymore. Can I walk please? It will be quicker."

He kicked her again, the pain from the blow to her ribs taking the breath away from her as she gasped. "You don't need to keep hurting me, I'm doing what you ask."

They reached the administration block and she stood as he kept hold of the chain, high on heroin and adrenaline.

"Move, you fucking bitch. Try anything funny and I will stick this through your neck. He prodded her with the blade before taking her set of keys and fumbled one into the lock. It didn't work. "Which fucking key is it?" he waved the set of seven keys at her.

She pointed to the one next to a larger gate key. "It's that one."

Opening the door into a large wooden building containing six offices, he shouted at her. "Is anyone else in here?"

She looked down, trying to avoid confrontation and eye contact. "No they're all teaching in the other building, I was the only one in here."

Again Rat Boy fumbled for the key to open the office before Stella interjected.

"It's a difficult lock, maybe you should let me open it?"

Bellingham turned, locking the outside door to stop an attack. He handed her the keys. "Do it, quickly."

She smiled. "It would be easier without the chain around my neck. You don't need it on me, what am I going to do?" She looked at him quizzically before shrugging her shoulders and forcing a smile. The feel of the metal chain's release from her throat gave her hope. If she could just play this right, she could survive.

The staff in the command suite sat in silence as they listened to an update from Sue.

"Okay, so at the moment we know that he has taken Stella Davis captive and is holding her at knife point. He has tied a chain around her neck and was making her crawl along the ground. They look as though they are heading for her office. I suspect that he is trying to either get to a phone, or work on a plan to escape. Do we have all the phones cut off?"

The security manager checked through his notes. "Yes Sue, they were turned off thirty minutes ago. All prisoners who were located in the education department are now back on their wings, and all teachers have moved to a secure sterile location. Bellingham can't get far."

Sue gave a grim smile. "Little does Bellingham know that his hostage was once the world kickboxing champion. I just hope that she keeps her composure."

Stella took the keys from Bellingham and fiddled with the lock before finally opening it. Bellingham pushed her out of the way, entering first and tipping the contents of her bag onto the desk. He rummaged through them before turning in triumph, holding her car keys in his dirty hands. His one second of elation evaporated as quickly as his escape plan as he realised that he had lost focus and was no longer in possession of the prison keys, and was out of reach of the hostage.

"Give me back the gate keys," he demanded.

"No problem, just calm down a bit. You have got what you wanted, you have me and you have my car keys."

Behind Bellingham a figure in black overalls hugged the outside wooden wall, listening to everything that was said through the open top window. The only thing stopping him grabbing the unsuspecting hostage taker were the thick window bars. He crouched listening to the conversation develop as Stella began to tip the balance of power. She wasn't ready to be dragged around the prison again. Enough was enough and if he intended to hurt her, let the little fucker try.

"I'll tell you what, you seem to like dog games," she told him, the anger in her voice evident. She tossed the keys through the open window. "Fetch!"

Rat Boy saw his only way out of the building sail past his head before the sound of the keys hitting the ground outside sent him into a rage.

"You stupid bitch!" Lunging forwards, he plunged the knife towards her throat but before he could blink, Stella stepped to one side and sent him to the floor with a hefty right hook. The knife clattered harmlessly onto the ground as she kicked it to one side before leaping onto his flailing body and pushing her forearm across his exposed throat. Rat Boy gagged as he tried to force her away from him but it was a one sided affair as her balance and strength quickly took away any hope he once held.

The sound of the scuffle alerted the officer outside that something was going very wrong. Whispering into the radio he called an urgent message to the command suite. *'The hostage is under attack.'* Sue acted instantly, calling the code word to assault the building.

"All units, Brighton Pier, I repeat Brighton Pier."

The teams rushed through the wooden door and into the

office, stopping for a moment as they looked at Stella on top of Bellingham pummelling him with crushing blows. He looked up, blood pouring from a split lip and broken nose.

"Boss help me, she's crazy."

Stella stood, blood dripping from her skinned knuckles where she had rained punches into his face. She looked back at her attacker one more time as the staff led her out of the prison and into the safety of a waiting ambulance.

Rat Boy lay bleeding and humiliated. The officers were unsmiling as he was handcuffed and taken to the segregation unit where two policemen greeted him with an official caution.

"I am arresting you for the murder of Micky McDonnagh. You do not have to say anything but it may harm your defence if you do not mention when questioned something that you may later rely on in court. Anything you do say may be given in evidence."

The words bounced around his drug soaked brain as he contemplated how a normal morning could have turned so wrong for him and the realisation hit that yet again he was taking the fall for someone else.

"I was told to do it, it was a planned hit. I was paid but if I hadn't done it, it would have been me next. It was Bigger, he made me do it."

The officers remained unimpressed with his pathetic pleas for leniency. "Save it for later son, in the meantime, we want all your clothes in these bags." They stood in front of him holding the paper evidence bags, his whining excuses beginning to hurt their ears.

"Stop talking and get changed son. We haven't got time to listen to your sob stories." He dressed himself in a forensic white paper suit and stood still while an officer placed handcuffs on him.

Signing the paper work for the reception officer, the lead policeman roughly grabbed the bar between the handcuffs, making them cut into Rat Boy's wrists. He winced in pain as the metal bar hit his wrist bone, the officers laughing at his predicament.

"Say goodbye son. You won't be seeing this place ever again."

Looking at the opening gates of Huntercombe Prison, Rat Boy realised that it would be a very long time before he would enjoy any freedom again, if at all. A tear dripped down his grubby gaunt cheeks as he watched the faces of the gate staff disappear into the distance. He was destined for a long night in Reading Police station before a daunting trip to HMP Woodhill.

Elsewhere in the prison, one person was feeling some of the heat that Rat Boy had left. The sun was starting to set, dipping below the prison fence as Bigger paced his cell. He knew what was coming - Rat Boy wouldn't keep him out of this for one second. He called out to Blue, a couple of cells down.

"If I'm moved, take care of business. I will drop you a line when I land at my new place."

The sound of his door opening and the view of half a dozen prison staff standing outside confirmed his thoughts. Rat Boy had wasted no time at all in trying to save his own miserable skin.

CHAPTER FIFTEEN

The bustle of number one court at the Old Bailey entered Luke's ears as he had sat waiting in a cell on his own, somewhere in the belly of this building. Shamus McCann now sat emotionless as Luke took the witness box supervised by a court officer. He had waited a long time for this moment to come, had lain awake for nights on end, thinking about how coldly they had taken Chris's life and then, without any concern for their actions, had destroyed his ambition of ever kicking a football again with one blow of that bar.

McCann looked up at the public area, smiling at friends who had come to watch the spectacle while the judge addressed the court. A comment shouted towards Luke caused the judge to scan the faces in the public gallery,

"Any further interruptions from those members of the public who are here to watch this trial will be dealt with by the court security staff. I will then have you charged and sent to prison. I hope that you all understand the gravity of this case." Silence swept back over the oak benches of this majestic room, a sight that had provided the back drop for many TV dramas.

McCann turned to look at Luke as he presented his evidence, showing a mix of emotions as he listened intently to the description of the murder. At some points he smiled at Luke, as though enjoying the memory before shaking his head while looking at the jury members in a sympathetic gesture. They weren't fooled by this pantomime unfolding before them as Luke gave strong, indisputable evidence. He had recalled every word and action and it flowed out and presented itself to the ears of the jury as the god's honest truth. McCann's barrister paused for a second as he read a written note handed to him from McCann.

"Your honour, my client has just presented me with some new instructions, may I take a second to clarify the position?"

The judge nodded before instructing the jury to retire. The barrister turned to McCann, a disbelieving look on his face. "Am I reading this correctly Mr McCann, that you wish to plead guilty after all this time?"

McCann spat onto the wooden floor of the courtroom. "Yeah, tell them that I did it. Tell them whatever you fucking like, they will never believe my story anyway. Any idiot can see that so try and get me the best sentence you can. I don't want to be locked up forever, do you understand me?"

The entire courtroom stood in silence as the judge returned to the bench. McCann remained standing, facing him, and for a brief second it felt that they were the only two people in attendance. Fixing him in his stare the Judge began.

"I have read the documentation regarding every aspect of this case. In my twenty-seven years at the bar, I have encountered many dangerous people, but something with you Mr McCann troubles me deeper than any other I have seen. You are a young man, so intent on creating harm to anyone who steps into your path, a young man so intertwined with gangland culture that I wonder if you could ever be saved? Would a further twenty years served in prison give you the opportunity to still live a useful life on release? Every instinct screams at me to give you a life sentence without any hope of release, but one little glint in your body language suggested that you are not a hopeless case."

Judge Peter Bell continued to sum up the case, describing McCann as, "a danger to all who cross his path, and any tariff on his life sentence must be long enough to make a difference."

McCann looked down at his barrister and hissed, "I fucking told you to get me a deal, you useless cunt."

Judge Bell stopped speaking at once as McCann continued his outburst. Pushing the court security to one side and vaulting the defendant's box, he assaulted his own barrister with a kick to his head as he sat motionless in shock. Security guards quickly regrouped and restraining him, led him back down into the holding cell area.

Judge Bell looked down and winced. "Are you okay Mr Noel?"

McCann's barrister looked up and smiled. "Yes your honour, just taken aback slightly by my clients final submissions." The Judge smiled briefly while looking back at his notes, before pushing them to one side.

"I will deal with this in your client's absence, Mr Noel, if that is acceptable? After looking at all the factors contributing to the murder in Reading Prison, plus the total lack of remorse and entrenched antisocial and violent personality issues with McCann, I hereby sentence him to a whole life term, without the possibility of release. I trust that you will convey the message to your client Mr Noel?"

Two years later

It was a bitterly cold day at the training ground, Monday January 15, 2001.

Ian Woodford stood in the drizzle, watching the ball fizz off the wet grass on the pitch. He had aged during the past two seasons; the expected push for a playoff place hadn't developed as Reading ended the season in seventh position and it was thought that the Chinese owners were thinking about replacing him with a high profile manager. Barry Turner, the former Sheffield Wednesday boss, had made himself available for management again after a brief illness and at thirty eight, he would be an energetic personality to have in the club. That would go well along with the recently retired former club captain, Steve Evans who was now the assistant manager.

What's more, Barry's history of getting the best out of players on a small budget seemed to fall into place with the clubs present financial situation.

Ian pulled Jake to one side. "Jake, you have played wonderful football for the team since your debut and it hasn't gone unnoticed." Jake laughed, he was tiring of transfer speculation about him which seemed to be occurring every other day in the local paper.

"I'm enjoying my football here, boss. We are in the play off places and if we keep pushing forwards we can get promoted. We're only four points behind the automatic places."

The enthusiasm Jake showed towards the club warmed Ian's heart. He knew that he could rely on him, he was the clubs leading goal scorer last season and had already scored twenty goals this season.

"It's not speculation this time Jake. Spurs are interested in signing you. They are offering the club five million and I think the owners want to sell you mate. It is out of my hands so you'd better have a chat with your agent."

A sense of disappointment tinged with excitement coursed through his body. Twenty years old and a top premiership club wanted to invest a load of money in him. Standing in the warm shower, Jake weighed up the pros and cons behind a move to North London's Spurs and he couldn't find many reasons not to go.

Steve Evans was waiting for him as he came out and dried himself. "I guess you have heard the latest gossip, Steve?"

His former captain nodded. "Bit more than gossip though Jake. This is real money talking, a bid has been made and the club have accepted. It's all down to you now, you can refuse and stay here, or you can go meet the Spurs chairman this afternoon and have a chat with him. What do you have to lose?"

Jake looked confused for a second, "So all this stuff has been agreed behind my back? Not even my agent knew about it?"

Steve shrugged his shoulders. "I know Jake, but this is the way with the big teams. Five million is nothing to them, but to us, it means that we can buy five new players."

Jake protested, more out of loyalty to Steve, "But I'm not even tested at that level and I may not be able to do it against world class defenders. Are you saying that I have to go?"

Steve shook his head. "No mate, I'm not saying that, I would love you to stay here and take us up to the premiership. Just go and speak with them, then you can make a decision."

Before Jake even had the opportunity to get in his car, a small crowd of young fans had congregated, eager to speak with their favourite player.

"Jake, don't go please. We need you at the club."

A reporter pushed his way through the group. "Hi Jake, we hear that you are moving to Spurs this afternoon. Do you have any words for the Reading fans?"

His head spun with the speed at which the news of his potential move had spread and he managed to answer, "I am a Reading player, I haven't spoken to anyone about moving to Spurs," before he brushed past the waiting supporters, gunned the engine in his car and set off down the M4 back to Newbury. His phone rang and he pressed the hands-free call on the steering wheel. It was Abdul, his agent, sounding as harassed as he himself felt. "Jake, where are you? I'm at the ground looking for you. The Spurs chairman has been trying to contact me all morning but I've been in meetings. They want us to get up to North London this afternoon."

It was all becoming a reality, like an out of control train gathering speed and pulling him along in its wake. "What, we just go up there and chat to them?"

Abdul answered immediately; he needed players like Jake, as agents with high profile players attracted bigger high profile players. Jake was still small fry in terms of profile, but within two years he could be a new Beckham.

"Yep, we have a meeting at a hotel at four this afternoon. If it's a success they have a medical planned for Wednesday morning and you could be playing away at Liverpool this weekend."

Jake slowed the car down as he spoke, finding it hard to maintain his concentration on driving. "I'm not sure Abdul, I haven't even had time to talk with my parents about it."

Abdul laughed. "You will be set up for life, Jake. I promise that the contract will be good. Fifty thousand a week, and five percent of the fee will be yours. You could buy your own place and pay off Mum and Dad's mortgage without even thinking about it."

Pulling off at his junction, Jake turned the car around and headed back to Reading. "Meet me at the training ground, Abdul, this news is spreading like wild fire so let's go talk to them."

The entrance to The Mayfair hotel in London was bathed in warm lights as Jake and Abdul passed under the fluttering flags high above the street. Entering the quiet surroundings of the plush foyer, a man in his early fifties stood dressed immaculately in a navy blue suit, white shirt and a Tottenham FC club tie. He walked over and shook Jake by the hand, his warm demeanour putting Jake at ease. "Hi Jake, my name is Clive Webb, thanks for coming over at such short notice. We weren't sure if you'd had the opportunity to eat after training so we have a table booked in the restaurant should you fancy a snack."

He gently guided the two men through into a private room where the round table was set for dinner. A younger man stood, dressed less formally in smart black trousers and a white shirt opened at the neck and held out his hand. "Hi Jake, Daniel Jackson, Chairman of Tottenham Hotspurs Football Club. I would very much like you to be a member of an exciting team that we are putting together." Inviting them to sit, he remained standing until they were all seated. He nodded to a hovering waiter and the door opened and trays of delicious looking Chinese food were carried through.

"I heard that you were partial to these dishes Jake, enjoy."

The four men sat, chatted and ate for a couple of hours before the subject of the meeting was raised again. Daniel wiped his face with a pro-offered warm towel before speaking.

"So Jake, here's the deal. We are amassing a squad of players this season who will challenge every other team in Europe. Our ambitions know no limits. We plan to spend two hundred million pounds over the next two seasons on players and we will aim to overtake United, Chelsea and Arsenal this season. Next season Real Madrid and Barcelona will know who we are so are you ready to be part of this journey? I have seen what you can do in the championship and I believe that we can take you to the next level. Succeed with us and an international call up for Jamaica or England will come, I promise." Jake rocked back in his chair and took another sip of the ice cold water in front of him before answering.

"Sounds great Mr Jackson, but will I get game time?"

Daniel laughed at the question. "I've been asked that question so many times. I don't care about your age, or apparent lack of experience. If you are good enough you will play, and trust me, I think that you are good enough. You will join up with the squad for the Liverpool game on Sunday where you may get on or you may not, I don't try to get involved in team selection but the manager certainly likes you. I would not be talking with you now if Carlos Conte didn't rate you as a player. Give it some thought, but I need to know your answer before Wednesday morning when I have a medical booked for you and a press conference to follow. I would look silly sitting there on my own."

Jake looked at Abdul. "Have you checked through the proposed contract?"

His agent looked surprised at the question. "Yes, of course. I read it all through earlier, it's a good deal Jake."

Jake didn't hesitate, he stood and held out his hand to the Spurs chairman. "It would be an honour to become a Spurs player."

Daniel punched the air. "Great news! Come over to the training ground for midday on Wednesday and we'll do the test and sign the papers. You won't regret this decision Jake."

As they walked back to Abdul's car, the pair of them could hardly contain their glee. "Jake my son, you have just become a millionaire over a sweet and sour pork dinner. Just wait until your family hear the news, I wouldn't take too long in telling them as you can bet that within an hour this news will be out there in the public domain."

Desmond and Kim were in the kitchen finishing cleaning up after the evening meal. Jake's dinner still sat in the oven keeping warm as Kim checked her phone for the fifth time.

"I don't know where he could have gone. He knew that I was cooking a big steak pie tonight but not even a phone call, Des." The door bell rang, followed by a sharp rap on the door knocker.

"Keep patient. I'm coming," Des grumbled as he opened the door to be faced with two sports reporters and a dozen Reading fans. The cameras flashed as he gazed out.

"What's happening? Has something happened to Jake?" Kim asked as she joined him on the doorstep.

A fat, middle aged man wearing a Reading football shirt with Jake's name on it shouted over the small garden wall. "Don't pretend that you didn't know, how can he leave us like this? He promised the fans that he would stay."

Des shook his head. "I don't know what you are talking about, Jake isn't going anywhere."

One of the reporters held out a press release from the club. "Oh yes he is, Mr Woods, he has just signed for Spurs for, it states, an undisclosed amount. We have heard five million, do you have anything to say?"

Des shook his head and put his arm around Kim. "We know nothing about this. I'm sorry but I'm sure that the football club will answer any questions that you may have."

He pushed the door closed and retreated back into the safety of the kitchen just as the phone rang. "Hey Dad, guess what has just happened?"

Des took a breath. "If you're going to tell us that you have signed for Spurs for five million, you're a bit late. We have a load of reporters outside Jake, so if you come back here it could be nasty. We also have a dozen or so fans waiting in the road so maybe you should stay in London tonight, book a hotel and phone us when you're there." He waited a second before adding, "Well done Jake, we are very proud of you."

Jake sat in his car, a little crestfallen that he hadn't been able to give them the news before it leaked. "It's ok Dad, I'm five minutes away so I'll come home and speak to the fans who are outside. Don't worry, leave it to me."

He pulled up into the small driveway where two or three of the fans came to meet him as he opened the car door.

"Jake!" One young girl, maybe only twelve years old was crying. "You promised in your last interview that you were staying at Reading - why have you changed your mind?"

Others gathered around to listen to the answer. He was nervous, this was the first time he had faced supporters who were disappointed in him. "I didn't know about this until late this afternoon when I was told that Spurs wanted to sign me. I'm sorry that I have upset you."

The press took some photographs while the other fans began to drift away, one stopping briefly to shout back to Jake.

"Good luck Jake, I don't blame you, I blame the board. We should be Premiership by now, then you wouldn't have to leave."

Taking his training bag from the boot of the car, Jake gave the girl his boots. "Please don't hate me, I'm just trying to do the best thing for my family and the football club."

She smiled up at him as he signed them before handing them over. "Look after them, hopefully they will be worth some money in a few years."

Closing the front door, he held out his arms to hug his mum and she buried her head into his chest, tears of pride welling up in her eyes. "My little boy is going to be a star, I can't believe it. But now I know that you are definitely going to move away from us and I'm going to miss you Jake."

Squeezing her tight, he chuckled. "I haven't even got into the team yet. We are playing Liverpool away this weekend and I'm in the squad so do you want to come?"

She looked up at him amazed. "Liverpool, already? You'll need to get some good food into your stomach before then, luckily I kept your dinner warm."

She took the plate out of the oven and put it on the table while Des took a seat beside him beaming with pride. "I knew that you could do this son. Go and be the best that you can, train hard and live a clean life." Jake nodded, tasting the delicious pie and trying to forget that he had a belly full of sweet and sour pork.

"I'm going to make sure that you never have to worry about money again," he said, smiling at both his parents, "and when Luke comes back home, he will be set up for the rest of his life."

Luke lay on his single, grey, metal framed bed listening to the sports news on his Roberts rambler radio when a five second football news item knocked him for six. His brother, the real murderer, was now on his way to unimaginable riches while he had to look at the back of a locked door as security lights outside flooded the inside of his cell, preventing him from sleeping. Where was the justice in keeping quiet?

Another eight years of prison life lay ahead of him. It should have been him making the headlines today, it should have been him that would move into an expensive apartment overlooking the London skyline. It should have been Jake eating crap food and fighting to survive everyday of this miserable existence.

Limping over to the light switch, he turned on his main light. Looking at the cracked glass on his cheap watch, it read 2.53, and as he had to study for the English 'A' level exams coming up, he threw himself back on his bed and opened his books. Yet another night of no sleep.

CHAPTER SIXTEEN

It had taken an age for Saturday to come around for Luke, he had barely slept this week in preparation for his exam on Friday, and when he did take it, he felt a sense of disappointment. It hadn't challenged him as much as he hoped and he felt that anyone could have passed. A massive feeling of anti climax had washed over him and his tutor, noticing his low mood had tried to lift his spirits. Luke was the brightest pupil that she had seen come through the system at Huntercombe, and had skated through all of his English coursework with excellent grades. She had thought long and hard before disclosing her plans for him and handing him a brochure for a degree course followed by a Masters in English. Luke had shown an interest in sports journalism and with the irreparable damage to his leg preventing him from playing sport, the nearest thing he could achieve to feeling the buzz would be reporting the action. He had looked through what she was offering before sliding the documents into his folder, promising her that he would think about it.

A call came out across the association area on the unit where Luke sat watching Football Focus on the BBC before the weekend games began. Apparently Spurs were expected to do well this season now the new manager Carlos Conte had recently taken over. As a former Spurs hero he had promised an attacking style of football which excited the players and supporters, and the discussion amongst the pundits was intriguing Luke as he sat glued to the screen. Someone shouting his name brought him back to prison life and he looked up as an officer opened the TV room door.

"You have a visit Woods, follow me."

Luke checked his appearance in the reflection of the window

and set off towards the visits area where he saw his mum and dad sitting waiting. He looked around for Jake as he greeted them. "Where's Jake? I thought that he was coming with you today."

Des cleared his throat. "He's up in Liverpool with the team as they're putting him on the bench for tomorrow's game. He says that he's sorry, Luke."

Luke kissed his mum. "But he's stopped writing as well so can you ask him to drop me a line?"

Kim held her son's hand as she made excuses for his brother. "We will see him tomorrow and I'll tell him to write to you. He's moving out of the house next week, the club have found an apartment for him near Barnet. It sounds nice."

Luke smiled. "I would hope that they would find somewhere nice for a five million pound player." The smile didn't disguise the bitterness in the meaning and Des heard it as he stirred his coffee,

"Come on Luke, it's not his fault that someone wanted to pay a lot of money for him. It's just football, you know that."

Luke took a drink from the can of coke on the table and decided not to press the issue. Des stood to go back to the counter to buy Kim another tea when a visitor bumped into him. Pushed back over the table, he lost his balance and knocked a chair over as the man turned and shouted at Des. "I hope your scum son gets relegated with that shit team." The venom in his comments was shocking while the arsenal badge on his jacket gave away his loyalty.

Luke sprang up and pushed the man backwards before punching him in the jaw sending him falling to the floor. The screams of children and other visitors drowned out the shrill sound of the distant alarm bell. Two officers grabbed Luke while one took the bleeding visitor outside.

"Everyone take your seats please," a large ginger-haired officer bellowed across the room.

The doors burst open and six officers ran into the room, quickly identifying Luke and escorting him away and down to the segregation unit. Des and Kim sat stunned at what had happened in the space of a few seconds.

A large white shaven-headed prisoner sitting alone on his table scowled at Des before shouting. "Your son is going to get fucked up for what he just did to my friend," before two staff grabbed him and dragged him out. He continued to shout before the doors closing behind him drowned him out.

Kim sat crying. "Des, he's going to spend all his life in prison. We didn't bring him up to be like this, what is wrong with the boy? If things weren't bad enough already, he didn't need to attack that person, he is out of control."

Des put his arm around her. "He was just looking after me Kim. Come on, let's go, the staff are waiting to show us out."

Luke sat seething in the segregation. The visitor had assaulted his dad and said things about Jake. In prison you couldn't let those things go. The cell door opened and the Duty Governor stood there with two staff. "What was that all about Woods?"

Luke stood and started to explain before he was cut off.

"Let me tell you something young man. You have just ruined an afternoon's visit for a lot of people and a number of prisoners are very unhappy with you, including Dawkins. That was his brother who you punched." Luke tried to speak again, a tear not far away. Yet again he was cut off.

"I'm not sure that you realise how the parole system works Woods. Let me spell something out to you and I will say it slowly so that it sinks into your head. You are in prison for a MINIMUM of ten years." He stressed the word and said it slower than the rest of the sentence. "But you are serving time for attacking and killing a person who was aggressive towards your brother. Today, someone was aggressive towards your father and you attacked them. How do you feel the parole board will view this incident?"

Luke stared down at the floor. "Badly sir."

"Yep, bingo! Badly is the exact word that I would use. They would look on it as a pattern of behaviour. Even though the court has placed you in prison as a punishment for what you did, it would seem that you haven't learnt from your mistakes." He turned as if to walk away before looking back at Luke. "I am ensuring that this incident is recorded in your file. That will possibly add another two years onto your sentence. By the time you get out of prison you could be a thirty-year-old man at the best. Let that one sink into your skull. Oh, and one more thing. If I have my way, your expensive education programme will be gone too - why should tax payers donate money to educate a thug like you?" The door slammed shut and the sound of the men walking away disappeared into the distance.

Luke lay back on the hard bed sobbing. His thoughts drifted back to the faces of his parents as he was escorted out of the visits room; the look of dismay on his mum's face was bad enough but the look of contempt on his dad's face was heartbreaking. The two people in the world who cared for him the most had been thrown out of the prison through his own actions, and made to feel like criminals themselves.

His door opened again and two young officers stood in the entrance way. "Tea time Woods, do you want water or coffee with it?"

He didn't care, any thoughts of hunger long gone. "Water please." They passed a blue plate to him, a grey coloured pie surrounded by grey mashed potato, diced carrots and a thin brown liquid, masquerading as gravy did little to tempt him to eat. He placed it on the small plastic table near his bed.

"Did that Governor mean what he just said? He would take everything away from me and get me another two years?" The staff looked at each other for a second before one answered.

"Yes, he could do all of those things. He's a new Governor who has just taken over all of the education and work placements. He's also in charge of all life sentence prisoners here so you don't want to piss him off Woods. Lucky for you, we both know who you are. I've told him that you're a good guy who has been working hard ever since you arrived. Your record was perfect until today so for fuck's sake, don't screw up again or he will do all of the things that he has said, and more."

Luke exhaled. "So if I keep all the good things going, I could still get out on my date?" The officer shrugged his shoulders.

"That's up to you Woods."

Pushing the pie around the plate Luke finally cut it in half, gristle spilling onto the plate along with a spoonful of bland looking mince. He decided against eating it in favour of just drinking the water, and lying on the bed sipping from the plastic bottle, he considered how he could apologise to his parents. However a bigger threat was heading his way, manifesting itself as a voice heard through his window.

"Woods, are you listening?"

No one had shouted these words to him for nearly two years and he didn't recognise the voice.

"Woods, I'm going to fuck you up when you get out of the block. You think that you can punch my brother and walk away? I'm gonna fucking cut your face open."

Luke's head spun. He shouldn't have to face these threats, life in Patterson Unit had passed so smoothly since Rat Boy, Bigger and his gang were moved away. Moving over to the window he replied.

"I don't want any trouble with you. I'm sorry about your brother but he pushed my Dad over. What was I supposed to do?" His tone sounded desperate and others were now joining in the conversation, some on Luke's side but most on the side of Dawkins.

"Your dad was in his way and he pushed my brother. I think your mum wanted to suck my brother's cock and your dad got upset. Anyway, I don't give a fuck what started the problem, I'm going to finish it. Watch what happens when you come out."

A ripple of laughter floated across the prison; the threat had been made and there could be no turning back. At some point Dawkins was going to attack him and Luke would need to defend himself by whatever means he could. The rest would just be down to fate.

He slept poorly all night, not through the threats that had been made, but more down to thoughts of his parents. It was now nine thirty on Sunday morning and for a second his thoughts flashed to Jake sitting in a posh hotel in Liverpool waiting for the match that afternoon. Suddenly his door opened and it was the Governor from the previous day. He had the same two officers with him, one handing Luke a few sheets of paper.

"These are your adjudication sheets. You are supposed to have these two hours before the Governor hears the case against you and gives you your punishment. Today we're in a rush so if you're happy to have your hearing before the two hours are up, the Governor will do it now."

The Governor, Mr Willis nodded as the officer spoke. Luke shrugged and managed a smile.

"Whatever, let's just get it over and done with."

He followed the staff to a small office where one of the officers searched him before they all stood at the far end of a rectangular table, an officer standing to his left and right.

The officer on his right barked a command. "Name and number to the Governor."

"PN34632 Luke Woods, sir."

The Governor checked the number against the sheet. "Take a seat please." Luke sat with his knees under the table, staff within touching distance.

The Governor continued. "Can you read and write Woods?"

"Yes sir."

The Governor continued through his check list.

"Have you been given a copy of the adjudication paper work and have you had sufficient time to read and understand it?"

"Yes sir."

"You have been charged with assault; on Saturday August the 14th you assaulted a visitor in the visits room by punching him in the face. Do you understand the charge?"

Luke's shoulders sagged as he replied. "Yes sir."

"Do you require legal representation during the hearing, or are you happy that we deal with it now?"

"No sir, I don't need legal help. Can we deal with it now?" Mr Willis smiled, to Luke he seemed a fair man.

"Excellent. Officer, please read the evidence to me."

The officer read the details about the assault and presented a copy of the CCTV. Luke cringed as he saw how bad his actions looked.

"Ok Woods, you have heard the evidence and seen the CCTV footage, how do you plea?"

"Guilty sir."

"Do you have anything that you might wish to say that will lessen the punishment that I am about to give you?"

Luke thought for a second. "Only that you can see that the man attacked my dad first. You could see that he was shouting at him as well. I was just trying to protect my dad."

The Governor sat writing on his documents before responding to Luke's plea.

"Yes I can see that there was some provocation; however, that's what my staff are in the visits room to deal with. You should have left it to them to resolve. As it is, you are lucky that the visitor didn't want police involvement." He looked at his officer. "Do we have any wing and conduct reports available?"

The officer looked down at his paperwork and read from a pre written sheet.

"Yes sir, the wing staff have reported that Woods is an excellent prisoner on the wing. He is employed in the education department, has no previous adjudications and no behaviour warnings at all. He is currently on the enhanced level of privileges and has held this position for a year."

The Governor looked sternly down the table at Luke. "This is a really disappointing day for you and the prison. You created a scene in the visits room and spoilt the day for a lot of people and your punishment will reflect that." He thought for a second, flicking through the paperwork before looking back up.

"I award you twenty eight days loss of TV, twenty eight days loss of association and twenty eight days loss of canteen. You will be allowed out to shower and make a quick daily phone call only. All of your education studies will be done in your cell and you will not be allowed to visit the education centre for another twenty eight days. Do you have any questions?"

Luke shook his head. "No sir, except when can I go back to the unit?"

The Governor looked at the staff and nodded. "You can go back now. Any further violence and I will take a much dimmer view of it, do you understand?"

The smile came back onto Luke's face. "Yes sir."

The officers stood and escorted him out of the room and back to his cell in the segregation. Luke knew he'd got off lightly and vowed to say out of any future trouble once back on the unit.

CHAPTER SEVENTEEN

Jake woke to his alarm, having only got to sleep at 2am due to nerves at the thought of his upcoming match. He had been given a room to share with an older player, Gary Melbrow, who had seen it all and done it all having represented England more than thirty times.

Gary spoke to him as he came out of the bathroom and saw him still in bed.

"Jake, get up and showered mate. We have breakfast in fifteen minutes followed by a team meeting. The boss doesn't allow anyone to be late for any meal - we can't eat until everyone is sat down and ready. It's one of his Italian habits and it drives me fucking nuts." He laughed as he continued to get ready and Jake climbed out of bed and into the shower. Another jolt of nerves went through his body as the warm water cascaded from his short hair and onto his shoulders.

Even walking into the breakfast room was daunting; it was the first time that Jake had met a number of his team mates as he had boarded the coach last the previous night and hadn't had the time to become acquainted with everyone. Looking at the faces of the players filling their plates from the self service hot plates was formidable. A few players from the pre season game two years before were still at the club, along with legends from around the world. Carlos Conte stood at the end of the room by his table wearing an immaculate suit and looking every inch an 'A' lister. Without a hair out of place and everything perfectly manicured, class oozed from every pore of his body.

Standing almost like a Roman Emperor, he peered around the room, smiling as Jake took his seat. As Carlos sat, the entire squad began eating and chatting; it was a world away from the routine to which Jake had become accustomed at Reading FC.

With the tables cleared, Carlos asked for the lights to be dimmed before giving a meticulous presentation where every strength and weakness in the team was highlighted.

Gary leaned over and whispered into Jake's ear. "We have trained for all of these things, the boss is really on it when he is preparing. They say he works twenty five hours a day." He stopped talking as Carlos prepared for his next part of the presentation, a series of short clips involving Liverpool scoring, conceding and how they organised themselves once they lost the ball. Carlos asked for the lights to be turned back on, clapping his hands a couple of times to regain the focus of the players.

"Ok, you all know your drills and your responsibilities. We have practiced for everything that they are capable of throwing at us. We are better than them all over the pitch so do yourself justice today boys. Any last questions?"

A brief spell of silence followed so Carlos spoke again. "Ok, get some rest, we leave at twelve forty five so do not be late."

He then beckoned Jake over and spoke to him on his own. "You will be on the bench today. I doubt that you will get on the pitch as the squad are drilled in our formation, but prepare yourself."

Jake nodded before going towards the elevator and back to his room on the fourth floor. He felt a small twinge of disappointment that he wouldn't be playing but a little relief that he would be able to be better prepared for the next game. Lying on his bed, he phoned his dad and the hum of the traffic in the background told him that his parents were already on their way.

"Dad, Mum, I will be on the bench today and I don't think that I am going to get on. If you want to turn around it will be fine."

His dad laughed. "Jake, we're only an hour away. It doesn't matter if you don't get a game, we just want to be there for your first time."

The support his mum and dad offered him all of the way through the academy had always been solid and even now, with little prospect of him playing, they still wanted to see him in his white Spurs kit for the first time.

Gary came into the room just as Jake ended the call. "Don't worry about what the boss said. If we are one nil down with ten minutes to go, he will bring you on, he loves the way you play." Jake looked surprised. "Really, why do you think that?"

Gary laughed. "Because he needs to get results. It's the old adage Jake, if you are good enough, you are old enough. Be focused for that minute."

Jake boarded the bus with fresh hope, he just needed a chance to show the boss what he could do and enough time to do it in.

The crowds of fans walking towards Anfield filled the pavements as the team coach made its way alongside the famous walls of the stadium. Scousers looked up and shouted at the tinted windows and a pie flew out of nowhere and hit the Spurs crest on the side of the coach, while Jake looked on in wonder. He had seen hostility from rival fans before, just not on such a large scale. The others had seen it a thousand times and just ignored it, all deep in thought or playing a video game with a team mate. They soon pulled through the red gates into the safety of the stadium. A tingle shot through Jake's stomach as he caught sight of the famous pitch, praying silently that today he would have a small chance to impress.

In rural Oxfordshire, a different chance to impress was presented to Luke.

His cell door opened again and an officer stood waiting to escort him back to Patterson Unit. They walked the fifty metres down the secure passageway before entering the unit and reaching the staff office where the segregation unit officer spoke to the unit manager.

"Twenty eight days loss of everything, including work. The Governor has said that he can have a shower and a phone call every day."

The manager wrote the details onto a large board in the office before speaking to Luke.

"You are a fucking idiot mate, you could have lost everything you have worked for. We're going to put you on a violence reduction course and give you some anger management training. If you don't do these courses you have no chance of any parole for a long while. Now get back to your cell."

Walking back to his door, Luke couldn't help but feel a little relieved. The manager opened the door before adding, "I'm going to have to take your TV away for a while. Do you have a radio?" Luke nodded, pointing it out to him.

"Good, and be careful, one of the guys on Mountbatten Unit is pissed off with you. He's telling everyone on here that he's going to attack you but the good news is that you won't be going anywhere for the next month. Maybe it will all blow over by then. Chin up Luke, we will get you back on track quickly."

Luke watched his TV being unplugged as he answered the officer. "I doubt that he will forget it, he has already threatened me. Everyone has heard him say it so I think that he will need to do something or he will lose face.

The unit manager walked to the door with the TV and turned to Luke. "You have a lot to lose Luke, let me see what I can do to stop it."

Luke lay down on his bed, but then noticed an envelope resting against his radio. In his two years in prison he had hardly received any letters apart from legal correspondence as everything was said either on the phone or via a visit. Recognising the writing on the envelope, he saw that it was from Jake, just when he thought that his brother had drifted off into his new celebrity world.

Ripping it open he eagerly read the news from Spurs and how things had occurred during the day of the transfer. The letter was warm and heartfelt leaving Luke with a smile on his face.

Jake took great pains in reminding Luke about the upcoming Liverpool game which was due to be covered on the BBC radio sports channel and that there was a slight chance that he would be involved. He had cheekily added a new squad photo of the team and Luke could see Jake standing on the back row, far left with the biggest grin he could muster. Checking his watch, Luke noticed that it was only twenty minutes until kick off and if he hadn't seen the letter he would never have known the game was on.

Turning the radio on to BBC 5 Live, Luke listened to the pundit's chatter before the game kicked off. Jake was mentioned briefly where it was felt that he was an expensive gamble and stepping up from Championship football to the Premier league at such a young age was a formidable jump. They considered that perhaps he would be a star for the future and may well head out on loan to a team from Germany but today would not be a great day to try to make his mark. Luke felt relieved that Jake would not hear the negative comments about him; he had the talent to make it to the top, he just needed the chance.

He lay on the small prison bed listening to the cut and thrust of the game, both teams giving their all but neither side managing the all important goal. Then out of nowhere, in the eighty second minute, Liverpool's key striker, Sandu Tabuk, picked up the ball on the edge of the area and curled in a powerful shot just beyond the reach of the keeper. From the substitutes' bench Jake looked around as the Anfield crowd erupted in celebration while the three thousand travelling Spurs fans stood watching in disbelief as three sides of the ground taunted them with the chant, 'You might as well go home.'

Carlos looked towards his substitutes to make a change. "Jake, go warm up. I need a goal so just be brave. You will get a chance to score, just take it when it comes along."

Luke punched the air in his cell silently as he listened to the commentary team announcing Jake's arrival on the pitch with six minutes plus injury time to go.

He sat up on the bed, the adrenalin pumping round his

own body as almost immediately Jake received the ball and drove into the heart of the Liverpool defence where a clumsy challenge from the Liverpool captain brought him crashing down two yards outside the box. Luke held the radio close to his ear trying to visualise the scene. He and Jake had practiced this moment numerous times in the local council park, but this time it was at the Kop end of Anfield. He could sense what Jake would do, Luke used to blast the ball at the keeper and Jake would always be there waiting for a rebound to put the ball into the net.

Jake sprang back up from the lush grass and grabbed the ball. Gary Melbrow strolled over and taking it out of his hands, covered his mouth with his hand as he spoke to him.

"Jake, I'm hitting this as hard as I can, be there for anything that drops from the keeper's hands." Jake nodded and moved away. He already knew what to do, he had spent a life time preparing for this moment.

The Liverpool players formed a wall ten yards in front of the ball, a seemingly impenetrable mountain of red shirts as Gary placed the ball down, looking at the keeper's position and hoping to catch him off guard. Taking two steps backwards he thundered a curling shot over the wall, the ball crashing off the bar and rebounding back into the area where another header from a spurs player arrowed it goalwards as the goalie hurled himself across the space, desperately trying to get a hand to the ball. The very end of his index finger pushed the football onto the woodwork again and the crowd roared at the magnificent save before a flash of a white shirt sprinted in before anyone else could react and Jake dived forwards among the flying boots of the Liverpool defence and headed the ball into the bottom corner of the net.

Back on Patterson Unit, Luke leapt into the air sending the radio spinning onto his bed, the batteries falling onto the hard floor making him scramble to replace them as the commentator painted the picture of the Liverpool fans who had been stunned into silence. It was now the turn of the

Spurs supporters to shout and Jake was euphoric, sprinting the length of the pitch to celebrate in front of them but not knowing what to do when he arrived. Kim and Des almost knocked each other over in jubilation while Carlos Conte watched stony faced from the side of the pitch before sending a message over. Gary grabbed Jake. "The boss says calm down, he wants you to press further up on the last defender. Go get them Jake, we have three minutes left to get a winner."

Four hundred miles away Luke settled himself back on the bed. He could hardly breathe through excitement as he turned the radio back on.

Liverpool restarted the game and sent the ball out wide where a speculative cross was easily caught by the goal keeper. He looked up and sent a long hopeful ball down through the centre of the pitch. Two players leapt for the spinning ball as it dropped from the sky, a spurs player glancing a header towards Jake who turned instantly and shot from thirty yards without a second thought. The ball smashed the underneath of the bar and bounced down into the net, a despairing lunge from the Liverpool keeper failing to keep it out of his goal.

Jake fell to the floor and was swamped with half a dozen of his team mates all screaming with excitement. The clock had ticked past ninety minutes as Jake jogged back into the Spurs half for the restart. Looking across to the bench he could see Carlos shouting at him to get back and help defend for the next few seconds before daring to take a brief glance up into the stands where his parents were sitting. He could tell that his mum was crying and Dad was still jumping around in jubilation. He smiled to himself before joining in with defensive duties.

Wave after wave of desperate Liverpool attacks tore forwards during the dying seconds, each one repulsed by a wall of white shirts. Luke could barely listen as the last two minutes of injury time felt like twenty. Then suddenly the final whistle sounded and Tottenham Hotspurs had found themselves a new hero. Jake Woods stood, arms waving to his parents as the moment sank in.

Luke shouted out through his cell window. "Anyone listening to the Liverpool game? That was my brother, he scored twice." A big cheer rang around, echoing through the empty exercise yards and Luke felt so proud about what Jake had done. He lay back on his prison bed and read the letter again. *'Sod these twenty eight days punishment, he thought, I can do them standing on my head.'*

CHAPTER EIGHTEEN

Twenty eight days later

Luke took his bag of revision notes over to the education department. He had not wasted a second of the days spent in punishment, completing an anger management course held on the unit and keeping his course work on schedule from inside his cell.

He didn't realise it as he woke, but today would take on a most sinister phase, a pressure that only someone who had experienced the misfortune of spending time in one of Her Majesties hotels could ever contemplate - the feeling of being caught in a trap where there is no escape and there is absolutely nothing that you can do to avoid it. The spider had been carefully watching the fly for two months, now he had flown into their web.

He took his seat in the classroom and looked around. The class was no longer one to one teaching and he could see another two places were set. The door opened and two young African boys came in, at first ignoring Luke as they chatted but eventually acknowledging him.

"You must be Luke? The teacher told us that you would be back today. We have just joined the class and we need our degree to be finished before we are deported back to Nigeria in two years time." Luke stood and shook their hands.

"Yeah, it's good to be back in the class. Why are you looking for a degree?"

They both laughed before one answered. "Because knowledge is power back home. With a degree from the UK we will be able to get a job in any business. We want to write for the papers, sports journalism. Maybe if we all get our heads together we can help each other out. This is Afamefuna or

Afam for short and I'm Adebiyi, or just Ade." They all sat down and Ade turned back to Luke.

"I've heard that you have a problem with a guy named Dawkins. He's on our wing and he is saying that he is going to cut your face open man. That's nasty stuff, we can't have our new journalist friend threatened like that. Leave it to us; African boys do this type of thing much nicer than you guys, but we will do this as a favour."

Luke shook his head. "No no no - I've just had twenty eight days in my cell with no privileges, I can't afford to be involved in this stuff."

They both laughed. "The guy is going to slice you open, I've seen the shank, but if you don't want us to help that's ok."

Luke frowned. "I'm in enough trouble as it is, I can't do anything that will hurt my parole. Do you really think that he will try something?"

Afam answered him this time. "A hundred percent he is going to try kill you, but we can stop him, we can make it go away."

Anxiety was creeping into Luke's thoughts. "What do you want from me? In prison nothing comes free, we all know that, right? So what do you want?"

Afam smiled at him. "We want you to be safe, but we also want you to pick up a little package that is going to be thrown over the prison fence into Patterson exercise yard. All you have to do is to offer to clean up the rubbish that has been thrown out of the cell windows first thing on Saturday morning. We have seen you do the job before, the screws trust you to work alone. Our package will be in a hollowed out orange, looks nothing suspicious at all. Just throw it in your rubbish bag, fish it back out when you are back on the wing and bring it to us. Simple, a one off payment for our troubles."

Luke thought for a second. "I only need to do this once?"

A wide smile from the other two indicated that this was a done deal. "Sure, just this one little job and your worries are over."

Zade Dawkins stood at the end of the landing on Mounbatten unit. Staff were busy resolving the Friday prisoner pay issues and preparing to lock the wing up prior to the evening roll check at nine o'clock. Dawkins didn't have too many friends on the unit, mainly due to his racist tendencies and poor personal hygiene.

Afam and Ade had waited for this exact moment; it was ten minutes until the wing were locked away for the evening and all staff and prisoners were preoccupied. They climbed the stairs from the ground floor to the first floor, prowling like two alpha lions hunting prey. Afam nodded to two skinny drug addicts who had been suitably paid for one minute's work and they silently walked ahead of the stalking boys, blocking all CCTV cameras with wet toilet paper. There would be no trace of evidence to what was about to happen.

They walked almost aimlessly towards cell 36, never taking their eyes from the ginger headed boy looking over the railings. As the last camera was covered, Dawkins looked up and saw what was coming. Ducking into his cell he tried to kick his door closed but it was too late as a broom handle shoved between the door and the lock made it spring back and the two lions rushed in.

Officer, Jill Weathers called out, "All away Mountbatten," as she began to close doors and count her landing. Normally Dawkins was trouble for the staff, always the last to go into his cell as he made a point of shouting from the landing to anyone who wanted to listen to him but this time he was not in his normal place. She hurried her pace, hoping that he was engrossed in some rubbish on his TV and hadn't realised the time. This could save Jill the regular five minutes of persuading him to go into his cell.

Looking through the half open door she saw him kneeling on the floor, blood dripping over the lino covering. He turned to face her and she saw the massive flap of skin that was once his cheek hanging loosely from his face. He mumbled something before falling flat onto his front, unconscious, an alarm bell sounding in the distance.

Luke lay on his bed watching TV; his wing had been locked up for thirty minutes when his attention was drawn to the glow of the blue flashing lights of an ambulance entering the prison. Jumping up to look through his window, he noticed that it had pulled up at the back door of Mountbatten unit. A single trolley was rushed out of the door surrounded by prison officers and ambulance staff. Even from this distance there was no disputing who was being loaded into the ambulance, Zade Dawkins.

A shiver ran down Luke's back, they had delivered on their promise and now it was his turn. Scanning the litter strewn exercise yard festooned with newspapers and toilet rolls he knew that sometime tonight the tooth fairy would come calling, and he needed to be there tomorrow to collect the package. He had been so intent on saving his own skin that he had failed to ask what was inside the orange, but he could already guess.

A face appeared at the cell observation panel. It was the night orderly officer, the person in charge until the day shift came back on duty. "Evening Luke, I was just looking at the rubbish on the exercise yard. If I get you out for seven in the morning, could you get out and sort it out for me before the day staff come on?"

Luke panicked slightly - surely this was a set up? Normally he would go out between nine and nine thirty.

"I can, but why so early? Normally on a Saturday I get out there a bit later."

The officer nodded. "Normally you do, but tomorrow isn't a normal day. We have the mayor of Henley coming in to have breakfast with the prisoners on here. Don't ask me why, but it's happening and we need the unit in pristine condition."

Luke nodded blankly back. "Ok, no problem, just get someone to unlock me and I'll take care of it."

He awoke the next morning as the same person opened up his

door. "Get yourself ready Luke, zoom around and do a good job and I'll make sure that you get another couple of quid in next week's pay."

Someone shouted the officer's name and he left, leaving the door open. Luke looked out of his window as he got dressed, noticing the piles of rubbish had doubled in size. Another pile of papers had been thrown out overnight, but also, sitting in the middle of the yard, was an orange. Tapping on the office door, Luke asked for the rubbish picking stick and a black bag. Quickly they were handed to him and a night officer opened the door to let him onto the yard.

"Just bang on the door when it's done Woods, I'll let you back in."

The morning promised a warm day ahead and all around him the prison was silent as people still slept. Luke wandered around, casually picking up the litter and dropping it into the bag, the orange still sitting looking at him. He wondered for a second about what was hidden inside - it could be a phone and some sim cards but he doubted it. It would probably be pills of some kind, and possibly some powder. He didn't care, it was irrelevant to him. If he was caught he was screwed anyway regardless of the contents.

As the sun hit his face he pondered the chances of getting caught and decided they were pretty small at this time in the morning. He continued picking until every last piece was off the floor and banged on the door three times before the sound of a key turning in the lock signalled that someone had heard him.

Three men stood in the doorway, one taking the sack from Luke. His tone was very different to the friendly Orderly Officer as he questioned Luke.

"Security information suggests that you are picking up a quantity of drugs from the exercise yard. We are going to take you into the segregation building to give you a full strip search and my friends here are going to go through the rubbish in your bag. Do you have anything that you wish to add?" Luke looked puzzled. How the hell did the staff know about this?

"Did you pick up an orange from the centre of the exercise yard? It was there twenty minutes ago, now it has gone."

Luke swallowed hard, they were onto the plan - the African lads must have sold him down the river. He answered confidently, "No, all I picked up was paper and ripped sheets, no fruit at all."

The guy in charge just smiled. "Yeah, of course you didn't," he said before taking him to the segregation area for a search. "Take your shoes and socks off and kick them over here."

The close nature of three officers and Luke in a small cell as he stripped off was intimidating so he blanked it out and followed instructions. Once they had finished their search, the lead officer looked at him, bemused.

"Ok Woods, nothing on you at all. Let's hope the orange in your bag doesn't come back to haunt you."

They walked back to the wing where two officers were already waiting by the gate.

"The bag was clear. No fruit, just paper and bedding. What do you want us to do?"

The man in charge looked at Luke. "Take him back to his cell and search it. That orange is somewhere and I fucking want it."

They marched him back to his cell and tore it to pieces. The Security officer came back and watched as the search finished.

"Still nothing boss, it's not here."

He snarled, looking at Luke as though he wanted to rip him to bits. "Fair enough, looks like it is one nil to you Woods, but I will catch you at some point."

They slammed his door as they left, Luke falling backwards onto his bed, half in exhilaration, half in sheer panic.

If they had checked the empty cell next door to Luke's they would have seen that he had thrown it through the open window seconds before the wooden door had been opened. Something within him had just told him to ditch it.

The security search team left the unit and the normal routine kicked in. Luke's cell was unlocked first. "Ok Woods, the bloody Mayor is in here, is the place tidy?"

Luke nodded. "Yep, apart from next door. The guy who was discharged yesterday has left it filthy - do you want me to rush in and clean it? He might want to have a look at a cell and it's our only empty one left."

The officer nodded. "Great idea, get in and do it quickly."

Flinging open the empty cell door the officer walked away without checking, before telling the wing manager that the wing was immaculate. Two minutes later the errant orange was hidden inside the laundry room, just waiting to be picked up on Sunday for the church service.

CHAPTER NINETEEN

Luke stood in the line of prisoners waiting to leave Patterson Unit to attend the Church of England service held every Sunday at ten o'clock. For the prison chaplain it was his moment to put on a good service for the prisoners and help them understand a little more about the bible. For the prisoners it was just the chance to get out of their cell for an hour and meet up with friends and enemies from other units within the prison. If you had a message or anything else to pass over then this was the time to do it. There were minimum staff on duty and as a result they were always rushing to get things done. Twenty prisoners waiting to leave a unit and less than two minutes to get them into the chapel resulted in no proper searching.

An old orange skin sat outside the laundry room window, the contents, now wrapped tightly in a plastic bag and brown tape, sat inside Luke's boxer shorts. Showing no sign of nerves as the officer motioned for him to raise his arms before giving him a five second pat down search, Luke felt a little guilt for what was in the package as he knew that someone within the prison would be feeding or developing a habit partly through his actions.

The chapel door opened and Luke saw another fifty boys chatting to each other as the chaplain lit candles. Afam and Ade sat in the middle, out of sight of the two staff who were now positioned at the back observing a sea of heads, a single chair left between them. Luke shuffled through and sat in it.

"Someone grassed us up, the screws were waiting for me when I came off the yard yesterday. They knew exactly what they were looking for."

The Nigerians looked at each other before Ade whispered,

"That is nothing to do with us, only one other person knew what was happening so it must have been that bastard."

Luke rolled his eyes. "Why did anyone else in here need to know about the drop off?"

Ade answered while Afam pretended to look through the hymns that they would be singing. "It's complicated man. She's a member of staff but refused to carry it through the gate. She was the one who knew where the yard was and told us about you. She threw the package over after she finished work on Saturday night. Next time she will bring it straight to me. She must have grown a conscience sometime during the night and reported it."

Luke puffed up his cheeks, "She nearly cost me everything, who is she?"

The boys laughed. "It has taken us six months to get this far, we're not fucking it up now. Where's the stuff?"

Luke looked briefly around and saw that the staff were reading the Sunday papers, disinterested in anything around them as the chaplain began his service.

He reached into his tracksuit bottoms and pulled out an egg sized package, placing it into Afam's waiting hand as he effortlessly slid it into a hidden pocket in his own boxer shorts. The congregation sparked up into a hymn while an old white haired prison volunteer smashed away at the keys on the piano in the vague hope of keeping up with the singing.

The service ended and they returned to their wings, the smell of the Sunday lunch wafting around the association area as the two boys headed back to the Mountbatten Wing, turning briefly to look at Luke as he walked towards his own wing. His personal Officer, Miss Nevis, was on duty and she stopped Luke as he wandered past.

"Luke, you have a visit today from your parents who haven't seen you for a month. They phoned to ask if we had space and the Governor has allowed it."

Luke grinned. "Cool, I thought that after the last visit the prison had banned them."

She put a hand on his shoulder. "No, it was just difficult for them to get here but they will explain when they see you."

Confusion showed on his face as he looked at the officer. "What do you mean difficult? They live forty minutes away and have a car. What was so difficult?"

She looked at him sadly. "They need to have a chat with you Luke."

Sitting on his bed, Luke's mind spun out of control. What could be so important that they couldn't visit? Were they getting divorced? Was there a problem with Jake? Was someone ill? His door opened and Luke collected his dinner but his appetite had gone and he pushed the chicken leg around on his tray until finally giving it away. Looking around for Miss Nevis she was nowhere to be seen, and without a further explanation about what she had meant, he would never be able to rest as he returned once more to his cell. Visits were due to start at two o'clock when the staff had returned from lunch but at one thirty his door opened. It was the prison chaplain.

"Luke, your parents are here. We thought that it would be nice to have your visit in the chapel where it's calmer and more private."

Luke stood up and tucked his shirt into his prison jeans. "I don't know what's going on, but this is freaking me the fuck out. Sorry, I didn't mean to swear."

Chris Thompson had been the assistant chaplain at the prison for the past five years and had seen and heard everything. He patted Luke on the shoulder.

"I saw you in church this morning, it was nice to see you had an interest. Maybe you will come more often?"

Luke nodded, but hoped not. "Yes maybe."

They walked into the warm chapel where Des and Kim were sitting drinking coffee. Both put their cups down before standing and hugging Luke. The look on his mum's face caught his attention first; she had seemed to have aged over the past month, her eyes looking tired, and Dad was more attentive than he normally was. Chris headed off to his office, leaving them alone to talk. Luke hardly waited for the door to close before blurting out, "What's happening Mum? The prison told me that you haven't been able to get up here for visits and I've tried to phone a few times but you were always out."

She took his hand. "I have some difficult news for you Luke. I found a lump in my breast nearly two months ago and I had the test results just after our last visit. I have breast cancer, Luke."

He felt as though a hammer had struck him in the face.

"No!" He started to cry, a sob that came from deep in his stomach. He was unable to speak, the words refusing to pass his lips, his mum holding his hand tightly as he tried to compose himself. Finally he managed to speak. "Mum, you can't die. I need you, please get better."

She smiled. "We're trying, Luke, I've started treatment at the Royal Berkshire Hospital. We have spent a lot of time there over the past few weeks which is why we haven't been up to see you."

His father who had been sitting quietly until now, letting his wife tell Luke her news, added, "We are just at the beginning, there are a lot of things that they can do at the hospital. With the treatments available at the moment a lot of people respond and the cancer is beaten. Mum may have an operation to cut the cancer out, we just need to think about what's best for her. We thought that you needed to know what was going on so you would understand why we weren't visiting as often.

The chaplain came back in with a glass of water for Luke. He took a small sip and he looked at his parents, trying to absorb everything he had been told. "So, you might be ok Mum?"

Kim nodded. "Everything will be ok, Luke. We are telling Jake this afternoon when we get home. We only see him at matches now, he has been too busy to come home so we'll call him and hope he answers."

Luke wiped his eyes with a tissue. "I've tried to call him three times but he never picks up. I had a letter from him last month but nothing since. It looked as though he was doing well."

Briefly a look of pride washed over her tired face. "Yes, they seem to like him and the crowd have started to sing his name a bit more. He has been substitute three times and started one cup game against Blackpool. He has already scored three goals, only Bryan Hearn has scored more for the team, and he is the England striker."

Des nodded, not looking quite so happy. "But he's starting to enjoy the football lifestyle as well. He's not drinking and partying because Carlos Conte doesn't allow it, but he has a nice new car and a bigger apartment around a place called Cuffley with some of the other players. I just hope that he keeps his feet on the ground."

Luke held up his hands. "I guess it's normal, he'll be fine. He just needs to remember what's important to him. Did I tell you that I sat my A levels? I'm trying for my English degree and Bachelors next. If I can't be a sports star I might as well write about them."

Both Des and Kim almost burst with pride. "Luke, that's brilliant news, two successful boys in the family," Kim said, giving him a big hug.

Chris patted him on the back. "And he has started to join us at the church service. I was very happy to see him this morning."

Des shot him a glance, neither boy had set foot in a church for as long as he could remember. "That's great news Chris, we tried to persuade them to join our local church so many times but they were always too busy."

Chris laughed. "I'm not kidding myself Mr Woods. They only come for a good cup of tea, a chat to the occasional young lady from the Henley congregation and time off the wing. But at least they still come in and listen, I can't ask for much more."

He looked at Des and Kim. "Unfortunately we will need to finish the visit, but I'll leave you alone to say your goodbyes while I complete some paperwork in my office. Is five minutes okay?" He strode back towards his small room while Luke and his parents continued to chat. The tears had ended and hope had replaced the initial despair in Luke's heart.

"Mum, just take it easy. I'm stuck in here but I will pray for you all the time. Speak to Jake, he could afford to get you some private treatment."

Shaking her head Kim replied. "There's no need. I don't think that I could have better treatment anywhere so let's just get this dealt with." They all stood and hugged as Chris came back into the room with an Officer.

"Luke, I'll take Mum and Dad back to the gate, the Officer will take you back to the unit. Miss Cummings, look after him please."

The attractive officer smiled at the group, "Of course I will, follow me Luke."

They walked back towards the unit chatting as though neither had a care in the world. What he didn't realise was that Sarah Cummings was the same person who had tried to wreck all hopes of his parole with a hastily thrown orange.

CHAPTER TWENTY

Jake sat in his apartment watching the large television on the wall, a young blond girl lying with her head on his lap. Two plates of half eaten curry from the Indian restaurant sat on a smart oak coffee table in front of them, and the wide open bedroom door showed the messy bed where they had spent the entire afternoon and early evening making love. His phone rang for the third time and looking down, he saw the call was from his dad as he tossed it to one side and let it ring out.

"I haven't got time to listen to another lecture about how I'm spending my money."

The girl laughed. Sam Walsh was seventeen years old and a dancer from a member's only club in Central London. They had met three weeks ago after a home game against Derby County when Jake had played well and scored one goal in a two-nil win. Afterwards their eyes had connected in the player's lounge as he sipped a cold coke.

They chatted for an hour that day, Jake virtually ignoring his parents as they sat in the corner, and since that meeting they were inseparable. Kim had grave misgivings about her motives, lecturing Des on the way home that evening. Half listening, he gave the customary nods in the correct places, and agreed and tutted every time she emphasised a point. Secretly he didn't like her either, but so long as Jake was happy, he was happy.

Sam got off the sofa and stretched. Wearing one of Jake's training tops and nothing else, the enticing sight had Jake making a grab for her as he contemplated returning to bed. She avoided him and walked over to the table.

"You should give your mum a call Jake, she will be worried about you. You can't avoid them forever.

Grabbing the phone, he pushed his mum's number and she answered within a couple of rings. She didn't give him time to speak before launching into her news.

"Jake, just listen to me for two seconds before you get annoyed with me. I have breast cancer, and I wanted to tell you before others found out."

Jake slumped back on the sofa. "No Mum, this can't be happening. I'm coming over right now and we can talk about what you need and how I can help."

Kim had to control herself, she wanted to see him so much but there was nothing that he could do.

"No, it's ok sweetheart. I have hospital appointments this week, when I'll have more news. I will then let both you and Luke know what they are planning for me. When was the last time you spoke to him?"

He shook his head. "I don't know, it's difficult. When he's in his cell locked up, I'm home and when he's out of his cell, I'm busy at work. I'll send him a letter."

Kim smiled to herself, she had used similar excuses not to phone home to Jamaica when she was exhausted from working.

"Just try to make a little effort Jake, he needs you too."

They said their goodbyes and hung up. Jake looked around and saw Sam bob her blonde head down to the table. He walked over as she hoovered up the last of a line of cocaine, another line sitting beside it. He looked at her smiling face, her hair falling in front of her glazed eyes as the drug kicked in.

"I've got a little present for you Jake, you've been a busy boy this afternoon and I need to keep your energy levels up for later. You didn't tell me that you had a brother in prison."

He studied the white line. "And you didn't tell me that you took cocaine. Are you fucking crazy? I have played less than a handful of games and you're trying to get me onto this shit."

She looked sad. "Come on Jake, they all take it during the week when they can't be caught. It will be out of your system by the time you go training, all the players do it."

Picking up the dirty plates he took them into the kitchen before returning with her jacket.

"The only thing that I want out of my system is you. Pack up your filthy shit from my table and leave. I've phoned a cab, it'll be here in a minute which is just enough time for you to shut the door and never come back."

She looked at him as though he were low life. "I don't need you anyway, you are just a boy. I can find a bigger and better player in ten seconds, the guys love my dancing. And by the way, within two years you'll be snorting bigger lines than that. You're all the same, but your loss."

Scooping the powder back into a bag, she changed into her own clothes and shuffled out the door and down the stairs and into the street. Jake followed, not to chase her, but to get in his car and go see his mum.

An hour later his headlights lit up the front of the house as he pulled into the small driveway. Hearing the car his mother rushed out of the front door and flinging her arms around his neck, she held him close. Eventually releasing him, she glanced into the car.

"Have you bought your girlfriend with you Jake? I'll put the kettle on." He followed her in, grabbing his Dad in a tight hug before answering.

"No, she's not with me anymore. I think that she enjoyed cocaine more than watching television and a Chicken Madras. I kicked her out an hour ago."

Kim laughed. "I could tell that she was trouble, we didn't bring you up to be with tramps like her."

Taking a mug of coffee from her, Jake took a seat in the lounge. "Is it okay if I stay over tonight Mum? We don't have any training on Monday this week so I can take you both out for lunch if you like?"

Kim smiled. "Of course you can stay, your room is always ready, as is Luke's. I still change your sheets every week just in case."

He carried his overnight bag upstairs. His bedroom seemed

even smaller after enjoying the pleasures of his large apartment and he couldn't help but take a look in Luke's room. Seeing his medals and clothes in the wardrobe tugged on his conscience. It could so easily been the other way round. If the witnesses had identified Jake, if Luke hadn't kept the secret, it would have been him in that cell. For the past three years he had taken it for granted but seeing the empty bedroom drilled home the point. He went back downstairs where his parents were watching television in the lounge.

"Dad, when you get your next visit, can you make it for a Sunday? I'll come with you."

As his dad nodded his agreement, Jake checked his phone. Three messages had been left already, all from Sam. He read the first message, her apologetic drivel annoying him even more than her drug taking. He read the second message which had been sent over an hour ago. *'Please come home baby, it will never happen again. It was the first time. I love you too much to lose you like this.'*

He scrolled down to the third message.

'Honey, I will do anything to have you back, I am so sorry about what I said to you. I didn't mean it. I was just angry that you had thrown me out like that.'

He typed out a quick response to her pleadings. "

'I'm at my mum's, I don't want you back in my life. Go and live your life however you choose to. We are done, please don't reply Sam.'

Turning his phone onto silent, he sat on the sofa beside Kim as they watched a film, and cuddled her in the same way that he used to do as a child. For all the things going wrong in her life at that moment, this brief moment made her feel well again.

CHAPTER TWENTY-ONE

Sarah Cummings tossed and turned all through Sunday night. Too hot to sleep and too much on her mind since the breakup of her last relationship, she wondered how she had arrived in this position after nearly five years as a prison officer.

She had received an award for the best recruit during her training at the Prison Service College and had been given the opportunity to take the fast track to promotion. But after fifteen years managing a large Waitrose store in Henley and with fifty staff to supervise during some turbulent times, she was finished with managing people. If the time felt right again to be a manager she would take it, until then she would learn the basics of the job and enjoy it.

When she met Peter Rogers on her first day in the prison, sparks flew. He was a much younger officer than her who had a lust for life, and his infectious personality was something that she craved after years of drudgery in her past.

They quickly moved in to an expensive rented house together, just outside the peaceful town of Marlow, sitting on the banks of the River Thames. They enjoyed the lifestyle that two decent salaries could provide with regular sunny holidays and spent nearly every other weekend out partying with friends around the country until she caught him seeing another younger officer at the same prison.

Once he moved out, the debts began to mount and the hectic lifestyle soon vanished as the mundane routine of survival kicked back in. He was a popular guy around the jail and he soon began spreading stories about her amongst the staff which resulted in Sarah becoming an outcast. She could live with the rejection, even the hurt caused by the gossip, but the end result for a person who couldn't find anyone else to talk to was that she began to spend more time speaking to prisoners.

In the short term this gave her some fulfilment; that was until she found an expensive gold chain discarded on the floor directly in front of where she was sitting supervising association. Picking it up, she could tell that it was valuable jewellery and probably real gold, so placed it safely in her pocket until someone claimed it as theirs.

After some time, she noticed a young black prisoner scouring the floor, crying in sorrow and guessing straight away what he was looking for, she called him over. Apparently Afam had lost a ten thousand pound chain that his mother had given to him before her death. Without it, he knew that the rest of his family would disown him instantly. The look on his face when Sarah produced it from her pocket was worth it as he fell to his knees in thanks before placing it back around his neck.

"My family will repay you for your kindness Miss Cummings. You have no idea what this chain means to us all," he told her in gratitude.

Even so, it came as a shock a few days later when she was approached in a Riverside bar near her home after the end of a long shift. An older black woman, immaculately dressed, sat down opposite her. "I'm very sorry to intrude Miss Cummings."

Sarah was taken aback that she knew her name. "Oh I'm sorry, have we met before?" she asked, a puzzled look on her face.

The woman shook her head smiling kindly. "No, but you did a very good deed for my nephew last week. You found something that he had lost. For that, my whole family wants to show our gratitude and I will be offended if you do not accept our thanks." She placed an envelope on the table in front of her before standing. "Kind people deserve nice things to happen to them, we hope that this helps you." She turned and left without waiting for a thank you.

Sarah spun the white envelope around a few times, as if in a game of spin the bottle, before opening it up. Seven hundred pounds all in fifty pound notes sat in her hand. The exact amount she needed to pay off the rent that month. Opening her bag she slipped the money in and smiled. *It pays to be honest*, she thought as she headed back home with one less headache.

It wasn't until the following week that she learnt the real intentions of the gift as Afam Musa slid a photo in front of her as she sat supervising association. It was of her taking the money in the pub.

"I'm not sure how this looks to you Miss, but to me it seems that you are taking cash from one of my family. Why would you do that?"

She didn't know what to say at first but countered, "I wanted to give it back, but she had already left."

Afam smiled. "So you reported that my Aunty had given you seven hundred pounds then? What did your security department say to you about that?"

She blushed. "No I didn't report it, I should have but I didn't. I will report it now."

He smiled again. "What, one week after you were given it, and ten minutes after I asked you where the drugs you promised to bring in are? How is that going to look for you?" His smile now gone, his tone turned sinister. "I don't give a shit about me, you people are kicking me out of the country anyway, but you will go to prison and lose your job. Your move Miss."

Shuffling uncomfortably on her chair, she realised the trap had been sprung as she looked at him in despair. "Ok you win, I did a good thing for you, and you are stitching me up. What do you want?"

Ade Ibrahim came and joined them. Rubbing his hand suggestively against her breast, she moved away before he grabbed her arm. "You will do whatever we ask, when we ask. Now go to the Waitrose store where you used to work after your shift tonight and be there for ten thirty. Sit on the boot of your car and wait for my friend; he is going to give you something to bring in."

She panicked. "I can't do that! They will see me and search me. What good is that to you?"

Afam shook his head. "The first time, I allowed you to throw it over the fence onto Patterson yard but we were nearly caught out so this time you will bring something in yourself. We know where you live, we have your bank account details and we can even prove you took the money from us."

She nodded, knowing they had her. "When do I need to bring it in?"

"Sunday, bitch. I need it in my hands on Sunday in the church. Don't fuck up."

Her mind drifted back to how she had thrown the orange into the exercise yard area and how she had regretted it immediately, her conscience forcing her into making a call from a public phone box to the duty night manager. He in turn reported the call to the Duty Governor and a trap was set, his searching staff waiting to intercept the package. Unfortunately Luke had been too smart for them and now she had to run the gauntlet again.

Returning home, her mind was swirling with anxiety. She had little choice other than to accept the second parcel and bring it into the prison.

Afam and Ade lay in their shared cell laughing at what they had started. "I grabbed her tits and she did nothing Ade, did you see it?"

Ade laughed back. "Man she's fucked, whatever way she goes."

On Monday morning the Security Manager was in early as usual to look through any security implications which had arisen over the weekend. A concerning email had been sent to him regarding Luke Woods and two Nigerian boys from Mountbatten Unit, Musa and Ibrahim. A knock at the door made him stop reading as he looked up to see one of his officers standing there.

"Hi Sarah, you're in early. I need to have a chat with you as I saw that you were in the prison on Sunday even though it was your day off. Why were you in the chapel?"

She reached into her bag to get out her letter of resignation. It was only a matter of time before the prison got wind of her arrangements so she had decided to pre-empt any fall out.

"Sure, that's why I came in. I haven't been able to sleep, I just thought that I could have a chat with the chaplain to discuss some things. He helps me since the relationship break up." Thoughts of the real reason she was in the chapel passed through her head. She'd been there to pass a bag of heroin to the boys, the chat with the chaplain was pure subterfuge. Had the prison already uncovered her motives?

Her manager shut down his laptop and faced her.

"I'm sorry to hear that Sarah, I'm sure that it will work itself out.

Meanwhile, we have an issue on Mountbatten where something is not right. I suspect that Musa and Ibrahim are at the heart of it, do you know them?"

Her heart thumped, how much did security actually know?

He continued. "I want you to report to your wing manager; he's expecting you. We need their cell searched before they are awake and can hide anything. We're doing the same with Woods on Patterson although I am not convinced that he's involved. Get up to the wing where I have a dog on route to help you. Take your time and be vigilant with everything that you see in there, I want to nail the people involved."

Sarah fastened her bag back up and turned to leave, resignation letter still sealed as he stopped her.

"Sorry Sarah, I'm so caught up in this drugs thing, did you want to speak with me about something else?"

She hesitated slightly before replying. "No, I just heard someone talking about a search as I came through the gate. I wondered if I could help." Turning for the door she could feel her face blushing with the guilt she felt. This had been the time to confess and face the music but instead she was on her own. Worse still, she was about to go into the cell of her tormentors and search them with a full security team. The tightness in her throat as she walked the two hundred metres to Mountbatten wing was a sign that her stress levels were raised. If the team found something, she would be the sacrifice made to save those two bastards' skins. However, if she was the first searcher to enter the cell, they would try to manipulate her into hiding evidence if they had the chance. And worst still, she knew for sure that the photographs of her were hidden in there somewhere.

A group of staff were congregated around the wing manager's office. Six staff had been designated to search, two for the cell and two each for the prisoners. Looking at them all standing there, she had a brainwave.

"Boss, can I be on the cell search team? Once you've lifted both prisoners out of the cell I can go in with another officer and rip it to pieces." Her scheming brain had thought of a way to save her own skin; this way neither prisoner would see her involvement, plus she would have the chance to move the photos.

"Sure Sarah, always good to have a volunteer, anyone else want to search with Sarah?" the wing manager asked.

As usual all the staff wanted to avoid her so the manager pointed to a new male officer. "John, you are searching the cell with Sarah, the rest of you sort your selves out. I want the cell opened and both prisoners moved to segregation for a full strip search. They must not be given the chance to grab anything before they leave. Any questions?" Silence indicated that there were none.

"Okay, let's go."

The cell door opened quickly as four staff entered. "Get up and stand outside the cell door now."

Musa protested and made an effort to open his locker door. Two staff quickly grabbed his arms and pulled him outside before handcuffing him. Ibrahim just stood in his boxer shorts and walked out, looking at all the staff's faces as he did so. He snarled, "You lot are making a bad mistake."

The manager nodded to the staff holding Musa. "Take him away," before instructing the other team to wait for the segregation staff to confirm that he had arrived before moving Ibrahim to the same area..

He looked at the prisoner. "Do you have anything in this cell that you are not authorised to have?"

Ibrahim didn't answer, instead just spitting on the floor by the manager's feet.

A call on the radio signalled that it was time to take Ibrahim to the segregation as the drug dog was brought onto the landing. Sarah and John watched as it was released into the cell. Within a second it signalled a hit on the locker Musa had tried to open. The handler looked at Sarah.

"Okay, there has been something in that area. I will call the dog back and you search it please."

Dressed in her searching overalls, Sarah moved in, her back blocking the staff's sight of where she was looking. A plastic folder sat on the shelf, and inside she recognised the back of the photo she had been shown. Beside it was a small tin box. She opened it and saw a plastic bag filled with round, blue tablets.

"Yeah, I have something here." She turned and put the box on the bed. The other staff came in and while they studied the tablets Sarah pushed the plastic folder into her pocket.

"Good work Sarah, Move back while I put the dog back in."

She stood and watched as the dog had another hit on Musa's pillow.

She took a deep breath, "Ok John, your turn. Take your time and don't miss anything."

Two minutes later a smiling John put a block of cannabis on the bed.

"Bingo! My first find." He smile only lasted briefly. "Hang on, what's this?" He noticed some ripped pages lying next to a copy of the New Testament and opening the book, he found a mobile phone concealed in a hollowed out section. "Bloody hell, we really have hit the jackpot," he exclaimed, pumping his fist in joy.

Sarah watched from outside the door, her thoughts going to what the two in the segregation were going to say once the evidence was placed in front of their eyes.

Musa and Ibrahim sat in a cell in the segregation, both now dressed in prison tracksuit. They chatted in a hushed whisper, each realising that their stash would be found." What are we going to do Ade? They will have found everything."

Ade thought for a moment.

"Nothing, we just admit everything and take our punishment. We are getting deported anyway in a few months so let's ride it out."

Afam looked at him. "We could do a deal with security, give that bitch up and save any extra bang up time."

Ade laughed. "That's why I'm the brains of this operation, you fool. Give her up and we have nothing, leave her out of it and we use her again if we manage to stay here. If they move us, fuck it, she's going to jail."

The Security Governor came to the cell door holding three evidence bags in his hand. "Right boys, you are firmly in the shit. It's time that you started telling me what is going on."

Musa stood up and faced him. "Ok, no problem, you have caught me," he shrugged. "I had a parcel thrown over the fence at the weekend and I was going to use everything myself. The tablets you found were steroids, the cannabis was mine, and the phone was mine as well to talk to my family. Ibrahim had nothing to do with it."

His admission was met with a laugh of incredulousness. "Do you expect me to believe that? I know the parcel came onto Patterson exercise yard and I know that Woods help deliver it to you."

Musa looked confused. "No, the parcel came onto Mountbatten yard and I had it pushed through my window. I only know Woods through my classes. He's an idiot, I wouldn't trust him. He's probably the one who grassed me up."

The Governor laughed. "Okay, have it your way, we are sending everything to the police. When they decide what to do with you, I will let you know."

Musa continued, feeling back in control. "Can we go back to Mountbatten boss? You have found everything I have. There isn't anything left for me."

The Governor nodded. "Yep, the pair of you can go back now, count yourselves lucky that we are deporting you. With what we have just found, a judge would have given you another two years in prison."

Sarah gathered her searching equipment and walked back down the secure passageway for a debrief meeting in the security office. As she approached the segregation unit, the door opened and Musa and Ibrahim were led out, on their way back to the wing. Musa looked at Sarah.

"Who's a lucky girl then, finding all my stuff? Well done, Miss." They walked past her without a backwards glance before Musa shouted back. "But Miss, me and you are still safe, I know that it's just business."

The search teams entered the security manager's office as he was collecting the evidence together. Sarah spoke first.

"Do I have a second before we start Governor? I need a quick break."

He nodded and she headed straight into the documents room and turned on the shredder to feed in the photographs and her confessional notice of resignation.

CHAPTER TWENTY-TWO

Jake took the ball under control in the middle of the training session and sprayed a thirty yard pass onto the feet of the advancing wing back, Jose Pepe.

He checked his run into the penalty area before appearing in between two defenders and volleying the ball high into the roof of the net. Gary Melbrow stood applauding the skill that he had just witnessed.

"Great movement Jake, and what a fantastic ball out to Jose; that would have split most defences wide open."

Carlos Conte didn't react, simply turning to his assistant and making another note in his already bulging notepad before standing on the half way line and blowing his whistle. The harsh shriek stopped everything else that was going on.

"Okay everyone, let's have a minute. Jake, I saw that bit of skill. Let's reset the play and see if you can do it again."

Once again the ball came to his feet but this time a midfield player tried to close him down. It was futile. Jake spun round and sent out the same ball to Jose who was now speeding down the wing.

This time the three defenders organised themselves, making it impossible for Jake to ghost in and make them look ponderous again but they needn't have worried as Jake cut towards them, and an instant before the ball was crossed, cut back towards the far post. Jose saw his movement and fired a high long cross above the heads of the apprehensive defenders and directly onto Jake's right boot. The ball fizzed into the bottom corner without the keeper touching it.

Carlos stood watching and laughing. "I think that between Jose, Jake and Gary, we had an unstoppable advantage. Well played boys, go and get ready for lunch.

Back in the showers the players joked about the session, the three defenders admitting that they didn't have a clue how to read the movement of Jake, or second guess the delivery from Jose. And anything Jake didn't reach, Gary smashed into the net. All in all their morning had been bloody miserable.

Sitting waiting for lunch, Jake's phone vibrated in his pocket. He looked down but didn't recognise the number. Carlos caught him looking down at his phone and called over, "Jake, what is distracting you over there?"

He blushed before admitting what was happening. He expected a fine for having his phone on. "Go outside and take the call Jake, it may be more important than you think."

Every eye in the room was on him as he made the walk to the door, it was unheard of for Carlos to allow anyone to leave.

As the doors closed behind him, he heard Carlos address the other players before phoning the number back.

"Hi Jake, it's Stuart Cobbs, the England Under 21 manager. I have selected you for the squad for the coming home game against Poland. Are you fit and available?"

Jake's heart beat uncontrollably. "Yes I am, but I need to speak to my manager first as he will need to agree."

Stuart interrupted him. "Already did that this morning, he was very happy for you to be involved. I will send you a message with all the details this afternoon. Well done on your first call up Jake."

Wandering back into the restaurant his head was about to explode with excitement. An international call up was unreal, and pushing the doors open, he saw a broad white smile from Carlos while the rest of the squad cheered and whistled. Gary stood and shook his hand. "You bloody deserve this, mate, get in a few games for the Under 21's and we will be leading the line at the next world cup."

Luke sat on his chair in his cell, his few possessions scattered everywhere. Everything in the room had been dismantled by a search team, the toilet had a camera pushed around the u-bend and even his television had been dismantled and reassembled. The searchers and the dog found nothing at all; he had been lucky this time as any trace of the drugs in his cell would have ruined his chances of getting a trusted job in the prison. His door opened and the Security Governor stood there on his own.

"Follow me Woods, I need a chat with you." They walked to the empty unit manager's office.

"Firstly young Luke, I'm happy that nothing was found in your possession. I have some faith in you and I hope that it's not misplaced. Secondly, however, I know that you have some knowledge about the two Nigerian lads in your classroom. They had a lot of things in their cell that they shouldn't have had. What do you know about them?"

The pressure on Luke was intense as the man looked him in the eyes waiting for an answer before he continued. "Remembering of course that you have an application coming up to be the orderly in the education block, a very trusted position that I would need to authorise before you got the job. And I don't think that I need to spell out that this is clearly a hurdle towards working for your parole. Now, what do you know about them?"

Luke calculated what he already knew and put together a plausible explanation. "They keep themselves to themselves in class. They work hard, but it's just to make a lot of money when they go back to Nigeria. I think that they might have had something thrown over the fence to them, but I'm not sure. They don't include me in conversations and speak in a different language a lot of the time."

The manager continued to look at Luke intensely. "What about the attack on Zade Dawkins, was that them?"

Luke realised that the guy was just fishing for information.

"I don't know, they are on a different wing to me."

The Governor started writing while still talking. "Yes, but is it a coincidence that Dawkins has an issue with you, the two Nigerian guys appear in your classroom and hours later he is sliced up?"

Luke struggled to stay calm. "Honestly Governor, I haven't a clue. Maybe he was the one who gave them the parcel and took some of the stuff for himself. It happens sometimes."

The Governor stopped writing. "Okay Luke, you just keep yourself out of trouble. Those boys are bad news, it's just a shame that no other prison will take them off our hands because of the immigration issues."

He took Luke back to his cell before adding, "You have got the orderly job by the way, don't fuck it up."

Musa and Ibrahim returned to Mountbatten unit, instinctively heading back to their shared cell before the wing manager stopped them in their tracks.

"Not so fast you two. Ibrahim, you are going onto another wing, I don't want you two together. Musa, you will be sharing with Dawkins when he gets back from hospital, I'm sure that you will enjoy that experience."

Musa jolted backwards against the wall, "He's a fucking racist, he will try to kill me. I'm not moving in with him, me and Ibrahim are not going anywhere else other than our old cell."

The manager smiled. "It's almost as if you and Dawkins have history." Musa looked down at the man's bulging stomach before shouting in his face.

"Fuck you, you fat cunt!"

The manager took a step backwards. "Ibrahim, I'm now giving you a direct order to move to Fry Wing. If you do not move I am authorised to use force against you, it's your decision."

The staff behind him took up a defensive stance, ready for action. Ibrahim snarled with anger, pulling off his blue t-Shirt revealing a ripped torso.

"Try take me then and see what happens." Musa tried to move to his side but was grabbed immediately by three staff, submitting as soon as he hit the floor without a fight. Ibrahim watched his friend being led under restraints to his new cell, the sound of his pain drifting away into the distance as his cell door was slammed shut.

"Okay son, your move," the manager said to Ibrahim, steadfast in his approach. This wasn't the first gun fight he'd been involved in.

"Are you moving, or are we moving you? One way is easy, the other way hurts." Ibrahim looked around and assessed his options. Of the two friends, he had the most courage so was tempted for an instant to fight.

"I'll tell you what, you fat prick. I will move, not because I'm worried about your staff, it's just because I choose to move, not you deciding for me." He turned and walked to the wing gates before adding, "I want to see your face when I come back one day and find you alone."

The manager laughed. "Join the queue, I've been around too long to be scared by a rat like you."

CHAPTER TWENTY-THREE

3 Weeks later

Des and Kim sat in the Royal Berkshire Hospital as yet another bag of chemo drained into her arm. Des sat beside her in a reclining chair that had seen too many patients, dozing in and out of sleep as the final bag was administered.

A young blond nurse, originally from Holland, walked past as the machine bleeped to signal the end of the bag. Playing with the settings, she said in perfect English, "Nearly there Kim, five minutes and you will be heading off to your football match. I hope that your son plays well, you must be very proud to have a boy playing for England."

But going to the match was the last thing she felt like doing as feelings of nausea started sweeping through her body.

"Des, I'm not sure that I'm up to driving all the way down to Southampton to see the game, I can hardly keep my eyes open." Her face looked grey as the rigour of the session took its toll.

Des fully understood what Kim was telling him, the treatment always knocked her for six. The tiredness would soon be replaced with the sickness, she would fall asleep and then the vomiting would start again. A familiar pattern had developed as the treatment poisoned her system, but without it there was little hope. He took Kim's hand and kissed it.

"I will stay here with you and we'll watch it on Sky. Let me phone Jake and explain, he'll understand."

Feeling her squeezing his hand softly gave Des all the reassurance he needed. He had made the right decision; now more than ever Kim needed him by her side so walking outside he phoned Jake before the pre-match routine would begin. It was still four hours until kick off which gave him time to digest the news.

He needn't have concerned himself about Jake's response, he fully understood. After sitting with his mum during her last session, he saw for himself how tired she got. "No problem Dad. It looks as though I could get the second half. If I score, I'll send you a message in the celebration. I have to go for a team meeting in a second, give Mum a hug from me please."

Des came back onto the ward just as the cannula was being taken out, the same Dutch girl rubbing Kim's hand as she finished. "I have just chatted with Jake, sweetheart. He understands the reasons why we can't go." Looking at the nurse's name badge he noticed that her name was also Kim. "Do you like football Kim?" he asked her.

She nodded her head. "I love it, my twin sister, Iris and I used to play back in the Netherlands. She is over here as well, studying to be a solicitor."

"Well, if you can both get down to the Southampton Stadium before eight o'clock this evening you can have these two free tickets. They will also allow you into the player's lounge after the game.

She looked stunned. "No way, we both live in Southampton and I'm off duty in twenty minutes. That's so kind, we can definitely go."

Des handed over the tickets. "And if you see our son Jake, say hello and tell him who you are. He will be pleased to meet you both."

The traffic on the way home to Newbury was thick but once there, Des made the sofa comfy with pillows and a duvet for Kim to snuggle under while he put the kettle on. He knew Kim wouldn't want to eat anything so planned on picking up a Chinese takeaway for himself once he had her settled. He brought her through a glass of water from the kitchen.

"Shall I get you some of the crispy chilli beef that you normally like?" he asked, trying to tempt her to eat.

Her stomach took a spin. "Not tonight Des, in fact can you fetch me a big bowl, I'm going to be sick."

Opening the cupboard under the sink Des found the plastic

bowl and a towel. There was nothing he could do other than be there as she learnt over the bowl and vomited, her poor stomach straining as she did so constantly for the next few minutes. Her face was ashen as she finished and collapsed back into the pillows.

"Okay, go and get your food, then we can watch the match. I will try stay awake."

Des stood in the empty takeaway in Thatcham. A glass wall between the waiting area and the kitchen showed the chefs all working hard behind the scenes as Des watched them blending ingredients together. A tap on his back made him turn around.

"Are you Luke and Jake Woods' dad?"

Des nodded with a smile. "Yes I am, Jake is playing for England tonight, his first international match."

There was no responding smile in the man's eyes as he stared at Des. "Yes, well you tell that black bastard of a son of yours who I hope is rotting in prison, that Robert Bell's uncle is waiting for him to get out. I'm going to gut him like a pig when I see him. Don't forget to tell him." The man turned and left without making an order.

A smiling woman came to the counter with a large white plastic bag containing his order. "There you are sir, enjoy."

Taking the bag, Des climbed back into the car, scanning the streets for the man who had threatened Luke. He wasn't anywhere to be seen. The short drive home was an uneasy one, people were not forgetting what Luke had done and life in this area would never be the same. Pulling into the driveway he wondered if they should just move and escape their history, but also knowing that it would always be waiting just around the corner with the next newspaper interview.

Opening the front door he steadied himself and took a deep breath. "Hi Kim, I'll just plate this up. Are you sure that you aren't hungry?"

The sound of the bowl filling up again told him the answer and he sat in silence in the kitchen eating the food before joining his wife.

Kim and Iris took their seats in the player's family section at St Mary's Stadium in Southampton. There was a good buzz in the stands where nearly twenty thousand people had turned up to watch the game.

Kim checked through the programme noticing that Jake's shirt number was thirty six and she scanned the players warming up below her before quickly spotting him. He was in his element, smiling and chatting to the other players, stopping quickly on the way back to the changing room to sign some autographs for a number of children waiting patiently. She liked the look of him and nudged her sister. "He looks nice, Iris, and he's the only player who stopped for those children. I hope he scores a goal tonight."

Iris smiled back at her. "Oh my God, my sister is in love with a football player before she has even met him."

The game started well with England scoring in the first five minutes, but without notice they then started to defend deep trying to protect the lead, allowing Poland to attack more often. Within the space of five minutes in the second half, England were two-one down and looking in need of some energy. The formation looked confused and there were no signs of the team even having a shot on target for a while.

A growing roar moved around the ground as Jake began to warm up. His reputation as a goal scorer was spreading across the premiership and a thunderous applause burst out as he took off his bib revealing his first ever white England shirt.

To Jake, it was just another game of football; he knew no fear in front of goal and everything came naturally to him when the pressure was on. He often turned, passed and shot without a thought going through his mind - it was pure instinct.

Jogging onto the field he casually looked up to where his parents should have been sitting, instead seeing two blond haired women smiling back down at him. Des noticed him looking for them on TV and laughing at Kim he spluttered, "He's forgotten that we are watching on television. Come on

Jake, focus! Let's go son."

The game seemed to be passing him by, every pass towards him a bad one. And five minutes of the game passed before he had the chance to touch the ball. Stopping it still thirty yards from goal he hit a pass out to the left hand side of the pitch where at Spurs, Jose would have been waiting. Tonight it just ran harmlessly out of play and a low murmur passed around the stands, the Sky commentator stating that he'd had an awful start to the game, one touch and a pass straight out of play.

Jake received the ball again and tried to turn the experienced central midfield player for Poland but it didn't work. Instead, the Polish player easily took the ball from him and passed it forwards, splitting the English defence. Before Jake could apologise it was three-one to Poland. His head was down, barely able to face his team mates as the captain, Brian Donaldson came over and had a word with him. "Come on Jake, you have to do better. Get your head back on and play football otherwise this could get embarrassing."

Before he had the chance to settle into the match, the final whistle blew. As debut performances go, it felt like it was a stinker.

Des stared at the image of Jake walking off the pitch holding his shirt over his face to try and hide from the public humiliation, the pundits all in agreement that this game had come a year too early for Jake. Des was astonished about how poorly he had played; he had never seen such a lethargic performance ever.

Kim and Iris made their way into the players area where Jake was standing alone as two older, overweight men wearing England blazers walked past him. One tapped him on the shoulder as they walked past and Kim heard him say, "Hard luck Jake, keep working hard and another chance will come along." If the words were supposed to motivate him, it had the opposite effect.

Kim approached him, a broad smile melting through his

hurt. "Hi Jake, my name is Kim. Your father gave me his tickets for the game, I'm a nurse at the Royal Berks hospital and I look after your mum when she comes in."

He held out his hand, looking into her eyes as he did so. "Thanks for everything that you're doing for her, we all appreciate it."

She held onto his hand for as long as she dared. "It's my job to look after poorly people, we'll get her through it."

"Yeah, I guess so. It's my job to score goals so I'm sorry I had such a bad game tonight, hope that I didn't let you all down too much?" He then caught sight of Iris. "Oh my God, I'm seeing double, no wonder I didn't score," They all laughed at his lame joke.

Iris could see some chemistry between the pair so she drifted off to the bar area and ordered a coke before chatting to a couple of the players' girlfriends who were standing waiting for the press commitments to be finished so that they could go home.

"So do you live in Reading, Kim?" He looked at her face and saw kindness, unlike the gold diggers he was used to hanging around the team, who just wanted free nights out. Shaking her blond hair she replied teasingly. "I'm afraid not, Jake. I share a flat with my sister in Southampton but it was nice to meet you though." She wandered over to where Iris was chatting before both headed out into the corridor leading to the stadium exit.

Jake followed her to the door. "Can I give you my number? If you want to talk, call me or send a message. If you don't want to, no worries," he hesitated, "but I would like to take you out for dinner sometime." He pressed his number into her hand and she looked at it before putting it into her small bag. "Maybe."

Jake re entered the player's lounge and sat on his own as the hoards gathered around some of the better known players, holding onto every word. Suddenly a bulky figure slipped into the chair beside him. He looked up from his phone to see Carlos Conte smiling at him.

"Tonight wasn't your fault Jake, the pass that went out of play was perfect. A better player would have picked it up and driven at the defenders. Look at what you do with Jose in training. And the rest of the tactics just froze you out of the play. When you were caught in possession, that was just down to frustration and you will learn from that. Everything came down the right hand side, or was pumped up past your deeper laying position. You did nothing wrong my friend and if you want my opinion, you are too good for these players."

Jake looked at him, waiting for the punch line to a well set up joke, but there wasn't one, he was as serious as Jake had seen him.

Carlos continued. "I have spoken to the manager; if he continues to play you in this role, we are all wasting our time. You could have won the game for England tonight very easily. I told him what I have seen so now it is up to him," He finished the small coffee he was sipping. "See you at training tomorrow, Jake." He walked away, brushing off a couple of reporters as he did so. The guy had style and the experience to support anything that he said.

As Jake sat thinking about what Carlos had just said, an England official came to his table and cleared his throat. "The manager wants to have a word with you, Jake, he's in the changing room."

Jake slowly pushed the door open to see Stuart Cobbs looking at his tactics on the large board on the wall. Acknowledging Jake, he asked him to join him at the board. "Jake, I got it wrong tonight. I played you out of position and didn't set the tactics to fit in with your strengths. It was my fault and I have given an interview to the press, saying precisely that. I will defend you to the end son, you are a great player and I promise you that our next game against Germany in two weeks time will be your first start. Let's show these gobshite journalists the future of English football." He shook Jake's hand. "Sorry buddy, stick with me. We will win the next European tournament together."

Jake headed down the A34 after the match as he wanted to drop in and see his parents before driving back to London. He phoned ahead to warn them and Des answered the phone. "Hey Dad, I'm on my way to see you, will you still be awake in half an hour?"

"Of course we will, we've just watched the game. They didn't give you a chance tonight."

Jake laughed. "Yeah, the manager has just apologised to me for the tactics - that's a first for me."

Des agreed. "He did more than that, he has just told Sky Sports that he was absolutely responsible for your performance, and that you would be a key part of the build up towards the Euro finals. We just need to beat Germany first to qualify."

"That's about the same as he told me. At least I get a chance to put things right. Oh, and by the way, I met Kim at the game tonight, she seems a really nice person."

Jake's phone signalled a message and when he arrived at his parents, he looked at the screen before getting out of the car. It was from Kim. "Dinner sounds good, tell me when you are free and I will book somewhere."

He had to read it twice before replying. Not only had she agreed to a date, she would make all the arrangements. His evening couldn't get any better.

CHAPTER TWENTY-FOUR

Luke mopped the education department corridor; lessons would be starting within thirty minutes and he needed to have everything ready for the start of the educational day.

Teachers drifted in and out of classrooms as they prepared themselves for the onslaught of another day's compulsory classes for the juvenile prisoners still of school age. They envied the teachers who were working towards 'A' level and above with the more academic prisoners. Sarah Cummings walked in with a clipboard in her hand looking officious.

"Hey Luke, how is the new job going?" Her attitude was carefree as she checked that the right names were on her list.

He smiled. "It's going well Miss, thank you. I'm back to having the lesson by myself after Ade and Afam were kicked off the course. Where are they now?"

"Afam Musa is still on Mountbatten, although I haven't seen him for a few weeks and Ibrahim went onto Rich Wing. Apparently he's very subdued on there and asking to come back to my wing. Not a bloody chance!" They both laughed before she made her way back to Mountbatten wing to unlock the prisoners on classes. Standing by the staircase leading to the second landing, the sound of a prisoner sweeping up caught her attention. She looked up and Musa appeared with a broom under his arm.

"See Miss, you can't get away from me. This is my new job, the Mental Health team sorted it out for me after I was diagnosed with PTSD." He carefully picked up a pile of dirt from the floor in a dustpan before continuing. "And the photo's you took from my cell, don't worry, I have more...plus pictures of you taking our money in the supermarket car park. I have enough to fuck you up and get you jailed for eight years so I need you to do something for me."

Sarah's heart sank, there could be no excuses now. She'd had the opportunity to report everything and didn't. What could she say to the Security Manager or the police now if she were found out? He stared into her face, so close his breath almost moved her hair as he spoke.

"I see by the look on your face, Miss, that you are in trouble. Do three little jobs for me and I will forget everything."

She started to walk away but he followed with the broom so she stopped abruptly and hissed, "What do you want me to do this time? I owe you nothing."

He placed the handle of the broom in front of her. "You owe me everything. If I had spoken up three weeks ago, you would have been heading to prison. You need to pay the debt you owe."

A male officer walked past and saw the look on her face as she spoke with the prisoner. "Are you Okay Miss Cummings?" he asked.

She nodded. "Yes, fine. I'm just explaining the cleaning schedule to Musa."

He nodded and left her alone with her tormentor.

"Move me into a single cell and make sure that Dawkins doesn't come back on here when he's finished with the plastic surgeon. And I have a package that needs bringing in, it must come directly to me, is that clear?"

She nodded in agreement. "And then the debt is paid?"

He looked around before grabbing her by the throat. "The fucking debt is paid when I say it's paid. Ten o'clock tonight, same place as last time."

She hated every last second of her shift, watching her blackmailer walking around without a care in the world, smiling when he saw her worried face. The clock hands dragged themselves around the dial until at last she was back out in the car park, fearing the drive home and what it that evening would bring.

She stood in her bathroom and dried her hair after a long

shower, thinking about the meeting tonight. She was dreading it and just hoped that it would be a quick drop off without questions or photos. The noise of her hairdryer masked the sound of footsteps coming along the wooden floor of her landing towards her steamy bathroom and as the door swung open, she dropped the dryer in shock, the casing cracking as it hit the hard white floor. Looking up she saw two enormous black men and a younger woman standing in the doorway staring at her.

The lead man, standing at well over six feet and with horrific scaring to his face, stepped into the room. His scruffy afro hair and the battered leather jacket which covered his enormous muscles made him look wild and dangerous and when he spoke, his thick London accent sounded uncompromising and menacing. "You should learn to lock your doors, Sarah. Anyone could walk in and do whatever they liked to you."

She looked at his face and noticed that a knife wound had taken out his left eye and a non-moving false one sat coldly in its place.

The girl began to laugh. She was dressed in skin tight black jeans and a small white denim jacket and her eyes looked vacant as she chewed on gum. The man ignored her and continued.

"You possibly don't know who I am, but lots of people do. They will tell you that I am not a man to be messed with, some even say that if you see me like this," he stopped speaking and gestured to her house, "then I am going to kill you, but that's not always the case. Mostly it is, I admit, but not always."

Sarah tried to grab her robe to cover herself up as the towel she was wrapped in made her feel even more vulnerable, but his large hands grabbed her arms and pulled down the towel. She stood naked in front of them.

He looked her up and down, his teeth glinting in the bathroom light. "You look good for an old woman - I bet you can still do your thing. Afam told us all about you and I did wonder how this would end."

The young girl shouted, "Fuck her, fuck her in the arse, the white bitch." He turned to her and slapped her hard around the face sending her dazed head into the wall.

"Don't you ever tell me what to do. Shut your mouth or I will bust your ass right now." She stepped back wiping the blood from her split lip, glaring at Sarah as the crack cocaine she'd taken before their call still spiralled through her system.

The man spoke again. "So now you know we can come into your house anytime we choose. If you move house, we will find you in less than a day. Put your robe on, take this fucking package and make sure that my friend gets it tomorrow."

She nodded in fear, before he added, "If you don't do these things I'm coming back here and I'm going to rape you so badly that you will pray to be dead. And my friend here," he pointed to the other large man, "he will film it and put it on line, and then when we change places I will film him. Do I make myself clear?"

Sarah nodded as she pulled the robe tightly around her. The parcel weighed a lot more than she anticipated and was solid rather than the softer drug parcels she had previously seen in prison.

"What's in the package? I need to know before I go through the scanner."

He stared at her. "Don't get clever, the scanner is only on when the security team decide to search the staff. I already know how your system works. Go into work early, take the package to Afam and he will do the rest."

They turned and left, leaving Sarah slumped, exhausted, on the cold tiled floor. She looked up at the package and knew it wasn't just drugs this time, it was a gun.

CHAPTER TWENTY-FIVE

Sarah parked her car in the staff car park, the package sitting in the bottom of her sports bag. She sat and watched staff going through the gate, looking for any signs that they were being subjected to searching this morning. The flow in and out seemed to be even and there were no sightings of additional dog support, unless the dog handlers had parked inside the secure compound.

She had two choices, walk straight in with her bag and if the searchers were there she would be caught, or go in without the bag and come back later to pick it up. This was dangerous as it would raise suspicion as to why she would go back out for her bag. Also, Musa was expecting the parcel first thing this morning. She made a decision, flicked the boot open and picked up her bag. In her anxiety, the bag felt ten times it's real size and came with a big sign stuck on top saying, '*Search me.*'

She walked towards the gate complex, her eyes peeled for anything that might lay in wait, heart thumping and almost struggling to breathe as she went into the sterile area before entering the prison. This was the moment that the search team would pounce if they were here, but with a mechanical trundle, the electronic gate slid open and to her relief there was no welcome committee for her.

"Morning Sarah," the officer said as he handed her the keys and took her blue plastic tally in exchange. "You have a note stuck on your keys this morning, saying you are going on escort so don't go to the wing. They need you in reception straight away, we've just had an incident in the kitchen where a prisoner has been stabbed. It looks bad but the ambulance is on its way. You can leave your bag here until you get back if you want."

She shook her head - of all the days for this to happen. "No, it's ok, I'll take it up to the wing, but the sound of the ambulance arriving outside spelt differently. The orderly officer poked his head out of his small office. "No time for that, this kid is bleeding out. Give me the bag, it will be safe here." She had no choice and handed it over.

"Bloody hell Sarah, what have you got in here? It weighs a bloody ton." Placing it down beside his desk, he continued to write up the escorting paperwork.

"You're in charge of this one Sarah. The prisoner's name is Ibrahim from Rich Wing. He just went into the kitchen to pick up some breakfast packs for new inductions, Dawkins saw him and stuck a carving knife straight through his throat. He has already been resuscitated twice but take care, he's a dangerous little bastard if he comes too. You'll have two of the PE staff with you as some muscle so make sure that they don't take their eyes off him. Any questions?"

She shook her head and headed for reception where Ibrahim was already lying on a hospital trolley with Healthcare staff and a doctor trying to resuscitate him for a third time.

"All clear," the doctor shouted as the defib machine kicked his heart back into life seconds before the ambulance staff arrived, the lead paramedic instantly assessing the scene. "We need to get him to hospital straight away, is everyone ready?" Sarah nodded and climbed into the back of the vehicle with her other two staff and a blare of sirens and blue lights filled the gate area as the ambulance rushed out, Ibrahim lying unconscious on the trolley, the handcuff chain rattling with every bump.

Looking down at his blood soaked body, Sarah hoped that he wouldn't survive as it would be one less issue to contend with. The other fear crushing her was the bag she had left sitting by the desk of the orderly officer. He was inches away from the weapon without knowing it and should the drugs dog be allowed to wander into the office, the scent of whatever else was in the package would trigger a search and she could arrive back and find the police waiting.

The other issue was that she didn't know when she would be getting back to the prison. At best it would be this evening when other staff could be identified to cover the night time escort and she knew Musa was expecting the package that morning.

Before she could worry any further, the first of her wishes came true. Ibrahim convulsed on the ambulance trolley and alarms began to sound as a paramedic shouted to the staff. "Get those cuffs off him, I need to shock him again."

Sarah quickly found the keys and released the metal cuffs from Ibrahim's limp wrists. They fell with a crash to the floor as the thump of electricity jolted his chest. "No pulse, let's go again." The machine buzzed as he placed the pads back on the still chest. It thudded again without response, the paramedic cursing. "Fuck it, don't give up on me now."

The prison staff stood back watching the frantic activity as the paramedic shouted through to the driver. "We're losing him, how long?"

A shout came from the front. "Two minutes."

The ambulance wailed through the busy streets as a third thump banged into the exposed chest before they pulled up outside the Royal Berkshire Hospital.

The doors burst open and frantic eyes looked on as the lifeless body was wheeled into the resuscitation room where a slim male doctor in his early thirties talked to Ibrahim as he worked.

"Come on, come on. Stand clear!" Thump! And the staff stared despairingly at the monitor.

"Nothing, let's go one more time." The fevered activity was starting to drift into normality as a procedure was being followed and the last jolt tried to kick start his heart.

Sarah stood silently at the side of the cubicle as the doctor said, "I'm calling it. Time of death, 09:06." The two gym staff looked at each other and shrugged before collecting the chains and handcuffs together and placing them back into a bag. One whispered into Sarah's ear, "Phone the prison Sarah, they need to know now."

Dragging her eyes away from what she had wished for, she took the prison phone from her pocket and rang the Duty Governor.

Sitting with the two staff in the hospital reception area waiting for their transport back to the prison, they chatted about banal stuff. They both poked fun at her about her relationships but quickly gave way to kinder subjects, it had been a tough start to anyone's day. A white minibus pulled up outside, a woman in the prison uniform driving. Sarah got into the front, chatting to the driver on the way back.

"He didn't have much chance, he must have bled out another five pints in the ambulance. At least we don't have to sit there all night I guess." Sarah sounded matter of fact about it all and Bev, the driver, nodded before speaking.

"The boss has told me that you all have to go to straight to see the security officer. The police have set up a full scale murder enquiry and Dawkins is already in police custody. They need statements from you about this morning."

Sarah's day couldn't have become more complicated if she tried and sticking her head into the orderly officer's office back at the prison, she looked for her sports bag. He took her by surprise as he bustled through the door with a file in his hand. "It's in that cupboard, Sarah." He pointed to a grey locker. "I fell over the bloody thing five times. You're needed with the police, they're in the boardroom. Take that bag with you, I'm sick of the sight of it."

Luke stood in the secure corridor on his way to education; he looked at his watch and wondered if it was worth it. He only had an hour and a half until he had to return to his cell. The two PE staff from the escort walked past him, chatting about Ibrahim and the hospital. Musa, also waiting to sweep the corridor when everyone had left heard some of the conversation. He jogged up to them. "I just heard you talking about Ibrahim, what's happening?" One of the staff turned and apologised.

"Sorry, everyone did all they could, he died this morning."

Musa sank to his knees as the staff kept on walking. Luke crouched beside him, Musa sobbing as he spoke.

"This is all so fucked up, we were going to walk out of here today."

Luke was surprised. "What, you were both going to be released?"

"No man, we were going to escape, disappear so that they couldn't send us back. We would have been gone today."

Luke put his arm around him as others started to drift off to work. "I'm sorry mate, I don't know what to say."

Musa kept his head down, almost whispering. "We were going to shoot our way out of here, like fucking legends. Now I have to do it alone." He looked up at Luke. "I need help to do it Luke. I have a gun and a place to stay where no one will find us, come with me."

Luke took his arm away. "You've got a gun?"

Musa nodded. "I will have today when that bitch Cummings brings it to me. We are gone this afternoon, meet me here and we'll grab a screw and walk out. Two o'clock, if you don't come, I will shoot as many as I can."

Luke walked over to the education building playing the conversation over and over in his head. It would be a blood bath, he couldn't be allowed to escape and why did he need him to help? Was he bluffing or was his story real? One thing was for sure, he needed to speak to the Security Manager in confidence. When he got to his classroom, he scribbled a note and passed it to a teacher. "Please Miss, I need this to go to the security manager, it's important."

She nodded and placed it in her bag. "'I'm going there for training in five minutes so I will do it then."

Twenty minutes later Luke sat studying in his classroom alone while the teacher was copying some coursework. The door opened and the Security Manager came in and closed the door. "I hope that this is important Woods, I don't normally leave a meeting with my team to come and speak with prisoners." A few minutes later he was walking briskly back to his security office, eyes burning angrily as he considered his actions.

Sarah sat talking to the police officer, the bag at her feet as the lead investigator finished speaking.

"Thank you Sarah, I have taken enough of your time today, I suspect that you need to get back to work but we may need to speak with you again before any court case against Dawkins."

Picking up the sports bag she headed back into the secure area of the prison, formulating yet another plan. Once this bag was dropped off she would report that she was too unwell to continue working and would take two weeks at home while the drama unfolded. Hopefully Musa would be killed by the police trying to break free and it could all still work out in her favour.

The long, cold, secure corridor to Mountbatten Wing seemed to last forever as she walked, the hum of the wing preparing for lunch time drifting towards her as she anticipated relieving herself of the package. A voice behind her interrupted her thoughts.

"Armed Police, drop the bag."

She froze briefly before dropping it at her feet. For a fleeting moment she wanted to run but instead she just waited for the police team who had shadowed her towards the unit to arrest her. She looked desperately at the arresting officer and blurted, "I have a parcel in the bottom of my bag. I'm being targeted by a criminal gang to bring it in as they have threatened to rape me if I don't do it. I don't know what's in the parcel."

There was no sympathy from the team leader. "Get on the floor with your arms outstretched, do not try to resist."

Bundled down with rough hands she lay in a haze, her once cosy life flashing before her, the prospect of twenty years in prison sending a numb feeling into her legs as she was hauled back up and into a waiting car. She looked through the rear window of the police car at the prison for the last time as she sat hand cuffed, avoiding the gaze of staff as she was driven through the gate area on the way to Reading Police station, the pistol and heroin securely fastened in police evidence bags.

Luke sat in the Governor's plush office sipping from a glass of cold coke as the Governor and Chief Inspector of Thames Valley Police spoke to him. He would be required to give evidence at court against both the officer and Musa, after which the parole board would be given a letter personally from the Home Secretary. If he behaved himself for the next few years, he would be successful on his first parole hearing after serving ten years. The beginning of the end had just crept into sight.

"Luke," the Governor looked him in the face. "I'm happy for you to remain in the prison until you have finished your degree and Masters, which will take you up to twenty-three years old whereas normally people leave here at twenty one. I have also given consent for you to have a laptop in your cell but it will not come with wifi I'm afraid."

The Inspector laughed. "You have made a brave decision today Luke. Your cooperation will not go unnoticed and we will protect your identity throughout the case." He stood and shook Luke's hand. "Now I need to go and prepare myself for the questions that are going to arise about how guns are so easily moved across my county. I guess that you will face similar difficulties Governor."

The Governor nodded. "But at least thanks to Luke we have stopped a massacre in here; I hope that Musa and Cummings receive the harshest of punishments. I'll be writing to the judge in your trial, he needs to know about this development."

"It will all help our case," the Inspector agreed, "based on the links Musa and his gang have to terrorist cells working in the UK, he should be looking at thirty years plus. Cummings will be getting at least twenty years for her involvement, regardless of whatever threats she has dreamt up."

CHAPTER TWENTY-SIX

Jake sat in an old pub restaurant in the New Forest, Kim sitting opposite him. She had dressed in casual clothes but still managed to look stylish. In seven days time the girls would be celebrating their twenty second birthdays in Ibiza and were really looking forward to it. It had been a long time since the pair of them had been able to let their hair down.

Jake looked across the table, she was a very pretty girl but not the normal type he chased after. This one was different, she had a great brain and career and on top of that she also had the social skills which would mean that she would be able to slide effortlessly into most of Jake's groups of friends. Choosing their meals, the two of them chatted effortlessly while eating and the hours passed quickly until the bell rang in the bar for last orders. After requesting the bill, he smiled at her. "Wow Kim, that evening has flown past. I'm hoping we can do it again soon."

Placing her purse on the table as she looked at the bill she smiled back. "I'll send you a message when we get back from Ibiza."

Jake took out his wallet and tried to grab the bill before Kim told him to put his money away, "This one is my treat Jake, you can pick up the next one if you want." Looking into his eyes she held his hand. "I've had a really lovely night, it would be great to do it again," she said before they walked out into the night air. Jake linked his arm with Kim's and strolled her back to her car where, leaning forwards, Jake kissed her for the first time. She responded before gently pulling back and finding her keys. "Slow down tiger. I need to get home, I have work in the morning. I'll phone you when I get back from our holiday. Play well on Saturday, I will keep an eye on your score."

He smiled, his emotions had taken a different twist with Kim - he knew that she would be good for him, and he would be good for her. "I'll try. Thanks for a lovely evening and you are very kind to pick up the bill. Have a great holiday, see you soon."

She pulled off, the wheels crunching on the gravel car park as her indicator flashed for her to turn left. Jake stood briefly by his car thinking about what had just happened. He wanted to see her again very soon but Ibiza was stopping that from happening.

Pulling out of the car park he gunned the engine back towards London. The familiar ping of a voice message made him look down briefly to see it was Luke. He listened and smiled as he heard his brother's voice sounding out around his car.

"Hey, about time you picked up your phone for me or dropped me a letter. I have loads of things to tell you Jake, I will try again tomorrow night at around seven o'clock. Please be waiting."

Checking the sat nav, he typed in Huntercombe and headed off in that direction, knowing that Luke's unit was close to the fence. He didn't care if a prison officer came out and questioned him, Jake just needed to hear his voice again.

Pulling down the single track road, Jake drove as slowly as he could, trying to keep the growl of the engine down. The large green metal fence towered above him as he carefully pulled to a stop and climbed out into the late night chill. Checking his watch, he saw it was 12.32am and still the sound of a couple of prisoners chatting from their windows drifted over to him. He had to be quick or his plan would fail.

"Luke Woods, are you listening?" There was a long silence before a voice came back.

"Yes, I'm here. Who is it?"

"It's Jake, man, I'm in the road. I need to be quick before the police get called. I love you brother."

Luke laughed out loud. "This is crazy, you are fifty metres away and I can't see you! Thanks for stopping in, shall I put the kettle on."

Jake smiled at the sound of his brother's voice. "No man, keep that stuff for yourself. Phone me tonight, seven o'clock. I will be waiting." A shout went up from the gate complex and two figures appeared.

"Got to go man, your prison officers are coming to arrest me."

The sound of the car turning around and blasting out of the driveway sent the prisoners who were awake into a frenzy. One voice shouted out, "That was your brother Luke, the guy who plays for Spurs, he was here shouting out to you like he didn't give a fuck about the law."

Luke smiled to himself before shouting back, "Yep, that's my brother, he's got my back you know."

A lone voice came back from a cell window.

"For real Luke? They are playing Chelsea on Saturday, tell him to have a bad game man, we need all the help we can get."

CHAPTER TWENTY-SEVEN

Jake was about to run onto the training field, still smiling about last night - a great evening with Kim, and then a quick illicit chat with Luke. Carlos stopped him before he could kick a ball.

"Jake, I need to have a chat with you before we start. Real Madrid have contacted the club, they are interested in signing you for next season. I'm not going to lie, they are assembling one of the strongest teams Europe has ever seen. They have asked me to manage them; we will be European Champions Jake and I want you to come with me. Say nothing at the moment, the club don't know anything about the conversations that have been happening with me. What do you think?"

Jake stood shocked, not only was his manager having a confidential chat with him about a subject that would send every news agency into meltdown, he was asking him to be part of the new revolution in Spain. "I think that it sounds exciting boss. But this is football, I'm a Spurs player until someone tells me differently."

Carlos smacked him on the back. "Great answer Jake, train and play hard and see what comes calling for you. Remember, not a word. I will not sign you if you talk to anyone about this, I need loyalty from my players." Jake nodded his agreement and jogged out to fetch a stray football.

As the days passed, and as much as he tried, he couldn't shake the thought from his head. In a few weeks time he could be playing for the best team in the world, but more pressing was the qualifier game against Germany coming up next week.

Des and Kim stood in the stands at Old Trafford, Jake lining up on the pitch while the national anthems of England and

Germany boomed out across a packed stadium. His thoughts drifted momentarily to his girlfriend, Kim, listening while working a nightshift with the cancer patients, and he hoped to make her proud. All they needed was a draw to qualify for the Under 21 World Cup and the chance for Jake to parade his skills in front of the world.

Tingles shot up his spine as the final words of God Save the Queen drifted away into the unseen faces at the backs of the enormous stands. The German team were a formidable outfit, unbeaten for forty eight games and topping the group with maximum points. The first meeting with England in Munich was a master class in pressure football, England crumbling to a 4:1 loss, the British press giving them little chance of reversing the score line after the Poland game, but Jake knew differently. He hadn't been fully involved in those games, now he was here, prepared for action, but more importantly the team was ready for Jake.

The absolute cut and thrust of the first seventy minutes had kept the crowd on the edge of their seats, Germany hitting the bar with a towering header from a free kick in the first half, and England coming close ten minutes into the second half when Steve Phillips, the tall central midfield player, crashed a thunderous shot off the foot of the post, both sides respecting the danger the others presented. Jake tormented the German defence with his darting runs into dangerous positions and only some last gasp defending stopped him getting a shot at goal.

As the game began to drift towards a draw, the English players counted down the seconds until the final whistle would blow marking their progression to the next phase. Out of nowhere the German midfielder picked up the ball and played an inch perfect pass to the striker who, shielding the ball from the last desperate lunge from the defenders, hammered a shot into the top corner of the net causing a small section of the crowd to celebrate wildly. Jake looked up at the clock as he walked back for the restart. Time was almost up and he glanced over to see the English Bench looking skywards in despair. Months of hard work and planning scuppered in the final minute of the final game.

Players looked deflated, some with tears in their eyes as Jake clapped his hands and shouted out, unconsciously taking charge for the first time. "Come on boys, this isn't over. Press forward, get the ball to my feet, we can still get something from the game."

The fourth official held up his board; four minutes of additional time was left.

England took the kick and looked after the ball, passing it across the pitch, searching for an opening. The clock ticked down as the German team dropped deep to protect the lead.

Bobby Baxter, the young Aston Villa midfielder, got the ball at his feet and drove forwards, a German defender bringing him down three yards outside the box. The large defensive wall lined up presenting an almost impossible task to hit the target as Bobby picked up the ball and worked out his angles. He cupped his hand around his mouth as he spoke to Jake. "I'm going top right hand corner, be aware of any rebound."

Jake didn't need to be told as he slid into a congested line ten yards away from the ball. He watched as Bobby ran and sliced the ball, almost touching Jake's head as it fizzed over towards the goal where a huge arm stretched out, desperate finger tips pushing the ball onto the post as it bounced back towards a sea of faces.

Jake anticipated the movement before anyone else and dived forwards, a boot thudding into his face as he got his forehead to the ball and sent the crowd crazy. Lying groggily on the turf, a sea of laughing faces looked down at him as the final whistle blew.

"What happened?" For a second Jake didn't realise where he was, the force of the kick to his head briefly knocking him out cold. Bobby stood astride him while the medics scampered towards them.

"You bloody legend Jake Woods! We're on our way to the

world cup, what a goal!"

Kim and Des had stopped the celebrating while their son lay motionless for thirty seconds until he finally sat up and took a drink of water. They looked around the ground as over fifty thousand fans jumped around in celebration. Their son had just helped England to the world cup finals in Brazil; it was a fairytale become reality.

Luke charged around in his cell punching the air in celebration. This was incredible, and as the rest of the prison quickly picked up on the score line, anyone in the area would have sworn a riot was in progress. What Luke didn't realise was that in a few short weeks he would hate everything that Jake stood for.

Carlos stood in the player's tunnel with another man who Jake didn't recognise, grabbing Jake in a bear hug as he walked by. The smell of a scent, so expensive that even Jake would baulk at the price wrapped itself around him.

"That's what I need on the new project Jake, you are a fearless leader, you just don't realise it yet. I want you to meet my agent, Sammy. He's a good Italian guy and has great contacts everywhere. I want you to talk to him. If you do the things that we have planned, you will be the best striker in the world. People will talk about you when they mention legendary players so think about that for a minute before you go back into the changing room. You can be a legend at Real Madrid."

Sammy took over the conversation. "I know your agent, he hasn't handled any big players and at the moment I have five of the top six players in the world with my team. I will make you hundreds of millions of pounds within five years. I will ensure that you are rubbing shoulders with the greatest players on the planet and I will also ensure that you belong with the elite. Sign with me and your dreams will come true."

Jake smiled at him before whispering, "Come get me at the end of the season, I will leave Spurs with Carlos and you will be my agent. Can I sign with you this evening?"

Sammy produced a contract from his briefcase. "I have

already taken the liberty of drafting one up. I offer a better deal with smaller commission, and the first contract is for one year. If you don't like the service, you can walk away with nothing owed to me. But after the first year I insist on a five year contract. What do you have to lose? I can take care of every detail for you."

Jake took a pen and signed without reading, trusting Sammy and Carlos implicitly.

Nothing else was on his mind. Thoughts of Luke were a million miles away, along with his mother's illness, his new relationship with Kim - nothing else mattered at this moment. He was going to chase his dream, earn more money and adulation than he could have ever thought possible. This was his time, he was twenty years old and the world lay at his feet. Nothing and nobody could stand in his way.

As he headed for the changing room, a reporter stopped him suddenly, catching him off guard.

"Jake Woods, England's hero tonight, do you have any words for Sky Sports after such a great game?"

He blinked into the lights as they shone in his eyes. "No, it was just a gutsy team performance and we deserved the result. Now let's see what happens in the finals next year." The next question threw him.

"Will you still be a Spurs player next season? We've heard rumours about a big money move to Real Madrid."

Jake paused; had someone deliberately leaked the story? "No, I'm a Spurs player, I enjoy playing for the team and the fans and I have had no contact with any other club."

At the same time that he was being interrogated by the press, Jake's agent, Abdul received a call from an unknown number.

"Hello Abdul, my name is Sammy Totti, football agent. I've been instructed by my new client, Jake Woods to inform you that his contract with you is terminated. My barrister has studied the wording of his contract and it is no longer enforceable. Please stop all professional dealings with him immediately or I will sue you for every cent you own.

Goodnight Abdul." The phone went silent.

Abdul phoned Jake straight away. "What's happening Jake? I just had a call from a guy named Sammy, he claims to be your new agent."

Jake took a deep breath. "Yes, sorry Abdul, I didn't realise that he was going to phone you before I had a chance to tell you. Sorry, but I need to move on."

Abdul pleaded, "Jake, we can move on together mate, remember that I got you the Spurs contract, we are good together. And we had plans to make sure that Luke was looked after…come on man."

Jake was sharp with his reply, a tone of voice Abdul hadn't detected in him so far. "Luke is a big boy, he can fend for himself now. Prison is easy for him. I need to move on and you aren't the one to do it. I need bigger people in my life now, if you have a problem, take it up with Sammy."

Jake hung up, leaving Abdul staring at a blank phone as his biggest client walked away from him. *Oh Jake, you're heading for a fall, my son*, he muttered to himself.

CHAPTER TWENTY-EIGHT

Luke sat pondering a question during his English lesson; he loved the subject and the way in which it made him look at things in a different manner. A gentle tap at the door didn't disturb him, but the Governor of the prison, Sue Bridges' presence did, and she was with the Prison Minister who had requested a tour of the establishment and a chat to staff and prisoners. Apart from the teacher, Jake was alone in the room and the Governor introduced her guest.

"Good afternoon Luke, this is David Jefferies, the Prison Minister, and by chance a big Spurs fan. He would like to know about your education course."

Luke jumped at the chance to explain the course content, along with his reasons for wanting to gain the degree and his Masters. The minister looked interested in what he had to say before looking through some of the work Luke had produced. "This really is excellent stuff, reminds me of when I was at university. The Governor has spoken very highly about an incident that you recently prevented from happening and I understand that the judge is relooking at your case as we speak. I know him well and suggested that maybe two years reduction in your sentence would show our gratitude towards your bravery in reporting terrorism and staff corruption. You could be home in five years Luke." He smiled at him. "Let me make a quick call to see where he has got to in his deliberations." The minister stepped outside and summoned his assistant.

Sue continued while the Minister spoke on his personal phone. "Luke, is there any chance that you can get the prison minister a signed shirt from Jake? His grandson is a massive supporter."

Luke was still in shock about the prospect of such a dramatic cut in his sentence and shook his head to focus on what she was asking. "Yes, sure, I will phone Jake tonight. If he answers, I'll ask him."

The Minister came back in with a smile on his face. "All agreed Luke, two years have been removed for helping our nation fight terror. You will be home before you know it."

The Governor patted Luke on the back. "Excellent news, that means another. three years with us, one year in an adult cat C prison and two years in a Cat D and then home." He turned to the Minister. "Oh, and Luke is going to arrange for you to have his brother's signed match shirt minister, I think that it's fair to say that we have all had a great day."

Luke dashed back to the unit, rushing to get onto the phone to tell his parents of his reduced sentence. Kim broke down when she heard the news.

"That's brilliant news Luke, two years off your sentence. I can't wait to tell Dad when he gets home. Have you told Jake yet? He phoned half an hour ago to try to find his passport - the club need it apparently. Also, I had a scan today Luke and the cancer has shrunk in size already. They've told me that I'm doing well... isn't that good news as well?"

A lump came into Luke's throat, the emotion of everything over the past week catching up on him. "Mum, that is great news, fingers crossed that it keeps getting smaller. I better phone Jake before they turn the phones off."

Luke phoned him straight away and Jake picked up on the first ring sounding irritated.

"Luke! Sorry buddy, my old agent keeps phoning me and he's pissing me off."

Luke was surprised. "Old agent? I thought that you were happy with Abdul?"

"I was, it's just that I found a better agency who'll take care of everything for me."

Luke shook his head. "It must be so difficult playing football for a living."

Jake, missing the sarcasm in his voice, answered, "Everyone wants some of your time all day long. It's crazy."

"Yeah, it must be hell Jake! Do you know how many times I've had a stranger search me or make me strip in front of them in the last month? Do you want to swap?"

Jake laughed. "No man! Anyway, you don't normally phone in the day, what's up?"

Luke left a dramatic pause before bursting out, "They have just cut two years off my sentence. I'm home in six years brother."

Jake let out a yell. "That's wicked Luke, we're going to have the biggest party when you come home."

Luke was beside himself with the relief he felt. "Oh man, I can't wait to have some home cooking and a nice soft bed again. The Prison Minister came in to the prison and told me about it. One small thing though, he wants you to give him a signed shirt, Jake. Can you sort one out for him?"

There was a short silence. "It's not that easy Luke, all our shirts are already promised to hospitals and charities all season. I will see what I can do but I can't promise anything."

"Come on man, the guy has just given me two years off my sentence and I said that I will sort him a shirt out. It's not much to ask considering why I am in here is it?" He was starting to get annoyed but in truth, the irritation had been building for years.

Jake spat back his answer, the conversation quickly going south.

"Luke, are you going to throw that in my face every time we speak? I was lucky, you were unlucky so don't try blackmail me over your prison sentence. Just do your time and get out."

The fury bubbled up inside Luke. "Fuck you man, you stabbed the guy and I'm doing the sentence for you. All I have ever asked for is one stupid shirt. You know what, keep the fucking shirt and I'll tell him that you're a super star arsehole who has forgotten his roots. Good luck with whatever you're doing next. Just remember Karma is a fucking bitch Jake, it will creep up on you one day and take a bite out of you."

Luke had hardly finished the sentence when he realised that Jake had cut him off. Banging the phone on the table next to him, he muttered, "Fucking, ignorant bastard, you're going to get what you deserve."

His Personal Officer, Miss Nevis, strolled up to him. "What's up Luke? You seem pretty pissed off."

He took a deep breath, "Yeah, just a row with my brother; he suddenly thinks that he's bigger and better than anyone else."

She nodded before taking the phone from his hand and placing it back on the receiver. "Come on, you need to calm down before you break something. Go back to your cell and we'll chat this evening."

The clunk of the cell door closing seemed harder today that normal. He'd had two years taken off his sentence but it still seemed a lifetime away and photos of Jake playing and scoring for Spurs adorning the cell wall further incensed him. He looked at his smiling face and felt a surge of anger again, ripping them all down and throwing them into the bin amongst the wet tea bags and tissues.

Looking around for something else to throw, he saw a letter waiting for him on his locker top. It was a handwritten note from another prison and intrigued, he opened it up. It was from Rat Boy who as usual got straight to the point.

'Luke, another guy has just landed at my prison, his name is Afam Musa, he says that he knows you.

He told me that you grassed him to the police to save your neck. He wants you dead and has paid people at your prison to do it for him. I know that you are not a grass but you need to watch your back, he says that he has already paid someone £500 to cut you open.

Bigger is in here with me, we're sharing a cell. He says that if he was still on Patterson he would make sure that you were safe. This place is crazy, the adult prisons are fucking brutal, I got a beating on the second day. Bigger was knocked out by a big Irish guy because he wouldn't get off the phone for him. We just keep ourselves to ourselves until we can get affiliated with the main Manchester gang running this wing. I am buzzing every night, this place has everything going on.

Try get yourself up here when they kick you out of there. I think the guy who has been paid is a kid from Somalia, they call him "skidz." Drop me a line back. Rat Boy.

Luke read through the letter for a second time; he didn't know anyone called Skidz on his unit or in education. He had two choices, ride it out and hope that Musa was just chatting prison crap to raise his own profile, or someone was actually planning to kill him in the same way that Rat Boy had killed a boy for the very same reason.

He asked around the unit to see if anyone knew of a prisoner nicknamed Skidz. A small African looking boy popped his head into Luke's cell that evening.

"I know someone called Skidz, he's coming here from Brixton prison for family visits. He gets here on Monday. He's a good friend of Musa's, they ran the same gang in South London a few years back. They call him skidz because the way he cuts people's face's with a double razor blade, looks like big tyre skid marks on the road when they heal up. He is a fucking animal Luke."

Luke's stomach sank at the thought of what lay in wait. Accumulated family visits were normally spread out over a four week period so if he could just stay out of the way for a few weeks he might just avoid any confrontation. He was sure, however, that this man would need to prove to Musa that he still had his back, plus the small issue of the money that he had been paid to do the deed. One way or another, the two of them were going to clash.

CHAPTER TWENTY-NINE

The prison van drove through the gates of Huntercombe Prison with a cargo of one. The steps clattered down as the security guard opened the cell door to a smiling Somalian prisoner.

"Okay buddy, we're here at last. Have a good few weeks and hope that your visits work out."

The man stretched out his slim six foot three frame and walked into the reception building for processing. He smiled at the officer who checked through his belongings.

"Mohamed, you have come here for four weeks without any property other than shower gel and toothpaste. Do you have any money in your account to buy things?"

He maintained his smile. "I don't need anything. The kids who grew up in this country have too much, they are fat and lazy and that's why we took over all of their business on the streets. At home I have nothing, all I need is a little food, a bed and to keep myself clean. Everything else will be down to the will of God."

The officer frowned, knowing this boy was trouble. "Good luck with that. We're going to put you onto the induction unit, all visits will be held on weekends and each of your visits will be for two hours. We have them booked for Saturdays and Sundays.

During the week you will be helping clean the wing, we will pay you £2.50 per week. If you screw up we have authority to send you directly back to Brixton. Do you have any questions?"

He shook his head. "No, it feels alright here, I may want to stay once the visits are over."

The officer took a look at his security file and laughed. "I don't think that you have any chance of staying here based on the past six months, your record is shocking."

The smile remained fixed. "Every person that I have hurt over the past few months has been a prisoner who disrespected me. I don't hurt staff and I respect all women. I won't be a problem to any staff, you have my word."

The officer looked down the long list of assaults. Seven serious attacks on people with a weapon, seventeen fights and five disobeying direct orders where staff felt that he was trying to incite a riot. "Ok, I've seen enough, in my view you shouldn't be here at all. Accumulated visits are a privilege, not a bloody entitlement. From what I see here it just looks as though Brixton are happy to get rid of you for a month. Pick up your stuff and follow this officer to your wing."

As soon as Mohamed left the reception building, the officer phoned the Duty Governor of the day, Claire Goodhill. "Who the hell allowed Mohamed to come here from Brixton? His record is amongst the worst I've ever seen and he's going to cause us problems, trust me on that. He is gang affiliated in South London and has strong links with Musa who we just shipped out to avoid a staff and prisoner massacre. We need to ship him back ASAP, Claire."

Claire was a well balanced manager who had cut her teeth working in dispersal prisons until moving to Huntercombe five years before her retirement.

"Let me go speak to the boss," she said, "this hasn't come through me so maybe she has agreed it directly with Brixton.

She tapped on the Governor's door. "Sue, we've just had a prisoner from Brixton arrive for accumulated visits. His security record is horrendous, how did we end up taking such a dangerous lad?"

Sue stopped working and brought Mohamed's details up on her screen. "Shit, I was promised that he was behaving. It was part of the deal for moving Musa out quickly. We have been tucked up Claire. Bloody Brixton, wait until I speak to them."

She picked up her phone and dialled the Area Manager's Office.

"Hi Steve, it's Sue, we have a problem here. We have been sent a prisoner way outside our security criteria." She listened intently for a few seconds before reading out Mohamed's name and number.

Claire could hear a rambling explanation from Steve Bagshaw, the Area Manager. Sue simply thanked him and hung up, her expression unchanged.

"Okay, he's ours for a month. The police want him to have his visits outside London and they'll be placing listening devices in his cell and under his visits table. It would appear that we are part of the bigger picture, Claire. Tell reception that he's staying for the month."

She nodded. "No problems, that stays in this office. I'll just tell the staff that it's a decision that was made between Area Managers, that way we are all going to be on the same page. Let's just hope that it works out for us."

Mohamed sat on his bed, his door open as association was about to start. A large white lad came to his door with a bag of canteen and goodies.

"These have been arranged for you by Musa, he has told me to get whatever you need." He tossed the bag onto the freshly made bed. Mohamed looked at it and then up at the boy.

"I do need something, get me a decent shank and look after it until I call. I need it this week."

Nick Jones, the boy, went a shade whiter. "Sure, I'll have one for you tonight. We took a large carving knife from the kitchen two weeks ago which is well hidden and security have stopped looking. Give me a couple of hours, it's not on the wing."

Mohamed stared at him. "Get it on the wing you fucking dumb ass. If I don't see it within an hour, I'll be leaving my calling card all over your fucking face. You get me?"

Jones turned to leave as quickly as he could. "Yes Skidz, no problems."

Mohamed stood and brushed past him, heading to the office where the security information on him had not yet spread. "Can I have a couple of razors please? I need to shave my beard off and one will not do it."

The young female officer pulled the cupboard drawer open and handed him two. "When you have finished bring them back to be changed."

He noticed that she hadn't bothered to write anything down and couldn't believe his luck. Two hours on the wing and he had his weapon of choice with a double razor to slash flesh open and a large carving knife to finish the job.

He went back to his cell and got to work melting the blades into a plastic tooth brush handle, hardly believing how easily this mission was falling into place. In a week's time Luke Woods would be lying dead in a pool of blood on the education floor and the bastard Governor who had ensured that Mohamed's brother received a life sentence would be wearing a Skidz mark for the rest of her life.

Bigger sat in his cell in Larkfield prison. Rat Boy had just scurried off to score some more drugs from the Manchester gang so while he was alone he scribbled a note out to a friend of his from Huntercombe. He didn't agree with what was happening, Luke was a decent person who was caught up in a world that he didn't understand. If he had chosen to, Bigger would have had him running drugs all over the prison but he chose not to. Rat Boy was a career criminal who didn't care about consequences and he could take the fall. Also, Bigger knew that Rat Boy was the real grass. He had allowed him to live until the gang connections in Larkfield could be established, then he would sell Rat Boy down the river. He was the only reason why Bigger was sitting in this hell hole looking at another fifteen years for conspiracy to murder. Rat Boy was facing a full life sentence and was way too stupid to realise that he had been rumbled.

He sealed the letter and addressed it to Blue, his long time general from his old gang. He was the only person left at Huntercombe who Bigger could trust to do a job, and now he was going to have to work overtime.

Luke swept the education building floor thinking about what Rat Boy had written to him. He had received some information from the prisoners on Howard that a new kid had arrived on the wing. His name was Mohamed and apparently he didn't talk to prisoners or staff and only came out of his cell to eat and play some pool in the evening. He was refusing to work cleaning the wing and was already becoming unpopular with staff and other prisoners. What Luke didn't know was that an officer was working on a plan.

An older officer on Howard, named Vince Neil, called in the rest of the cleaners. In total there was a team of five prisoners assigned to keep the wing clean and he took them into an empty classroom on the unit.

"Listen lads, I don't trust that new fucker who has just come onto the wing. He's giving it a lot of attitude to everyone and it could make life a bit tough for you all if he's allowed to continue throwing his weight about. Do you know what I mean?"

A muscular Indian prisoner standing at over six feet asked, "do we get a bonus if he wants to go back to Brixton?"

Vince put his thumbs in the air. "Yep, nice bonus for you all if that happens. Nothing too drastic though boys, I don't want him dead."

The big guy laughed. "I will take care of this myself, he might wish that he were dead after I finish with him."

Vince clapped his hands. "Okay boys, back to work. We have an hour to get this place clean - I've left a few cell doors open so that they can clean their own cells if you know what I mean."

Mohamed brushed his floor and looked down the empty landing. He'd been in the system too long not to be suspicious. Why would they leave his door open when the staff had already made it clear that they didn't trust him? Listening intently as the clicking and sweeping noises of a brush cleaning the stairs approached his landing, he knew that whatever was planned would happen now.

Looking down the landing again he spotted Ansh, the

Indian, cleaning. He seemed an imposing figure standing looking at Mohamed as he brushed the imaginary piles of dust. Mohamed retreated back into his cell opening his drawer and placing his toothbrush handle in the palm of his hand, waiting for the burst of action that would come in the next thirty seconds. He stood at the rear of the cell, his back against the wall ready to defend himself as a shadow appeared before the massive frame of Ansh filled the entrance to his cell.

"Mohamed, you better fuck off this wing by lunchtime. If you don't go down to the block by then, I will break you up."

This wasn't the first time he had faced these threats over the past few months and he stood his ground, feeling the plastic handle hidden in his palm.

"Well you better come in here and fuck me up then because I'm not going anywhere until I finish what I came here for."

Ansh sprang forwards, his athleticism almost catching Mohamed off guard before he twisted and threw Ansh onto the bed, pulling out the double razor and pressing it firmly against his eye. "If you want to be blind for the rest of your life carry on struggling, otherwise fuck off back down to your cleaning party, and tell your little screw friend that if he tries to have me hurt again, I will come and find him when I am released and sew his lips together with fishing line before I let him watch me rape and kill his wife and family. What do you say?"

Sweat poured down Ansh's forehead as he mumbled, "No problems with me, sorry man."

Mohamed stood, letting his attacker get up from the bed before drawing the blade across the back of his neck. A trickle of blood ran down the back of his blue t-shirt and he winced, holding his hand to the cut before looking back at Mohamed. "Okay man, I said no problems, you didn't need to cut me."

Mohamed just smiled. "Go wash yourself little boy, fuck with me and I will take your life," he said before tossing the blade back into his drawer.

Ansh walked back past the wing office where Vince, seeing the blood splattered down his back, rushed out and took him into an empty office. "What the fuck happened? You said that you could deal with it."

Ansh shrugged his shoulders. "Fuck that man, I'm not going back in against him, he's a fucking crazy guy."

Blue stacked the weights up in the gymnasium where he had recently been given the job as the orderly. He didn't mind the cleaning side of things but he absolutely loved working out on the weights, his powerful frame capable of bench pressing one hundred and eighty kilos. No one in the prison could keep up with his strength.

He leant against the white wall in the gym corridor watching the prisoners from Howard walk into the changing area and heard the officer standing at the gate with the clip board say the name, Mohamed. Blue watched him as he sauntered through without a care in the world. He needed to assess his enemy, Blue had spent too long in different institutions to underestimate anyone.

The prisoners broke into small groups to train on the equipment. Mohamed stayed by himself and lay on the multi gym bench and pushed some medium sized weights with ease before increasing the weight to something more challenging. Blue was impressed with what he was doing; he was a slim, light person but was still lifting way above his body weight. Eventually, sensing he was being watched, Skidz approached Blue and held out his hand. "I'm Mohamed. I'm here for a month and I need some help, I can pay you."

Blue nodded. "What do you want?"

Mohamed looked at him for a second, assessing if he was worth the risk.

"I'm looking for a person named Luke Woods, what wing is he on?"

Blue didn't answer the question. "You said that you are paying for my help. I don't see anything coming to me."

Mohamed looked frustrated. "I will get fifty paid into your account from outside. A letter will arrive next week with a postal order. What wing is he on?"

Blue answered, "Patterson Unit, he comes up here on Friday afternoons for physio work on his leg and some weights. Why do you want him?"

"Because we were friends from a long time back, I wanted to surprise him."

"Bullshit!" Blue had heard too many stories. "You're going to shank him, I can tell man, don't lie to me."

Mohamed spoke softly so he couldn't be overheard.

"He's an informer and I'm putting his grassing arse in a box. Can you help me?"

Blue grabbed him by the shirt and pushed him backwards into the wall. "No I'm not helping you, but I'm telling you, if you touch my friend, I will take care of you. Now fuck off out of my space."

Mohamed turned and walked back into the showers cursing under his breath. He had lost the element of surprise and would need to act quickly or lose his chance.

The gate to Howard opened and the officer shouted out to the staff inside. "Twenty back on from the gym." Mohamed at the front of the line spotted Jones, and as he passed him on the way to his cell whispered, "Go get me the shank, I need it now."

Hurrying in to his cell, he grabbed the hidden razor blades. Jones returned a minute later, the knife hidden inside a pillow case. Mohamed snatched it, telling him, "Good, now fuck off and say nothing,"

He dressed quickly and concealed the weapons before heading back to the gate. A young officer was standing there, counting prisoners from the education classes back in and he saw his chance.

"Miss, I've left my stuff in Education, can you just run me over there? I have a watch in my bag, it belonged to my mum. Please Miss."

She looked around seeing the Howard staff were tied up with other things.

"Come on then, we need to be quick," she said and opening

the gate, they headed over to the education block.

CHAPTER THIRTY

Jake sat watching the morning news on TV before taking the short twenty minute drive into training. His days seemed to have become more active since the arrival of Sammy as his agent and he was constantly needing to check the diary that the agency sent him each morning. Every hour during the day seemed to be accounted for this week despite his request to be able to take time to visit his mum.

He scanned through the agenda for that day; nine until two thirty was booked for training and lunch and at three thirty, he had an interview with BT Sports at The London Golf Course followed by a golf lesson from the new British Open champion, Tom Vine. He was going to use a new virtual simulator which BT Sports and the golf club were in partnership promoting.

His bank balance was building at an accelerated rate, however he hadn't seen his girlfriend Kim or his parents for nearly two weeks. Jake phoned Sammy's PA.

"Can we cut down on the work for next week please? I need some family time. My mum's not well and I need to see her."

The phone went silent for a second before Sammy took over the call. "We can scale it down Jake, but I had some exciting things mapped out for you to do. Only small details but for instance the owner of Real Madrid wanted to entertain you and your lady friend on his luxury yacht out in Dubai next weekend during the international break. Shall I cancel that one?"

Jake stopped eating his toast "Is that for real or are you joking?"

Sammy's voice didn't change. "No, it's booked along with two days reserved in Monaco as a guest of Ricky Turner, the Formula One world champion. He wants you to have a kick about with his son and he's offering you half a million dollars to give him a lesson and a game of one on one. Shall I cancel?"

Jake laughed. "No, I think that we can fit them in at a push."

"I thought that you might say that. Phone your girlfriend and tell her that a private car will be picking her up at two thirty on Friday afternoon. We have checked her rota and she's free. Remember your passports, sun cream and massively growing address book. I told you that life with me would be more impressive." Jake could hear Sammy flicking pages.

"Take the week off at the start of next month Jake, I haven't booked anything for you then so you can see your mum for a couple of days."

Jake drove along the busy roads towards the training ground and phoned Kim before she started her shift at the hospital. "Hey, I have a couple of good events happening over the weekend, are you free?"

She sounded a bit sleepy after a busy evening shift the night before. "Sure, what do you have planned? I was hoping that we could spend a couple of days relaxing."

"Oh, I have a couple of things….how about on Friday night we visit a billionaire on his own boat in Dubai followed by Saturday and Sunday in Monaco at the luxury home of Ricky Turner, the best Formula One driver of all time? Not only that, he's paying me half a million dollars to play football with his son. All travel is on a private jet and everything is already paid for."

Kim remained silent for a second. "I would rather us book into a nice little hotel in the forest somewhere, just you and me. All this travel stuff just seems like business to me and I don't think that it's my sort of thing Jake, sorry."

Perplexed he pulled into the training ground and switched off his engine.

"Are you being serious? Most people would jump at the chance of this type of lifestyle."

She sighed. "But I'm not most people Jake, money doesn't impress me at all. I'm a nurse, I see rich people and poor people all dying of the same illness - cancer. Flying around the world on our weekend off just seems tiring to me."

Jake exhaled; this hadn't been the reaction he had expected at all. "Look, this is just part of my life, it's what we do. I'm going with or without you Kim, this time next year I could be living in Spain. I suppose that you wouldn't want that to happen either?"

She laughed. "To be honest, no. I love my job, and I like living with my sister. Why would I want to go to Spain and sit by myself while you play football and visit rich friends?" Her voice raised a little. "I know that your life is planned by an agency, every bloody minute of the day, and that's not for me. You're changing Jake, since that bloody Sammy Totti came into your life, everything else has taken a back seat." She paused for a few seconds then continued sadly. "Let's give it a break for a while. I don't have time for this at the moment, it's too complicated."

He could feel his temper starting to boil. All the things that he was offering her, she was throwing back in his face.

"Have it your own way. If you're sure about a break, I'm okay with that. Have a great life." He ended the call without waiting for a reply and took his bag into the changing room, confused about why Kim was not impressed with the chance of a fabulous new life. His phone rang again and this time it was Mum calling.

"Jake, I thought that I would phone early as I'm having treatment all day so I may not feel like talking later on. Can I see you this weekend?"

Already annoyed by his former girlfriend he didn't think before answering. "No Mum, I'm busy this weekend but maybe next month, I'm trying to take some time off from my schedule."

Her silence was more difficult than any answer and feeling a bit guilty he continued. "Sorry Mum, life is so busy. I've asked my agent to give me some time off so I will come and see you, I promise."

Her clipped tone made it clear what her thoughts were. "Maybe ask your agent if he can book me in, perhaps between two and two thirty one day. Just remember that I may not be around forever, I have cancer Jake, not a cold."

"I know Mum, Look, I have to go, I'm late already, I'll phone you tonight."

She sat in her lounge all alone, tears running down her face as her chest heaved with a continuous sobbing. She had lost one son to prison, and the other was quickly vanishing into celebrity status. Des was out, driving in London; he was a good man but he needed to earn extra money while she was unable to work. What she really needed today were her boys, just to hug for a second, but they weren't there and she felt betrayed. A horn peeped outside of the house; Des had arranged a friend to drive Kim to the hospital until he was able to join her.

She sat in the back seat, a feeling of total exhaustion sweeping over her even before the start of the latest batch of treatment. The driver, knowing all too well that Kim just wanted some peace, left her alone to rest and set off along the A4.

Dozing off, her thoughts kept jumping back to Jake - he wasn't the same boy who had left home for Spurs a few months earlier. He seemed cold and distant whenever they spoke on the phone and both Des and Kim had long since stopped going to the games. He never seemed to have time to talk to them afterwards and was always giving interviews or planning to go elsewhere with new friends. Sadness hit her again as she thanked the driver and made her way towards the ward. Kim was waiting for her, the usual smile missing from her young face.

They had their customary greeting but neither of them seemed energised, making some small conversation as the first bag of treatment made its way down the clear tube. "How is my boy treating you Kim, nice hopefully?" Jake's mum asked.

Kim turned her nose up slightly at the question. "We're not together anymore, we called it a day this morning. I think that his life style doesn't fit in with mine and we're both far too busy to give each other time." She paused for a second, "Well actually he is far too busy, I think. It's a shame but for the better I guess."

His mum sighed deeply. "I don't know what has happened to that son of mine, but he better snap out of it." She closed her eyes and let the drug flow into her body, speaking softly as the bag began to empty. "He is heading for a fall, and all of his friends at the moment are not real friends. I hoped that he would settle down a bit after he met you but it just seems that this agent and people around him have made everything twice as bad."

CHAPTER THIRTY-ONE

Luke sat in his late afternoon class, the teacher running through some revision notes needed for an upcoming test. A scurry of feet outside the classroom made him take note; he had just cleaned and polished the floor and some idiot was running up and down it.

A distant alarm bell sounded and the crackle from one of the staff's radios emitted a warning. "Urgent message, armed prisoner has just assaulted an officer and is loose in the education centre."

Knowing what was coming, Luke tried to rush towards the door to block it, as his teacher tried to get out of the room and to safety. She had placed one foot outside the room before a hand struck out at her and she fell to the floor with blood dripping from the top of her arm. Mohamed stepped over her and into the classroom.

"Sit," he shouted at Luke before pulling a filing cabinet in front of the door. "I take it that you are Luke Woods?" Producing a large carving knife from the rear of his jeans he walked over and looked at the name written on the blue band around Luke's arm.

"Yeah, you're Luke Woods. Do you know why I'm here?"

Luke nodded. "Because someone has told you a bullshit lie about me."

Mohamed shook his head. "No, no lies, my friend doesn't deal in lies. People call me Skidz and I kind of like the reputation. You grassed my boy Musa and he's looking at life because of you. He doesn't like you at all."

A voice came through the door, it was a hostage negotiator.

"Mohamed, my name is Paul Tucker, do you want to talk?"

Skidz ignored him, still talking to Luke. "My friend wants

you dead, I want you dead and the guy outside wants us both alive. Someone is going to be disappointed today."

Through the classroom window Luke could see the remaining prisoners from the education building rushing past, heading for safety. He wished that he was one of them as the negotiator continued to try to make dialog.

He turned back to Mohamed. "Look Skidz, I didn't grass anyone, I think it was the bent screw who gave them all up. I was in the frame as well, Musa had me bringing stuff onto the wing for him. She tried to get me arrested too but I was lucky."

Skidz waved the knife in Luke's direction. "Musa said that you were smart, he told me that you would try talk your way out of it."

A scream went up from outside the door, the negotiator shouting at the top of his voice. Both Luke and Skidz looked up in amazement as a huge figure dived head first through the glass of the window. Blue stood up and brushed the glass from his short hair. "Now you have a fucking problem, I told you not to fuck with my boy."

Pulling a bar from the back of his tracksuit bottoms, he moved towards Mohamed, who now held the large knife towards Blue. It was clearly going to be a fight to the death.

Luke stood un-noticed as the two prisoners faced off. Picking up the heavy, grey, metal chair which he had been sitting on, Luke smashed it down onto the back of Mohamed's head, sending him crashing face first onto the floor. Blue jumped forwards and kicked the knife away while stamping hard on Musa's face.

Looking up at Luke, Blue smiled. "We make a good team Luke, I thought for a moment that we were both going to get sliced up." Using one powerful arm he pulled the heavy cabinet to one side, pushing Luke through the open door and into the plastic shields of a team of waiting officers.

"You can thank Bigger when you see him again, he just saved your ass. Now I have to finish this fucker off before he comes back for me." He kicked the door closed and picked the knife up, grabbing Mohamed in a rear choke hold as he regained some consciousness. Blood dripped down the Somalian's forehead where a large gash gaping open on the top of his head oozed blood over the visible white bone of his skull but he showed no fear as the sharp blade was held against his exposed throat. "So what are you going to do gym boy? If you don't kill me, I'm coming back to kill you, it's only a matter of time before me and Musa fuck up your black ass."

Blue thought for a second. "That might be true, but I'm out of here in a few months and you're now in here forever." He dragged Mohamed to his feet as though he weighed nothing and pulled him towards the door. Unlocking it and pushing him through, he hoped that the staff would deal with the rest.

Mohamed stood in front of the team and before any of them could react, pulled his razor blades from his sock and sliced his own neck in a vicious cutting motion. His carotid artery erupted in a fountain of foaming blood and spinning, he faced Blue and smiled before falling into a pool of his own pumping blood, each spurt becoming less powerful as he bled out in front of the stationary team.

Blue looked at the stunned staff as he walked towards the door with his hands on his head, the negotiator standing in shock, staring at the carnage lying before him. Blue's face remained unaltered as he looked down at the dead body before adding with comic timing, "I bet that you didn't expect this when you ate your porridge this morning."

Luke sat in the Heath Care Unit with Blue, no other prisoners present. Both started to laugh with the release of stress from their ordeal as the staff watched on. "Blue, when you came flying head first through the window, did you have a plan?"

Blue picked some more glass from his bleeding ear. "No man, course not. Bigger just asked me to look after you so that's what I did. The screws were just about to lock the outside door as I walked past and I knew that he was going to slice you up so I thought, fuck it, what's the worst thing that could happen? I didn't like him anyway."

A tall woman in a suit came into the waiting area. "Luke?"

He stood up. "Yes Miss?"

"Your parents are here, we had a duty to tell them about what happened. The visits room is empty for you to use."

Blue looked a little deflated before she continued. "And the Governor has just agreed to your request for a weekend at home, Danny."

Luke looked up. "Who's Danny?"

Blue answered quickly. "It's me you idiot, and if you tell anyone, you will wish that our friend back there had finished you off. Can I phone my mum to tell her?"

She nodded. I have already made the arrangements. I'm sure that she would love to hear from her little boy.

Luke was sure that Blue's massive biceps flexed in anger for a second before he burst out laughing. "Miss, you are a joker! Thanks, I won't let you down."

CHAPTER THIRTY-TWO

Jake's plane touched down again at Luton airport; he was exhausted from a weekend partying on the boat of Ralph Hyatt, the President of Real Madrid and from spending hours in the night clubs of Monaco. He looked at his watch, it was 06:35 on a rainy Monday morning and training was due to start at nine thirty. It was the last thing he felt like doing as an equally tired official checked through his passport documents.

Sammy had enjoyed his weekend just as much and had taken enough cocaine on the boat to keep him awake for days. Jake hated these excesses but it seemed as though he was the only one not indulging. However he had no such problem with the girls wandering around on the deck, one of whom had kept him occupied all night. His football status and muscular athletic body ensured that he'd had more sex in the past twenty four hours than during the whole previous two months. Sammy tapped him on the back as the two of them prepared to go their separate ways, him back to bed for a few hours and Jake to get his training kit on and run around in the rain.

"So Jake, this weekend you have seen what money can really get you. If you want the deal with Real Madrid it's there with twenty five million pounds on offer. That sort of money puts you into their league within a year and you will earn more cash in a season than half of the Spurs squad will see in a lifetime. Think about it, playing under Carlos in that magnificent stadium where you will be a hero in the city. Talk it over with your parents, we have a meeting on Wednesday with your new sponsor and we can discuss it more then."

Two private cars pulled up. "You could have just earned financial stability for your family for the rest of their lives Jake, see you on Wednesday."

Jake sat in the back of the warm car, fatigue finally kicking in as he headed home to take a shower and collect his training kit. He knew what he was going to do, it was a no brainer. Earn as much money as he could, invest sensibly and play great football in the sunshine of Spain. Whatever he had left he would share amongst the family, but just for once he would think about himself first, just as Sammy advised him to do. Carlos stood in the car park at the training ground, waiting for Jake to arrive.

"I spoke to Sammy this morning, it sounds as though you have had a good weekend," he greeted him. "Just have some massage this morning, if you train when you are tired you will hurt yourself." He followed Jake into the building. "I think that my story is going to come out this week so you may have some questions thrown at you. Remember that you don't know anything; if a reporter asks why you were on the boat this weekend just say that it was a trip with the new sponsor. The club will not believe you and offer you a new contract to stay here but don't sign. There is far more on offer in Spain. If the masseuse asks questions don't tell them anything, the club use them to get information"

Jake nodded although this was starting to feel outside of his comfort zone.

"Sure, just give me a second, I need to give my mum a ring."

Kim lay in bed still feeling the effects of Friday's chemotherapy session. Des had taken a day off and brought a cup of herbal tea up to her as the phone rang.

"Hi Jake, this is a nice surprise," she said, pleased he could spare her a few minutes in his life.

"Sorry about last week Mum, this whole thing is just running out of control. I need to chat with you and Dad." She pushed the button to ensure Des could hear them speak.

"Dad's here, what's wrong?"

Jake had got back in his car to ensure that they weren't overheard. "Another team want to sign me for next season, they're a bigger club."

"Who wants you Jake?" Des asked. "It would have to be a big offer for Spurs to sell you. Who is it? Liverpool? United?"

Jake paused a second before answering. "No, neither Dad, it's Real Madrid. They have offered twenty five million for me, that's why I was away this weekend. I had a meeting with the owners and club president. What do you think?"

They both answered together, the message in strong unison. "Take it Jake!"

"You only get these chances once in life, go and enjoy the country and the football," Des added.

"My treatment is going well, so as long as you keep in contact with us and visit from time to time you will have our blessing," his mum said. "I guess that this is still a secret?"

Jake sighed a long breath of relief. "You could say that, just keep an eye on the sports news this week when things will start to become clear."

The road leading out of the training ground was blocked with reporters by the time the players began to leave. Jake was ready for some sleep but the bustle around Carlos's car told him that the cat was out of the bag.

A message flashed up on his phone. "Tune into Sports Talk, the boss is getting smashed."

Pressing the button, he heard the familiar sound of Carlos denying all rumours of leaving the club and he sounded so convincing that Jake wondered if it was true.

Another message pinged onto the screen. "Are you going with him?"

Jake ignored the question, why would anyone put two and two together like that? Security finally gained control of the area as the players drifted away and Jake drove home before slipping into bed and catching up with sleep after a weekend of clubbing.

The harsh tone of an incoming call brought him back around to his senses and he sleepily answered. "Hey Sammy, sorry I was just getting some sleep."

"No time for that Jake, have you seen the news?"

"I saw the reporters grilling him at the gate."

"Yep, but that's not all, the press know about the offer from Real Madrid. Spurs are going to make a statement this afternoon confirming an offer of twenty five million has been made. What a surprise! Expect the Spurs chairman to call you today, he will need details before he can address the press. He will want to tie you down with a bigger contract which is just what I anticipated."

Jake yawned. "But I turn that offer down? Carlos told me not to sign."

There was a silence for a few seconds. "It's a bit of a game that we are playing Jake, Spurs hear that you and Carlos are going and they double your contract and you both stay at Spurs."

Jake was confused. "What the fuck are you talking about? All this stuff from the weekend has just been a game to get more money from the club, none of it was real?"

Sammy laughed. "Welcome to the dark side of football, you have just doubled your salary at Spurs."

Jake cut him off. "I am going to Real Madrid Sammy, if you and Carlos were using me as part of a game it has backfired. I'm going to Spain with or without Carlos."

"No Jake, we were never going to actually go," Sammy stuttered. "Think of your family, how about if I guarantee you that your parent's house will be paid for by the club?"

Jake was becoming increasingly angry. "You have used me in a fucking game Sammy, what about the trust?"

Sammy started backtracking fast. "Look, it's not my fault that Carlos didn't keep you in the picture, it happens all the time in our game. All of the big transfer rumours that you hear, why do you think that they are leaked? More money, Jake, it's all about the money. That's why I'm looking after the biggest names, because I get the biggest deals. If you thought that it was all bullshit at the weekend, do you think that you could still have behaved normally? You would have given the game away in seconds. Real will still come calling next season, I'll just explain why the deal couldn't go through. The club refused to release you, your mum's health, any fucking reason Jake."

Jake's phone indicated that another call was waiting and seeing it was the Spurs Chairman, Daniel Jackson, he ended his call with Sammy.

"Jake, would you kindly let me know what's happening?" the Chairman's voice boomed in his ear. "I have the world's press sitting on my doorstep telling me that you are a Real Madrid player. Can I just remind you that you are contracted to this football club?"

Jake felt out of his depth, this should have been Sammy's job.

"I haven't agreed to go anywhere Mr Jackson, I've been told that an offer of twenty five million was made and in my contract it says that if anyone offers this amount it triggers a clause. But as I just said, I haven't signed to go anywhere."
Jake could tell that Daniel was considering something.

"This bloody agent of yours, Jake, is bad news. What do you want, double money? Is that what it's going to take to make you stay? Carlos has just had a similar conversation with me and he wants you to stay at the club."

Jake took a deep breath. "I'll stay for one more season, Mr Jackson. I will sign a new contract with a bigger release clause, however if Real still want me at the end of next season you must promise me that I can leave."

"You have my word Jake, just win us some bloody cups. If I'm doubling your money, the least that you can do is win me a trophy. I will send another contract to your shark of an agent."

CHAPTER THIRTY-THREE

Luke looked at the calendar on his cell wall, not believing that another year had past so quickly. He'd had very little contact with Jake since the argument over the signed shirt, only messages passed through Des and Kim. It had been a good year since the Skidz incident, his mum was in remission and had returned to work full time, his dad had given up the driving job in London and had recently received a job driving for Reading buses where the money was regular
and he was able to fit his shifts around Kim's three monthly hospital appointments.

He was checking through his course work when a knock on his cell door distracted his attention and one of the more junior wing managers, Gary Elkins, stood looking in.

"Morning Luke, I've had an idea that I've been discussing with the Governor. I was wondering if you were still interested in football? I run an under nine boys' football team in the local town - my youngest son plays for them - and we're going to be training in the prison gym and on the Astroturf this winter. Would you be interested in helping me coach them?"

He didn't need to be asked twice. "Oh my God, Mr Elkins, that would be terrific! When do you come in?"
Gary laughed, he had hoped for this reaction. "Every Wednesday evening, seven till eight. We play on Sunday mornings in the Reading league and have some excellent players in our squad. I'll have a chat with them during the week while you have a think about some of the things you did with the Reading academy and write down some routines. I think that between us we can put on some good sessions."

The course work was quickly put to one side as Luke began to recollect things from a previous footballing life. He briefly considering calling Jake for ideas from Spurs training sessions before dismissing the idea, they had not spoken for over a year, the letters had dried up and it seemed that the bond between them had been destroyed irreparably. Even their parents couldn't persuade Jake to put things right after the harsh words had been said.

A short time later, Gary returned to the cell to tell him the Governor was waiting to see him in the wing office. He followed the officer along the landing and entered the office to see Sue Bridges sitting behind the desk, her tight, frizzy, grey hair and glasses which perched on her nose and moved up and down as she spoke reminding Luke of his old head teacher. Her broad northern accent rung out clearly across the small office.

"Now then Luke, Mr Elkins here has put a lot of work into you helping out with the football sessions so don't let him down, Chuck." Luke shook his head; he knew that something else was coming so kept his mouth shut.

"The Prison Service Managers at our HQ are a bit worried about letting this happen but I have promised that you will not screw up. If you mess up it will make things difficult for every other lad serving a long sentence to do anything different. I don't mind taking a risk, Chuck, but please act responsibly. There's a chance - and it is only a slim chance - that I will allow you to go out and watch a game one Sunday morning. Your parents will be allowed to come as well, so be good and make me proud."

A feeling swept over Luke as for the first time in three years a chink of light was revealing itself to him. Someone was willing to trust him again, and for that one little second he became a person again and not a prisoner. He cried as he stood up and shook her hand, feeling embarrassed because he hadn't had these emotions for a long time. He wiped his eyes on his sleeve. "Sorry Miss, I'm just so happy to be given this chance."

Sue had seen it all before but it still always moved her.

"Just do a good job Chuck and before you know it, you will be going home." She stood and left, leaving Luke and Gary Elkins looking at each other.

"So there you have it Luke, if you didn't have a big enough target to aim for already, this one will prove to be your first steps to freedom. There is one other thing that I haven't mentioned yet."

Luke looked at him quizzically. "What's that Mr Elkins?"

"You're going to have to put those English qualifications to good use as I want you to write a news report for the team every week. I'm going to be filming each game and you will need to watch it and write a full match report. Are you ok with that?"

Luke nodded his agreement. "So long as the Education Staff let me use a lap top that can show films, the one I have in my cell is only for course work."

Gary smiled. "Already sorted Luke, you'll see the first game on it tomorrow where we won five-two. I'll give you a list of the squad players and their shirt numbers, you work out the rest."

As moments go in a young man's life this may have not have been a seismic moment, but to a former professional footballer convicted of murder and who had been written off by the rest of the world, it was enormous. "I won't let anyone down Mr Elkins. I've already worked out a few training drills for Wednesday and I can't wait to get started."

Wednesday evening came along and Luke was in the gym placing out sets of cones for skills training. Gary had agreed that he could run the warm up this evening but Gary himself would take the session while Luke got to know the boys. The door to the main gym opened and twenty two young boys came in and stood on the white line, chatting amongst themselves while Gary prepared the blue and red bibs. Not one boy tried to kick one of the ten balls that sat on the gym floor and Luke was impressed with the discipline.

Gary handed out the bibs and stood in front of the line up. "Ok boys, great result at the weekend, top of the table by five points and looking good, let's keep the run going. I have asked one of my friends to help out on Wednesday nights; he was with Reading Football club until he broke his leg. His name is Luke and he is going to put you through a good warm up before we start. Luke and I have decided to up the quality of our training sessions and believe it or not, these training sessions over the winter are the same ones used in professional football clubs. Luke's brother plays for Tottenham, you might know him, his name is Jake Woods."

Twenty two smiling faces looked back at Luke and he knew he had the credibility with the group to make them do anything he wanted and his own confidence grew. This was the first time that he had ever given any instructions to anyone and he opened his mouth and every player obeyed his commands.

The hour passed quickly and Luke saw that two or three of the young players had enough ability to play at a higher level. He spoke with Gary as they watched them put an attacking manoeuvre in to practice. "Those three in the blue bibs are decent players, Mr Elkins."

"You can call me Gary in here Luke, this is training not prison. Yep, they are special and the dark haired lad is mine. Palace and West Ham have shown an interest in taking him on trial but he isn't interested at the moment."

Luke looked surprised. "Why not? I thought it was every kid's dream."

Gary laughed. "I was premier league for ten years, playing for Fulham, Wimbledon and finishing my career at Swindon Town. There's plenty of time for the boys to enjoy playing before they get eaten up by the academies. How many players did you see not make it Luke?"

Luke nodded in understanding. "Almost everyone except me and Jake I guess."

"There you go, they deserve to enjoy kid's football before it all gets too serious. How about you pack up the kit while I take the boys out the gate, the parents should be back in the car park by now. Did you enjoy the session?"

Giving a corny thumbs up, Luke beamed. "I loved it, for an

hour I felt I wasn't in prison. Will the boys ever know that I'm in here?"

Gary shrugged his shoulders. "That's up to you Luke, maybe when you feel the time is right you can tell them although, knowing these boys, they will have sussed it out already when you don't follow us out."

Gary's life had taken its own complicated path, a hard working boy from a solid hard working family, his talent had been spotted at an early age when he was picked up by Fulham before going out on loan to Exeter City. A badly broken leg had nearly signalled the end of his career before it had truly begun, and when he fully recovered another London football team, Brentford, showed an interest in signing him. Fulham reluctantly agreed to the sale, not thinking for one moment that bigger and better things were waiting just around the corner.

The manager of Wimbledon had previously cast an eye over Gary and snapped him up into the premier league for a cut price fee, where he thrived for a number of years before age began to creep up on him. One last move to Swindon Town who were chasing promotion beckoned and Gary moved west to quickly win over the fans with his solid defending and deadly accurate passing.

He finally ended his career to begin his new venture in the Prison Service after having a conversation with a friend who worked in the local prison.

His true passion though, was training young boys and girls in the skills of playing football and he became a well known figure in the town. His spring and summer football schools were always fully booked with a bevy of excited children from the ages of four to sixteen, thus his involvement with the local children's football team became cemented.

Luke continued to tidy up the equipment as Gary came back into the gym.

"I think that tonight went really well, Luke. The kids like you and have already worked out why you didn't come out with us.

I have spoken to them and also their parent's and everyone is okay with our arrangements. How is the match report going from last weekend?"

Luke bent down to his bag and took out a few pages of A4 paper. "This is the style of writing that I was thinking about, Gary, what do you think?"

Gary read it in silence, the buzz of the overhead fluorescent lights suddenly loud as Luke waited in anticipation, hoping he'd like it. Finally, he looked up.

"Bloody brilliant, mate! This will be in the paper next week - keep up this quality and we are all doing well."

He flicked off the lights in the large gymnasium hall as he took Luke into the secure corridor and back to Patterson. "How long do you have left on your sentence Luke?" he asked as they walked.

Luke thought for a moment. "Around four and a half more years if I get parole. The Governor is going to let me stay here for maybe one more year before I need to move on." They reached the barred gate to Patterson Unit.

"One year? We can do a lot of work in a year Luke, the time will whizz past." The door opened and the reality of being back in jail hit him.

"I hope so Mr Elkins. Do you think that you can take over as my personal officer? Miss Nevis is good, but if I am going to be helping you, maybe it will make sense for the parole reports to be written by you."

Gary thought for a second. "It would be a good idea, but let's just keep things separate. I will give Miss Nevis a report on our work so she knows how well you're doing. Let's not get the football and prison stuff mixed up as plenty of staff in the prison do not want you helping out at all. Let's not give them an excuse that I'm doing you favours by becoming your personal officer. Anyway, Miss Nevis is better than me at writing parole reports. Remember I was a footballer, she was a university graduate." He looked through to the wing office and gestured to Luke to tell them that he was back on the wing.

"See you tomorrow." The gate clanged shut and he was gone.

Luke thought for a second before speaking to the Wing Officer. "Can I make a quick phone call before I go back to my cell?"

He stood by the phone on the wall and dialled Jake's number. The phone seemed to ring for ever until it was finally picked up.

"Hi Luke, it's been a long time since you rang. What can I do for you?" His voice sounded very matter of fact as he spoke.

"Nothing Jake, I just thought that we should have a chat as it's been a year since we spoke."

Jake didn't respond immediately, leaving a few seconds before giving his reply.

"Yes, I remember what you said to me when I couldn't get you a signed shirt."

The conversation wasn't going as Luke had planned, further emphasised by Jake's next words.

"Just remember that I'm the super star arsehole brother and Karma is coming to get me. I think that they were the words you used Luke. Have you phoned to apologise?"

Luke shuffled on the spot as the barbed words dug into his flesh. "Yeah, I'm sorry Jake, I was under a load of pressure with prison and Mum's illness. Can we just put it behind us?"

Jake answered instantly this time. "I can but I'm not sure that you are capable Luke. Look, I have put some money in an account for you. When you come out it will be enough to buy a little place to live. I have also paid off Mum and Dad's mortgage so I'm doing my little bit out here to keep things going, but as things stand, I can't afford to be dragged away from football and into your prison issues. I have to go Luke, I have an interview with the BBC but I'll try to write a letter to you at some point when I have time."

Luke said goodbye but knew that the line was already dead.

CHAPTER THIRTY-FOUR

The bright floodlights of White Hart Lane shone down onto the glistening pitch as Jake ran out to screams from the home fans. The Arsenal fans at the other end exploded into abuse as the white shirts streamed onto the field, before turning things into a carnival as the red shirts joined them.

The North London Derby, one of the hottest fixtures in the entire calendar was about to kick off with Arsenal sitting in third place, three points behind the leaders, Spurs. A victory this evening would ensure that Arsenal would overtake their old enemy on goal difference with two games left to play, an unthinkable thing to happen in front of the home support.

Relationships had become increasingly strained between Jake and Carlos Conte over the contract agreements, Jake refusing to sign any further extension to ensure that Spurs could cash in with a bigger transfer fee before his proposed move to Real Madrid. It was becoming an open secret that talks were ongoing, but not one of the Spurs supporters thought that he would be allowed to move.

Carlos cut a lonely figure on the sideline as he watched his young star work his magic. He regretted using the marketability of Jake to try boost his own wage demands and ego. While Spurs pleaded with him to stay and keep Jake at the club he and Sammy sat in the background watching the pound signs going up. Never for one moment had he thought Jake would actually move to another club but now that nightmare was very real. Sammy had one job, to persuade Jake to stay in North London and abandon dreams of playing in Madrid but it was a mission that he was destined to fail in.

Jake was electric on the field all evening, the England manager watching him closely, admiring the vision of his passing and his ability to split open a defence with one pass, or his silky, unseen runs into the opposition penalty area where he would appear and cause panic and confusion amongst opposition defences.

With the score at nil-nil with less than a minute to go on the clock, Jake was fouled twenty five yards from the goal while making another run at the heart of the Arsenal defence. He grabbed the ball and held it under his right arm as he watched the Arsenal team muster the defensive wall, the goal keeper moving them one step to the left to prevent a shot into the top corner.

The weight of expectation from his own supporters came from all around him in a deafening crescendo of excitement and anticipation, a chance to finally get one over on their bitterest enemies, but in this moment of mayhem Jake only heard silence and the slow deep breaths coming from his chest.

The Arsenal fans facing him behind the goal hardly dared to watch. After the performance that they had just witnessed from Jake, they would have happily taken a draw. Placing the ball down he had a plan; in every film he had watched of the Arsenal team that week, the captain, Tony Jennings, jumped as soon as the ball was kicked. He was at least six feet four and managed to get his body in the way of more than half the free kicks, those that cleared his head sailing harmlessly over the bar.

The referee blew his whistle and Jake ran in to take the free kick. Jennings strained every muscle to jump high to stop the danger but Jake double bluffed him as his shot cut across the top of the turf, directly under the feet of the jumping captain. He looked down in horror as the ball shot under his right foot, but it was too late, the goal keeper not seeing the ball until the last second by which time it was in the back of the net.

Spurs were six points clear of Arsenal, and two ahead of Manchester United with two games to play as Jake stood in front of the stunned Arsenal fans and crossed his arms nodding as he was mobbed by his Spurs team mates. Plastic cups and bottles hurtled through the air towards him but he didn't care as he jogged past a prostate Jennings.

The final whistle sent three sides of the ground into unbridled joy, the red section long since drifting out and into the night heading under a close police escort towards the safety of the underground station. Jennings shook Jake's hand with a smile on his face. "You had me over Jake but that won't happen again. The sooner you piss off to Spain the better for me."

Jake laughed. "We may still have another season facing each other, Tony."

He looked back at Jake surprised. "Well, I'll tell you something Jake, a full England call up is coming old son. Brian Travers was watching the game tonight and if he doesn't select you after this season's performances, I will tell him that I don't want to play for England again. You are the future son so don't fuck it up if you move over to Spain."

Jake walked down the tunnel to a rapturous ovation from the celebrating fans. He thought about Luke and his apology for a brief second before a sky sports interviewer grabbed him to one side. "Jake Woods, you are the Sky Sports man of the match tonight. Another super performance as you led the line, and what a strike for the goal. You must be pleased with how your first full season is going? You could win the league in two weeks time."

Jake was used to these interviews by now and knew how to respond.

"One game at a time, Everton away will be a hard game. If we don't get a win, United could go top by a point so we have it all to do. Let's just focus on Everton."

The England Manager, Brian Travers, walked into shot, the reporter asking him to join Jake. "Brian, what else does Jake Wood need to do to get into your world cup squad?"

He looked displeased with being put on the spot but answered the question.

"Jake has had an exceptional season, but so have three or four other top level strikers. We will select the squad next week based on a number of factors, but Jake is in our thoughts. You will have to wait along with the rest of the nation for the final squad." He shook the reporter's hand. "Now I do need to go, we have our own business to attend to before the upcoming international games, and it's very unfair of you to take away this moment from Jake. The plaudits that he deserves for his performance tonight must be the focus of your interview. The England team will be announced soon, but Jake has to focus on Tottenham Hotspurs for the next two games. After that we will see how it goes. Good night Gentlemen." He turned and left the spotlight as Jake was presented with a bottle of Champagne, Jake wondering if his chances of playing for England had been hurt by that ambush interview.

The reporter concluded the piece to camera but Jake stayed once the live feed had ended and accosted him. "If you ever do that to me again it will be the last interview I hold with you. If questions need to be asked about me playing for my country, I will ask them in the correct way and in private. I will not have the England manager or anyone else embarrassed for the sake of your viewing figures. Do I make myself clear?"

The reporter nodded, knowing he was in the wrong. "Sorry Jake, I thought the public needed an answer."

Jake handed back the mike and walked away without another word. He had found his voice and his confidence, he was no one's fool anymore. He turned the corner towards the changing room and found Brian waiting for him.

"I listened to the rest of the interview with that idiot, it isn't the first time he has done that. Thanks for what you said off air, it means a lot and he had it coming. That's just what I'm looking for in my players for the world cup. Keep your phone on for next week, we will be having a chat and I think that you may be pleased." He turned and left without waiting for a reply, leaving Jake buzzing with the thought that he could be going to the world cup with the senior team and not just the under 21's.

CHAPTER THIRTY-FIVE

Jake sat in the changing room at Everton for a Wednesday evening game. Manchester United had lost 1.0 at home the evening before so all Spurs needed to do was to get a win tonight to be crowned champions. The entire left hand side of the ground had been sold out to Spurs fans, thousands making the trip hoping to see the trophy lifted.

For the past two weeks the race had been cut down to Man Utd and Spurs, the pundits favouring the Manchester team as on paper they had the easier of the last two matches. Last night, the hotel the Spurs team were staying in just outside Liverpool erupted as a last minute own goal sent United to their first home defeat of the season.

Jake felt some tension as the two teams ran out onto the pitch where the theme music from the 1960's Z Cars TV programme which was played on every Everton home game seemed to make the situation even more real for him.

Looking up into the stands, he caught sight of his parents, there for the first game they had watched for a few months, and waving up briefly, he stretched his muscles in front of a seething arena of fanaticism.

The whistle blew and Everton wearing the famous blue shirts poured forwards from the start, putting pressure on the Spurs defence with relentless attacks. Before twenty minutes had past they had scored a terrific goal, one of the Spurs defender's slipping, leaving the Everton striker to sprint fifty yards and unleash an unstoppable shot into the roof of the net. Three sides of the stadium erupted into a bubbling sea of smiling faces and bouncing bodies and Jake looked over to see a young girl sitting on her father's shoulders in the front row by the half way line, spinning her scarf around her head as she sang a song. Feeling the weight of momentum washing over him and the team, it was like the crowd had given Everton an extra player.

Carlos stood watching, unable to stop the tide of blue pressure from crushing his title dreams. And then in the forty-forth minute the unthinkable happened as Everton got their sixth corner. The ball crossed deep in the Spurs area before the man mountain of an old fashioned centre forward, Tommy Buxton, crashed through and headed the ball into the bottom corner making the score 2.0.

Music blasted around the stadium once more as the excitement levels rose to near hysteria. Everton were sitting outside the top seven and had only pride to play for but tonight it seemed that this pride would win.

Directly from the kick off Jake received the ball thirty yards from goal just as a defender crashed into the back of him. Jake immediately felt his ankle ligaments scream with pain and collapsing in agony, he lay motionless. For a second he thought that he had broken the bone until the team medic assessed him.

"That's you done Jake, you've ripped the ligaments. Sorry mate, that's your season over."

The words hit him hard, 'Season over,' and he suddenly felt very vulnerable lying in pain in the full glare of the world's media. The pain was constant and crippling and a mask was pulled over his mouth as the team doctor told him to breathe in the gas. Sucking it in, he felt a little light headed as the initial sharp stabbing pain died down to a long, constant ache. There was a blur of motion around him as he lay there, and the crowd, realising the significance of the injury, watched on in silence before a stretcher was called for. As he was carried off the field, all the supporters clapped him but Jake didn't care, he had just two thoughts in his mind; the move to Madrid if he was out with a long term injury, and the world cup starting in a few weeks time. Pulling his shirt over his face to hide his emotions, he was carried down into the depths of the ground before a waiting ambulance took him to the Royal Liverpool hospital for x-rays and scans.

A young female doctor who looked as though she had worked far too many hours, stood at the foot of his bed with his scans in her hand. "You have ruptured the ligament in your ankle joint. You also have some severe tendon damage which is a very painful injury and will need surgery. It's called a Brostrom lateral ligament repair, and you will require a great deal of rehabilitation work after the operation. I'm afraid it will be many months before you play football again, Mr Woods."

Jake was devastated. "Operating tonight? Is there any other choice? I need to be fit for the world cup." His mind was a little groggy from the pain killers and he was finding it hard to grasp the full severity of his injury.

She shook her head. "Mr Woods, count your blessings if you kick a ball again in the next six months. Let us do our work and then it will be down to you and your club. The surgeon will speak to you shortly." She left, leaving Jake bemoaning his luck where one tackle had cost him so much. The curtain was pulled open and Jake recognised the person coming in - Seth Jackson, the same defender who had caused the injury.

"Sorry Jake, I didn't mean to hurt you mate. I just came in a bit quick to win the ball and caught your ankle, I'm gutted mate."

Jake held out his hand. "It's good of you to come in, Seth, I know that it was an accident. When you kicked the ankle, my studs got caught in the turf - just one of those things, mate."

Seth looked as upset as anyone could. "If you need anything Jake, give me a call. Your parents are outside, I better get going, mate."

Jake nodded but with the pain killing medication he had forgotten about the game and he called him back. "What was the final score Seth?"

He smiled. "You got a 2.2 draw mate, with a last minute equaliser. You lot are still in the hunt for the title, just one more win Jake." He turned and left, passing Jake's parents as he did so.

Des and Kim came through the screen and looked at their son in a hospital gown, with mud still on his knees and the seriousness of the situation written all over his face. "Mum, if you take my shirt you can give it to Luke. I don't think anyone will miss this one and I don't want to see it again."

She took it from the chair and put it in her bag. "I think that he'll like that. What are the doctors saying Jake?"

He repeated the information to them both and he cried as he told his parents about the world cup. Kim sat by the bed and took his hand in hers. "Jake, we didn't realise that you were going to be selected. I'm so sorry darling but you are still young and will get another chance."

He squeezed her hand as she spoke to him and Des handed him a tissue before adding, "Jake, the guy from Madrid was in the stands watching. He's going to get in touch with Sammy this week after they know the extent of the damage."

Jake nodded. "That one is down the pan for a season at least. The doctor thinks that it will be six months if I'm lucky. They're operating tonight as luckily I haven't eaten anything."

Des agreed. "The good part, Jake, is that half of that six months is pre season so you might just miss the first couple of months. Let's get the operation done and start rehabilitation."

The surgeon entered in time to hear Des's words.

"I've looked at the scans and my initial thoughts are that it's not as bad as some that I have seen in the past. If everything goes well tonight there will be no reason why you can't return to some very light work in eight weeks. Let's get you back onto the pitch, Mr Woods, your country will need you for the Euro's in two years. Unfortunately this year's world cup is a definite no go."

Jake lay back staring at the lights on the ceiling as he was pushed along near empty corridors to theatre, the porter chatting aimlessly about the state of English football. Jake let it wash over him until the sound of a heavy door crashing against the trolley made him open his eyes to see a tall athletic man dressed in blue scrubs standing next to him. "You will feel a small scratch on the back of your hand and I'd like you to count to ten for me please."

"One, two, three……," and the warm woozy feeling was quickly replaced with darkness.

Jake woke up in a hospital bed, Kim and Des sitting beside him.

"Hello Jake, welcome back," Kim said, sounding tired. "We've just seen the surgeon and he said everything is repaired and there was much less damage than they expected to see. Apparently because you are still so young your ankle had more flexibility than most. The football club are transferring you to a private clinic tomorrow."

His throat was still dry from the anaesthetic. Kim noticed him licking his dry lips and handed him a small glass of water. The ping from Des's phone almost went unnoticed and he read it twice before looking at Jake.

"What is it Dad….although I think I can guess." A wave of tiredness came back over him as he lifted the sheet and tried to inspect the bandages around his calf and ankle.

"It was Sammy, the Madrid deal is off and it looks as though Spurs will keep you for another season. They want to offer you a better contract." Des was furious as he spoke. "Bloody man, he doesn't care about you, only the money you can bring him. Get rid of him Jake, he's a bad man."

Jake lay motionless, letting the news sink in. "They're all bad men, Dad. At least with this one I know him. I'm going to sign a new deal; if this injury doesn't let me play again, at least I'll have five years on good money."

CHAPTER THIRTY-SIX

Luke sat listening to the football reports on the radio while waiting for breakfast. News of Jake's injury had begun to trickle through with everything from six months to maybe an entire season missed being discussed. He listened but didn't really care, he had done everything that he could to patch up the relationship but Jake didn't want to repair the damage. England, Spurs and his career were a bigger deal than Luke sitting out of sight behind his cell door.

The shuffle of feet signalled unlock for breakfast and checking his watch, he saw it was indeed eight thirty. The shouting coming from the windows all night had kept him awake, so grumpy and tired, he stood in line waiting for his turn to be served.

A large black lad, Liam Miller, recently sentenced to eight years at Snaresbrooke Crown Court, cut to the front of the line, the staff turning a blind eye as they tried to prepare for the coming day. Luke looked around, waiting for someone to say something but nobody did, everyone standing with their heads down looking at the floor.

Miller looked across at his London friends, a big smile on his face as the last two bits of bacon were placed on his tray before the default option of hardboiled egg was placed onto the servery top.

Luke didn't want the bacon but that wasn't the point. If this clown started to take advantage of weak staffing and prisoners too afraid to stand up to him, life would become tough for everyone. He looked over at the Wing Manager; she had seen what had happened but didn't seem to care. He called over to her, the rest of the wing falling into silence. "If you aren't going to do anything I will." He put his tray down and approached

Miller.

"Go sit down, Woods," the Manager shouted across the room. It was too late, Miller had seen the challenge and he didn't like it.

"Yeah, go sit down, screw boy," he said, putting his tray down on the nearest table.

Luke didn't need a second invitation and hit him hard in the face, forcing Miller to step backwards. He hissed at Luke, "Suck your fucking mum, screw boy, fucking batty boy." Miller spat blood onto the floor, but he didn't come forwards again.

Luke waited for him to make a move but it didn't materialise. Picking up his tray Miller walked to his table unsmiling before shouting back, "me and you, it's on."

Luke walked up to the table and took the bacon from his tray. "Why wait Miller? Let's do it now."

Miller's cracked jaw shot bolts of pain through his head. Never did he expect anyone to challenge him and Luke had hit him harder than he had ever been hit.

"No man, the screws will stop it. We'll sort this out on our own." He desperately tried to save any scrap of credibility he still possessed while the London prisoners looked on in disbelief. The big man who had kept the entire wing awake all night had been chopped down by someone who nobody even rated.

Luke didn't show any signs of emotion, not even bothering to think about any consequences. He sat back in his own seat, the rest of the wing shocked into stunned disbelief. A couple of the prisoners tried to praise him but Luke wasn't listening to any of it. "You fuckers were ready to just let him do whatever he wanted, what sort of friends are you?"

He ate the boiled egg, leaving the bacon to one side before the wing manager called him and Miller over into the office. The rest of the wing drifted off to work as she sat looking at the two of them. "Okay, that was my fault. I should have sent you to the back of the line Miller, but that doesn't give you the right to start a fight Woods. You will be placed on report."

Luke nodded. "I don't care, the guy kept us all awake last night, and then cut the line. What did you think would happen? If you don't deal with it, I will." Miller sat in silence before mumbling through his broken jaw.

"I asked for it, he didn't do anything wrong, I slipped in my cell this morning and banged my jaw, nothing happened. If you nick him I will tell the Governor that we were only playing around."

She looked at Miller. "Is it all over between you two?"

He nodded before looking at Luke. "If it's over with him, it's over with me, I'm cool."

Luke looked up at him and nodded. "It's done with me." Holding out his hand towards Miller, the two shook hands.

"You hit hard Luke." Miller tried to smile but the sharp reminder of how hard he had been hit came back to visit him again.

Luke didn't respond, all his thoughts were focused on keeping his football coaching position and gaining parole as Miller stood and left the office looking sheepish as he headed back towards his cell.

Luke remained seated. "Is this going to affect me Miss? I don't want to lose the football job, it's my only escape at the moment."

She sat shaking her head. "It bloody well should do Woods, the number of people who believe in you. I'm not going to tell Mr Elkins, that's your job and keep your mouth closed about this on the wing, that lot out there will forget about it in a day. If the Governor finds out that I let you off with a slap on the wrist she will come looking for answers, is that clear?"

He nodded his head, the relief showing in his expression.

"And you can get that stupid smile off your face as well. Go to work, I don't want to see you again today."

Hurrying out Luke ignored the smiling faces of the cleaners still out of their cells, packing his books before joining the line of prisoners waiting to go to the education block. Gary Elkins was standing at the main education door ticking people off as they entered, oblivious to the morning's events.

"Mr Elkins, can I have a quick word with you once you've finished?"

Gary looked up from his list. "What have you done you fucking idiot? It's written all over your face."

Luke waited to one side until all other prisoners had passed through. "I just got involved in a fight on the wing. I'm not in trouble but I need to explain myself to you."

Gary listened before putting down his clip board and looking around before answering. "I'm trusting you with a group of children including my own son, and you can't even keep your temper in a breakfast queue. So fucking what that he pushed in, what are you going to do if I take you out to watch a game on a Sunday morning and a parent upsets you, are you going to break their jaw?"

Luke blushed. "No Mr Elkins, I promise that I wouldn't do that; if I had let this guy walk all over me life would be impossible."

Elkins didn't even look back at Luke as he walked away. "Get to work, you have let me down badly and I need to think about what I'm going to do."

The morning dragged past and he swept the corridor in deep thought five times, hoping that Mr Elkins would reappear and tell him what the decision was. Luke could deal with the consequences of what he had done, but the uncertainty was tearing him to pieces.

Finally the clock ticked around to eleven thirty and classes were over for the morning. Elkins returned and checked the names from the board before calmly stating, "Stay where you are Woods." Luke stood in the corridor until it was once again clear of prisoners.

"If you ever do anything like that again, Woods, I will make it my mission to ship you out to a prison so far away that your parents will need a plane to visit you, do you understand me?"

"Yes Mr Elkins. Am I still on the team?"

Gary nodded. "Just make sure that I get my match report by

the end of today."

Grabbing his books Luke headed back towards the unit, not seeing the smiling face of Gary Elkins watching him disappear back through the metal gate.

"Luke!" An urgent voice called out to him from near the pool table where a really young looking Asian boy beckoned him over. Luke knew him as a friendly version of Rat Boy, always up to something, but with Hussain it was never malicious.

"Hey Hussain, what's up?" He bumped fists with him.

"That new guy that you hit has just come back from the hospital, he wants to see you in the shower. Careful Luke."

His head spun briefly, they had agreed to leave the trouble behind them so either his London friends wanted him to have revenge or Miller had just gone back on his word. Either way, there was no way that he was going to walk in there and be attacked. "Hussain, go and tell him that I'm not playing those games. If he wants to speak with me he can come out here. I'm not moving."

Hussain scuttled off and into the steamy shower room while Luke's mind drifted back to his first days in prison when Chris was murdered. Hussain returned.

"Okay, he says that he doesn't want any trouble, he just needs to speak to you in private. He's on his own, everyone else has gone. I'll watch the door for you."

Luke walked over and pushed the door open to see Miller sitting on a wooden bench with a notepad on his knee. The door slammed shut behind him as Hussain did his best impersonation of a doorman.

"Hey Luke, I didn't think that you would come. My jaw isn't broken man, so maybe you don't hit as hard as I first thought. Those idiots from my area want me to fuck you up, trouble for them is that I'm not into that. If they want you beaten up, they can come and do it themselves, and guess what? They haven't got the courage."

Luke looked confused. "So what do you want to talk about?"

Miller opened his notepad which was full of beautifully

written pages. "I write songs and poetry man, the others can't know about it, it's embarrassing."

Luke smiled. This was a different man sitting in front of him, not a thug but someone who enjoyed English as much as he did.

"I could do with a hand Luke," Miller continued. "I have written twenty tunes, they just need a bit of refinement. Could you speak with someone in the education department to see if they'll take a chance on me? I know that I can get these tunes out there, I can sing mate so if I get a chance anything could happen."

Luke read through a few pages, Rap song followed Rap song, all of them gritty and describing life and issues from his area of North London.

"These are great Miller, you've put a lot of thought into the words so why change them?"

Miller's eyes had never left Luke as he read through his most intimate thoughts on paper.

"Really? I just thought that I should use different words." He sounded surprised by the encouragement.

"No, the words are great - if you change them, you change you. People will love them because they are so real. But I'm going to speak to my teacher, she holds a course on creative writing and you have some real talent here."

Miller took the book back and slid it into his pocket. "What are we going to do about the other London boys?"

Luke thought for a second. "Let's go and speak to them together."

The three London lads sat together at the far end of the association room while staff rushed around dealing with administrative issues, not one of them noticing the developing friction. Luke took a soft blue chair and sat down in front of them. They looked at him silently as Miller stood beside him.

"Me and Miller have no beef with each other, it's done. I was wrong and I have told him. He just put me on my arse in the shower so I don't need any more trouble."

One of them looked at Miller. "Is that right? You put this screw boy on his back?"

Miller was thinking on his feet. "Yeah but it's over now, he won one, I won one. He's a good lad and I like him. He has a lot of heart, he walked straight into the shower and had it out with me....just this time I was ready."

They all smiled at Luke. "See, you don't fuck with my boy, that's what you get." They stood triumphantly and walked back to their cells, shouting loudly back at Miller. He had his pride back and Luke had some peace at last.

Miller held out his hand as soon as they had walked around the corner. "You didn't need to do that Luke. Word will go around that I have really done it."

Luke shrugged. "So what? Let people think what they want to think, it doesn't matter to me. Tomorrow I'm getting you involved in education and I'm also going to ask the music teacher to speak with you. They have a small studio in the education building but only take six people on the course. They have real live artists coming in every now and then and last year four of the guys on the course appeared at a Princes Trust concert. More than forty thousand people watched them perform - they were on stage directly after Elton John. Can you imagine that?"

Miller's eyes were rolling in his head. "Shit, that's heavy man. Forty thousand people? What did they sing?"

Luke tapped his notebook. "Stuff they wrote themselves, like this in here."

CHAPTER THIRTY-SEVEN

Jake sat alone in his apartment. It had been six weeks since his operation and five weeks since he had bothered to phone his parents. The rehabilitation work at the training ground had started well and already Jake could feel some movement coming back into his ankle. A new five year deal had given him some comfort, but Spurs losing out on winning the Premier title on goal difference after a 0:0 draw at home on the last day of the season had hurt everyone involved at the club.

A confidential email sprung up onto his screen two minutes before the scheduled kick off time for the England game. It was from the club doctor.

'I have recently received the reports from your surgeon. The healing process has already ensured that you have stability in your ankle and the ligaments and tendons are recovering well. Please attend the club training ground tomorrow morning at 10.00 for a further assessment.'

He had already realised that the operation had proved to be a brilliant piece of surgery with the tendon and ligaments already in an advanced stage of repair. The recent scans at the clinic clearly showed that he could begin some light fitness work to strengthen his ankle and potentially he would be allowed to kick a ball again in three weeks time.

Finding the tv remote, he flicked on BBC just as the England team lined up for their quarter final game against Spain. It had proved to be a painful business watching the stuttering progress of the national team, knowing that he would have had the chance to shine on the world stage.

Two draws against Switzerland and Nigeria, followed by a last gasp winner against the USA had put them through as a best runner up in the group. It just meant that they would face one of the strongest teams in the competition now.

The phone sitting beside him on the leather sofa vibrated again and he looked down to see his mum's name. Tutting, he spun the phone in his hand before deciding to ignore it. She would only complain about the lack of phone calls from him and he wanted to watch the match. It rang again a minute later and irritated, he pushed the answer button.

"Hello mum, aren't you watching the England game?"

There was a second's pause before she answered. "Jake, is that anyway to greet your mother? It's been five weeks since we spoke and I've been worried sick about you. If the papers hadn't kept me informed about your recovery, I would have known nothing."

He rolled his eyes as she gathered momentum. "Mum, just take a breath for a while. I'm fine, and I'm also a grown man. I don't need to keep phoning you all the time. I'm really busy trying to get a clothing range sorted out in my name and I hardly get a break."

"Good for you Jake, how about your brother sat in prison. Have you bothered to contact him?"

"No Mum, I haven't. He said a lot of bad things about me and I've had enough of it. I'm through with all this stuff, it's not my fault that he went to prison and I didn't. He needs to grow up and do his sentence instead of crying that I should be in there with him."

Kim could barely control herself. "You are turning into a selfish young man Jake. We didn't bring you up like this."

He cut her off before she could say anything else. "Selfish? I paid your bloody mortgage off for you, without me you would be still in debt."

Her response was instant. "And a lot happier Jake Woods. I don't care about the mortgage or money, all I want is for our family to be back together instead of fighting."

He took a deep breath before letting the words flow out. "And your attitude is the reason that I'm not calling you. I don't need lectures from you about how I should live my life. You just worry about Luke, Mum and let me get on with my own life for once."

He cut the call and tried to concentrate on the game. England were out of the game within the first thirty minutes, Spain galloping to a two nil lead before sitting back and controlling the match for the final sixty minutes. The media screamed for a change in management and threw out statements about how young players under performed when in pressured conditions. They revisited the age old question of why the English players didn't seem to have the same technical skills as the best teams in the world and it seemed that every pundit had all the answers to the questions but not a clue how to implement them. Not one person mentioned Jake at all and it was as though he was the forgotten man of the squad. The picture became clear to him, unless you were performing on the football pitch, you were a nobody. When he was fit, he would be starting from square one, and probably with a new national manager to try impress.

Jake picked up his phone and dialled his friend, Noel Reader, a young midfield player who was presently playing for Chelsea.

"Hey Noel, how about hiring a big boat and cruising around the Med for a couple of days? We could pick up some girls from Marbella and chill."

He didn't need to wait long for an answer. "I'm up for that bro, fly down in a nice private jet, pick up some champagne down there and have some fun. You get your guy to sort out a boat, I'll get mine to get us a plane and I'll bell you tonight with details. Let's make it Thursday to Tuesday, how does that sound?"

Jake was already looking forward to the break. "Sounds good, I'm in for treatment tomorrow morning so I'll tell them that I need a few days away."

Dialling Sammy, he was already thinking about the best place to pick up a couple of girls who would just jump on a luxury boat and party all weekend.

"Hey Sammy, I need you to book me a nice boat with crew to

cruise around the Med between Thursday and Tuesday."

Sammy was as excited as Jake. "No problem Jake, am I invited?"

Jake's thoughts whizzed around his head; if he agreed it was assured that the boat would be the best available. "Course Sammy, but leave your powder at home, I don't like that stuff."

Sammy laughed. "One day, Jake, you will taste it, just not yet. We need you to be in top shape. Madrid have been back on the phone asking about your fitness, I've told them that you will be back kicking a ball in three weeks so don't fuck it up on some two bob brass from the south of France."

Jake laughed, almost hysterically. "Mate, I don't care what you say, I have been living like a monk for six weeks, I need to blow off steam." As he ended the call, his phone immediately rang again. It was Luke.

He answered coldly. "Luke, what's happening?"

The sound of the prison wing buzzing around in its evening routine drifted into Jake's apartment through the phone.

"Hey Jake, I just wondered if you could send me a little bit of money? I need to buy some new trainers for football training. I'm coaching a team of lads from the town near the jail."

Jake thought about his reply for a few seconds. "You don't contact me for nearly a year, then phone me and want money? Yes, I will send you some cash, enough for you to stop begging. I'm putting two thousand into your prison account so just don't bother ringing no more, me and you are done."

Luke felt hollow inside, he had thought that they might chat as brothers again, but from the opening words he could hear his own desperation. Twenty times he had practiced his opening line, *"Hey Jake, I am sorry for how it has been between us..."* but as soon as he heard Jake's voice everything went out of his head. He stammered, "Come on Jake, we are brothers, let's just pick it up again."

"Yeah, I know that we are brothers, nothing can change that fact. But whenever we speak you threaten to tell everyone that I should be in prison and I'm fed up with it. If you want to make it official, do it Luke, if you don't, just shut the fuck up."

Luke protested, "I'm not going to say anything Jake. Forget it man, keep your money. I don't need your charity."

Jake spat back, "Well don't fucking ask me for it every time you want stuff. It's always been the same – you're a loser Luke, you would have never made it as a pro. You, Mum and Dad are all the same, trying to control my life. I'm sick of it, always trying to please everyone. Prison isn't difficult, all you have to do is eat sleep and work, everything is done for you. I could have done that easy. Anything else you need from me?"

The phone went dead.

Luke felt like smashing the phone against the wall, his brother had become a stranger who he no longer liked. He headed back to his confined space which was so easy to put up with and the clunk of his cell door closing behind him signalled a finality to any friendship.

The boat sailed out of Marbella, five ice cold glasses of champagne sitting on a table packed with tasty treats. Three girls lay on sun beds soaking up the sun as Sammy shared the contents of a small ornate box of white powder with them. Stroking the back of a Spanish nineteen-year-old, the pair of them disappeared down into his cabin as the forty-five thousand a day gin palace cut its way through the calm blue waters.

Noel rubbed sun tan lotion into the back of a dark haired French girl whose name he couldn't pronounce. She took the box from the table top and arranged two lines of cocaine. Glancing up at Jake, Noel shrugged his shoulders before snorting the powder through a thin, steel tube. "Don't worry man," he said after seeing the look on Jake's face, "it'll be out of my system by the time we get home. It's a holiday man, relax."

Jake took a cold glass and drained the contents before a waiter appeared and refilled it for him as the sun, alcohol and hedonistic feeling of the trip began to wash over him. Sammy reappeared with the girl and noticed the tin had been left open.

He looked at Noel who was busy kissing the girl on a double sun bed.

"Noel, have you been a naughty boy?"

He looked up at Sammy and laughed. "Snooze you lose," he said before taking the girl's hand and whispering into her ear as they disappeared below deck. The third girl appeared behind Jake and wrapping her arms around his neck, kissed him suggestively on the shoulders.

Sammy looked up and winked, tapping the top of the box. "Are you sure Jake? This girl looks like she's going to need all the energy you can find."

Shaking his head Jake took her hand. "I think I can manage Sammy, see you in a few hours."

The lights dimmed on the deck as six plates of a seafood salad were offered to the guests. Jake picked through the lobster as he thought of what was happening. He was on board a boat in the middle of the ocean and he was the only person not taking Sammy's magic powder. It seemed as though he were the only person in the world not to have a little fun and let his hair down.

"Sammy, how long have you been taking that stuff?"

Sammy emptied his plate before replying. "I don't know Jake, around five years. Why? Are you interested in giving it a go?"

Jake nodded. "Everyone else is doing it, why not?"

One of the girls smiled, a little white powder on the end of her nose, her heavily French accented English very clear as she tried to warn him.

"Why not give it a try? That's what I thought at eighteen. Now I am twenty-one and spending all my money on it. You have the world at your feet....get involved in this shit and your talent will go, as quick as my dreams went." She bent down and took another line. "But you are a big boy, it is your life."

Noel was about to take another line before stopping himself at the girl's words and looking at Sammy as he prepared another line. "Sammy, the girl is talking sense, you need to get

this shit off the boat now. Throw it in the sea or I throw you in."
Noel was deadly serious as he looked at Jake.

"The girl is right, Jake, until today I had never wanted to take a drug, now I'm thinking of buying some when I get home. Fuck that stuff, you may be an addict Sammy but don't bring us into your world."

Sammy looked sheepish as the two players lectured him, Jake taking the box and throwing it as far into the ocean as he could, knowing that he had nearly given in to the pressure of celebrity.

"You either sort yourself out, Sammy, or I'm going to Carlos and telling him about you."

Sammy staggered a little, the combination of drugs and alcohol taking their toll. "I think that you need to keep your mouth shut, son, without me the Madrid deal is dead in the water."

Jake's face flushed with anger before Noel grabbed Sammy by the throat and pushed him half over the railings, a night time dark blue sea beneath him. "And if you don't get the captain to drop you off at the harbour tonight, you'll be dead in the water."

The boat chugged back out of the Marbella marina an hour later, Sammy standing at the quayside watching them heading back towards the horizon, muttering words of revenge under his breath as he searched for a cab to take him to the airport.

Jake popped another cork. "Okay ladies, let's get this party started."

CHAPTER THIRTY-EIGHT

Graham Matthews trotted onto the training ground at Tottenham. After scoring thirty goals for Brighton the previous season he had put himself in a great position to be snapped up by a bigger club. With Jake's injury, the Tottenham Chairman had taken a chance on him keeping a title challenge going before the goals dried up and the opposition disappeared into the horizon.

A six-foot, heavily muscled twenty-six-year old unit, he had tremendous skill with his feet and head and in the pre season games it became clear that he was the real deal, scoring a hat trick against Inter Milan in a tournament held in South Korea. Plus, with Sammy as his new agent, Spurs was his only destination.

Jake watched the team training through the window of the treatment room; the rest of the team had taken easily to Graham, quickly adopting his nickname of 'Matty,' and a sense of jealousy had crept over him as less and less of the team dropped in to see how he was recovering. Carlos spent time watching Matty's playing style and adopting team formations to suit his style of play. He seemed to have everything in his game, plus that extra strength that Jake was missing at the moment.

Time after time the ball was played into him in the area, sometimes crashing a header or a shot past the keeper, often holding the ball up to bring others into the game, but always deadly. Sammy stood on the side of the pitch watching. Jake hadn't spoken to him since the Marbella trip and was not looking forward to their next encounter. He didn't have long to wait.

A tap at the door followed by the smooth Italian accent

meant only one thing, Sammy was in the room. He pushed the door closed, leaving just the two of them together. "I take it that you liked your little joke on me Jake? Making me look stupid and having to find my own way home - but it looks like the tables have turned a bit on you now, Jake. My new boy is doing very well, it's as if the team don't miss you. Carlos has told me that they seem a little more solid with Matty's strength up front. What do you think?"

Jake sat up. "What are you getting at Sammy? Spit it out."

Sammy took a seat on a comfy leather sofa. "You just need to know that you aren't irreplaceable. A season on the side lines injured and you will always have that reputation of a player who can't get through a full season. People will forget you, maybe a drop down into the championship could restart your career but it rarely works. That's how fragile your life is, Jake. I fought for everything that you have at the moment, and you treat me like an idiot."

An under 21 player briefly opened the door before sensing the atmosphere and leaving quickly. Jake paused slightly before responding.

"Nobody treated you like an idiot, it's just the bloody drugs Sammy. I don't want them around me."

Sammy looked awkward for a second, looking around as if to check for anyone who could hear. "That's all in the past, I have dealt with it. But listen to me, if you ever pull a stunt like that on me again, I will make sure that you never play for a top team again. I know everyone Jake, one call from me and no club will touch you with a barge pole."

Jake flopped back onto the treatment table, knowing Sammy had crushed him in the space of two minutes. "Okay, okay Sammy, it won't happen again. I'm sorry. Can we move on?"

The smile returned to the Italians face. "Sure Jake, just like old times."

A shout from out on the field made Jake look up again as the keeper picked the ball out of the net and Matty ran celebrating back to the centre circle. Jake flexed his ankle, he felt that he was ready to step up the training. He couldn't stay on the treatment table any longer; things were starting to overtake him.

Four weeks later

Jake sat in the dugout, watching the Under twenty-one game whizz past in front of his eyes with the same feelings he had experienced at Liverpool on his debut.

Weeks of physio, strength and conditioning work had culminated in this game behind closed doors with QPR. The managers had an agreement that when Jake was introduced for the final twenty minutes, there would be no heavy tackles on him. The Rangers players didn't care, it was a nothing game for them. Jake on the other hand felt the need to be tested and Carlos sat high in the stands watching everything.

The first team had suffered a stuttering start to the season, winning the first three games with Matty scoring two goals but then losing away at Bolton and again at home to Sheffield Wednesday. The players had seemed to lack the spark that had been evident the previous year and friction was developing between some of the more senior players and the new style of play needed to keep Graham Matthews in the game. It was too direct and the midfield players were feeling cut out of the game. It wasn't the Spurs way.

The online forums were a little clearer about their assessment of the problems. Jake Woods was needed back in the first team to link up play, maybe even he and Matty could hit off a partnership to get the team back onto a winning run but without him, things looked bleak.

On seventy minutes the manager looked up at Carlos and nodded, and within a minute Jake was warming up before taking up his position on the field. A few of the QPR players tapping him on the back as he jogged past them - it felt good to be back in some kind of action.

At first it was hard to get back into the pace of the game,

everything seemed to be speeding past him until a long ball out of defence landed at his feet. Jake spun, putting pressure on the old injury before exploding past two defenders and slamming a shot just past the post. He flexed his ankle joint for a second, and realising that he was pain free, he relaxed and picked up the pace, causing confusion in the QPR defence every time he picked up the ball. Finally he got what he was waiting for and after skipping past the QPR captain one too many times, retribution followed.

Darting into the penalty area, Jake steadied himself for an easy goal, the keeper was committed to diving to his left and Jake was about to flick the ball to the right when a thunderous tackle onto his ankle flattened him into the turf. Everyone fell silent until a fight broke out between the Spurs and QPR players when they realised the unwritten rule had been broken,

Jake lay still, waiting for the familiar pain to kick back up his leg. The trainer sprinted on with his bag, expecting the worse as Jake had not moved. "Shit Jake, where are you hurt?"

Jake rubbed his ankle. "He caught me on the scar, just give me a second." He lay on the grass for a moment more before sitting up, a wide smile coming over his face. "No, it's all good."

He stood and walked over to the scuffling players, holding out his hand to their captain. "No hard feelings, it's just what I needed," before picking the ball up and smashing the penalty into the top corner.

Carlos had made his way down to the side line as the final whistle blew. "How does it feel Jake?"

Jake smiled. "Like I have never been away boss. Am I in the squad for Saturday?"

CHAPTER THIRTY-NINE

Eight months later

Luke sat in the office as his personal officer discussed his progress during the past year.

"Things are going very well Luke, your English studies are on track, I'm just reading the reports from your tutor. She thinks that you are on course to get excellent grades. Mr Elkins has also given me a written report, the coaching sessions have progressed well and he states that you are writing weekly articles for the local newspaper. I wasn't aware of that Luke, why didn't you tell me?"

He shrugged his shoulders. "Sorry Miss Nevis, I just thought that Mr Elkins might talk to you about it. I didn't think much of it to be honest."

She shook her head. "I need to know everything that you are doing, it's me who writes your reports for parole."

The word parole shook him to the core, this was the first time that they had even talked about it. For a second he visualised walking out of prison on release, his parents standing smiling by the prison gate, the car parked in the leafy car park that he could nearly see if he went up onto the top landing and looked out of a cell window. It was starting to seem real as she continued.

"We need to plan your next moves. You are able to finish your exams in another prison if needed, we do that all the time to the lads from Patterson Unit. But it's important that we get the right place as they need to be able to keep your education going, plus we could do with the Wallingford News talking to the local paper where ever you go to. You could have a great career in journalism Luke, let's keep the momentum going."

Something about the conversation make Luke feel uneasy.

"Do I have to move? Can't I stay here and study, where we all know each other? Why do I need to move on?"

Miss Nevis didn't smile while responding. "You're going to have to move Luke and it may be sooner than we first planned. If you want to get out on your parole date, you have to jump through a few hoops first."

Luke looked at her, the pieces falling into place, "I'm moving today aren't I?"

She looked down at the floor not wanting to make the eye contact which would give her away.

"Luke, I'm not allowed to tell you when and where you will be going, all I will say is sort out any unfinished business that you might have here." She picked up her notes from the table and stood up.

"Take care Luke, I'll keep an eye open for you in the national papers one day.

The office door opened and Luke didn't need to be told who was coming in.

"Luke Woods?"

He nodded looking at the two officers standing holding a large black leather bag. "Let's go and pack your stuff, we're leaving in fifteen minutes."

Puffing out his cheeks, he turned to follow the staff, leaving Miss Nevis standing by the desk looking awkward. "Miss, you could have at least told me that this was going to happen."

She shrugged her shoulders, a red rash appearing on her neck caused by either embarrassment or stress. Not wanting to leave the comfort of the office he continued to wait for her response. A strong hand grasped his arm to lead him out and he shrugged it off.

"Get your hands off me man, I can walk by myself." Feeling the flush of rage surge through his body Luke readied himself for the inevitable scuffle, the type he had seen a dozen or more times in this very spot. His breathing steadied to a controllable level and he was able to think clearly. "Ok boss, it won't take me long, just let me walk without you pulling me please."

The hand released him and Luke walked towards his cell, a cluster of faces appearing from the shower window as he walked past.

"Can I phone my parents before I leave please sir?"

The second officer shook his head. "No, you'll get a call when you're there. It's just the rules we have to follow for life sentence prisoners, nothing personal Woods."

Taking a large plastic bag Luke crammed his belongings inside, letters and personal items that had been hidden away and read repeatedly during long nights suddenly exposed to the eyes of the unit. Grasping it in his right hand, he scanned his cell, searching for anything that he might have forgotten, mind drifting back to the days of Bigger and Rat Boy and the drama of the drug package. He turned and walked out, not bothering to watch the prisoner rush in to clean the cell and steal anything else that was left.

It felt strange walking away from the place where he felt that he had grown up, and the familiar routine and jokes with his favourite staff fell away behind him as he was escorted to the reception building.

"Where am I going boss?"

The two staff looked at each other. "Winchester, they have a unit there for people like you. It's where we work, we just dropped one off who is going into your cell. Look on the bright side, you're working your way out, that poor bastard has just started a twelve year sentence. Which one would you prefer?"

Luke smiled, the thought of working his way out felt good. "What's the unit like?"

The two staff seemed relaxed as they checked through the paperwork and applied the handcuffs around Luke's wrists.

"A hundred and twenty-nine prisoners, some working outside in the community, others doing trusted jobs or working on higher education. You'll like it, it's all adults and all the silly behaviour that you see in these places will be a million miles away."

The sliding door of the white transit van closed as Luke sat on the seat next to one of the staff while the other got in the front to drive.

"I hear that your brother is Jake Woods? He's signing for Real Madrid next week for thirty million or so the papers say."

Luke rolled his eyes. "I don't know anything about it, we haven't spoken for a long time. He's a football superstar and I'm a prisoner. Why would he have anything to do with me? Good luck to him."

The officer stared at Luke. "Really? He just dumped you? What a twat."

Luke laughed. "My thoughts exactly."

The van trundled onto the A34 and headed south as Luke closed his eyes and thought about what faced him, the weight of the handcuffs bumping into his wrist bone every time they hit one of the numerous pot holes. Finally the van slowed as they drove through the outskirts of the city, the hospital looming on his left and the tower of the Victorian prison looked down from the right. The huge brick walls added to his feeling of anxiety and a tightness grew in his throat as the nerves kicked in.

The officer sitting next to him noticed his look of trepidation. "Calm down son, this part is not for you. We just need to go in this bit to get you booked into the reception. Your unit is called West Hill, it's outside the walls, a bit like the place that you just came from but better."

Luke didn't believe him, he had heard the same thing said to everyone who had left Huntercombe. The large brown wooden gates slid open as the faces of two staff peered out towards the van before waving it into the cavernous throat of the jail.

The voice of the van driver echoed as he called out. "Alright Billy, just the one back from Huntercombe, he's going to West Hill in a moment.

One of the officers peered through the window at Luke, smiling at him as he did so. "Poor kid," Luke heard him say to the woman sitting behind a desk in the gate office, "look at him, he had it all and threw it away."

The van pulled into the forecourt and Luke's bag was carried up a flight of stairs and into a building marked 'reception'. Looking at the officer sitting next to him as he removed the handcuffs, he said, "Are you sure that this place is better than Huntercombe?"

The officer looked up and smiled. "Just give it a couple of days, son. I work down there remember?"

Standing in front of the desk, Luke checked through his property as the man standing behind it checked off the list. "You can have that, that and that, he pointed to some items in the large bag. You are not allowed that radio, or the training shoes. One pair only, and you have a pair on your feet. Sign here."

Luke didn't argue, he had learnt that it was pointless to do so. Taking the pen, he scribbled his name on the property sheet before a young, overweight man took his photograph. "Keep this ID card safe as you will get nothing without it. If you lose it you are fucked, Understand?"

Luke nodded. The atmosphere of the building was crushing, a processing plant for humans without time for an ounce of empathy. An older man appeared behind the desk holding sheets and a blanket. He smiled as he saw Luke.

"Morning son, how are you?"

Luke was taken aback. "Good thank you."

"Ok, don't look so worried, we're heading down to West Hill right now. It's a different type of place to this one - grab your stuff and we'll get going.

CHAPTER FORTY

Jake sat at a table on the edge of the pristine football pitch, looking at the contract for Real Madrid sitting in front of him. He was in the very place where dreams were built up and smashed down by the Spanish supporters hungry for success.

The flashlights in the Santiago Bernabéu Stadium made his eyes blink as a familiar white football shirt was presented to him to wear for the obligatory photographs. Peeling off his t-shirt and revealing a well defined six pack to the fans, Jake proudly pulled on the number nine shirt before turning to the mass of cameras and news reporters. A ball was rolled towards him as the crowd sang out his name and flicking the ball around the back of his right leg, Jake displayed his skills by magically juggling the ball up and down with feet, knees and shoulders as the flashlights continued to cover him with an illuminated cloak of invincibility.

Ten thousand fans had flocked into the ground to see their new striker who would propel them all the way to the champions league final again. The pressure was immense from the first second as question after question poured down from the waiting media congregating in a press section on the side of the pitch. Every response given was translated into a pulsating Spanish rhythm of conversation swaying the audience into a well-choreographed feeling of euphoria.

"Why did he think that he could succeed where others had failed over the past three years? Why had he snubbed a mega deal at Barcelona? Why didn't he consider staying at Spurs after they had offered to match the wages offered?" He had expected all of these questions as the Real Madrid press office had vetted every one that would be asked. And the answer to them all was obvious, "I want to play for the best team in the world."

Just as the press conference was coming to an end and Jake stood to wave to the fans again, a young woman reporter put her hand up to ask a last question. The well oiled media machine ready to stop the circus and move on tried to guide him off the playing field and into the board room for a meeting with the club president but he paused, intrigued by the way she looked at him. He pointed at her and said, "Last question," whereby the press officer went into a controlled panic as she began to speak.

"Is it true that your brother is in prison for murder Mr Woods?" she asked, her accent portraying perfect English. She said no more, just waiting for the answer.

Stunned for a second by the nature of the question, he wished that he had taken the hint and was drinking the promised fresh orange juice and talking crap with the club's management. Seeing his hesitation, the press officer abruptly answered the question for him.

"Jake Woods has a brother whom he no longer has contact with. His criminal behaviour has been an embarrassment to Jake and his family. He wants to try forget about the actions of his brother and put it behind him. Real Madrid do not and will not accept acts of violence."

The media scrum raised the volume as Jake was ushered out of view and into the players' tunnel before heading up an impressive staircase towards a large meeting room. The thick oak door closed behind them and ensured instant silence from the bedlam below, as Jake looked out of the window over the snooker table of a pitch to where he could see the live news reports already in the process of reaching around the world. Understanding the consequences of the official press release from the media department regarding Luke, Jake shivered at how his family would receive the news.

He turned to the well dressed man with the clipboard and angrily hissed, "Why did you say those things? That's not what I wanted to say. That bullshit will be all over the British press tomorrow."

The official shrugged. "You need to understand this football club Mr Woods. This is not Tottenham Hotspurs where you were a big fish. This is Real Madrid, the biggest club in the world where you are a very small piece of the jigsaw. The club own you, they will dictate everything that you do and say for the next five years of your contract if you last that long. We have the most successful business model ever seen in the history of football. We will not be tarnished by outside influences, ever. Your brother will be history, you will not tie him to this football club through your words or actions. It is written in your contract if you had bothered to read it fully." He fixed Jake with an unsmiling, uncaring look before continuing. "Be warned Mr Woods, this club has crushed the dreams of a lot of players bigger than you."

A number of people in the room looked over, unaware of the problems brewing. Jake reflected on his position, where a dream day was suddenly turning brutal and the reality of his position was seriously denting his ego. He was owned, no longer calling the shots about tactics or training. He was nothing more than an employee who had better perform brilliantly, day in, day out, on and off the pitch.

Just then, his negative thoughts halted as a beautiful young woman walked seductively over towards them, a deliciously manicured hand held out towards him. "Hi Jake, my name is Sara Paolini, my father is the Director of football here. Welcome to Real Madrid. I am sure that you will be huge hit with the fans - I hear that you have no problems scoring." She shot him a glance that was missed by the media team.

"Thanks Sara, I hope that my lucky run continues," he said, giving her his best smile before she turned and headed to her father, glancing back momentary before busying herself with keeping sponsors happy.

A steward from the club approached Jake and introduced himself.

"Mr Woods, your luggage has been taken to your apartment

in La Moraleja to the North of the city, near the training ground. You are booked in for the next six months or until you find your own place."

He handed Jake a set of keys and headed off before Jake could tip him. He suddenly felt out of his depth again, unsure of etiquette in this jungle of football.

Everywhere he looked were images of greatness or great days; player's pictures hung like royalty from every wall, smiling down as if to dare him to better their achievements. He shivered a little inside, feeling awkward and lonely, and for the first time, he wished that Mum and Dad were here with him.

Taking a sip from an ice cold orange juice, Jake looked around for a little friendship within this scrum. It was nowhere to be seen, but the money making machine were pressing flesh. The mass of suits made their way slowly over towards Jake, stopping and greeting everyone as they approached.

Antonio Paolini, a proud Italian man, approached and held out a heavy hand, clutching Jake's hand tightly in his. "Where are your parents Jake? Normally I get the chance to meet everyone in the family?"

Jake felt a little intimidated by the massive presence of this man. "Sorry Mr Paolini, they are still in the UK. Everything happened so quickly that I didn't have time to tell them to come over, they both work during the week. I'm sure that they will come out for the first home game."

Antonio looked at him a little suspiciously. "Make sure that you do Jake, we Italian men are very much into family harmony if you understand what I mean? It is a value I want to share with the Spanish people within the club."

Nodding weakly Jake felt like a kid back at day one in the Reading academy. "You have my word Mr Paolini, they wouldn't miss this for the world."

Paolini nodded and held out his hand. "Dial your mother and give me the phone." Jake did so, feeling sheepish.

"Hello, Mrs Woods, my name is Antonio Paolini. I am the

director of football for Real Madrid. I understand that Jake didn't invite either you or your husband to our party today?" He listened attentively to her reply while Jake could only guess what she was saying.

"Please come to Madrid next week as my special guest. I will have a plane waiting for you at Heathrow, my P.A. will send you all the details. And please accept my apologies for not personally inviting you here today, it will never happen again."

He handed the phone back and looked deep into Jake's eyes. "Treasure your parents Jake, they have given everything for you to stand here today," he said, his Italian accent conveying the message loud and clear,

A steady flow of well wishers took selfies with Jake for the next twenty minutes until the well practiced meet and great came to an end. Sara came back over to him with a warm smile on her face. "Well done Jake, you have survived your first ordeal, I guess that you need a little time to yourself before meeting the players in the morning. I've been asked to look after you for the next few hours before the playing staff take charge. I will show you to your apartment, and take you to dinner tonight if that's ok?" Jake stood stunned by the professionalism of this club as she continued. "And then tomorrow morning at eight thirty I will also show you to the training ground and introduce you to the manager. He couldn't make it today as he is preparing the team for Wednesday's Champions League game against Bayern Munich."

Nodding again, Jake followed her down the trophy laden corridors within the hallows of the stadium to a smart private lift with white doors and the club crest emblazoned across them. A large security officer guarded the entrance as they headed down and into a private covered car park and within two minutes, the roar of a smart Ferrari heralded Jake's entrance into this glamorous club as they headed through the busy streets of Madrid towards the exclusive area inhabited by multi-millionaire football gods.

He sat in wonder at the magnitude of what was happening

around him, people staring through the tinted windows to try gain a glimpse of the special cargo within. He turned to the woman beside him. "Sara, this just feels so gigantic, the experience is swallowing me whole...is this normal?"

She laughed as her foot pressed down further on the pedal, the acceleration pushing him back in his seat.

"Same for everyone Jake, first day nerves. I have only seen two people not effected by the fuss - John Beckford who you obviously know from England and Rossi from Italy. They both seemed to own the place from day one. You'll meet them both tomorrow. They are nice guys, both married with families living close to your place. I'm sure that you will be invited to John's home, it's a duty that all Madrid captains have during your first week, Chill, you will be fine."

The car turned sharply from the road and headed towards a large gated commune where imposing black iron gates swung open as the staff recognised Sara's speeding red car. She barely needed time to slow down as the armed guard waved her through with a smile. Row after row of huge villas with carefully manicured lawns were positioned in such a way that each offered the required seclusion. Small children played on one of the lawns, kicking a ball into a full size goal. Sara pointed them out.

"They are John's children, it's half term here at the moment. This is such a lovely place to live, where the fans can't get in and bother you."

The car took another twist into the private driveway of a smaller cottage. Orange lights adorned the thirty metre driveway as they pulled up to the large white door. Jake sat and stared at the ornate exterior. It was the most beautiful house he had ever seen, the grass surrounding it so lush and green and cut as short as that in the football stadium he had just left. A large white fountain puffing up arches of sparkling water sat in the centre of the paved driveway, with a huge triple garage incorporated into the building on the left hand side.

Sara turned off the engine. "This is your home for the next

six months or longer if you choose. It's only five years old so everything is pretty new but the club will alter anything that you don't like."

Jake climbed out of the car. "I thought that I was having an apartment?"

She smiled again. "Compared to the size of some of the places on this estate it is an apartment. You have four bedrooms and your own cinema room and gym - positively tiny Jake."

She took the keys from him and opened the door. Fresh flowers were arranged throughout the twelve rooms, the scent drifting fragrantly around every turn. "We have people who will come in everyday of the week and clean the place. The flowers are replaced every three days. Follow me, I will show you where everything is. I lived here last year while I looked for my own place."

Jake followed in awe of the magnificence of the building, where everything he ever wanted was catered for. Sara opened the kitchen door and when Jake stepped in, he saw it was the size of the whole of his last apartment.

"We have stocked up the fridge and cupboards ready for you. All of your favourite products are here."

Opening the fridge he could see that she was right. "This is incredible Sara, how did you know?"

Winking at him she tapped her nose. "We do our homework Jake."

A pool pump kicked in as Jake approached a gleaming set of bifolding glass doors, and looking through onto a large expanse of patio, he saw several sun beds placed ready for action around a glistening blue pool. Looking at Sara he blinked in disbelief.

"This is unreal, I can't believe it."

Pulling the doors open she sauntered to the edge of the pool, bending down and splashing the water playfully. "Fancy a swim?" she asked, her openness taking him aback slightly.

"We don't have our costumes," he answered lamely.

Slipping off her flowing white dress she stood naked for a

second before diving in and swimming the length of the pool before resurfacing "Always ready for a swim Jake, this is Spain. Don't stand there looking all English on me, are you coming in or not?" The pile of cloths left on the hot stones and a splash told her the answer as he stood chest deep in the warm water.

"You're not afraid of coming forward Sara, what next?" he asked, his question loaded with meaning.

She ducked her head briefly under the water again. "What next? Not a lot at the moment Jake, this is just how I am. Love me or hate me, I'm not shy. Now, let's get ready for dinner and we can talk about other things."

Brushing her bronzed arm across his muscular chest as she took the stairs out of the pool, Jake tried to keep his cool, lying on his back floating effortlessly in the water as he watched her get dry on a large white fluffy towel. She knew that he was watching every sensual movement and enjoyed the feeling of him wanting her. Pulling her flimsy dress back over her head she turned and faced him.

"Is it ok if I sleep over tonight? I have some clothes with me - it will save me driving across the city during the dark."

She watched him for a second as Jake processed what was happening. A beautiful young girl, a similar age to him, had stripped in front of him and jumped into the pool before drying herself seductively. Now she was asking if she could stay the night. Holy shit, yes she could stay!

CHAPTER FORTY-ONE

Des and Kim sat in the visiting room at Winchester Prison waiting for Luke to arrive. They could sense that this was a far more secure environment to the one that they were used to. The far door opened and a number of prisoners dressed in grey tracksuits and orange bibs trooped in, Luke in the middle peering around the sea of tables until he spotted them both. A broad, white smile cracked across his entire face as he cuddled them, never wanting this moment to pass. Sitting down he opened the packet of cheese and onion crisps that Des had just bought from the kiosk. Kim looked Luke up and down before speaking.

"You seem to be very happy sweetheart, and you look healthy. How is it here? It seems very strict."

The smile hadn't left his face. "I'm not in this part, my unit is outside the brick wall where we just have a fence like Huntercombe had. There are just over a hundred prisoners on the unit and it's relaxed. We have rooms with our own keys and we don't have to be locked in our rooms all night, we can chat in the corridor area for as long as we like. Everyone seems friendly in here and it feels like I'm on my way to freedom, Mum. For the first time I feel that I can do this."

Both Des and Kim smiled back. The old Luke was sitting in front of them, full of hope for the future. "And better still, I'm writing for the local paper every week. They love my articles about the football; I think that after this is over, I can get a job in the media." Des nodded, loving the positive feelings coming from Luke.

"How is Jake doing, Dad? I heard that he was with Real Madrid now?"

The smile left his parents faces for a second.

"We think that he's doing well but apart from a brief phone call with his manager yesterday we've heard nothing from him. We didn't even know that he was signing for Madrid until the papers told us." Des went silent again, he didn't need to say anything else, it was written all over his face.

"I think that he has said some bad things, Luke, the papers are full of stories about you," his mother added.

Luke looked confused. "I haven't seen the papers today, what is he saying?"

Kim held onto Des's hand while she answered him. "The papers seem to say that that he doesn't care about you anymore." She began to cry. "I don't know what has got into that boy, it's as if we never existed."

The anger built inside Luke as his mother spoke. Wiping her eyes she controlled her breathing. "Des, I'm going to get a tea, can I get you two anything?"

Luke looked over towards her as she stood behind three other people waiting in line. This was his time to clear himself of a burden and the words seemed to blurt out carelessly. He hadn't considered that this moment would ever arrive.

"Dad, I'm in prison for Jake." He let the words sink in for a second, wondering how the next minute would unfold. Des looked back in bewilderment, the creases across his craggy forehead looking deep with anxiety.

"What the hell are you talking about Luke? Why are you here for Jake? Tell me what's happening."

Luke took a breath. "It was him who killed that man, I didn't do anything at all except try to break up a fight. Just before we were called back into court to find out the verdict, he told me the truth. He stabbed him during the fight. I have kept silent for the past few years while I've watched him grow apart from everyone but I'm not taking it anymore, you deserve to know the truth. Please don't tell Mum, it will crush her."

Des looked at him in disbelief. "Tell me that you're joking Luke, this can't be right," he said, holding out his hands as if questioning everything he had ever known to be true.

Kim reached the front of the line and placed her order, glancing over at the two of them chatting intently.

"Dad, it's a hundred percent the truth but he doesn't care. He even told me to report it to the police if I wanted to, he knows that after all this time I have nowhere to go with an appeal. I'm stuffed, my life ruined, and all to protect him and his career."

Two cups of tea and another can of coke bumped down on the table.

"Whatever were you two talking about? You look like you've seen a ghost, Des. Are you ok?"

Des shuffled in his seat. "Yes Kim, we're fine. Luke was just telling me about some things that happened in Huntercombe. Best that you don't know sweetheart." He took a sip from the cup and looked at Luke in sorrow. This was a conversation that would continue later.

Unaware of the devastating news Des had just received, Kim continued to smile and praise Luke. "We are so proud of you, twenty-two years old and writing for a newspaper and in another year you will have a degree. We just can't wait to have you back home again."

He pulled back the tab from the can. "It's starting to feel real Mum, three years and I can come home hopefully. The Governor of my unit had a chat with me, he said that because I have completed all the courses set out for me while I was at Huntercombe, there's no reason why I shouldn't be able to be released on parole. But if the family of Robert Bell object to their son's alleged killer coming home, it could be more difficult to get through. They haven't said anything to the papers about the articles I'm writing so either they haven't seen them or they don't mind me trying to get my life back on track."

Kim squeezed his hand. "Hopefully they have forgiven you. From what I've heard they are rebuilding their lives and campaigning against knife crime in the area." She took another sip of her tea and looked more composed than earlier.

Luke nodded. "I did write to his parents last year as part

of a restorative justice course. They contacted the chaplain and told me that I was forgiven, but they didn't reply to my letter. Fingers crossed that they have realised that it was all an accident."

Just then a gruff voice bellowed out across the visits room. "Finish of your visits please ladies and gentlemen."

A flurry of activity gave the officer the response that he was looking for as visitors drifted towards the door, some thankful that the agony of seeing a husband they hated had come to an end for another two weeks, others wiping tears as they filtered through the single door. Des sat still for a second, he was still processing the information.

"Luke, give me a quick call this evening if you can, we still need to talk." Kim was pulling on her jacket and missed the whispered message.

"See you in two weeks Luke, be good and study hard." She waved as she backed through the door, not taking her eyes from him until he was out of sight.

Luke sighed, trying to consider if he had made the right call in telling his dad. He wasn't sure that he could deal with what he had just been told, Luke wasn't even sure that he was totally believed, although he suspected that Dad was swaying towards the truth. Returning to West Hill, Luke headed back to his single room, flopping back on his bed and turning the TV on. He checked his watch, estimating it would be around an hour before Mum and Dad were home. He would wait until later to phone Dad's mobile, he needed to hear the rest of the story.

The light was fading as Des walked down to the end of the garden before answering the call. He listened intently as Luke filled in the details of the entire night of the stabbing and the conversations that he'd had with Jake since the day. He felt disgust that his son had not had the courage to face up to what he had done but this was overshadowed by the anger already boiling over inside him. The fact that Jake had openly discussed Luke's guilt with them in their own lounge after the trial, the cheek that he had shown in breezing through life without a second thought for his innocent brother getting attacked in the prison shower, and even when Luke limped into the visits room in Huntercombe, with a leg so badly broken that he could never play football again, still Jake showed no remorse.

How could two boys be so different, one a tower of strength against adversity, the other a coward? He ended the call with Luke after a half hearted promise not to bring this up with Jake was made. He knew that he wouldn't keep his word though, how could he? For the first time in his life he hated his own son, despising his lack of morals and values. Everything that Jake had built was a lie formed on the strong shoulders of his innocent brother. He looked skywards and whispered a prayer, something so spiteful he wondered if it would ever be heard.

CHAPTER FORTY-TWO

Jake checked himself out in the mirror; he was looking good in his two thousand euro shirt, his five thousand euro trousers and fifteen hundred euro leather shoes. He was spending more money every week than his family earned in a year and the cash seemingly still poured in quicker than he could cover himself with it. He walked through to the lounge where Sara was waiting.

"Hey Sara, you look stunning." She spun round in front of him, her tight fitting dress clinging to every curve of her body. He was mesmerised by her style and confidence and visualised them sharing his large bed on their return from the evening out.

"Thank you for the compliment, but I already know," she said with another gorgeous smile before asking, "Am I driving or do you want to have a go in my car?" Jake thought for a second, he would rather her have a couple of drinks to ease the deal along, and besides, who wouldn't want to drive that Ferrari?

"I'll drive, it'll be fun."

She tossed the keys to him as he eased himself into the opulence of the leather seat. The engine growled at him as they pulled out of the driveway and headed through the secure gate. "Just tell me where to go, and I'll get you there without a scratch on your body work," he promised, looking over towards her smiling face.

"You leave my body work out of this conversation you randy boy. All of you single players are the same - you are single aren't you?"

Jake nodded. "As free as a bird, Sara, no ties at all."

She threw back her head laughing. "It won't stay that way for long, trust me on that."

Pulling up outside a plush, neon lit restaurant front, a smartly dressed man came round to the driver's door. "Thank you sir, I will look after the car, please follow my colleague and have a pleasant evening."

Jake handed over the keys and followed Sara through into a dimly lit room where private cubicles surrounded the main dining area, each leather seat perched above an enormous aquarium filled with patrolling sharks and whichever other exotic fish were able to survive their roommates. Jake looked down in awe at the pure theatre of the place, his look not lost on Sara.

"Special isn't it Jake? It took five years for my uncle to build this place. He spent millions to create the look and the food is as good as the setting." Before she'd finished speaking, two plates of seafood were slid almost invisibly into the centre of the table, a sharing platter that could have fed four.

"I hope that I have chosen well Jake, I seem to remember that this is one of your favourite dishes."

He looked down at the plate. "Perfect Sara, all my favourite things in one place."

She smiled, just as a third person slid into the cubicle. It was Rossi, the Italian striker who was the record goal scorer for Madrid. Jake was taken aback, he had admired him as a player for years but had never met him in person.

Jake held out his hand. "Pleased to meet you,"

Rossi smiled, his teeth and skin perfection. "Hey Jake, hope my girlfriend is treating you well?" he said as he took his hand and held it for a second. "We're going to tear this league to pieces Jake, I've been watching you and we are perfect for each other.

He leant over and kissed Sara on the lips before taking a prawn from the plate. "I need to go and meet up with some friends Sara, are we still good for this evening? I can pick Jake up tomorrow for training."

He stood and shook Jake's hand again. "Eight o'clock

tomorrow Jake, be sober please, the boss is a non drinker."

Winking at Sara he left as quickly as he appeared, leaving Jake in shock. "Wow, one of my idols Sara! Sorry, I had no idea you were together."

She shrugged and mumbled almost apologetically. "It's only been two months but he's very possessive. I'm going to have to drive over to his place this evening, sorry. He'll take you on from here but maybe catch up at some point?"

He nodded and took a delicious piece of smoked fish from the plate. "It's no problem Sara, let's just enjoy the evening. I can't wait to taste what is coming next."

Outside, Rossi sat in the car park texting furiously. Sara's phoned pinged a second later and she frowned as she read the message. "Sorry Jake, I need to go. Mr Possessive is outside waiting for me to join him and his friends...I'll see you soon."

She slipped out of the cubicle and spoke to the waiter on the way out. Jake sat back into his chair feeling stood up and deflated. Two cold glasses of wine were delivered on a silver tray, the waiter standing attentively. "Sir, Sara has told me that you can order anything from the menu. We also have someone who would like to join you for the meal. A stunning Russian girl with blond hair and a dazzling smile took Sara's seat, helping herself to the lobster.

"Sara asked me to be available, she guessed that she wouldn't last the entire evening. I hope that you don't mind Mr Woods?" Jake raised the glass of wine and chinked it against hers.

"Is there anything that this club can't arrange?"

Before he could discover any more about the woman in front of him, his phone vibrated in his tight trouser pocket and looking down at the screen, he saw it was his dad.

Rejecting the call, Jake was mystified. It was ten at night and a strange time for family to be trying to contact him so he quickly sent a message. *Home in half an hour, will call you then.*

Speaking to the waiter Jake gave him a generous tip before taking his new dinner guest by the hand.

"I'm really sorry that our dinner date has only lasted for

twenty minutes, maybe we can do this again sometime?" Flashing her perfect teeth she nodded as they exchanged numbers, Jake realising that he had already forgotten her name. The immaculately dressed waiter came back to the table. "Your cab is at the door sir, will there be anything else?"

"No, if you can just make sure my friend leaves safely, I would be very grateful." Handing over another banknote, Jake stood and apologised once more for the surreal evening before heading home.

The phone only rang a couple of times before Des answered.

"Jake, it's been a long time."

"Hi Dad, what's up?"

Des was fighting to remain calm. "Jake, I visited Luke in his new prison this afternoon."

"I didn't know that he was moving anywhere. Is he okay?"

"Yes, yes he is fine. Just very upset with the press release about him serving a prison sentence," the phone went very silent for a few seconds, "and you apparently disowning him so publicly. That hurt us all."

Jake sagged back in his seat, he had expected this to come out, just not so soon.

"That's not how it happened, Dad, if you had seen and heard the question you would understand."

Des cleared his throat. "If you had invited us to be in Madrid we wouldn't have this confusion now would we?"

Jake immediately felt defensive. "I just didn't have time to make the arrangements, it was all so fast."

"All too fast, how ironic! Your brother has sat in prison for nearly five years Jake. Do you know what he told me this afternoon? He told me today that he was innocent."

A knot came into Jake's stomach. What had Luke said? "What did he tell you Dad? You know that we fell out a while ago so what exactly is he saying?"

Des didn't hesitate. "He told me that you were the killer, that you had not told anyone about stabbing Mr Bell until the jury were about to give the verdict. Only then did you confess to

Luke. The wrong man is in prison Jake, and you have had five years to rectify that problem, but maybe you haven't had time."

A difficult few seconds of silence sat heavily before he replied. "Believe what you want to believe Dad, I'm telling you that he is a liar. I didn't do anything that night." As the lies tumbled out, Jake realised that it sounded fake and his voice gave him away, the same high pitch that he had always used when trying to hide the truth. The tell tale signs were clear for Des to see.

"Do you hear yourself Jake? I know when you are lying, I understand everything that you do, or I thought that I did. How can you leave your brother like that?" It didn't come over as a question, more as a demand made in anger.

Jake's head was spinning, he didn't understand where this was leading, but he wasn't ready to confess to something from so long ago. He couldn't give up all that he had worked for, just to save his brother.

"If you think that I have set Luke up, that's up to you. Do what you like, but be warned. I will have the best legal team in Europe if you continue to throw allegations at me. I will take everything from you. Remember who bought that house for you, and who keeps you in holiday money. If you want to accuse me of murder, you better be ready. Do you have anything else to add, because it will be a long time before we speak again." Jake hung up and threw his phone against the wall. "Fucking bastard!" he yelled before pouring himself a large rum from his well-stocked bar.

Des walked back into the kitchen from the garden, the call with Jake having told him all he needed to hear. Kim was already upstairs getting ready for bed and stood in the bathroom drying herself off as he came into the bedroom.

"Is everything okay Des? It sounded as though you were angry on the phone. Were you talking to Jake?"

Des was still apoplectic after the call. "Yes, that boy is not a nice person, I'm done with him Kim, he can make all his own decisions."

She hung the towel up on the heated rail and walked through to the bedroom naked.

"What has he done now Des, is it money?"

He got undressed and climbed into bed. "No, it's nothing to do with money. Don't worry about it, I will resolve it with him."

CHAPTER FORTY-THREE

A car horn beeping from the driveway was Jake's signal to grab his sports bag and leave. Closing the door he turned to see a smiling Rossi sitting behind the wheel of the enormous Mercedes 4 x 4.

"First day training is always different at Madrid, Jake," Rossi told him as they drove out of the secure compound. "The standard is way above what normal players see in an entire lifetime. I'll give you one tip though, Beckford will fizz in a hard pass to you at knee level, he's trying to test you in front of the boys. He catches everyone out with it."

Jake laughed. "Yeah, I've read about that test. Ian Johnson had two seasons here before leaving and he spoke about it in the papers."

Rossi nodded. "Yeah, he didn't settle in. Thirty goals a season in England but unfortunately didn't get off the mark here. You're a different player, Jake, you play with your head. He was all muscle and no brain."

The car soon reached the wide gates of the training ground and Rossi parked up before the two of them jumped out and grabbed their kit bags from the back.

"I'll show you around before we start Jake, we have nine full size pitches here, all with a playing surface the same as our home ground. We even let fans in to watch from time to time as it's the best training complex in the world." Jake looked at the magnificence of it, his mouth open.

"We have everything here Jake, apartments for the players, cinema, warm up, warm down areas. Every single thing has been thought of. Come on, we're meeting the others in the players VIP lounge.

He pushed the door open to where a dozen or so players were

relaxing and chatting about the upcoming Bayern game. One or two ignored Jake as he was ushered in but John Beckford stopped his conversation and came straight over. Dressed in pristine training kit he looked every inch the multi millionaire football star.

"Hi Jake, welcome to Real Madrid."

The others had all stopped talking by now and filed over to shake his hand. "It will all make sense by the end of today, mate," Beckford reassured him, "this is a massive club with big expectations. Luckily no fans are invited in today as we're getting ready for the semi final game on Wednesday."

Jake shuddered inside as he looked at the footballing greats sitting around in shorts and flip flops. "I don't think that I'll be involved in the game John, maybe a bit soon for me."

Beckford laughed. "What are you talking about? All week we've been practising getting the ball quickly to your feet - you are starting buddy, there's no hiding place here."

Jake smiled while inside he was shaking. This would be the most intimidating training session he had ever had and his main antagonist was talking to him as though they were about to have a picnic.

The door opened and the manager, Gregorio Benito, walked in dressed in full training kit. He was a legend from the history of the club, and at present proving himself as the best manager in Europe. Showing his class, he walked straight to Jake and shook his hand, ready to discuss tactics from the off.

He had researched every strength and weakness of Jake's game, studying every kick he had ever made.

"Here at Madrid we will turn you into the best you can ever be. As you have already seen we give you the very best but in return we expect the best." He flashed a big smile at Jake. "But you already knew that." Holding out his hand again he pulled Jake close to his face, whispering, "I don't expect to smell alcohol on your breath again. Train well." He turned and walked towards the door leading to the pitch and instantly everyone stopped what they were doing and followed him.

Benito took his place by the touchline as the players slowly jogged across the pitch, warming up their muscles under the Spanish sun. A small team of coaches walked onto the field and chatted with the boss, sacks of new footballs scattered around the touchlines.

Instructions were shouted out, firstly in Spanish and then, to Jake's relief, in English. They were going to work on counter attacking Bayern Munich. Everyone seemed to know the drill and Jake looked lost until John told him what was expected.

"We break forwards down the left or right and we want you to link up between the midfield and Rossi, getting up to support him whenever you can. He is looking for you, you look for him - simple really when you have the best players in the world around you.

Eleven of the under 21 team trotted out dressed in Bayern colours, showing nothing had been left to chance. Benito shouted out, "Ok boys, let's get going. Hit Jake when you get the chance and he will do the rest."

The Under 21 team broke forward, quickly losing the ball just outside the Madrid penalty area. In a flash the ball appeared at John Beckford's famous right foot; he looked up once and saw where Jake was running, the ball hissing towards him at knee height. Jake was ready, bringing it down in one simple movement, turning the defender and sliding a precision pass straight through to Rossi as he darted into the box. Without breaking stride he smashed it into the roof of the net. Jake looked up and everyone was smiling.

Ten minutes later the same situation arose again, Beckford this time passing directly to Jake's right foot. Rossi darted across the area taking a defender with him, a gap appearing for a split second - just long enough for Jake to smash a shot into the top corner before the keeper could move.

The whistle blew and a booming voice sounded across the grass. "Ok lads, take a break."

Benito jogged over while the other coaches prepared for the next drill. He called Rossi and Jake over towards him, speaking in perfect English. "Good work you two, I think that we are onto something."

Rossi nodded. "Yes boss, there will be a good chemistry between us, we just need to work on positional. Maybe when we have finished we'll stay with the younger lads and work on something for Wednesday."

Jake stood back and listened; these were the margins that made a good player into a great player and he belonged on the field with these legends.

The others headed back to the warm down area as Rossi picked up a ball and called a few defenders over. Twenty minutes later they had a good understanding. As they walked off the pitch, Rossi took the opportunity to quiz Jake.

"So, what did you think about Sara last night?"

Jake could see a trap when it was presented. "She was fantastic, made me feel very welcome. Just a pity that you couldn't stay and eat, I had to share my food with a Russian girl."

Rossi smiled. "Yes, she likes to keep the new boys entertained." His smile disappeared. "Stay away from Sara from now on, she's off limits, understand?"

"No problem," Jake quickly agreed, "you two guys are a good match, hopefully she has a nice friend."

Rossi slapped him on the back. "I'm sure that we can find a nice girl for you. Let's get cleaned up, dinner's on me."

CHAPTER FORTY-FOUR

Luke sat in his cell looking at the calendar stuck to his wall, a mass of crossed out days spread behind as he looked forwards at the months instead of years spread ahead of him. Twelve months left before he could be eligible for his first parole release date.

He looked at his face in the mirror; the boyish looks of a seventeen-year-old young man had long gone, he was a stone heavier with solid muscle throughout his body, the limp in his leg had faded to a memory but his love for football still burned brightly.

A pile of newspaper cuttings and magazine articles gave testament to his ability to paint the picture of a game of football into a work of art, and a number of football publications were using his regular articles, all written under the name of 'Woody', at the insistence of the Ministry of Justice.

Radio Berkshire's sporting commentator for Reading FC had visited him the month before with exciting news. A position within the team working with the new online media team and assisting with match day broadcasts was planned for the next year, and if he was released, the position would be his. Luke had jumped at the chance - what parole board in the world could turn him down for release with all these promises dangling in front of him?

A knock on his room door brought him back into the reality of prison life. It was a member of the security search team who Luke had only spoken to last week.

"Hello Mr Barker, how can I help you?"

The look on his face indicated that this was not a social visit. "We're moving you to another prison Luke, it's only for a couple of months but there's a specialist media presentation course that the Governor has just been told about. Apparently your probation officer from Newbury has insisted that you attend."

A flush of annoyance ran quickly through Luke. He didn't like change when it happened this quickly as it normally meant trouble.

"Where am I going? I was due a visit this weekend."

The officer nodded. "I've been told that you can phone your parents to tell them about the move. It is an open category 'C' prison in East Sussex called Northeye, near a town called Bexhill. It's only an hour and a half away from here - I went there to drop a lad off a couple of months ago. It's an absolute doddle there, you won't want to come back."

Puffing out his cheeks Luke looked around at the contents of his room. "I've heard about it, one fella came back from there a couple of months ago. He told me that it was a good place for the screws because they didn't have to do anything as the doors are unlocked all day. But he said that it was bad for the prisoners. Apparently there are drug gangs running around everywhere with no one to stop them. He even told me that stuff is thrown over the fence to order - there are more drugs in the prison than outside. I don't need the hassle of that place Mr Barker."

He wasn't listening and instead two large clear plastic bags were tossed onto the bed. "Pack your stuff up, we're leaving in an hour." Without waiting for an answer, the officer turned and left.

Luke hurried outside and along the passage way towards the Wing Governor's office. Seeing the light on, he knocked on the door before pushing it open.

"Mr O'Shea, do you have a minute?"

Looking up from a pile of papers on the desk O'Shea smiled.

"Hello Luke, what can I do for you?"

Luke liked him, he always had time to talk to people when they were in need and this wasn't lost on the prisoners who treated him with the utmost respect.

"Do you know that they are moving me out to another prison this afternoon boss?"

O'Shea nodded before holding a hand up in explanation. "Yes, I was told around an hour ago and I've looked into it already. I was on my way to see you about it before the officer gave you the order to move."

Luke sat down on the chair opposite the desk.

"Do I have to go? I'm coming up to a parole hearing so I need to stay here."

"You are staying here Luke, I have already agreed it with the Governor. We're keeping your room free for you as the course only runs for eight weeks. There are just three of you doing the training which has been funded by a media company called Global Coverage who want to trial it before asking the Government to fund them for a five year programme. They asked for you personally to be on it, so think about it Luke. You've been writing for the papers for the past two years, people love your articles and now a big media company have asked you to attend the training before your parole hearing. Join up the dot's Son, they're going to employ you on release. Do the course and you could be home in a year." Luke took a huge gasp of breath.

"You think so Mr O'Shea?"

He nodded. "I know so, I've been on the phone with the company not half an hour ago. Do you think that I would just let someone jeopardise the release plans of one of my star prisoners without checking? Go do the course and I will see you in a couple of months." He held out his hand to shake Luke's.

"If it's any consolation Luke, I don't think that you should ever have ended up in prison anyway. Something just never added up to me." Luke shot a look back at O'Shea that told him all he needed to know. "Just as I thought Son, now go get yourself packed."

The large, metal, green gates of Northeye Prison clanged shut as the mini bus trundled through. An old 1950's RAF camp converted into a category 'C' prison, it looked its age. Clusters of single story billets which were once living accommodation for radar staff sprawled over the large site. Groups of prisoners walked around aimlessly, some chatting in the spring sunshine, others walking towards large factory style workshops. Luke looked around at the scene; the prisoner at Winchester was right, there were no staff to be seen.

The only thing keeping these four hundred and fifty prisoners from running out into the prison staff's housing estate was a fourteen foot high metal fence with razor wire crowning the top, and by the look of the torn clothing flapping in the cool breeze, it appeared that a few had tried. The van stopped and the side door slid open as the driver grabbed one of Luke's three plastic bags. "Come on then Woods, let's get you into reception."

The gentle warmth of the sun lapped over his arms as he stood looking around, stunned by the sudden freedom these prisoners appeared to have. Words echoed around in his head, the advice that he had been given by a prisoner whose name he had long forgotten in Reading Prison. He had played the game right and now he had the sun beating down on his back again. It felt exciting and almost liberating.

Two young staff stood behind a desk in the reception building; gone was the officious look of over busy staff on an already over busy evening. They were relaxed, even friendly in a strange way.

"You ok buddy? Just put your bags down over there - are you the guy from Winchester who has come on the course?"

Luke nodded as the man checked through the documents before speaking to the driver. "Cheers mate, we'll take it from here. If you want a cup of tea before you drive back, we have a mess room by the gate."

Luke stood, unsure what was going to happen next.

Historically for him, this was a time when the staff would confiscate half of his property because it wasn't allowed, but not this time.

"Sign here Woods. If you want to leave any valuable property with us for the next two months, we can keep it safe, otherwise I will take you to your billet. You're staying in number 16, I'll show you the bed. There are another four guys sharing the room so follow what they do. The evening meal is at five and everyone eats out together - it will take some getting used to after all your years of bang up. If you want to use the gym, it's open every evening, just go and give them your name when you leave here." The officer pointed at a larger building in the middle of the prison.

Luke looked up at the blue skies and could hear the children playing just outside the fence. The officer laughed. "I guess it's been some time since you felt like this hasn't it?"

Luke could only nod at first, suddenly realising that he was feeling emotional.

"You could say that sir. It feels as though I'm coming to the end of a nightmare."

Billet 16 stood at the top of a fairly steep path, the officer pushing open the unlocked main door and finding Luke's room. "Here you go, this is where you will sleep for the next eight weeks."

It was a large dormitory room with four beds adequately separated to give privacy. Luke imagined the RAF people who would have been sleeping in the very same conditions before tossing his bags onto the bed as the officer turned to leave.

"Oh and by the way Woods, if you hear a siren sounding you must always come straight back to your room. It goes off at midday, five o'clock and nine in the evening. The only other times that it may sound spell trouble. Enjoy your course, the tutor will come and get you after breakfast tomorrow."

Unpacking, Luke wondered why anyone couldn't put up with life in this prison, it seemed idyllic compared to what he was used too. A shuffle of feet behind him alerted Luke to the fact that his roommates had arrived.

Two large Nigerian men, possibly in their thirties and a smaller Chinese man who appeared a lot older flopped onto their beds, eyeing up Luke before one of them spoke.

"Where are you from brother?" He didn't sound hostile in the least, and the others were only watching events out of curiosity.

"Winchester, just here for a course they're running. My name's Luke."

The others nodded before the man added, "Welcome Luke, although I think that you have come at the worst possible time."

CHAPTER FORTY-FIVE

Jake looked down at his phone, debating whether to dial or not. It had been nearly a year since he had last spoken to anyone in his family and the bitter taste of the argument that he'd had with his dad was still occasionally keeping him awake at night time. He had been exposed as a liar by his own father and his cowardice in not facing up to his own actions had been driven into his heart by his dad's words. Luke sat in a prison somewhere in England knowing the truth of what the European top goal scorer was really about. And here he was, sitting in a multi million pound luxurious home overlooking Madrid, with his choice of whatever he wanted to eat, where to eat and what girl he would choose to keep him company. He also had the football world at his feet, a regular goal scorer for his national team and expected to be England's record goal scorer should he continue playing like a god.

Real Madrid had signed him into a longer term contract with a club record salary after his first full season. His twenty-five goals had eclipsed every other player in the league and even the famous Rossi had bowed down to him at the end of the Spanish Cup Final, Copa del Rey, as Jake scored the third goal of his magnificent hat trick that day against Athletic Bilbao

And yet here he was, still feeling that he was the under achiever in the family. He threw his phone down onto the plush leather sofa and stepped into his heated indoor swimming pool mumbling to himself. "Fuck them all, if they want me, they know where I am," before diving in and feeling the warm water wash away the guilt for the hundredth time. Drying himself on the soft, white, fluffy towel, Jake nodded at the house keeper as she busied herself keeping his empty home clean. The phone vibrated softly, and nestled amongst the soft silky cushions, Jake looked down and noticed the familiar number of his new agent, Sasha Williams, flashing up at him. He picked up.

"Hi Sasha, what's happening?" Her friendly, deep, Welsh accent brought him a little instant comfort.

"Hey Jake, I have something for you to consider. Man United have just been taken over by an American family, they are planning a revolution and are over taking Real Madrid as the richest club in the world. Just one problem is that they have to start winning some important trophies again." As she took a breath, Jake cut in.

"Are you saying what I think you're saying Sash? We've just signed a record deal here, Madrid would never consider selling me. Apart from that, I'm happy here."

She laughed. "Hold your horses, cowboy, I have just got off the phone with the new owners, they will double your weekly money and think that a world record bid of £38 million will persuade Madrid to let you go." Jake looked around to ensure that the cleaner wasn't spying on every word he uttered; it was common knowledge among the Madrid players that the cleaners vetted by the club also had a duty to report any signs of bad diet or other vices.

"Are they serious? That's a shit load of money to pay out. How do we do this without Madrid and the fans hating me for wanting to go?"

She expected this question and answered straight away. "Just leave that to me. I know that Madrid needs a lot of money, the debt is rising and a new president is due to take over. Word has it that he was against the wages that the club have offered you. He has told some influential backers that you will take a pay drop to stay at the club."

Jake could see where this was going. "And you plan to turn him into the bad boy who makes me leave?"

"Bingo Jake, you have learned the game well. Maybe I could turn you into a super star agent one day."

Jake almost choked on his diet Pepsi. "What, and live a

devious life like you and your gang out there? Do you have any idea how many times your friends have asked me to screw you over during the past two months?"

She sighed. "That's just the way of the world Jake, of course I know about them. I do the same thing to them, how do you think I ended up getting you onto my team? Dog eat dog Jake....are you in or out of this potential deal?"

Her tone was back to professional, and she was serious again.

"Sash, just let me think about it for a couple of days, tell them that it's a maybe."

"Will do Jake but they won't wait forever, they have a big name South American player on the radar. If they think that you are not interested, they'll move for him. Trust me, United are going to dominate world football for the next twenty years."

The buzz around The Santiago Bernabéu Stadium grew into a frenzy of adulation as the team coach inched through the crowds and through the gate. The swell of noise still reverberated from the concrete walls as the players entered the changing room. Jake looked around at the magnificence that surrounded him, not just the wealth of talent that stood shoulder to shoulder with him against the best players in the world, but the adoration from the people who gave up so much to share their love of the team with the players.

It was more than a club, it was a family, a team of brothers brought together to bring perfection to these tightly manicured pitches. Could this feeling of belonging ever be repeated at any other club in the world? Would he ever get the same feeling driving into a wet afternoon in Manchester?" The frenzy from the crowd bubbled into every crevice of the stadium and even the seasoned staff felt the tingle of this fixture. Barcelona were in town.

Walking out onto the pitch thirty minutes before the kick off sent a shiver through his body. This was much more that a game, it was life. It was going into work tomorrow in the local factory with your head held high while the Barcelona fans hid away from ridicule. It was waking up happily and looking at the news headlines reading Real Madrid beat Barca again. It was everything to players and fans.

Kneeling, he re-tied his boot in the centre circle, looking up for a second and taking in the scene. Eighty thousand people sat watching in anticipation, gazing at every flick and trick during the warm up. Was there anywhere else in the world that he would want to be at this moment in time?

Glancing up at the director's box he could see the party starting even before the first ball was kicked. They were expected to win, no it was more than that, the people demanded that they win. Suddenly the flash of the director's box door glistening in the sunshine caught his eye for a brief second as it opened. Then he saw why, Mum and Dad were staring back down towards him.

Waving up towards them and wondering why they had decided to come and make the peace, Jake walked back towards the players' tunnel, signing autographs and posing for photos as he did so. Instead of turning right into the Madrid changing room, he continued to the lift where the two members of staff smiled and shook his hand before pressing the button for the top floor.

The grey doors slid open to reveal a room full of people drinking, eating and chatting in a multitude of languages. Des and Kim were standing alone outside, looking over the pitch.

"Hey, Mum, Dad, what brought you here?" His tone wasn't friendly, still feeling the sting of his father's words after twelve months.

Des looked up, surprised that Jake wasn't in the changing room.

"The club invited all the parents to the Barcelona game. Apparently it's tradition, Jake." Des's tone didn't seem any friendlier than Jake's. Kim looked between them both, her face creased in an anxious anticipation.

"Does it have to be like this? I just hoped that you two would have moved on by now. I don't know why you fell out but you need to sort it out please." Jake looked at her, he had stood with them now for a minute and hadn't even touched them.

"Well that's up to Dad, he seems to know all the answers. Why don't you tell her Dad? Go on, tell her that you think that I'm a murderer and belong in jail."

Des grunted. "Not now son, now's not the time." He turned to look at the other parents staring at the uncomfortable exchange. "You need to go out and do what you do best."

Jake half turned before retorting, "I'm busy after the game, I won't have time to see you. Enjoy the match."

The people in the lounge made way for Jake to leave, the stony look on his face giving a clear signal.

Kim hugged Des. "What does he mean? What on earth has gone on between you two?"

Looking into the distance Des didn't reply but the shake of his head and the faintest glint of a tear told its own story.

The game flowed along, neither Des or Kim having a heart to watch or even take any interest in what was happening on the pitch. Des had a dull feeling in his chest and realised that he truly knew what it felt like to have a heavy heart.

Jake played with an aggression during the first half that none of his team mates had ever seen before, reckless and unthinking of any consequences, picking up his first ever yellow card in the thirty-seventh minute for a lunging foul on the Barcelona captain.

Rossi jogged up beside him. "Chill brother, you'll get a red card if you carry on. Focus on the game."

The words bounced off Jake, the hatred and energy that came with his anger burned so deep within his stomach he could feel its fire. The game became unimportant as everything that had lay dormant within him suddenly came to an uncontrollable boil, a furnace that coated his senses.

Lunging in for another tackle, he missed the player by a fraction, the ball rolling out of play. The referee standing beside Jake knew him well from other games and quietly spoke to him.

"Jake, calm down. You will give me no choice other than to send you off if you carry on." At the same time he looked at the Madrid manager, Gregorio Benito and shook his head, a gentle movement not picked up by the cameras, but Benito saw it and recognised the meaning. A large illuminated board was held aloft by the fourth official showing Jake's number, he was getting substituted in the first half for the first time in his life.

He looked up, almost in disbelief as the crowd gasped. "No boss, I'm fine, leave me on."

The number remained burning brightly as Benito shouted back in English.

"Don't disrespect me or the club, get off the field now."

Jake sauntered off, applauding the fans as he did so, the insane chatter from the media boxes trying to fathom out what was happening. Then Jake did the unthinkable, ignoring the outstretched hand of the manager and rushing directly down the tunnel. The crowd's cheers turned to jeers and cat calls - no one player was bigger than Real Madrid.

Kim stood watching in disbelief as those sitting around her shook their heads.

"What the hell is wrong with that boy, Desmond?"

Des looked back at her. "A cross between conscience and karma, Kim. I will tell you everything back at the hotel, it's time that you knew."

The half time whistle blew almost before Jake had climbed out of the shower, head still buzzing with a mixture of aggression and annoyance at being substituted so early in the game.

The large screens in the changing room told him that it was still 0:0 and a pretty unimpressive match till then. The door thumped open and the players walked past, each one of them ignoring Jake. He didn't care. Still in his mind he had done nothing wrong other than to ignore the handshake gesture of the manager.

Gregorio Benito calmly walked in once everyone else was sitting ready and wasted no time in addressing Jake. "You played the first half like a lovesick fool, thinking of nothing more than yourself. Fuck your team mates, fuck me, but worst of all fuck Real Madrid."

All eyes turned to these two people while Jake struggled with a response, his words stuck firmly in the back of his throat as he heard the smooth Italian dialect cutting him into small pieces.

"I do not need that type of attitude in my football team, in my family of sons that I gathered so carefully around this football club. You might hate your own father, you might disown your brother, but you never, ever turn your back on us! Do you understand?"

Jake sat still, torn to shreds by the barbed comments as Benito continued his tirade. "Do you think that the club president doesn't see and hear everything? You are a fool, Jake. Now go and sit in the seat that you should have taken when I substituted you. You will sit there and wait for the team to come back onto the field and win this game. Go!"

Jake pulled on his track suit and wandered back past the photographs of historic footballing greats who had worn the famous white shirt. It was a lonely walk back to that vacant seat under the eyes of millions of people sitting watching at home. He glanced up, his parents were gone, obviously ashamed of what they had seen. "Fuck you all," he mumbled as he pulled his hood up to hide his shame.

Kim was the first to enter the hotel room, a mixture of emotions coursing through her body. "Tell me what the hell is happening, I need to know every detail," she demanded as soon as the door had closed. Des patiently covered the conversations he'd had with Luke and Jake, recollecting every comment and emotion. He cried as he discussed the horror Luke felt, the moment that Jake had confessed in the court waiting area and the guilt and silence that had followed. She sat and listened without comment until he finished, shaking her head so vigorously that Des thought that she would dislocate her neck.

"Des, this is rubbish, none of these things have happened. Jake hugged me in our lounge straight after the verdict and talked about what had happened. Luke actually said these things to you? It's all lies Des, not one word is true. What wicked things to say - and you confronted Jake about this? You actually told him that you thought that he was guilty? And you sit there wondering why he feels bitter towards you." She got up and stormed into the bathroom, closing the door loudly behind her.

Des sat back, astonished by the reaction. Everything had been so clear to him when he spoke with Luke, the evidence so compelling. Could he have got everything so wrong? Could Luke be trying to establish a new identity for himself before the parole decision? Could Luke be lying after so long sat in a prison cell? He replayed everything back through his head until he got to the moment he confronted Jake on the phone. The cold manner in which he dealt with the threat to his own liberty, and the tell tale tick that Des recognised as a lie. No, he was right, Luke was telling the truth and Jake was a cold arsed killer.

The bathroom door opened after a few minutes, the steam edging from the gap in the door. Kim had been crying, and Des noticed her tears. "Kim, it will be okay, Darling, we will work it all out between us. Luke will be home soon and we can all be together again."

She shook her head. "No Des, it's not that. I've found another big lump on my breast. The cancer is back."

CHAPTER FORTY-SIX

Luke continued to unpack his bags, laughing at the thought that he'd arrived at the easiest prison he'd ever seen at the wrong time.

"What do you mean, the wrong time?"

The bigger guy came over and shook Luke's hand. "I'm Elvis." He stood back, belly laughing. "My mum was a fan before you ask. My friend here is Johnny - not sure where his mum got that one from." Both men were now laughing. "And the Chinese dude, you call him whatever you like, he doesn't understand a word that we say. He was caught with a house full of cannabis plants according to the court papers he carries around with him." Luke shook all of their hands, a little relieved that he was in a room with three other good guys.

Elvis continued. "This prison is great, don't get me wrong. It's just that there are not enough staff around to watch everything. Plus we have two big gangs running the place, a Jamaican group of around fifty guys, and a big gang of white guys from the South. They are both having regular packages thrown over the fence and this place is awash with drugs. There are more people getting addicted to smack in here than ever happens outside, it's crazy. We stay well away from it all and I suggest that you do the same. But trust me, the Jamaicans will come calling for you pretty soon."

Luke placed the last of his things inside his locker. "They can come all they like, I'm not interested in that stuff and my parole is just around the corner."

Elvis gave him a knowing look. "Come with me, I'll show you everything that you need to know for the next few weeks." They stepped back out into the sunshine and walked back down the hill towards the gym.

Entering the main door, a young muscular prisoner wearing a brand new Adidas track suit came over. "Hey Elvis, do you want booking into the session this evening?"

Elvis nodded. "And my friend here too, this is Luke, arrived today."

"Sure, you're both booked in, good to meet you Luke. Seven o'clock, don't be late."

Walking back out of the brightly lit gym they headed towards a large, drab looking building. "That's where we go to eat, the food is good here."

Luke looked shocked. "What, everyone eats out together?"

"Yep, the screws unlock us slowly to stop everyone arriving at the same time, but yep, four hundred and fifty of us all sitting down to lunch, crazy ehhh?"

Luke stood and tried to get his bearings. He guessed that the entire prison site was a little larger than the Reading FC training facility and that was twenty five acres, or so he had been told while they jogged around it one winters morning, The entire site for accommodation and workshops sat on a large slope enabling him to gaze over the fence and over the marsh land on the far side that seemed to sprawl out for miles. A separate area was fenced off at the bottom end on the right hand side where the regulation double vehicle gate with a smaller pedestrian gate beside it seemed to be the only way into this flat sports area. A well looked after football pitch sat on the right hand side of the field, and bizarrely it appeared that someone had put in a nine hole golf course.

Looking backwards up the hill, twenty four old single floor accommodation billets dating back to the RAF days clustered all the way back to the high, green, metal fence which encircled everything. Popping their heads above the fence on the left hand side was the obvious cause of the noise of children playing. The 1940's style chimney pots sat on top of council style housing showed where many of the staff lived.

But the most enjoyable thing for Luke was the calm, warm breeze which seemed to blow years of prison dirt away from his soul and he closed his eyes for a second to allow the sun to kiss his body. The freedom he was feeling at that moment was so foreign to Luke; what he considered as relaxed at Huntercombe and West hill at Winchester were nothing compared to the emotions he felt at this moment. He shook his head before speaking to Elvis.

"It's hard to believe that there are four hundred and fifty other prisoners here, it's so silent."

Elvis agreed. "Everyone has to work in this place, gardens, education, kitchen or workshops. If you don't want to work you leave and go back to a bang up jail but not many take that choice. It gets busy later on, trust me." An older officer perhaps in his late fifties approached them both as they stood chatting.

"How are you doing Elvis? I take it that this is Luke?"

Luke nodded. "Yes sir, I'm here for the course starting tomorrow."

"Great stuff. If you come with me, I'll introduce you to the team. Both teachers are in the studio now getting ready so let's go down and say hello."

Luke was taken aback. "Studio?"

The officer smiled. "I'm Mr King, and yes I did say studio. Come with me, I think that you will like the set up." They walked into a large building that Luke guessed must have held aircraft equipment a few decades ago, before he stopped in his tracks at what he saw. To his right there was a full mock up of a TV studio, complete with cameras, and on the left hand side was a full radio station complete with working switchboards.

"Oh, my days, this is unreal!" Luke stood with his jaw open.

Two young women came over. "Hi Ted, thanks for bringing Luke down. We can take it from here. I'll send him back up to his room when we have briefed him." The officer bowed in mock homage to the teachers and backed out theatrically through the door.

"Luke, I'm Julie and this will be your home for the next eight weeks. We're going to teach you the art of radio and TV work and by the end of the training you'll be able to work within any media environment. It's a recognised qualification for any of the companies employing out there and for you that's important. SKY, BT Sports, nothing is off bounds."

The smile hadn't left Luke's face yet. "But what about my criminal record, surely that will hold me back?"

She didn't bat an eyelid. "Nothing could be further from the truth. Trust me Luke, if you prove yourself during this course, and believe me it's a tough thing to pass, you will have a job when you're released. The boss of our company is a big fan of your writing and he's the one calling the shots. He is why you are here."

Luke looked shocked. "That's mad, I don't even know who he is, and the guy is taking a risk in me. Why would he do that?"

She shrugged her shoulders. "I think that his son put in a good word, Gary Elkins from Huntercombe. I believe that you know him?"

Luke laughed out loud. "Yes, I do know him, I thought that I owed him a lot at the time, now I don't think that I could ever pay back his generosity."

Julie nodded in agreement. "Yes, they're a good family. Come on then, I'll show you what you are going to be doing for the next few weeks."

4 Weeks later

The visits room at Northeye Prison was busy and Luke looked through the door waiting to be allocated his table. He could see his parents sitting at the far end of the room but there was something wrong with their body language. Normally Mum would have been staring at the door, waiting to see him and then getting up to give him a hug. This time she just sat as he joined them and bent down to give her a hug.

"Hey Mum, you look tired. Is everything okay?" He looked at her and the familiar sight of someone ravaged by chemotherapy stared back at him. She didn't need to explain.

"How bad is it Mum?"

Dad shook his head. "We don't know yet Luke, the hospital have put Mum on another course of treatment. In a month or so they will scan again and then we will know more. We just wanted you to know first."

Luke stuttered, not wanting to accept his mum's mortality again.

"Have you told Jake?"

Kim laughed sarcastically. "He doesn't want to speak with us at the moment, I will try to talk to him tomorrow."

Des spoke over her last words. "He didn't want to speak to us a few weeks ago when we flew over for the Barcelona game. Let's just say that he wasn't pleased to see us."

Kim butted back in, seemingly annoyed. "Did you tell Dad that Jake killed that boy Luke? Is that what you honestly told him?"

There was no hiding place from the oncoming conflict now. "Yes Mum, that's what happened. It was all an accident but Jake had the knife in his hand and he told me that he did it."

She waved a hand in disbelief, dismissing the notion that this could be true.

"The problem is Luke, that you have told yourself so many times that Jake was responsible that you've started to believe it yourself. I will not hear another word of it, do you understand me?"

Des nodded towards him, signalling that the conversation was over.

"Yes Mum, you won't hear me say it again."

As if a cloud had parted to reveal the sun, her smile broke through the gloom as she gently stroked the side of Luke's face. "You are a beautiful man Luke; you will be back with us soon, just keep strong for us all."

Struggling to maintain his composure Luke leant forwards and kissed her on the cheek. "I will Mum, this place is the nicest one that I've stayed in. I'm in the sun everyday, just like we always promised, plus the course is going well and I have the offer of a job if I pass. Mum, life is starting again - you will be proud of both of your sons again, I promise."

She held his hand, her once strong grip feeling weaker. "I have always been proud of you Luke. Just keep working hard and you'll be back home by next summer. I can't believe that I'm saying that!"

Luke smiled. "It has felt like a long time, Mum, but the past four weeks of the course have flown by. I'm loving it and I'm not sure that I want to go back to Winchester. I feel like I have the key to the door to freedom in my hands."

Des slapped him on the shoulder. "That's what I want to hear son." He looked at Kim and noticed her grey face. "We better get going Luke, Mum gets a bit tired with this treatment. You remember how it is, she needs to build up her strength."

Luke nodded, looking at Kim and feeling a gut wrenching sense of loss, not just the loss of his youth in prison but from a deep fear that he wouldn't return home to his mum. This time things just felt differently, as if she was preparing for something so frightening that she couldn't face it herself.

Standing to hug his mum he could feel her ribs, her weakness and her vulnerability. Sobbing he whispered into her ear. "Mum, you will see me released, trust me and stay strong."

Holding him tighter she whispered back. "No doubt, Luke."

Luke walked back towards 16 billet, his thoughts all about his mum and how he could help her. A deep voice beside him made Luke look up. "How are you doing bro?"

A large Jamaican guy with huge biceps stood there in a tight white t-shirt designed to accentuate what years of hard work in the prison gym had given him.

"Blue! Bloody hell, when did you get here?"

Blue didn't smile, instead he looked around at the billet windows surrounding the pair. "Come with me Luke, we need to talk."

The pair of them strolled down into the empty gym building where three PE officers sat in the office in between classes. One of them called out as they walked past. "Blue, when you get a second, set out the equipment for tonight's circuit."

He nodded back in their direction. "Five minutes boss, I just have to show my boy something."

Blue pushed open the laundry room door and ushered Luke in before pushing the door closed. "Listen Luke, I've been told to get you onboard for our boys. We have about fifty soldiers ready to fight, and it's all going to kick off at some point so you need to stay clear of it. It's going to be big and will definitely fuck your parole up. You listening to me?"

Luke acknowledged him. "What am I supposed to do, how can I stay clear?"

Blue thought for a second.

"It's my job to recruit you and they're watching me. If I fuck up I'll be beaten hard."

Luke took a deep breath, wondering about the ruthless nature of people able to scare Blue. "They are serious guys, Luke, but I have an idea that could save us both. Catch a parcel that's going to come over the fence tomorrow night. When the screws sound the siren at nine o'clock for bang up the parcel will come over by billet 24. All you have to do is catch it and throw it through the open toilet window in billet 18. Do that and they will be happy."

Luke's mind drifted back to the parcel at Huntercombe and how one parcel was never enough.

"No Blue, I'm sorry mate, I can't do it. I have too much to lose, and you know that these people are not going to let me walk away from that. Once I'm in, I'll be in. Tell them that you have told me that I have to join them and I will join them once the course is over. Up until then I will still jump in and help them if it kicks off. Just cover for me Blue, my life is in the balance with this course, I need it."

Blue nodded, bumping fists. "Okay, I'll get someone else to pick up the drop tomorrow. I'm not sure if they'll buy your excuse and they will come calling again Luke." He pushed the door open.

"Now fuck off and stay safe. I have work to do."

CHAPTER FORTY-SEVEN

The floodlights burnt brightly over Wembley, the smell of hotdogs drifting over the turf as Jake stretched his muscles before kick off. England needed a draw against Poland to qualify for the European finals but more importantly for the self-centred Jake Woods was the fact that he only needed ten more goals in an England shirt to become the leading England goal scorer in history. The referee sounded the whistle to get the action started, England going on the attack straight away with Jake bossing the game and dictating the patterns of play from back to front. Tirelessly he worked the front line well, running the Polish defenders all over the pitch, creating enough space for the attacking midfield players to surge into the penalty area on two occasions, scoring both times. The crowd were delirious that the team was on the verge of qualifying for the next world cup in Spain.

England broke free again with a counter attack down the left hand side. Ashley Grimes tore past the last defender before a lunging tackle sent him sprawling to the turf and the referee pointed to the penalty spot, the large clock on the scoreboard indicating that there were still twenty five minutes left of the second half.

Jake took the ball and wiped it on his shirt before placing it on the spot. He could already hear the cheers from the crowd before he kicked the ball; only nine goals to becoming a legend and never had he felt so confident of scoring as the ball sailed towards the bottom left hand corner. Only this time the goal keeper had guessed right and diving down, tipped the shot around the post.   Jake stood looking in disbelief as the Polish defenders laughed in his face before thinking *'Fuck them, we're going to Spain.'*

Poland broke down the field from the next goal kick and scored a lucky goal, the ball deflecting from a defenders knee and looping into the top corner. The scoreboard changed to 2:1 as the anxiety in the crowd grew.

Poland broke forwards again with ten minutes left, Jake lunging in to make a last minute tackle and caught the heels of the Polish striker. The referee pointed to the spot, the resulting penalty tucked effortlessly into the top corner and the scoreboard changed again. 2:2. The English team were falling to pieces in front of a sell out crowd, fear hung heavy and every mistake was met with a chorus of booing.

Then the unthinkable happened. England poured forwards in the eighty seventh minute, and sensing victory, Jake picked up the ball and took on the last defender, his first touch clumsily giving the ball away and Poland once more pressed forwards in numbers. The captain picked up the ball and hit a thunderous shot into the top corner of the England net. They were losing 2:3 with two minutes to go, and as it stood, out of the cup. A crescendo of jeers grew as the clock ticked towards the ninetieth minute, and wave after wave of pressure built onto the Polish defence.

"How long left?" Jake shouted to the referee,

"Two minutes."

One more desperate attack was launched, Danny Wilson the young central midfielder picked up a loose ball and smashed a shot which left the keeper standing, the ball crashing back from the bar into Jake's path, both he and the keeper lunging for the rebound. Jake made contact a split second before the keeper's boot hit Jake's left leg, the sound of a rifle crack alerting the surrounding players to the gravity of the injury. They recognised the noise created when a leg bone was broken, a sound drowned out for others by the roar from the crowd. 3:3, the game was over and England were through.

Jake lay crumpled at the edge of the pitch, the team doctor placing an oxygen mask over his face as he tried to ease the discomfort radiating from the unseen broken bone, the same feeling that reminded him of Goodison Park. The ambulance staff rushed from the tunnel area and quickly took over putting Jake out of the pain which convulsed his body as they gently manoeuvred England's prize asset away into the busy traffic of North London. Jake floated in and out of consciousness but managed to mutter, "Is it a bad break?" through the oxygen mask, the young doctor sitting beside him barely hearing what he said.

"It looks okay from the outside, hopefully just a clean snap. Let's wait for the x ray." Jake winced as the sharp prick of an injection entered the back of his hand before darkness crept over him again.

The harsh lighting hurt his eyes as he opened them. "Jake, are you with us? You need to start waking up."

Looking around and trying to make sense of his location, the memory of the accident came back to him and licking his dry lips he nodded. "What's happened?"

The door opened and an older woman who Jake guessed was the surgeon, came to the bed side. "Good evening Mr Woods, I have just reset your leg. Luckily I didn't need to operate, you were very fortunate, but the break was a bad one and it's going to take a great deal of care to recover fully. I understand that they are flying you back to Spain tomorrow morning where I'm sure that they will give you the best treatment available. Take care and try to rest." She turned and left before Jake had even realised that the conversation was over.

"When will I be able to play again?"

The nurse tidying around the bed just shrugged. "Try getting walking properly before you think of that one. Like the doctor just told you, it was a bad break."

Jake muttered, "Yeah, I guessed as much. Has anyone contacted my parents?"

The nurse checked through the notes. "Yes, they are aware of the accident, but it says here that they weren't able to make it to the hospital." Jake took a tissue and wiped his nose.

"Really? It's only an hour and a half from their home."

She carried on cleaning the trolley. "I don't know Mr Woods, that's between you and them." Tossing the wet wipes into a sterile bin, she left the room without looking back.

Twenty-four hours later Jake lay in a different room, this time with a stunning view from a private clinic in Spain. A Real Madrid translator on permanent call loitered around and seemed to get in the way of everyone as he stood listening to the doctor as he examined the x-rays. "Jake, the doctor has looked at the break and it's more complicated than they thought in the UK." Continuing to listen to the medical terminology the translator looked concerned. Jake was tired and irritable,

"Don't sugar coat it, just tell me what he has said."

The doctor stopped talking and waited for the message to be passed. "He thinks that you will never play football again Jake," he paused for a second, "I'm so sorry my friend."

Jake felt a numbness creep around his body as shock kicked in.

"Why, what has gone wrong? I have to play again, without football I have nothing." The doctor listened sympathetically as the questions were fired back and forth like a morbid verbal game of ping pong.

"The break is such that the areas surrounding the injury will never regain the strength and flexibility needed in a professional football player. He says that he has dealt with a dozen similar injuries in sports people and no one has ever returned to previous levels."

The doctor continued briefly while the translation continued.

"He suggests moving into coaching or media if you want to continue in the football world. You will be able to kick a ball with your children in the future, but nothing else more strenuous." Jake pulled the pillow over his head hoping that it would all go away and when he took it away again the doctor had left.

The interpreter carried on when he saw Jake was once again

listening.

"They are discharging you from the clinic this afternoon and the club will take care of your rehabilitation. You are still under contract for five years. Real Madrid are going to take care of you Jake."

Jake barely heard him; his own thoughts focused on how he was going to survive. He thought that he had saved a lot of money but it wouldn't last forever. He had enjoyed a couple of seasons on top money but had spent a lot of cash also and his outgoing were massive. A short career was the last thing he needed.

He wracked his brain, trying to find a solution. Maybe if Madrid bought him out of contract he would make a few million but fifty percent paid back in tax, and his lifestyle costing almost ten thousand every month, his savings would be gone in a few short years. He needed a plan B and that plan would have to involve the UK.

CHAPTER FORTY-EIGHT

Luke stood in front of the assembled media, course leaders and a very proud Des as he studied the hard earned certificate that he held tightly in his hands.

The other two candidates had fallen out of the programme during the last three weeks, the TV coverage module proving to be too much for them to cope with, or that was the official line for the press. Two failed drugs tests for opiates was far closer to the truth, however the Ministry of Justice didn't need the public to be made aware of the epidemic that was sweeping through every prison in the country.

A short speech and an interview for the Inside Times was halted when the CEO of Global Coverage, Eric Elkins stood to give the Prison Service a pledge for a fully funded five year course across the English Prison Service. He held in his hand a signed document, Clement Atlee style, his dream was to offer the most talented individuals serving prison sentences a way into the world of media.

Luke shook his dad's hand. "How's Mum doing?"

"As well as we could expect Luke, she's sorry that she had to miss today, she just wasn't feeling able to make the trip. We get days like that from time to time."

Eric came over to speak to them both and this time he held a new document in his thick hands.

"Mr Woods, Luke, I have something that may be of interest to you," he said, passing Luke the sheet of paper. "I would like to offer you a position in our studio. It's for a trial one year period and will ensure that you work with our top football presenters, providing some live up-to-date match analysis from ongoing games straight to TV, and working as an assistant to our lead presenter, Jimmy Carter."

Des looked at the document. "My God! Mr Carter is on every channel in the country at the moment and he hosts the yearly sporting legends awards. What an opportunity."

Luke looked on in disbelief. "I would love to take you up on the offer, Mr Elkins, I just need to get my parole first."

A tall slim woman who had been waiting close by shook Luke by the hand.

"Hi Luke, my name is Sarah Harding from the Ministry of Justice where I'm the Director of Prisons. I've already studied your parole documents and they look very positive, this work has been the cherry on the cake. The director of the department responsible for parole decisions is also very pleased with your determination to rehabilitate yourself. We can see no reason why you shouldn't be released, but that is just our thoughts. You do have to present your case to the parole board shortly but I think that you may be pushing on an open door."

She shook their hands again and smiled. "See you on TV soon, Luke."

Luke sat in the dining hall picking through his meal, his head full of that day's events and for the first time in years he allowed himself to see the finish line. It was a big mistake.

A mountain of a man lowered himself down on the bench in front of him, his plate piled high with pasta and tuna. "You have had a warning from your friend already and you told him that you would be with us when your course was over. Well, it's over so time for you to deliver on your promise." Luke continued to pick through his salad wondering how he could get himself out of this mess as the man continued. "You see, it's an easy choice - Blue gave us his word and that's on him. If you don't come over to see us tonight in billet 24, Blue will pay the price for failure. And when we hurt him, and we will hurt him badly so what do you think he is going to do to you?"

Luke looked up, alarm written over his face. "Okay, I'll come over, this is on me, not Blue."

The man leant over the table, inches from Luke's face, the

smell of fish filling his nostrils. Without warning he crunched his forehead into Luke's nose, splitting it open. "Eight o'clock, if you don't come I will find you and carve your face open." He held out a razer sharp knife - not a hand made effort - this was a small hunting knife designed to gut and skin. "Make the right choice."

He picked up his plate and left Luke bent double, holding his once clean shirt over his nose to try stop the flow of blood which had seeped onto his plastic dinner plate. Looking around in the vague hope that a member of staff would help him, he was out of luck. The few who were on duty were supervising the meals being served, so standing, he made his way out into the sun, the other prisoners looking at the sight of his blood stained clothing.

Elvis looked up as Luke staggered into his room. "What the fuck has happened to you?" he asked, grabbing a white towel and trying to stem the trickle of blood as he spoke. "Oh let me guess, the Jamaican gang have caught up with you. Don't get involved, you'll be out of jail by next spring if you can stay out of trouble." He checked the cut again, satisfied that it didn't need further treatment. "It's only a cut man, you'll live, it's already stopped bleeding."

The door opened and Officer King walked in. "I saw you walking out of the dining hall, what happened?"

Luke looked up, dried blood smeared over his nose and mouth. "I slipped Mr King."

"Slipped? If I had a pound for everyone that slipped over this month, I wouldn't need to do this shit. Be careful Luke, there are only four staff on duty tonight as the union have told us not to work overtime. We had the full complement of seven but three staff have already gone home. It's bubbling out there and nothing can stop it."

As he uttered his last words, the emergency siren sounded. "Fuck, it sounds like it may have already started" he yelled as he ran off towards the noise of a disturbance. Luke looked at his watch, it was nearly eight o'clock and as he and Elvis followed the officer outside, they could see groups of prisoners running down towards the sports field gate. Elvis shouted to one of his friends who he recognised in the group.

"What's going on? Where the fuck are you all running?"

Someone from the group half turned. "It's all kicking off, the staff have been attacked. We're following this officer down onto the sports field to try get out of the way - they are killing each other."

A hand clasped onto Luke's shoulder and a familiar deep voice whispered into his ear. "It's eight o'clock, are you a soldier or not?"

Elvis stepped forwards. "No he is not a fucking soldier, he's a civilian heading to safety with me." The glint of the blade slicing forwards stopped the conversation as Elvis sank to his knees, hands trying to hold the gaping wound across his throat closed. He collapsed as Luke bent over to help him but he could see by the look on Elvis's face that it was already too late. Looking up at the killer Luke screamed. "You have killed him!" He desperately tried to revive Elvis as the man strode off without a care, but it was clear that he was dead.

He needed help, but all Luke could see was chaos and destruction as the hospital building burst into flames with a boom and the sound of windows shattering filled the air. A small group of prisoners broke through the hospital door, ransacking the pharmacy, handing drugs out like Halloween candy without any thought. Other prisoners were swallowing whatever they were given and the signs of drug use were evident everywhere as looting rioters ran around, high and out of control, screaming like animals seeking a kill.

Before the man could return and finish Luke off, he turned and ran. Unsure as to where he would go to stay safe from the mob, he dived into the nearest billet, turned the lights off and stood listening to the carnage. Elvis was dead in a pool of his blood, his body lying motionless by the main path leading to the dining hall as gangs of hooded men rampaged and fought with each other. Luke caught sight of Blue as ten other men attacked a small group of white prisoners. Blue pulled a metal bar from his jacket sleeve and split a small skinhead's skull open before moving on to attack others, his ferocity fuelled by drugs.

An officer with a torn white uniform shirt tried to move in between the billets hoping to not be seen. Hugging the shadows, desperately looking for an escape route, Luke caught his attention and the young officer climbed through the window, his radio blaring out frightening messages of attacks. Luke barked an order at him. "Turn that thing down or we are both dead."

A huge explosion rocked a workshop as gas canisters exploded in a fire somewhere down the hill and in the light of the flames Luke could see that the officer was in his early twenties and was terrified. His eyes were wild with terror as he began to babble. "I've seen four prisoners killed, they are strapping them onto gas cylinders and throwing them into fires."

Luke ducked down as another group of fighting prisoners bounced against the billet wall. Another louder explosion sounded and the power was cut all over the camp, throwing an already terrifying scene one step further into chaos. The emergency generator tried to kick in before it too was burnt out in the inferno.

The officer carried on talking. "We need to get to the gate, Woods, or we are dead." Luke was surprised that the officer knew his name but his panic was becoming contagious and Luke had to control his own emotions.

"We can't move sir, if we are seen they will attack us both. Some have run down to the sports field with an officer, maybe if we manage to get down there we will be safer."

The young officer shook his head. "They were with me, we were ambushed half way down by a large gang and everyone has been dragged into the gym as a hostage. They are threatening to burn them alive, I only just managed to get out. They stole my keys but I managed to hit one with a weights bar before leaping out of the window. I thought that I was going to die." He began sobbing but Luke quickly snapped him out of his self pity.

"Get a grip, we need to stay calm otherwise we will both be stuck here."

The last of the generators spluttered to a halt as darkness descended in full, the only lights showing coming from the multitude of burning buildings and casting weird shadows and patterns around the room. The officer slumped to the floor as another window was smashed close by. He was calmer now, trying to explain the process to Luke.

"The staff will be arriving at the gate soon, they would have heard what is going on. A message was just passed on my radio that the police are coming, so if we stay here listening to the radio for instructions we might make it."

Luke laughed. "I have a better idea, instead of hiding, why don't you tell whoever is listening where you are? Maybe they can help us get out of here."

The officer shook his head. "The gangs have at least two radios. Mr King is up there somewhere, they beat him up really badly before stripping him naked so they have all his equipment, poor bastard. If I say anything they will hear me and kill us both, we need to just listen."

Two shadows ran past the window, and as Luke watched, they climbed over the fence before disappearing into the night darkness on the other side. The officer laughed in despair.

"That's at least sixteen who have gone over the fence. Fuck me this is dangerous."

A muffled voice came over the radio.

"Any call signs in the prison, the police are going to cut the fence in section twelve. Get there as soon as you can."

The officer stood up, seemingly reinvigorated.

"Ok Luke, the hole is going to be cut up at the top of the hill on the right hand side. We can move up there in the cover of darkness but I need to get this uniform off. What have you got?"

Luke opened a drawer and pulled out someone's denim jacket. "This isn't my room, but put this on. If you get seen at least you will have a chance."

They both looked through the open door, the scene from the bottom half of the prison resembling Dante's inferno with every building except the gym ablaze. Shadows and silhouettes of rampaging groups criss-crossed the entire site and tribal screams rang out over the crackling roar of the numerous fires raging out of control. They saw a shower of sparks arcing out into the darkness by the top fence. The officer nudged him. "There we go Luke, they're cutting through, let's go."

Climbing through the window, the two men sprinted towards the new hole in the fence. Out of the corner of his eye Luke noticed a semi naked body kneeling in the darkness and stopped as the officer ran on without him. "Mr King!" He grabbed his arm and pulled his bloody body to his feet.

"Come with me, I know a way out of here."

The two of them limped slowly towards safety, the sea of faces and lights behind the freshly cut hole so close it was almost within reach. A roar went up behind him as the officer disappeared through the safety of the hole.

"There's the screw!"

Luke pushed Mr King through the gap, turning to see the crowd descending on him and recognising the wild eyes of Blue leading them. Looking back, he could see the policeman covering the hole screaming at him to move. Life turned to slow motion as he made a last second dive towards the fence, almost within reaching distance but still feeling a mile away. Luke looked back again seeing Blue and two others frantically raced towards him as he tried to scrabble the last few feet. The metal bar swung by Blue crashed into his already injured leg making him fall to the floor, almost in touching distance of the fence and the strong hand from a burly arm reached out from the dark and dragged him the last few feet to safety. Heavy police shields placed against the hole kept the rioters inside as the mob pounded upon the Perspex barrier and the high pressure water hose directed into the rioter's faces pushed them back into the hell that they were creating.

Luke lay on his back, the pain screaming from his bleeding left leg. Over twenty police officers were gathering and two ambulances stood ready to receive casualties. A police officer patted Luke on the back. "You just saved the life of that officer, what's your name?" Luke looked up but couldn't see the man's face under his riot helmet. "Luke Woods. Please help me, my leg is broken again." The policeman waved over to a waiting ambulance.

"Come and look at this lad, he's a bloody hero," he said before dashing back to the hole in the fence to help his colleagues.

A paramedic came over and looked at the damage under a flash light. "Looks nasty son, but I don't think it's broken. Anyway there is nothing we can do tonight, there are no staff to come with us."

Two police officers walked past holding up Mr King who was dressed in a set of police overalls. Luke recognised him although his face was bloody but smiling as he looked down. "Woods, I knew that you were a good one right from the start." He held out his hand. "That young fucking officer ran straight past me, but you stopped to help, I will never forget that."

He waved one last time as the police put him in the back of the waiting ambulance. Another policeman then arrived, helping Luke to his feet. "Get into the van son, we'll take you down to the prison staff."

Luke limped into the van, where another two frightened faces looked up at him from the darkness, unable to speak as the horror of what they had faced still bubbled in their brains. Less than a minute later the van stopped near the main prison gate and the door slid open. An officer's voice rang around the darkness of the vehicle. "Ok all out and follow me."

The three were quickly transferred into a white prison van, pulling away from the fire and smoke and into the relative calm of the roads, the orange glow disappearing behind them as they headed away. It was only after twenty minutes that anyone questioned where they were all going and a gruff voice from the front retorted, "Lewes, you lot will regret what you have done for the rest of your fucking sentence."

The bright lights of the prison welcomed them as the van pulled through the gates of the aging Victorian buildings of Lewes Prison. Luke looked through the van window and sighed, it was a carbon copy of the drab Reading Prison which spelt one thing, a return to being locked up in a cramped stinking cell. A large group of staff waited as they were disembarked, all on edge and waiting for trouble. "What's wrong with your leg son?" a nurse asked as Luke limped into reception.

"I was hit by a metal bar, Miss."

Taking him to one side she slid his tracksuit leg up to reveal a large gash covered with dry blood which was starting to swell. "I don't think that it's broken but we won't know until the morning. I'll give you painkillers and in the morning come back to see me in the hospital. We will have a better look at it then.

A tired looking officer interrupted. "Woods, follow me, we have a cell for you tonight. Tomorrow you will be allocated another prison as the Northeye staff phoned us before you got here. We know what you did for the officer so don't worry about anything. You'll be going to an open prison after breakfast, HMP Ford.

CHAPTER FORTY-NINE

Jake sat by the pool, his leg still throbbing but it was good to be home. A call from the side gate made him spin his head around - he wasn't expecting visitors.

Rossi stood smiling with a cold bottle of wine in his hand. "Hey, that cast on your leg looks serious man, when do the doctors think that you can come back?"

He pushed a glass towards Rossi and watched as the bubbles filled to the top.

"Never, the guy told me yesterday that I will never play again." He started to get choked up again. "The doctor told me that this type of injury will stop me ever playing football again. What the fuck am I going to do mate?"

Rossi sat down beside him. "Fuck man, I had heard that it was a bad one, but not that bad. Listen, this club have the best facilities, if anyone can get you back on the pitch it's them. Don't give up, just give it a try Jake, promise me."

Jake forced a smile. "Yeah, I'm going to try my best. If anyone is going to make it, it will be me." He drained the glass. "I'm not sure these pain killers mix with booze Rossi, you're trying to kill me." He took a deep breath and regained his composure. "Let's give it our best shot."

Six Months Later

Jake stood at the edge of the training ground, the muscles in his leg already building back to their previous strength. He could feel the desire for football returning after months of rehabilitation - the pronounced limp in his left leg was still there, but getting better week on week. A stray ball came towards him and he couldn't resist it and for the first time since the England game he sent a twenty yard pass straight to the feet of Rossi, and better still he had no pain. All heads were turned to him and a cheer erupted, echoing around the empty stands, and for the first time in a while Jake felt as though he had a sense of purpose back in his life.

He waved and laughed before heading back to his daily rehab session. He and the medical staff had become the best of friends and the worst of enemies during their sessions, his leg stretched and twisted in ways Jake had never felt possible. Some days the pain of the treatment was worse than the initial injury, but mostly it was the boredom of not training with the team, or being part of the preparation on a Saturday or Sunday for another massive game that killed him. Madrid was going to pick up the Spanish title again this season and Jake's last memory would be of storming down the tunnel with the crowd jeering him for ignoring the manager. It couldn't end like this.

Joe, his daily torturer told him off as soon as he lay on the treatment couch. "I told you last week Jake, no kicking a football until after next week's scan. You could undo the good progress we have made," he nagged, his thick Irish accent so out of place in Madrid. "If you fuck yourself up on my watch we are both finished."

The week had dragged for Jake, with all his thoughts on the scan that afternoon. With a good result he could restart some gentle jogging and putting a little pressure on his left leg.

The buzzing of the machine seemed to take forever, two of the clinic's consultants watching every join and shadow appearing on the screen. After what seemed an hour the machine stopped its examination and a nurse came into the room. "Thank you Mr Woods, you can go into the changing room and wait for the doctor to come and see you," she told him, her English heavily tainted with an American accent.

Pulling on his Real Madrid track suit, Jake sat waiting. He had worked so hard for this day and his anxiety levels continued to rise as the minutes ticked past. Finally the consultant knocked on the door and took a seat.

"So Jake, we've had an initial look at the scans." Jake's heart pounded as he waited for the news. "It's not as good as we hoped, but there is a very definite improvement in all areas. Whether it is good enough to survive the rigours of full training we don't know, but all I can say is that the injury is now as good as it will ever be. You can try some light jogging from today....it may work out and you have no reaction, or it may just break down, we simply don't know."

He listened to the consultant, taking out the key information, mainly that he could run that afternoon and a full report was on its way to the club.

Hurrying back across the city and rushing into the training ground, Jake found Joe. "Get the treadmill warmed up mate, I have the all clear to run."Holding up his hands Joe brought him back down to earth.

"Wait one minute, I have to read the report. You bastards have caught me out too many times with your recollection of what a consultant has said."

He flicked the report up on his screen. "Okay, this is interesting. Basically they are saying that it's as good as it's going to be without years of work. They think that if you can build up some running strength followed by light football sessions we may be back in business. The guy also thinks that we have a sixty percent chance of establishing full movement. There is no promise that you will be able to compete again Jake so one step at a time."

He turned on the treadmill. Let's set it at a slow pace to start with, if we manage fifteen minutes that will be epic." Quickly making some notes Joe turned back smiling. "Go stretch and warm yourself up Jake, we don't want to pull something before we get going."

The belt began to turn as Jake began to walk briskly. "Remember Jake, any pain at all tell me," Joe told him.

The walk turned into a slow jog, each step feeling like a move towards fulfilling his ambition towards picking up medals and becoming his country's top scorer.

"Feels good Joe, I've lost a lot of cardio fitness but it feels good to be back."

Upping the speed a little, beads of sweat began to roll down his forehead, and then a gentle ache started to develop across the injury, followed by a sharp stabbing pain that made Jake stop.

"What's happened Jake?" Joe's voice was full of concern. Jake's head was already down, tears of frustration flowing onto the black belt of the treadmill.

"The injury Joe, it's back. The pain is as bad as ever, look at the swelling for fuck's sake." Jake slumped back into a chair while Joe looked at the leg.

"Okay Jake, we're heading straight back for a scan, don't jump to conclusions."

This time the journey to the clinic was not as joyful as Joe sat beside him in a cab, the consultants already waiting to inspect the damage. Jake was a multi million investment, a top priority and either needed to be fixed, or written off for insurance purposes. The machine clicked and whirred again and this time the news was more definitive. The bone had suffered a hair line fracture, it would repair itself again fairly quickly, but not if Jake ever played football again. His football career was over.

Joe sat in disbelief. "Are you sure? Is there anything else we can try?"

The consultant shook his head. "I'm sorry, there is a zero percent chance of ever playing any sport again to a competitive level."

CHAPTER FIFTY

Jake sat by the pool alone, he had told nobody about the diagnosis but somehow everybody seemed to know. His phone rang, looking down he could see that it was his agent, Sasha.

"Hi Sasha, cancel the move to United," he said sarcastically.

Sounding unimpressed she answered, "Yes, I saw it on Sky Sports last night, why the hell didn't you tell me? We have talked nearly every day through the rehab and now when everything goes wrong you clam up."

Jake took a sip of his coke. "Yeah, sorry. I wasn't thinking straight."

She gasped. "Well it's lucky for you that I'm thinking straight. I have spoken to Real Madrid and England this morning. We can get a substantial pay off, that will help you clear any debt that you have amassed on private boats, planes and house rental."

He listened to her for a second, before cutting in. "Calm down Sasha, I'm fine with money, I have loads saved up."

She sounded impatient this time. "No you don't Jake, your debts are going to be crippling. The accountant you use has given you bad advice. From my estimates, once you have paid your tax this year you could be five million out of pocket. Bloody wake up! You have lived like the rest of the squad for the past two seasons. The difference is that they are already millionaires and they have made solid investments. You have got nothing left Jake, you have over spent by a long way. The only thing that was saving you from going under was the salary and now that's going to stop."

He dropped his glass and it shattered on the patio. "Are you being serious? I'm broke?"

His head was spinning, how much more bad news could

he take in one day? He checked his account quickly on his Samsung. "Jesus Christ!" She was right, all accounts were in the red and reality kicked in quickly. No job and no cash, he was screwed.

Sasha tried to calm him down a little. "Yep, but I have come to an agreement with Madrid that you need to sign. They will buy back your contract for five million pounds and they will also settle your tax bill. The FA have agreed to split the cost with them."

He pulled his trainers on to avoid cutting his feet. "What, and then just walk away?" He could hear her typing on her keyboard as she spoke,

"Yes Jake, but I have lined up some work for you with the BBC. They want to take you on as an expert for the next football season and this could then lead to a full contract. It keeps you in football, in the public eye and in money. Have I done well for you or what?"

He thought for a second. "I would need to move back to the UK?"

"Yes, It's the best we can do at the moment Jake. You are still young and maybe have another five years football in you if the injury heals. Who knows what can happen?"

Sasha heard a muttered curse before he spoke again. "Send over what I need to sign, I'm coming home next week."

Luke sat on his bed in Ford Prison, it had been six months since his move and a lot had happened. He still could not believe the good fortune he had faced; a simple act of kindness in dragging Mr King out of Northeye Prison had resulted in him going to a totally open jail. Able to work outside the prison every day in the charity shop in Chichester was even better than he could have ever hoped for - all the freedom with zero violence and a parole hearing booked for March, five months away.

He lay back, considering all the scrapes he had been through over the last eight years. The death of his friend Chris at the hands of Shamus McCann and his gang in Reading and the chances he took at Huntercombe which could have screwed everything up. But out of all the incidents, the riot at Northeye had burned deep into Luke's conscience, not only because he had barely escaped with his life, but he had seen a man stabbed to death in front of his face and not given it a second thought. The things he had seen and had to do just to survive the process of a life sentence had harmed him in ways that those who never needed to step foot behind the walls of a prison could ever imagine. His mum suffering cancer twice while he couldn't be there to help, his brother finding fame and wealth, and then turning his back on the entire family and conveniently forgetting that he was the reason all of this happened so long ago, and now here he was, preparing himself for release back into society but emotionally empty for anyone other than his mum and dad.

For one second he felt self pity coursing through him as the armour that he had protected himself with for the past few years started to fall apart, piece by piece as the purpose of protecting Jake's reputation was stripped bare by his betrayal of the family. Older prisoners had told him about the dangers of letting down your guard before it was time, and here he was unpacking his emotional bags before it was time to check out of the hotel. He shook his body from head to toe as the prospect of parole nibbled into his brain again for the umpteenth time this week, before grabbing hold of his coffee mug and taking a long gulp.

A knock on his door brought him back to his senses and a prisoner looking in his late sixties stood there smiling. "Hello Luke, do you mind if I come in? My name's George. I've kept an eye on you from the first day you turned up here so can I tell you something nipper?"

Luke was perplexed for a second, he'd seen the guy shuffling around in the library a few times but had never spoken to him. Thankful for the distraction but trying to work out what blag he was trying to run, Luke invited him in. "No, go ahead, I was only feeling sorry for myself."

The man chuckled. "Yep, that's why I'm here. Sometimes I share a story, but only to the people who deserve it and I think that you need to hear it." He barked out a chesty cough before continuing. "I was fifteen when I first landed in prison, a robbery that a few of the local lads committed on a clothing warehouse. We made ten quid each back then, but the police saw us spending the cash and put two and two together so we spent the next two years banged up working on how we could make honest money." Luke stirred some sugar into a second coffee and handed it to George as he spoke.

"Then at seventeen I was released. I caught the train from Ashford in Middlesex to central London and found myself standing on Paddington Station, minding my own business with two quid in my pocket. A tap on my shoulder changed the rest of my life." He laughed exposing his lack of teeth in his craggy face. He took a sip and lit up a cigarette.

"I had known this kid before prison, he was the only one who escaped getting caught in my little warehouse robbery, but he had a plan. All I had to do was follow him into Clapham where a barrister lived alone who had forty thousand pounds sat in a safe in his house. Apparently someone had seen him win it in a game of cards the night before. You see, my mate told me that the guy was a queer and wouldn't fight back, he said that he would just hand over the cash and keep his trap shut in case we told everyone that he was a poof." He took a drag from the cigarette and watched the smoke float to the ceiling.

"We kicked his door in, expecting to find him shitting himself, but he was there with his wife and kids - it turned out that he was straight. And guess what, he didn't want to give us his hard earned cash. He dropped my mate with a punch to the jaw and knocked me on my arse too. I had a knife in my pocket so I stabbed him nineteen times, right in front of his kids. I was then rooted to the spot and ended up trying to stop him bleeding out. Fucking stupid thing to do, I should have legged it. My mate ran, he never served a day in jail for the murder as I didn't give him up. But I've served fifty years so far." He stopped and looked at Luke.

"Bloody hell George, that's a long time."

He nodded. "I'm going to die in here, I have terminal cancer now. I could have been released five or six times, the parole board wanted me out. Said that I was fixed, I just knew that they were wrong. You see, at thirty years old it was a joke, I liked drugs and had everything I needed in prison and the next time they came knocking I had nothing left for me outside. I was nearly forty, what family I knew that I had were dead. What the fuck was I going to do? So I failed a drugs test just before the board came knocking. I did the same thing another three times until they gave up on me.

I guess what I'm saying son is grasp life while you still can. I can see the fear in you as parole approaches, it's written all over your face. Don't make the mistakes I made. Life is just starting for you Luke so go out and grab it."

Luke sat there contemplating what George had told him before shaking his hand. "You are right mate, you are so right."

George just nodded and stood up. "I will be dead in a month son, lung cancer is going to take me. Do me one favour if you want to."

Luke looked him in the eyes. "Shoot."

"If you get out of here, take my ashes with you. I don't want to spend eternity on a lawn somewhere in this shit hole. Take my dust and spread me somewhere nice. Will you promise to do that?"

Luke had a lump in his throat. "Of course mate, it will be an honour." George clapped his hands together before lighting up another fag.

"You have made my day son. I'll speak to the Governor and tell him my good news. God bless you nipper." The door swung shut and George was gone, his chesty cough disappearing into the distance.

CHAPTER FIFTY-ONE

The easyJet plane landed at Gatwick at nine twenty seven on a chilly October morning. Jake stepping onto the tarmac with a back pack on his right shoulder, and he wondered for a second what sort of reception he would receive as an English football hero. He need not have bothered as with the exception of a young lad sitting next to him on the plane, no one looked at him twice.

Clearing customs he stood outside the terminal and for the first time in a few years he didn't have a car waiting for him. Taking out his phone he called Sasha.

"Hey Sasha, I've just landed, where are we meeting?"

There was a second's silence before she answered. "We have a meeting up at the BBC sports office in Manchester in two days time, that's Thursday at three o'clock. I'm meeting you at Euston station at eleven. I have the tickets so don't worry, apart from that your time is your own, visit family or something."

He felt a little deflated, life in the real world where you were not wrapped up in cotton wool and told what to do every second suddenly didn't feel very appealing. "Ok, thanks, see you on Thursday."

He thought for a second before finding the station and boarding the Newbury train. It was a nice journey through the countryside, the first he had really seen of it since he was a kid at Reading FC. He watched the fields and villages pass by, considering what to do with the rest of his life when the realisation hit him for the first time. The big time football striker who had ignored his entire family for years was returning home with nothing. The settlement from the football club had been paid but Sasha had invested it all for him. He had just twenty thousand pounds in his bank account and a few shares in some companies that were worth nothing.

The train pulled up at Reading station and Jake limped his way around to his platform before boarding a train which looked as though it was made from cheap plastic. He looked out of the window wondering where he would start the conversation with his parents. The last time they had briefly talked was in Madrid, at the match against Barcelona. That day seemed so long ago and for Jake it was another world away - like a dream, his friends still doing what he loved, but he now an outsider.

The countryside soon turned into a small town as the Victorian station of Newbury came into view. Getting off the train Jake crossed the footbridge before taking the streets that led him towards the taxi rank.

A couple of young lads shouted over the street at him as he entered the town centre and he laughed and waved before passing the Snooty Fox pub on his right hand side. The doors were still locked but he managed to see in. The place was unchanged and the table where all the trouble began was still in the same place, unoccupied and waiting for this afternoon's drinkers to turn up.

Cutting through the Kennet centre shopping mall, he looked at the very different shops than he was used to in Madrid, the Pound Land store living up to its name as he walked past the door of Ladbrokes bookmakers and into the market square.

And there he stood, looking at the restaurant where nearly nine years ago the fight had happened. It was still the same, as if life had just washed down the cobbled square and marched on regardless while opposite, two taxis sat patiently waiting as Jake approached. It was a surreal experience after all this time.

Looking out of the back window as they drove past the Newbury Police station his mind fluttered back to the night in custody before the first court hearing. How scared he was, and how deep he wanted to bury his lie once he realised that he hadn't been seen. The warm feeling of embarrassment flushed over his face before the true realisation of what he had done swept into his mind.

The driver's voice broke into his thoughts. "Here you are son, that's seven pounds please."

Taking out his wallet, he gave the driver a ten pound note. "Keep the change mate."

Looking up at the semi-detached, small house Jake suddenly felt like a child again, the road unchanged with the exception of the neighbours' new extension. Surprisingly his parent's bedroom curtains were still closed and checking his watch he saw it was almost lunch time. The old white door bell was the same one he and Luke used to press when they had forgotten their key on a late night out, waking Mum and Dad up again to let them in. He pushed it tentatively and waited for a minute before he heard the door being unlocked as the face of a very ill woman appeared in front of him, almost unrecognisable from the memory that he was just having. "Jake, we weren't expecting you. What are you doing in England?"

He stood still, a feeling of sorrow pouring over his body.

"Mum, what's happening? You look ill." He hugged her before walking into the house. "What's going on Mum?"

She sat on the wooden kitchen chair, still wearing her dressing gown. "The breast cancer came back a year or so ago, they're trying to treat it but it has spread to other places." She gave him a tired smile.

"Why didn't you tell me Mum? I would have come home."

She laughed. "I'm sure that you would have done Jake, but you just didn't want to talk to us at the time. Anyway, that's history. We hear that you had an accident?"

Jake shrugged, his leg didn't seem very important at all when his mum was dying in front of his eyes.

"Yes, I've taken a break from football until I recover. I'll be doing some work on the TV instead. How is Luke doing? Does he know that you're ill?"

She gave a gentle nod. "He's been through a lot, Jake, but he's doing well now. He's at a prison in West Sussex named Ford where it's easy to visit him. It's an open place where he works outside in Chichester everyday. We usually go to the city and see him at lunchtime, no one minds and we can buy him a nice lunch. I haven't been for a month as I'm too tired, but Dad goes every week."

She scribbled down the address of the shop. "Why don't you go and surprise him? He'll like that. Just don't worry him about me please. I have good and bad days, today is a bad one and Dad is on his way home to take care of me."

Jake couldn't take his eyes from her and he hugged her again, feeling nothing but skin and bone. The sound of the door opening made Jake spin around as Des walked in.

"Hey Dad, surprise! I'm going to stay over tonight if that's ok – I'll buy us some dinner this evening."

Des dropped his work bag at the bottom of the stairs and hugged Jake. "Great to see you back son, and sorry about the leg. I've been reading about it, how long are you here for?"

Jake shrugged his shoulders. "It's a long story but I guess it starts with an apology. I've treated you all badly but I'll make up for it."

Des nodded. "You certainly have put us through a hard time, but that's not so important. Are you going to come with me to see Luke tomorrow?"

Jake smiled. "Yeah, we need to talk. There has been a lot of water under the bridge since we fell out."

Des picked up Jake's bag and took it upstairs. "I'll give you fresh sheets, you make the bed. I'll put the kettle on for us all while you're doing that."

He went back down and spoke with Kim, Jake listening from the top of the stairs.

"Shall I phone the doctor Kim? I haven't seen you this bad before." There was some mumbling before Des shouted up to Jake.

"Jake, I'm just taking Mum down to the cancer ward at the hospital, they want to run some tests. Can you look after yourself for a couple of hours?" The question was rhetorical as the door closed a second later.

He sat on his old bed looking at the thousands of photographs his parents has put around the walls. He had never been forgotten, and hearing the car pulling out of the driveway he whispered to himself, '*Okay Dad, see you in a bit. Good luck Mum.*'

The silence was deafening as Jake sat alone in the lounge, the hedonism of life as a top striker consigned to history. This was reality, the part of life that he hadn't cared about as he boarded private jets and boats to fly five hundred miles for a two thousand pound steak at a fancy Mediterranean beach shack known only to the mega wealthy.

The times when he threw his phone down cursing his family, if only he could have that time back, share the planes and boats, give them an experience of a lifetime whenever they needed it. If only….

CHAPTER FIFTY-TWO

Jake's phone rang waking him up. He looked at the lounge clock as the TV played an online roulette gambling programme - it was two o'clock in the morning. "Hi Dad, what's happening?"

There were a few seconds of silence before he heard his dad's voice trying to answer him through tears. "It's not good news Jake, they think that Mum is going to die soon. She has got a problem with her breathing and they've put her on morphine while they try work something out. They don't expect her to last the week." He broke down sobbing again as Jake tried to talk to him.

"I'm getting a cab down there now, is there anything that you want me to do?" Another few seconds of silence followed.

"Someone needs to tell the prison, Mum needs to see Luke before it's too late. Can you phone them and see if he can come to the hospital tomorrow, even if it is for just one day?"

"I'm on it Dad. I'll speak to the night manager, give me an hour and I'll be there."

Going online, he found the prison number and dialled. It rang for a long minute before someone answered.

"Good evening, HMP Ford, how can I help you?" Jake composed himself for a second, this was the hardest piece of news that he had ever given.

"Sorry to phone you so late. My brother, Luke Woods is one of your prisoners and I need to pass on some bad news. Our Mum is in hospital and the doctors think that she is going to die very soon. We need to get him to the Royal Berkshire Hospital Cancer Unit in Reading if possible. Could someone please try to arrange something?"

He could hear the officer writing something down.

"Do you know his prison number sir?"

"No I don't sorry, his name is Luke Woods."

The sound of a key board being tapped sounded very loud in the darkness.

"Yes sir, I've found him on the system. We do not pass this type of news during the night. First thing tomorrow I will tell our chaplain and he will need to speak to the cancer unit and find out what the position is. Just looking at Luke's files it seems as though there will be no problems getting him to the hospital. Someone will phone you just after eight o'clock on this number. Will you be picking him up Mr Woods?"

Jake answered immediately. "Yes, I can be down there waiting at eight o'clock. I can talk to the chaplain personally if that will be better?"

"Okay, I will pass that on. I'm very sorry to hear the news Mr Woods, I hope that things get better for you all."

The cab slowly pulled up outside the house, the exhaust fumes billowing upwards in the freezing night air and twenty minutes later Jake passed over the last of his cash before heading into the warmth of the hospital where around a dozen people sat on plastic chairs waiting to be seen. Fifteen minutes later he was standing at the end of his mum's bed where she was peacefully sleeping on her side while his dad sat in a blue chair watching her. He was more in control now, the initial shock of the news blunting his emotions slightly.

"Can I borrow your car Dad?" Jake whispered. "I need to drive down to the prison for eight o'clock. The night manager thinks that there will be no problems letting Luke out. The prison chaplain is phoning the hospital as soon as he comes into work and once that's done I can bring him here." Des smiled and patted Jake on the shoulder. "Well done. Yes, just take the car, we have enough fuel to get you there and back. He took out his wallet and handed him forty pounds. If you need more just use this Jake." Not thinking, he took the cash and put it into his empty wallet. Des was in Dad and husband mode, he didn't care about anything else. Kim continued to sleep, a tube attached into the back of her hand.

"What's in that bag Dad?" Jake pointed to the plastic bag above the bed, Des explaining without looking up. He was busy texting his manager to explain why he wouldn't be in for work.

"Oh, that's just to keep Mum with enough fluid in her body, her blood pressure was very low. They give her morphine as well, but that's a different type of thing." Jake looked at his mum's face. "I knew that she was ill as soon as I saw her. I can't believe it Dad, I thought that you were both going to be around forever."

He looked around and saw that his dad had drifted off to sleep, and not wanting to disturb him, he sat silently on a chair beside the bed, gently stroking his mum's hand. He watched the clock until a nurse came in and checked Kim's blood pressure, waking Des as she did so. It was nearly six o'clock and time for Jake to leave if he wanted to be at Ford by eight. "Dad, I'm going to drive down to get Luke, we should be back at lunch time so tell Mum that we won't be long."

Des nodded. "She knows that he will come and she's going to stay strong until he gets here. I know her so well, trust me."

Just after eight o'clock Jake pulled up in the staff car park, the frosty grass portraying the temperature outside the car. He wondered if Luke had been told the news yet and he didn't have long to wait for the answer.

A smartly dressed man in his late fifties came through the gate and made his way towards the car. "Hello, Mr Woods?" Jake nodded and held out his hand.

"I'm the Governor, we've spoken to Luke and the chaplain has contacted the hospital. Luke will be out here in twenty minutes, we are just sorting out a licence for his day release. He must be back here by seven o'clock this evening, is this possible?"

"Yes, I'll bring him back myself. Thank you so much, we all appreciate it."

"Thank you Mr Woods, I'm so sorry to hear about your mother, please keep me informed." He handed over his card with a direct line number. "We'll do everything that we can do to help you all and especially Luke."

The gate opened as the Governor was still talking, and Luke stood looking for the car. Jake held out his hand one more time and thanked the Governor before walking towards Luke.

"Luke, I don't know where to start, is there anything that I can say that will make things better?" Luke laughed at him. "What like eight plus years of my life gone because you couldn't tell the truth? Maybe in time Jake, but for today, let's put it to one side." Hugging each other they got in the car.

"It's been a long time since I was in a proper car without handcuffs, the last time was just after we passed our test before the trouble happened."

Jake looked over as he started the engine. "Yeah, I remember how you drive so I'll take the wheel today."

The pair chatted nonstop for the two hour journey about their parents, prison and football. Jake checked out his brother's muscles.

"Bro, I'm a professional sportsman and you are as hench as me. What are they doing with you in there?" Luke flexed his biceps. "I think mine are a bit bigger Jake, anyway it looks like we both have screwed up left legs. Mine's not going to get any better, how about you?"

Jake shook his head. "No, mine is ruined. I had the best treatment and it still broke again although maybe with a bit of time it will get stronger."

The chat drifted away as they reached the hospital car park, driving around for the fourth time until a space became available. Both walked in silence lost in their own thoughts until they reached the corridor leading to the unit.

"Luke, just be prepared, Mum looks bad. She's knocked out on morphine at the moment."

Luke looked at his brother with concern etched over his face. "Yeah, it was starting to go that way six months ago. She looked bad when I was in Northeye and she's slipped back ever since. I think that this is as bad as it gets Jake, I just wish that I could have been out to be with her."

Jake stayed silent, his own conscience biting into him.

Pressing on the bell by the locked unit door, Jake waited for the click which signalled the door was open before pushing it and leading the way to room 4. The door was closed and the window blinds down as they approached. He entered apprehensively but was amazed to see his mum sitting up waiting, a weak smile crossing her face as both boys entered.

"Boys, you've made it. I asked the nurse to stop my drugs until I spoke to you both."

Des stood up making room for Luke to sit down. "I'll just go down to the shop for a minute as you three have a bit to catch up on." Striding purposely out through the door he struggled to contain his unseen tears, sad that pride and ego had got in the way of so many wasted years.

Luke sat by the bed holding his mum's hand and chatting softly about times when they were children. She listened and laughed a little, sometimes closing her eyes as both boys chatted to her before eventually drifting into a restful sleep. The boys held a hand each as she dreamt beautiful things, her father waiting for her with open arms. She muttered in her sleep, the boys not catching what she said, but she knew.

"Daddy, I can see you."

Des came back in and saw Kim looking at peace, asleep. "She fought so hard to stay awake for you both, I guess she managed to do what she wanted to do. Thank you, both of you."

Jake and Luke shared a glance before both folded up in tears. Des stood between them both hugging them until their sobs came to an end. Jake wiped his eyes and looked at his watch. "Luke, we need to get back to Ford, we're going to be late."

Luke exploded. "No, I'm not going back!" He gained his composure before continuing. "I've missed eight years of Mum's life for some bullshit and I can't leave her now."

Des hugged him. "It's okay Luke, Mum understands. You need to get back - you have a lot to lose if you're late. I'll phone you tomorrow." Luke held her hand again, whispering into her ear softly and kissing her cheek. "I'm so sorry for not being here Mum, please forgive me." He backed out of the room, crying floods of tears until the door closed, and he and Jake were gone.

The sun was setting as they heading back towards West Sussex and hardly a word had been spoken until Luke made a suggestion.

"Jake, I have swallowed nearly nine years of prison to protect you, I don't want anything in return." Jake could sense a 'but' coming. "Would you do one thing for me? Let me stay with Mum for her last few days, you can pretend to be me at Ford, no one will notice the difference."

Jake laughed a little nervously. "Are you serious, how would that work?"

Luke had it already planned out. "We're identical, we swap cloths and you walk in as me. I have already booked myself off work so just act normally and no one will know. Then we'll swap back at the funeral and I finish the sentence. Mate, it's the least you can do, just give me a couple of days with Mum, please?"

Jake continued to drive before finding a service station and pulling in.

"Okay, let's do it, two weeks at the most Luke and then we have to come clean. I need to phone my agent to rearrange an interview tomorrow but she'll understand." Both headed to the toilets to reappear minutes later, Luke checking himself out in the reflection of the garage shop window.

"Okay Jake, now you are me." He passed him a written note containing a drawing of the prison. "This is where I sleep, just follow the plan and it's easy. We wake up at seven thirty, just follow everyone else." Jake listened, looking at the plan and nodding. This is my prison ID, you will find everything you need in my room. Any questions phone me on your number. I will need everything you have, wallet, ID driving licence. You can't have anything on you that relates to your true identity or they will find us out."

Jake handed everything over. "My agent is called Sasha, she may phone you. Just go with what she says, it will be fine, she hardly knows me at all." They pulled up in the prison car park as Luke held his breath. "Thanks Jake, we're quits again. Just keep cool, I'll wait here for a minute to make sure nothing goes wrong."

Jake laughed. "It'll be fun bro, trust me. But if nothing has happened after two weeks, we swap back. You come down to where I will be working and we change, deal?"

Luke shook his hand. "Deal! Be brilliant mate."

Jake picked up Luke's small bag and wandered towards the gate, Luke chasing after him. "Wait, there's something in the bag I need."

Jake laughed. "Fuck me, I thought that you had changed your mind."

"No mate I have an old friend in the bag, George. I made a promise that I have to keep, I almost forgot him."

Jake screwed up his face. "You have a dead guy in the bag?"

"Yeah, I'll tell you later, take care."

Luke waited with his heart thumping as Jake walked through the gate. If the plan was going to go wrong it would be now. He peered through the fence Jake would need to walk past to get to his room. Five minutes later Luke saw him walking towards his new accommodation for the next few days - they had pulled it off.

The family car leapfrogged out of the car park before gathering speed, Luke barely able to conceal his joy at returning to be with his mum. Ten minutes later he was driving as though he had never stopped and tapping the wheel, he muttered, *'like riding a bike.'*

The door opened again as Des sat with his eyes closed, Kim still asleep. He didn't look up before speaking. "Did Luke get back on time?" The voice which answered made his eyes spring wide open.

"Luke, what the hell have you done?"

CHAPTER FIFTY-THREE

Jake threw the bag on the bed and checking through the drawers he found all of Luke's possessions. Turning on the small TV in the corner of the room he climbed into bed before a knock at the door caused him some panic.

A young officer came in and spoke as if he knew him. "How did it go Luke, are you okay?"

Jake responded as if it were the most natural thing in the world. "Yes thanks sir, she isn't good but we will see how this week goes. The hospital don't think that she will last much longer." He found himself getting upset as the officer patted him on the shoulder. "Well done for getting back Luke, that was the toughest test that you have faced." He turned and left without any other questions.

Jake turned off his light and pretended to be sleeping. He had passed the first two big tests, now he had to last the next few days before getting back out into the real world again.

The noise from outside his room woke him up and turning on the TV he saw that it was nearly eight o'clock in the morning. "Shit!" he exclaimed, and gathering the wash bag on the locker top he made his way to the communal washroom. Other prisoners pushed past, stuck in their own routine. No one spoke until a voice came from behind him. "Luke, I need your help." Jake looked in the mirror and saw a youngish, slim, blond lad, around twenty two standing dressed and ready for work.

"You're the only one that I trust Luke, and you have a good brain. Can you come to the gym with me to chat to the gym screw?"

A fizz of excitement came over Jake; here for a few hours and a bit of excitement already. He turned. "Yeah, why not, let me get dressed and I'll be ready in two minutes. Tell me the plan as we walk." The cold air bit in deep as they walked towards a large building, the prisoner chatting incessantly.

"I just need to talk to the screw. If I'm on my own he'll take liberties with me so you're just moral back up." Jake skipped with the buzz of prison life; this was cooler than he thought.

They entered the gym where a stocky young officer in a PE tracksuit was sitting completing paperwork in the office. He was alone and they knocked on the door before the officer looked up.

"Yes Jones? I hope that you haven't come back again to talk about your parole report. I'm not writing lies for you, you are a trouble making shit house, and the sooner you realise it the sooner you will get out." He then looked at Jake. "I'm surprised that you have got yourself involved in this Luke, you don't normally go within a mile of this cretin."

Jones pushed Jake into the office and kicked the door shut before pulling out two large knives from his bag and passing one to Jake. "Change my fucking report, you're not leaving here until you've done it."

Jake looked down at his knife and froze, just as the door to the office opened and another PE officer looked in and pressed the alarm bell. Jake heard the call on the radio. "Urgent message, two armed prisoners holding a member of staff hostage in the PE office."

He looked around at Jones. "Fucks sake, this isn't what was supposed to happen."

The officer held hostage remained calm as Jones tied his hands together. "I really hope that this was worth it Woods, your parole has just flown out the window."

Before Jake could answer, the door was kicked open and six staff entered, grabbing both Jones and Jake before they could respond. "You two are fucked! Say hello to Belmarsh, the pair of you," they were told as the knives clattered harmlessly onto the floor.

Jake sat in a single cell in the escort van, his initial thoughts were of how he would explain this to Luke. When they swapped places, he was in a nice easy prison but when they swapped back at the funeral he would find himself in a whole different world. He smirked a little, thinking of how he would start this conversation. It wouldn't matter because the parole board had all the reports ready and they were good. This one misunderstanding would be resolved quickly when Jones gave his story about holding the knives and Jake would return to comfort anyway. The van pulled through the gate and Jake's confidence evaporated as he realised that this was a serious place to be.

Standing flanked by staff he was searched roughly, the duty governor watching as Jake failed to realise the consequences of what had occurred.

"Governor, I need to have a day release to go to my mum's funeral in the next couple of weeks. She's about to die in hospital."

The Governor looked at him and laughed. "You aren't going anywhere sunshine other than our segregation block. Say goodbye to parole, goodbye to your mum and hello to another ten years added onto your time in prison, you piece of shit."

Jake's hand was thrust into a biometric reader where his finger prints were taken and a DNA swap was pushed roughly into his mouth. A large policeman stood waiting for the tests to be finished.

"Luke Woods, you are under arrest for the unlawful detention of Mr Peter Scholes at Ford Prison on the 28th October 2009." The rest of the caution rattled around in his head as he heard it and he tried to explain again, "but I'm not Luke Woods, I'm Jake Woods, there has been an error."

The Governor looked at the screen in front of him. "No son, we have your fingerprints and DNA here. You are fucking Luke Woods. Take this scum to the block."

The policeman smiled. "We'll be back to interview you next week as your little mate Jones hasn't fared so well. He took an overdose in the back of the other van and he's a dead boy so you're facing this one alone." Three staff in full protective equipment shoved Woods towards a thick metal gate and escorted him to the segregation unit. Jake shivered as he entered, a feeling of despair running through him. He looked hurriedly around at the soulless unit, the desperation leaking out of every doorframe as lost eyes stared at the new boy coming to join them in their own hidden world. Even most prisoners in the jail had no idea what occurred within this hellish area.

He looked around at the staff bustling him towards his own bare, cold cell. There was no pity in their faces, only a hatred towards this bastard who wanted to kill a fellow prison officer.

"Can I phone my dad please?" he asked, his voice sounding childish.

"No you fucking can't, you should have thought of that before you threatened one of the staff with a knife, you cunt. You ain't phoning anyone for a long, long time. As they say out here on the wings, *go fuck your soon to be dead mum.*" A howl of laughter erupted from the staff as the door was slammed shut.

He stood staring at the back of the graffiti covered door, where extracts from the minds of countless years waxed lyrical on hopelessness. The room spun as a tightness grasped his head, a thick black fog enveloping his feelings while the dizziness whizzed from his head to his feet. He wanted to vomit but nothing came up other than a foul tasting yellow bile which hung from his chin as he tried to mindlessly wipe it away with his shirt.

He could still hear the laughter of the staff as they made their way back into the office and his knees buckled for a second as the realisation swept over him. This wasn't a game, it was real life, a billion miles away from the luxurious training grounds and Spanish apartments he had become accustomed to. There were no Real Madrid Mr Fix-its who could make every situation vanish into a steamy Madrid evening air and at last the tears flowed, chest heaving as he could barely get his breath. "Fuck no, this isn't me," he cried out to nobody.

Jake sank onto the hard floor and curled up into a ball. "Please help me, please let me see my mum."

The stench and stickiness of the grey floor seemed to glue to his wet cheek as he lay face down, before he recovered an ounce of decency and climbed back onto his knees. The tears dropped onto the dirty lino making a pattern like heavy rain would on a hot summer pavement before an early evening thunder storm. His mind buzzed with ideas about how he could save himself. If only he could get to a phone, he could ring his dad and everything would be sorted out. Dad always knew what to do, he could tell Luke to hand himself in and explain everything. With what had happened to their mum, they would understand. He forced himself to stand again, waiting for the thick blanket of stress to rise from his thoughts.

Looking up at the tiny window, he again felt hopeless. Life was carrying on only a few hundred yards from where he stood, people just getting on with normal every day activities. Why had he thrown it all away for a few seconds of fun in Ford Prison? Sitting on the hard bed he tried to plan a way to save his own neck again. Dad needed to speak to Luke, it had to work and then this would be over by tomorrow. He would be back in his bed in Newbury planning for his media career. All he needed was a minute on the phone - surely they would give him that?

Another wave of self pity took control of him and the sobbing recommenced. A prison officer looked through the observation panel and smiled before turning and shouting something to another officer. A burst of laughter erupted and Jake knew it was all about him.

Hammering his hands on the back of the cold door he shouted a pathetic tearful threat. "Get me on the phone or else, I need to talk to my dad." A voice shouted from the next cell. "If you don't stop crying you little pussy, I'll cut you open in the morning."

Jake threw himself back onto the bed and pushed the thin

pillow over his face to stifle the sobs. It didn't make any difference and they lasted all night.

The milky October sun made its way through Jake's small cell window. He hadn't slept at all, petrified by the shouting coming from the cells around him as threats bombarded him until the early hours. The noise of the cell next door opening made him sit up as his cell flap opened and the wild eyes of a prisoner looked through at him. Jake stared back at him and feeling like cornered prey, he couldn't even maintain eye contact, looking away and hoping that the man would leave and get on with his day. It wasn't to be.

An officer's voice called out harshly. "McCann, get away from that door now." The vicious rasp of McCann's voice sounded almost triumphant.

"I knew that it was you, Woods, you little grassing cunt. It's a small world in prison, it was only a matter of time before I caught up with you. There's nowhere to hide now, grass."

McCann remembered the last time he saw Woods in that dirty Reading shower room and anger burnt into his eyes. A lot had happened to McCann over the past few years and he ran a finger over a freshly healing scar across his cheek that came after an attack on two black prisoners the month before.

"See this scar, black man? One of yours gave me this just before I cut his stomach open. Now you're going to wear one just like this when I bump into you on the wing, you cunt." He slammed the flap shut and walked away whistling. Jake was left sitting in terror, trying to piece together what had just been said to him, before remembering something from his visit to Reading Prison where McCann's name was mentioned. He also remembered the fear on Luke's face when he talked about him.

The cell flap opened again but this time it was a friendly face. The door opened and the two segregation staff stood each side of a man in a dog collar.

"Good morning young man, I'm the prison chaplain, Graham Jennings. When did you arrive?"

Jake sat up. "Last night, my family don't know that I'm here. I need to call my dad, Mum is in hospital and she's going to die this week. I need to call him."

The chaplain looked at the staff. "Is this true?"

One of them nodded, "Yep, I think so. He tried to take an officer hostage at Ford but the staff stopped him, that's why he's here. We've been told not to give him anything and that includes a phone call."

The chaplain nodded. "Okay give me a minute, I need to speak to the Governor but I'm sure that we can give you a one minute call to let people know where you are."

The door was closed and the sound of footsteps disappeared. Jake lay on his bed, his heart thumping as this one ray of hope had appeared before him. This was his own key to getting out of there. *Fuck Luke, he can look after himself. Me, I'm going home.*

The smile came back onto his face as the door reopened a few minutes later. It was a grinning chaplain. "Luke, I have permission for you to make a quick call, but I must be present and it's for a minute only."

Jake dialled his dad's mobile number, his breathing feeling tight as he hit the last button and the phone began to ring.

"Hello, Des Woods here." He voice sounded a little hushed as he spoke.

"Dad, it's Jake. I need Luke to come clean, he needs to come to...." The phone went dead as Jake tried to continue. "Dad? Dad?" He looked down at the phone as though he could see what was going on through the plastic covering. "I need to try once more," he told the chaplain as he pushed the buttons again. This time Des sounded annoyed. "Look, stop ringing, it's upsetting everyone. Mum hasn't long left, I'll phone the prison when I know. Just be calm Luke," Des said before ending the call.

The name Luke sent a shiver down Jake's spine as the chaplain looked at him and gave a weak smile. "He will phone when he has news Luke. Maybe we can pray together when the end comes." The staff waiting by the open door stepped forwards and grabbed Jake's arm before pushing him hard back through the cell door.

"Try that shit with anyone else and it will be the last thing you do. Remember this Woods, you get fuck all down here, no one cares about you." Jake lay back on his bed. "Why did Dad call him Luke? What the fuck was going on? How the hell am I ever going to swap places with Luke," he thought as the desperation returned.

CHAPTER FIFTY-FOUR

Luke sat by the bed holding his mum's hand as Des sat back in the reclining chair trying to sleep. Kim had been restless all evening, the morphine now flowing as a constant drip to keep her pain free, the nurse mopping her forehead every hour as she checked on the lines.

Something made Luke look up, he didn't know if he had heard something or her breathing had changed, but there was a subtle difference. Des opened his eyes at the same time, as though feeling Luke's concern. Kim's chest heaved up one more time and stopped with one last gasp. They stared at her for what felt an age hoping for another breath before Des stood and walked to the side of the bed, feeling her wrist for a pulse. His body sagged in that moment as he looked at Luke and shook his head. "She's gone Luke, can you call for a nurse?"

Luke sat looking at the motionless body, unable to contemplate life without her, before standing and walking to the door as though on auto pilot. "Nurse, I think Mum has died." The words came out bluntly, resulting in the unit sister putting her finger to her lips. "Shh, others can hear."

Luke felt affronted that he was castigated for such an innocent slip at the most vulnerable time in his life. He was going to give her a piece of his mind, but swallowed the words just in time as the nurse entered the room and closed the door before checking Kim's pulse.

"I'm sorry, she has passed away. I need to call the doctor so do you want to sit with her for a little longer alone?" The question sounded so absurd and unsure about what to do they shook their heads. "There is nothing more that we can do is there?"

Des asked.

The nurse took Des's hand. "No, not at the moment, she's at peace. We will take care of everything tonight and if you want to come to the clinic tomorrow morning to talk about anything at all, you are welcome. We will be able to give you Kim's possessions then if you like."

The words were entering their heads but they seemed unable to process the meaning, just nodding, hoping to get out of there as soon as they could. A nurse came and took over from the Unit Sister. "Would you like to come with me Mr Woods? I will take you to the door and in the morning you can come here and ask for me, Sue. I'm on duty all day. I'm going to look after Kim this evening, I'm so sorry for your loss."

The clinic door opened and swung shut behind them as they left Kim for the final time. Des looked at Luke. "What the hell do I do now? I've been with Mum since we were young," He didn't cry as he spoke, the shock masking all emotion.

"I don't know Dad, we need to phone the prison to tell Jake, then I guess we swap back. I love you Dad but I won't be in there long. We'll work it all out when I get home," he promised, embracing his dad as though he were the child.

"You're right Luke, I would do anything to keep you out here with me. Jake phoned earlier but I couldn't talk to him because the nurse was in the room and I could tell people were listening to his call. It was a mobile phone and there was someone in the room with him. Is that normal?"

Luke looked at him puzzled. "That's weird, normally he would just use the phones. There are plenty in our billet and no one ever listens to our calls, there is no need."

A sense of unease crept over him. "What the hell is going on back at Ford? That sounds so wrong."

Making their way down to the car was surreal as they walked against an endless stream of visitors coming from the other direction, no one realising or caring that their world had just ended. Thirty minutes ago, Des was still a husband, now he was a widower with no plans for the future.

They sat in the car, Des thumbing the card given to them by the prison Governor. The phone rang twice before he picked it up.

"Good morning, Governor speaking."

Des took a breath before speaking. "Morning sir, it's Luke Woods father, Des. I'm sorry to tell you that my wife has just passed away - could someone tell my son please? Also, is it possible for him to come home again?"

Luke's heart sank as he listened, knowing that he had only a matter of hours before returning to custody. The look on Des's face however gave another story.

"What do you mean he has been moved? What incident? What are you talking about?"

Luke sat glued to the conversation, his fears coming true. Jake had been unable to last even a few days without screwing up. Des listened for another minute before hanging up and looked blankly at Luke. "Jake has messed things up badly." A look of absolute amazement came onto his face. "He's taken a member of staff hostage with a knife and they have moved him to Belmarsh Prison. He's in court today. His parole is cancelled and he won't be allowed out to the funeral under any circumstances." He dropped the phone onto Luke's lap.

"What the hell has that boy done? He has cost you all that you have worked for." Des was devastated, still trying to process the events in the hospital and now he was hearing that Jake had condemned Luke to many more years in prison.

Luke looked at his dad with tired, red eyes. "Maybe not Dad. Remember something, he is Luke." Des looked at him, not following his thought process,

"What are you saying?"

Luke stared out of the window speaking in a matter of fact manner. "He made me do nine years in prison for something that he did. Why should I do the rest of my life for something else that he did? He is Luke, Dad, I am Jake. You are the only person in the world who knows differently." He turned and looked at his father for confirmation that the message had been delivered.

Des stared back at him. "What, you want to stay out here and live Jake's life?" His voice sounded as though he was about to add the punch line to a bad joke.

Luke nodded, unsure as to where his dad's allegiance sat.

"Unless you have a better idea, Dad?

CHAPTER FIFTY-FIVE

The Old Bailey

"Luke Woods, you have proven yourself again to be a violent and calculated thug of knife crime that the public should never need fear facing again." The words echoed around Court Number one at the Old Bailey as the packed gallery hardly dared draw breath.

"You will serve the rest of your life in prison with no hope of release. Take him down Officer."

A cheer went up from those watching while a member of Robert Bell's family shouted out, "Rot in hell, bastard. You should never have been considered for parole in the first place."

The judge looked up and silenced them. "Order please, anymore outbursts and you will be removed."

Jake looked up from the dock at the public gallery where Luke and Des were sitting observing the scene. He shook his head briefly before the two staff ushered him downstairs and out of sight. Des looked at Luke and gave a half smile. "This is not going to be an easy job, Jake, we need to be together on this son." Luke smiled when he heard his new name. "I can live with being Jake, Dad, our secret."

The Old Bailey cell door banged shut behind him as it had on tens of thousands of others during its long and famous history. Jake hardly had the time to process the sentence given by the judge before the sound of the key in the lock caught his attention.

"You have a visitor Woods, you will get five minutes until the van goes back to Belmarsh."

Escorted into a small cubicle he saw his father sitting behind a break-proof screen.

"Where is Luke, Dad? I thought that he would be here."

Des didn't even blink. "Jake has gone for an interview with the BBC in London Luke, he didn't have time to come down with me. The BBC had a car waiting for him but he said that he will be in touch when he has some spare time on his hands."

Jake stared back but couldn't raise a smile. "Is this how it is Dad - you two fucking me over for the rest of my life?"

Des nodded. "I think that you have brought all of this on yourself son. Count yourself lucky that you were protected for so long."

The door behind Jake opened and a court officer told him to finish the visit. He looked at Des. "Please Dad, don't do this to me."

Des stood and turned towards the door before replying. "I'll write to you next week Luke, stay safe son."

CHAPTER FIFTY-SIX

The studio buzz faded as the voice in his ear piece counted down from five.

"And.....Action!"

"Good evening everyone from the Match of the Day studio where we have four belting games to show you tonight." The VT rolled as a number of action shots flashed before the public as they sat glued to their screens across ten million homes in the country.

In what seemed just ten minutes the famous theme tune rang out its anthem, spelling out the end of yet another goal packed Saturday night. Luke sat looking at his co-hosts as the cameras finally stopped rolling and his heart beat managed to finally drop below the hundred and forty rate it had pumped throughout his first show on this famous program.

The producer, Sue Cummings, almost floated out in front of the desk holding a fizzing glass of bubbles. "Jake, you are a natural and the public will love your fresh delivery. I'm so happy!"

She took a sip from her glass before raising it to everyone in the studio. "I think that we have our new face for the show. Welcome on-board Jake."

Luke sat almost numb from the internal panic he'd felt for the entire hour. John Diamond, the former Manchester United captain turned pundit, laughed. "Jake, you were a good striker, but bloody hell mate, you made us look like we were first timers. You are so easy in front of the camera. Remember when we had a big argument at Old Trafford? Tell Sue what you told me that day."

For a second Luke froze; these were the moments that he dreaded, the little things that could trip him up.

He smiled. "John, you've been telling that same story every time you give an after dinner speech, I will leave it up to you. The story gets better every time." As he listened to John ramble on once again, Luke studiously took in another anecdotal bit of information that might come back around again.

The people remaining in the studio roared with laughter and Luke settled back into his Jake persona. After the story had ended he took Sue to one side. "Is there anything else that I could do to make the show better? I felt so nervous."

Giving him a knowing smile, she placed a hand on his shoulder.

"Jake, I remember Gary saying the same thing to me when he finished his first show. You were equally as good as he was, and he certainly was the best we have ever had so far. Just be yourself, it's all the public want from you."

The way that she looked intensely at him made Luke think, for one brief second, that he'd been rumbled, before discarding the notion as quickly as it came. Impossible! There were only three people who knew."

She winked at him and turned to go edit the recordings for the evening show. Turning at the last second before entering the editing suite, she said, "I know these things Jake."

John came back over, looking buoyant from the performance of the team while Luke was still in a state of flux. "What did she know?"

The small tell-tale sign of a fleck of white powder on John's nose gave away his renewed vigour, and noticing Luke's enquiring eye, he wiped his nose with a tissue.

"Jake, you even managed to make me look good tonight, fancy a couple of drinks? I'm meeting up with a few of the Chelsea lads later, they'd like to catch up with you."

Luke gave him a warm smile. "No mate, I have a few things to catch up on. You go ahead and I'll see you next weekend."

He left the studio and made his way back to his car where he took his phone out and rang home.

"Hi Dad! Get ready for some questions from the press, I just finished my first ever recording of the show." There were a few seconds of silence while Des considered what to say. He was immensely proud of what Luke had achieved in just a very short time in the media world.

"I'm very happy for you son. Just remember the lesson about keeping your feet on the ground, one superstar ego was enough for me."

Luke listened and understood. "Not me, Dad, see you tonight."

His phone rang again as soon as he had ended the call. It was Sasha, his agent.

"Hi Jake, Sue just phoned me, they want you to sign a longer term deal already. She couldn't be happier with you. Can we meet up again on Monday at the office and discuss her proposal? And one more thing, I've changed your accountant as you suggested. You were right not to trust him, and we have moved all the bank accounts to a new home. You were also right to not trust Luke to try get into the account. He tried to withdraw a few hundred on Friday but lucky for us the bank noticed the attempt and have helped us shift everything into a new account. We just need a few signatures from you when we meet up."

He had been right second guessing what Jake would try to do. It wasn't the fact that Jake even had a lot of money in the account, by last calculation he was showing just short of a million after image rights were calculated by Real Madrid. Now all contact was broken the team didn't care about him anymore and a new hot shot was scoring the goals for them. The real issue for Luke was repositioning everything to avoid any questions from nosy accountants who knew Jake's business inside and out. Sasha had ruthlessly purged them all and seemed to enjoy the process

Tapping into his phone, he made the appointment for Monday lunchtime at the Mayfair office Sasha had made home. He had yet to visit it but visualised the plush surroundings and sporting memorabilia on the walls as busy staff hunted for new clients.

One final ping of conscience tugged his brain as his mind raced back to a hasty phone conversation he'd had with Jake in the prison the week before. He had sounded broken, as though he finally realised that there was nothing he could do to try to reverse the situation as he desperately looked for a way out of his predicament. But this was never going to happen, Jake had betrayed everyone who loved and trusted him, he had changed beyond all recognition, putting money and fame before family, and was still willing to let Luke rot in jail. And even now, after screwing up Luke's chance of freedom and building a life back for himself after nine years in prison, he still wriggled like the snake he was, pulling every trick to get Luke back behind bars. But this time it was different - Luke held all the aces.

His final plea for money was familiar and Luke recognised the desperation in Jake's voice. He had actually begged Jake for money a few years ago when he was made to feel like a tramp in the street. Sometimes karma really did have this peculiar habit of hiding in the shadows until it was show time, and now the stage lights were burning brightly.

"Please Luke, I need a couple of hundred pounds to buy some new trainers for the gym - I will pay you back at some point."

Luke had sighed. "Look please stop calling me by that name, you are not fooling anyone. If you insist on pretending that I have taken your identity, ask the police to check our finger prints from when we were convicted. Oh, wait a minute, we were juveniles and they were destroyed after five years. I'll send you some cash, but this is the last time." He almost held his breath as he sensed the reaction that was going to explode from a caged animal. The sound of the phone crashing against the Belmarsh prison wall could almost be heard in Newbury.

CHAPTER FIFTY-SEVEN

5 years later

Jake lay on his bed in his single cell in the vulnerable prisoner unit in Belmarsh, his walls bare of photographs, but a small stack of letters stored in an old sardine can box sat on his locker.

The staff hated him due to his attack on one of their own, the prison population hated him because he was known as a grassing nonce, possibly the worst label to hold in a high security prison, and there was a price on his head with plenty of drug hungry prisoners willing to play bounty hunters and get their rewards. He had no choice other than to stay on his landing twenty-four hours a day as even to attend the visits room was too dangerous a risk. Instead, he was forced to use the wing phone or letters to keep up communication, his brother Luke only managing to speak to him during gaps in his busy work schedule.

A loud tapping on his wall alerted him to the fact that the paedophile in the next cell wanted to talk. Jake shouted out, "Hey Ed, what's happening?"

A weasel like voice hissed back, "Turn onto BBC One, Luke, you will like it."

Irritated by having to communicate with scum to survive, he turned his TV on to see that The Sports Personality of The Year programme had just started.

He watched as a video clip of the Manchester United team winning the league again was shown followed by a reporter standing outside a chilly Old Trafford, before cutting back to the warm studio and the host of the show, Jake Woods.

Jake stared in disbelief as his brother, dressed in a suit looking like it cost a million dollars, effortlessly took the show to heights it had never reached before. He tried to take his eyes away but felt compelled to continue watching, hoping that he would make a terrible mistake, but knew that it was never coming, every delivered line impeccable.

The weasel voice next door cackled with laughter. "Your brother's on every TV programme at the moment, he must be rolling in cash. I bet you wish that you were him.

The End

AFTERWORD

Thicker than Water gave me the opportunity to write about people and events I experienced during my years in the prison service alongside my life-long love of football.

With the character of Luke, although written as fiction, I drew on my knowledge of gang culture within the prison community, and many of the characters such as Bigger and Blue were based on real boys I knew during my time at Huntercombe. While an officer there, I did indeed have a boy who was very interested in football help me train the local boys team I was involved with, as Luke does in the story.

I was involved in a real riot at Northeye back in the 1980s and my description of it in the book comes from a lot of my memories of that night......sometimes the truth is better than any fiction.

On the other side of the story, Jake's football career follows the dream I had as a youngster, picturing my football prowess leading me to stardom on the field....but it was just that, a dream, which as an author I can now live out on paper!

If you'd like to find out more about me, visit my website www.adrianodonnell.com

ACKNOWLEDGEMENT

Thank you for reading my latest novel....I hope you enjoyed it. Please could I ask you to leave a review on Amazon, as for all indie authors, reviews are a critical part of getting our books out there.

Thanks also goes to all those who support me with my writing, either through editing, constructive feedback, or simply through reading my books....particular mention to my wife Jo, Adrian Whiting, David Saddleton and Angie Haylor.

For more information on my books and upcoming releases, please visit my website.

www.adrianodonnell.com

PRAISE FOR AUTHOR

'O'Donnell's 32 years in prison service lends the book a feel of authenticity that adds credence to the story...'

'The plot was intriguing, and the suspense was so intense in spots that I had to take a break – but the story kept drawing me back in.'

'A page turner that out kings Stephen King!'

'Can't put it down thriller...lock the doors and windows before you read it.'

'Adrian's writing style is not dissimilar to David Baldacci'

- HIGH RISK

'Addictive! What a thrilling book!'

'A real insight into the life of a prison officer, prisoner and criminal.'

'Great follow up for first book in this series.'

- RESOLUTION

'The third book in an amazing trilogy was another masterly crafted suspense thriller.'

Adrian makes use of his real life experience to provide detail throughout the book.'

'This would make a great TV drama.'

'Adrian's experience in working with some of the country's worst offenders shines through this work.'

- *BETWEEN THE SHADOWS*

'Thrilling, fast moving fabulous read.'

'Another stonking good read!'

'just couldn't put it down'

'great book, look forward to the next one.'

- *VENGEANCE IS CALLING*

BOOKS BY THIS AUTHOR

High Risk

The Byfield Trilogy, Book One

Visit www.adrianodonnell.com for excerpt

Resolution

The Byfield Trilogy, Book Two

Visit www.adrianodonnell.com for excerpt

Between The Shadows

The Byfield Trilogy, Book Three

Visit www.adrianodonnell.com for excerpt

Vengeance Is Calling

An Ernie Stocken adventure.

Visit www.adrianodonnell.com for excerpt

Printed in Great Britain
by Amazon

21169039R00226